HAWKWOOD'S SWORD

HAWKWOOD'S SWORD

BY

FRANK PAYTON

Fireship Press
www.FireshipPress.com

HAWKWOOD'S SWORD: By Frank Payton
Copyright © 2012 - Frank Payton

HawkwoodAll rights reserved. No part of this book may be used or reproduced by any means without the written permission of the publisher except in the case of brief quotation embodied in critical articles and reviews.

ISBN-13:978-1-61179-253-9: Paperback
ISBN 978-1-61179-254-6: ebook

BISAC Subject Headings:
FIC014000FICTION / Historical
FIC002000FICTION / Action & Adventure
FIC027050 FICTION / Romance / Historical

Cover Work: Christine Horner

Address all correspondence to:
Fireship Press, LLC
P.O. Box 68412
Tucson, AZ 85737
Or visit our website at:
www.FireshipPress.com

Chapter 1
Lombardy 1361

The attack came as I had half expected. I had felt for some time a strange unease about the darkling woodlands through which we rode. No birds sang. There were none of the familiar rustlings of small beasts scurrying about their daily business.Suddenly, my fears took shape. A shrill blast of trumpets rent the air, and as the leaders of the vanguard emerged into the sunlight of a clearing, groups of mounted men-at-arms hurled themselves forward in attack.

Whirring volleys of crossbow bolts swept in from either flank. Our men reeled under the shock, the first two ranks going down to bloody ruin before the rest were able to gather their wits. I slammed down the visor of my helmet, unhooked the shield from its place on my saddle, and, thrusting my left arm through the straps, took a fresh grip on Boy's reins. Sword in hand I plunged into the fray, urging the big bay destrier to the front. Smashing aside the shield of a tall man-at-arms, I ran him through under the mail coif of his helmet. Bright blood poured over his armour. He screamed, choked bloodily, slid sideways and fell under trampling hooves. To my left, a long-handled mace swept towards my head. I caught it on my shield and pushed mightily, overbalancing the rider so much so that he fell forward across his saddle bow and took a blow from my sword across his unarmoured neck. His horse carried him away, and several of my men engaging lustily with the enemy swept in front of me as I turned aside to seek new opponents.

Hawkwood's Sword

"Stand! Stand! God damn you all!" Will Preston, the vanguard commander, roared at the top of his voice. "Spread out at the front! Let more men through!"

I called to him, flinching as a bolt clanged off my shield. "Where are those crossbows, Will?" He waved his arms to either side and shouted something I could not hear above the surrounding tumult of clashing weapons, shouting, screaming men and neighing horses.

"Get back to Master Ashurst," I told Ralph Blount, my page, who rode close beside me, his own weapon crimson to the hilt. "I want sixty or more archers up here. Quickly now!"

"Aye, Sir John." He disentangled himself from the melee, turned his mount and rode off as if the Devil were behind him. I returned my attention to the fighting. More men under Jack Onsloe, their marshal, had ridden up to swell the ranks of the van. I called to him.

"Dismount half your men, Jack. Send them out to either side. Save the horses, and deal with those goddamned crossbowmen." He raised his sword in reply, and gave the order.

His men-at-arms flung themselves off their horses and moved off into the woods, using shields and the trees as cover against the whining bolts. The crossbowmen were well hidden. I imagined them furiously winding their clumsy weapons to get in another shot against the advancing swordsmen, who would hack them to pieces when they got to grips.

The grinning face of Giles Ashurst, my captain of archers, appeared, bow in hand; behind him followed a jostling throng of archers.

"We're here, Sir John. What's to do?"

"Bring your men up to the front, and out to the flanks. Break up that cavalry. You know how."

He showed his teeth. "Aye, we know the way." He called to his men, who ran up to the back of the press and deployed themselves on either side of the men-at-arms. They began to shoot. It was near point blank range, and the long yellow shafts sped almost

FRANK PAYTON

horizontally into the enemy ranks. Horses went down screaming in agony under the deadly torrent, as the bodkin points bit deep into their flesh. The riders fared little better as the arrows pierced mail and flesh alike. After a space the pressure on the vanguard eased, and slowly we began to push the unknown enemy back.

I met Jack behind the main line. His voice boomed hollow behind his visor. "We should throw in an attack now, Sir John. The archers have scattered them."

"Very well, I'll follow up with my guard." I turned and waved my men on to follow me.

Jack wheeled his horse about, calling to his men, together with Will Preston's troop, to follow him in the charge. I followed, but even as we went forward there came again the sound of trumpets rising above the clamour of battle. Hearing the signal, the enemy cavalry, whoever they were, turned and withdrew as quickly as they had come. Many of the crossbowmen melted away with them, clinging to the horses' stirrup leathers.

The tall marshal trotted his horse over to me. He removed his helmet and wiped a cloth over his sweat-streaked face.

"Well, that's that, I suppose. I wonder who they were." Jack always relished the excitement of battle. "Why did they not stand and fight?"

"Not surprising, is it? Look what they've lost." I pointed to where the ground was littered with the dead, men and horses, and groaning wounded. The loss of some of the horses was a great pity. We were always in need of good mounts to maintain the Company's numbers. Fighting men were easier to come by.

Ralph's voice broke in upon my thoughts. "I'll take your sword and clean it, Sir John." I handed it to him absently, my mind still on the ambush. As Jack turned away to rejoin his men, I called after him. "Where were the fore riders? Why did we have no warning?"

His brow furrowed. "That's what I wondered. I'll find out."

Hawkwood's Sword

The badly injured on both sides who were like to die were despatched cleanly with a dagger thrust, as was the custom, but two of the enemy crossbowmen were relatively untouched. The first, an older man, had taken an arrow through his upper arm. One of Giles' archers broke the shaft off short, and as I watched he pulled out the other part. The man gritted his teeth and groaned with pain. Then, muttering something in his own tongue, he bound up the wound with a white scarf which he took from about his neck.

The other survivor was but a boy, or so it appeared. Also a crossbowman, he leaned unsteadily upon his weapon and stared at his captors. He seemed to be suffering from a broken, or at least a badly sprained ankle. I dismounted and went over to him. He was a sturdy, dark-featured lad, who looked me boldly in the face. Suddenly my mind took me back to England years ago when I stood before one of the King's officers who travelled through the land seeking men for the assault on France. Memories flooded back.

"So, you're an archer, lad," the King's officer had said to me. "How good are you?"

"I can knock a pigeon out of a tree at fifty paces, or kill a fox at a hundred," I answered boldly, looking him in the eye.

"Hmm, you'll do," he grunted, handing me a shilling. "Go, stand over there with the others."

Thus I became an archer for the King, long years ago.

Now there stood before me a young lad, a Genoese crossbowman, much as I had been. I remembered how I had felt and had difficulty in stifling a laugh, but I addressed him kindly.

"What's your name, boy, and his?" I asked, nodding towards the other prisoner; but he shook his head, so I repeated my question in French, which he seemed to understand somewhat. "I am Marco di Stoldo Bandini, of Genoa," he announced with some pride. "And my companion is named Ugo."

"Was this your first fight?" I asked. He looked so young; I could not help but be curious.

Frank Payton

"No, I have been in such skirmishes before. This time I expected to die when the swordsmen came at us, but I was too busy to care at the time. Yes, I was afraid, yet it was exciting. As it is, I am still alive, though I am your prisoner." He cast his eyes down.

I spoke to him, softening the tone of my voice. "What do you know of your master? Is he the Count of Savoy, and where does he presently lie, and in what strength?"

"Our master is the Doge Boccanera of Genoa, and we were engaged by the Count of Savoy for his own ends, and what they are I know not."

"But who was your commander in the field?" I pressed him.

"Federico Orsini." He was very wary.

"And your Doge gave him instructions to attack us, I suppose."

"No. On our way here we were met by knights from the Count's household, and their horsemen. Messer Orsini acted upon their orders. Until this day we did not know who we were to fight. You were too strong, and too many for us," he finished ruefully.

His companion, Ugo, swayed upon his feet and clutched his arm, muttering in his own tongue. Marco caught him as he began to fall and lowered him to the ground.

He looked up at me. "He is very weak, Signor. I fear he will die."

"Hmm. We will speak again later. Ralph! Take this Marco and his companion to Master Turton to be held securely. They must give up their weapons, but they are to be well treated, and fed properly. See that our healers attend to their wounds."

I watched as the two lads went off, followed by the older man, whose arm still bled freely through the white scarf. Ralph and Marco seemed to be much the same age, and might make fine friends for each other if matters turned out as I began to hope. An idea was forming in my mind.

*****

Hawkwood's Sword

Gradually the Company began to shake itself back into marching order. The captured horses taken into the Company's service to make up for losses from death or lameness. All the weapons of the slain were taken into the care of Will Preston until they could be stored in the baggage train, which was a day's march ahead under the command of John Brise, my burly senior marshal.

At last the column moved off again, but not before Jack took me to one side and amongst the trees showed me the body of one of the foreriders. His throat was slashed from side to side, so fiercely that the head hung half off the man's neck.

"Do we know who he was?" I asked.

Jack shrugged, and turned down the corners of his mouth. "I've seen him before. I'm sure he's one of Belmonte's men. Shall I ask around?"

"No, not now, later will do. But at the right time I will find out. Get two of the men to bury him and say a couple of prayers for his soul. I don't want his spirit following us."

Grave suspicions were beginning to arise in my mind, but there was little I could do about them at the time. Small happenings of that nature had arisen before, especially since the Battle of Brignais, when we of the Great Company defeated an army sent against us by the French, who were anxious to clear us out of their country for good and all. It was then I joined my band to that of the Almain freelance, Albrecht Sterz, who I had chanced to meet many years before at Coblenz, when the Emperor of the Holy Roman Empire had appointed King Edward to be one of his lieutenants. Over the years we met at intervals, on one field of combat or another, and regarded each other as comrades in arms.

His Holiness the Pope eventually agreed to pay the Companies to leave France and fight in a cause dear to him. Thus the White Company took up the sword on behalf of the Marquis of Monferrato against his long-time enemies the Viscontis, Dukes of Milan, who for years had sought to add his territories to their own.

Frank Payton

Bearing in mind what happened earlier in the day, and the suspicious death of the forerider of our company, I determined to keep a close watch on events.

*****

Later, I sat over the evening meal with Jack, Will, and Giles. Our night camp was in an area of pasture-land hard by a small stream. The site afforded us a clear view in all directions. The stream made one boundary for defence, and for the other we relied on a fence of roped stakes such as the archers used in a pitched battle. My small tent was set up, as we were on the march. The others had their own tents and bivouacs. We set regular guard patrols. With men and horses trampling the ground the fresh smell of the crushed grass took away the stench of blood and mire.

Four of us sat around a small fire, for the evening air had begun to wrap its chill fingers about us. Above us the clear black sky showed its familiar array of stars. Jack was speaking quietly, as was his way. His dark features were reddened in the firelight.

"I lost three good men today, Sir John," he mused. "All knocked down by bloody crossbowmen hidden amongst the trees. They didn't even see who killed them. They never got in even one blow against the cowardly knaves. Now I'm told we have two of these men as prisoners. What for, I'd like to know?"

"Jack, think on this. They could be very useful, and at some time not too far ahead we may want to recruit some of their fellows for our own ends. This has been in my thoughts for some time now."

"Haven't we enough archers already who can shoot faster?" he growled.

"Yes, we have, but in a siege speed doesn't matter so much, and at such times crossbows can be better. Don't forget, we don't know this country. We're riding blind, and much as I trust Albrecht Sterz, there are those amongst his following about whom

Hawkwood's Sword

I have grave doubts. These prisoners may be of great help to us if we treat them well."

"I suppose so," he grumbled. "But it won't give me back my men, will it? Three of my best they were, who'd been with me for years. Little Robbie Marshall was one. A rare young limb of the Devil, he was." He shook his head grimly.

Will laughed. "You'll soon get over it. Have some more wine, Jack. In our trade we all know we could be dead by the end of any day. We've lived with Death at our elbows for years."

Jack heaved a sigh, relapsed into silence, and spoke no more. He cared for his men, but his temper was well known. I had heard from others that years before in England he was a villein bound to a cruel landlord who exacted harsher fines than usual from all his people, who chafed helplessly under the yoke. One day the lord's son came upon Jack's daughter as she worked in the fields. He took her off on his horse to a place in the surrounding woods and there raped her. She was greatly distressed, being but a maid of thirteen years. At last she escaped and made her way home, where she collapsed sobbing in her mother's arms. When Jack learned what had happened, he went out and found the culprit. Dragging the young man off his horse he beat him to death with a flail.

That same night his lord came to Jack's house with two armed men. They fired the thatch and drove out the family. As they fled, the two young boys were cut down straightaway, and Jack was seized. His wife and daughter were raped and butchered before his eyes. Jack broke free, wrenched an axe from one of the killers and hewed off his lord's head with one stroke. He fled into the forest.

Despite the hue and cry raised by the Lady of the Manor, over the next few weeks Jack hunted down and slew both the retainers who had raided his home, stalking each man as a cat would stalk a mouse. Afterwards he vanished from the familiar woods and fields where he had lived since he was a boy, and walked to Southampton. On his arrival he found a great stir, as the King was making ready to lead yet another foray against the French.

FRANK PAYTON

Offering his services to the first knight he met, Jack began his military life as a humble spearman at two silver pennies a day. Even that was seven times as much as he had from working in the fields.

Over the years Jack rose in the world of battle and constant strife, so that by the time he joined me in the White Company he rode a fine horse, owned costly weapons and armour, and fifty men followed at his back. He had become a leader of men, but in all the time that I had known him, never once did I see him smile. Many times I wondered what he held close in his heart, but on that he was silent. After hearing of his beginnings I always tried to be a good friend to him, but only partly succeeded, due to the harshness of his character.

Of a sudden there came the sound of hooves in the darkness outside the camp, hoarse shouts, challenges and replies. A guard ran towards us, as we sat around the fire.

"Sir John, Sir John, the Almain knight, von Felsingen, and his escort to see you."

On his heels came a familiar tall figure, that of Werner, Ritter von Felsingen, followed by his close companion and lieutenant, the blond Conrad Harzmann, always a sinister figure to my mind. He was devoted to Werner, but to little else, apart from his own ends. They were both in full armour, carrying their helmets. At my word the ever-attentive Ralph brought more wine and food, and we shuffled back from the fire to make room for our unexpected guests. I glanced at Jack, who raised an eyebrow in enquiry, but I could only wonder, and shrugged my shoulders.

"This is a surprise, Werner. We did not look for guests so late in the day." I lifted my cup. "Good health to you both."

"Thank you, you are most kind." Werner drank off the wine and held out his cup for more. "It is thirsty work riding about on patrol at night."

"I am surprised that you are not in your own camp," I said. "That must be well ahead of us here, surely."

Hawkwood's Sword

"Yes, it is. We have seen your John Brise and his men. But Albrecht sent us out, and I felt we might be able to guide you a little if we could find you."

Harzmann sipped only once from his own cup, I noticed.

"We have heard that you have been attacked. How was this? Have you suffered much loss?" Werner asked.

"We lost twenty dead, we have several wounded, and we also lost a few horses. But we saw our attackers off, whoever they were. Their losses were greater than ours, over fifty so I'm told. We did gain twenty or so horses, which is much to our advantage. It was an unwelcome affair, but we came off best in the end," I said, and wondered how the two of them knew of the attack.

Werner's eyes gleamed in the firelight, leaning forward eagerly. He set his cup upon the ground and rubbed his hands together in the warmth from the fire.

Werner von Felsingen was Albrecht Sterz's senior marshal, but I never quite trusted him, nor he me, so I believed. He was some fifteen years younger than I, and I know he resented the fact that I was second in command of the White Company, not he. As with all of us, he had learned his craft in the wars in France. He was a hard young man, and a good soldier, but we found little to like in each other. He held out his cup for more wine, sipped, and then gave me a sly look.

"Jack, there is more to tell, is there not? We hear you have prisoners. Have you questioned them yet?"

I confess I was taken aback by this. How, I asked myself, did he know this? Did we have a spy in our own camp? I decided to bluff my way out of the situation.

"I have, and they had nothing of interest to tell me. One is a mere boy, the other sore wounded and like to die this night."

"We should help him on his way, not keep him alive. We should kill the boy now too, before he has chance to escape and report what he have seen to his masters. This is weakness," Werner sneered. "You were ever too soft, John. Where are they?" He stood and began to draw his sword from its scabbard.

Frank Payton

"Not so, Master Almain." Jack rose to his feet. "You see no further than the end of your long nose. A dead man is of no use, a live one may well be."

"Do not presume to speak to me, peasant!" This last was almost spat in Jack's face.

In two heartbeats the point of Jack's dagger was pricking at Werner's throat. I held my breath. Once in a killing mood Jack was not easily stopped.

"My word is given, whether you will it or not," he said between clenched teeth. "I am as good a man as you at this trade, and I have killed better than you many times in the field, so beware when you name me peasant."

Werner's face turned pale and fear was in his eyes.

"Jack!" I said. "I think he regrets his hasty words. Isn't that so, Werner?" He nodded, carefully, and slammed the sword back into its sheath. Jack sheathed his dagger and resumed his seat at the fire, ever watchful of the two Almains.

Will Preston stood, and drained his wine cup. "Well, I'm for sleep," he said. "We've had a long day. Come on, Jack, you too. Good night, all." He yawned widely.

Jack rose and tossed the dregs of his cup into the fire, causing it to spit and smoke. He loomed over Werner, who continued to gaze into the flames.

"Keep away from me, you whoreson bastard, if you value your head," Jack snarled, then nodded to me. "Good night, Sir John." So saying, he stalked off into the darkness.

Harzmann sipped his wine, and spoke for the first time. "Yes, it is late, and I think we must impose upon your hospitality for the night, Sir John. In a strange land it would be unwise to blunder about in the darkness seeking our own camp, some leagues away."

"Well said, Conrad. You are wise to avoid a night ride. Of course you and your escorts are welcome to stay here until the morning." I could not turn them away, but I was concerned about their presence. The matter of the murdered forerider lay heavy on my mind.

The Almains were quartered in some spare tents, and eventually the whole camp settled down for the night. Soon, only the low voices of the patrolling guards broke the silence, apart from the rustling and scratching of the small birds and animals of the night, and the louder calls of hunting owls. Before retiring to my own tent, I sent for two guards from my most trusted men and assigned them to watch over our prisoners. "I do not want them to run off into the night," I informed them, "nor do I want them murdered in their sleep. I have plans for them." Only then did I retire.

As I drifted off to into what became a fitful sleep, I wondered how Werner had learned of the attack upon us. Also, where were the other foreriders? Did they still live? Only the morning would tell.

Chapter 2
Treachery

I emerged from my sleeping quarters early next morning to find the camp shrouded in heavy mist. The sky was clouded over and the sun invisible. Ralph had just rolled out of his blanket; he stood knuckling his eyes and yawning.

"I'm sorry, Sir John. I should have been about earlier than this. I'll bring you food and drink directly." He pulled on his boots and made off in the direction of the cooks' tents.

I sat at the long table placed in the open and let the events of the previous day drift through my mind. It became clear to me that we would soon have a hard fight on our hands. It was even possible that Werner was pursuing some little campaign of his own making, although at the time I could not even guess where it was to lead.

Ralph returned ere long with cheese, bread, good red apples, and a jug of watered wine. On such simple fare I usually broke my fast.

Shortly after Werner appeared. He joined me at the table and chewed gloomily on an apple. "This mist is not good for us, John. It holds some pestilence, I have little doubt. I would be away were it not for this." He lifted and gulped at a cupful of the watered wine. "Faugh! What in Hell's name is this you drink?"

I called to Ralph. "Pour the Ritter von Felsingen some wine. I'm sorry, Werner, but wine at this time of day does not sit well upon my stomach. However, you are welcome to what we have."

Hawkwood's Sword

He muttered his thanks, and drank the wine. Ralph brought in more food and we sat and ate in an uneasy silence. Soon we were joined by Jack Onsloe, Will Preston, Will Turton, and finally by the cold presence of Harzmann.

Chased away by the morning sun, the mist gradually lifted and our spirits rose likewise. The Almains made ready to leave, and I walked over to where Werner stood waiting for his horse, a dappled grey, to be brought to him.

"Thank you for your hospitality, Sir John," he managed to say with some effort. "It is bad that we do not see eye to eye. We should be better friends. He held out his hand, and I took it a firm grip. Our eyes met and I felt that we were both trying to read the other's true mind.

"I agree, Werner, we must. At least we must try for the greater good of all. We wish you a safe journey back to your column. Give my duty to Albrecht, I beg you, and wish him well. God speed."

His lance-bearer brought his mount as we talked; he swung himself up into the high peaked saddle and settled himself for the ride. The others of his party were already mounted, and as they set off I was struck yet again by the precision with which the Almain riders positioned themselves. They rode in twos, each pair exactly behind the two to their front. This pattern of march never seemed to vary or falter.

I turned away to make my own preparations for the day, but first I set in motion a plan to discover the answer to a question which had plagued my mind all the previous night. I sent for Will Preston, who bustled up full of protests about the need to push ahead with his duties in organising our column to make ready to move off.

"That won't take long, Will. But you may find the task I have for you takes more than a little longer. Most importantly, you must be very wary in its execution."

"What can this be, Sir John? I have too much on my hands at this time." Anxiety showed in his round face.

FRANK PAYTON

"Yes, and I understand, and I won't expect you to come to me before the morrow, perhaps not even then. I want you to ask each of the foreriders who rode between our column and the Almains which of them told of the attack upon us yesterday. Be careful not to suggest that there is anything wrong in having done so, or you will not come at the truth. Do it all very quietly, in a roundabout sort of way. Say nought to anyone else of this."

Will's eyes widened. "What is this all about? Do you suspect treachery?"

"I'm not sure. My mind will be easier when I know whatever you find out, whether it be good or bad. Again, I say, not a word to anyone else. Now I must to my own preparations. The sun is higher in the sky than I would have liked."

He saluted, and left to go about his duties, but his face wore a worried frown. As for me, I called for Ralph.

"Come, boy, help me with my armour, and where is my horse?"

*****

It seemed an age before the column was ready to ride on. I fretted with impatience as Ralph and a fellow page helped me into my armour. The well-worn straps broke more than once, and this meant further delay whilst an armourer was fetch to make further repairs. Finally, I was armed and ready. Then Tom Steyne, our Horse Master, reported my horse, Boy, to be lame. As a replacement, the best he could produce was a willing but fidgety young colt.

On this questionable mount I rode to the head of the column to my place just to the rear of the vanguard. Will was there, cursing the men for their tardiness in getting into their proper order.

"Problems, Will?" I ventured, when the tirade had abated a little.

Hawkwood's Sword

"Not so much, he replied with his crooked grin. "But I felt like waking up the idle knaves this morning, to let the sluggards know I'm awake if they're not."

"Ready to move now, Master Preston," a voice called from the very front of the van, and with that the whole column jingled into movement. At last we were on our way again, riding four abreast to cut down the length of our column. A more compact body made more sense in open country, where we could see the approach of an enemy. Off to each side and to the front rode a screen of foreriders on light, fast horses. Those furthest out could, at need, make contact with the other two columns ahead of us. John Brise and his men were on my right, and the Almains under Albrecht to my left. However they were both perhaps a day ahead, and I expected they would already be settled in camp by the time we joined them.

We journeyed on, and before long we were unexpectedly met by a patrol under John Brise. "Well met, Sir John!" his homely Essex voice boomed through his beard. "You have made good progress. We are not so far from our camp, and that of Master Sterz."

"Well met, indeed. I'm glad to see a familiar face in this strange land." I held out to him my hand, which he grasped and shook heartily.

He swung his mount alongside mine, and his escort distributed back along the ranks of the column. John screwed his neck round as he realised that there was a new face behind us.

"Who's the stranger? He looks a likely lad," he asked, turning back to me.

"A new recruit to our ranks, and he will be very useful to us here in Italy." I then told him briefly the happenings of the previous day, even to the visit we had had from Werner and his men. I didn't mention my suspicions however, formed after Werner had revealed that he had known about the attack upon us.

"How d'you think we shall fare with the Almains, Sir John?"

Frank Payton

"It all depends upon how matters fall out. If we are successful, I see no hindrance."

"And if not, what then?"

"We shall see. But let me tell you something for your ears alone. When we were in Avignon, I was lucky to make the acquaintance of a Tuscan merchant who lives in the city, a very shrewd man, by name Francesco di Marco Datini. He hails from Prato, a small city near unto Florence, and has been in France as a man of business for the past twelve years. Apart from anything else, he deals in arms, and much of our new equipment, including armour, was supplied by him. As well, he has large stocks of arrow shafts, points and fletchings, so our archers will not want for those. Francesco has also given me the names and residences of some of his agents, and letters of introduction to them, so I know that we have something that Albrecht does not, which at need could work very much to our advantage."

"Ha! What does he want in return?" Brise asked.

"Gold, what else? He is a merchant. Also he wants protection for his goods in passage from Italy to Avignon. I will need help in a strange land from time to time. We can aid each other. That is the bargain between us."

A tired silence fell between us. As we jogged onwards I recalled my first dealings with Datini. I had walked the streets of Avignon with Ralph at my side. The great Papal palace rose up to dominate the whole city, and the riches of the people—or a good many of them—could be seen on all sides. The palaces of the Cardinals and other princes of Holy Church were both opulent and ostentatious. Their retainers were dressed in rich stuffs, laden with gold and silver embroidery. Even the horses of the great wore gold-encrusted harness, with gold on the bits and bridle mounts. Those of us who gained access to the city streets, captains of the Free Companies encamped outside the walls, marvelled at these things and spent many hours discussing the chances of relieving the city and its people of their riches. In truth the task was beyond us, as we had no siege engines nor means of scaling the steep rocks and

Hawkwood's Sword

walls which surrounded Avignon. Thus, when allowed within the walls, we could only gaze in wonder, see but not take, touch but not carry away save by purchase.

I recall looking through the open door of a merchant's shop at the various pieces of armour lying about on the floor, with weapons hanging from the walls. There were many other items of trade displayed: decorated caskets and chests, rich hangings and cloths. In the shadows, the bright gleam of gold and silver plate was to be seen.

I noticed also several bales of wool, such as I had seen years before in the warehouses of London and port towns of southern England. From somewhere unseen wafted the scent of warm exotic spices from the East.

As I gazed at these riches I espied also, sitting at a high sloping wooden desk such as those used by money-changers and bankers, a serious-looking young man dressed in sombre brown. He was bent over a parchment book, pen in hand, making entries with quick, deft strokes. Perhaps he sensed he was being watched, for suddenly he looked up and spoke in strange tongue. I shook my head and uttered but one word—"English."

"Ha, Inglese," he said, standing up and laying his pen carefully on the desk. "Come within, Signore. I have a little of your speech." This was said with such a heavy accent I found it difficult to grasp at first, but I accepted his invitation, and we entered the shop.

"I am Francesco di Marco of Prato near Florence in Italy. You are 'capitano' of one of the Companies which sit at our gates?" he asked. He stood with his right hand resting on the polished wood of the desk, and I noticed the fine shape of his hand, with carefully trimmed nails, almost womanly. On the thumb was a gold ring set with a red, engraved stone.

"Yes, I am John Hawkwood, a knight of England, and I seek weapons and other equipment for my men. I see you have such things here."

"Indeed, Signore. I buy and I sell. Sometimes after battles and campaigns I buy a great deal. Presently I have a good store of weapons and armour. If you require the finest armour, I can obtain it from Milan. But not immediately, you understand." He paused. "Perhaps you will take a cup of wine with me."

"Gladly. You are most kind," I told him.

I followed him into the room behind the shop, where stood a table and several chairs, all of the plainest fashion but of good quality. A glazed window opened on to a much larger hall, which appeared to be the warehouse. We seated ourselves, Ralph taking his place behind my chair. No sooner had we done so than a serving maid appeared, carrying a pottery jug of wine and two silver cups. She said nothing, and neither did Datini, but my eyes must have told him that I thought her comely. He smiled.

"Only a slave-girl, Signore, from Tartary, bought in the markets of Constantinople. A pretty enough little thing, but a heathen. Your health, Signore." He raised his cup, and I followed suit, and waited for him to speak again. His dark eyes watched me shrewdly.

"I hear that the Holy Father is to offer you and others employment in Italy," he said, sipping his wine.

I was taken slightly aback that this should have become common knowledge. "It is possible," I countered, "If the pay is good."

"I would have an alliance with such a man as you. It could prove useful to me, Signore Haccuud."

That was the first time I met the Italian awkwardness with my name, something which was to follow me all my days.

Datini leaned forward. "You see, Signore," he went on, "most of the goods I have here for the delectation of my customers are from Italy, from Florence and other cities. They must be brought here by pack train, over the great mountains which lie between my country and France. Armed escorts are very necessary to guard against the thieves who prey on honest travellers. At times I would be very grateful for your protection of my goods."

Hawkwood's Sword

"What do you offer me in return?" I asked. "And why do you ask this of me? You do not know me. I am a stranger, and a foreigner to boot."

"Let me say that I have heard of you from others, who told me that your Prince gave you knighthood. That is enough for me to know that I may trust you. What do I offer you? I do not offer you money, but I will discount the price of anything you may buy from me. In addition, I will give you letters to my agents in several cities of Italy. My offer would be most valuable to you in a strange land, would it not? However, if I request guards from you to travel with my goods, I shall expect you to pay them. That way, it is clear where their loyalties lie."

He drained his cup and set it carefully on the table.

*****

So it was that I bought much of what Datini had to offer in the way of equipment. He kept his promise, and I received letters of introduction which would engage his agents to assist me when required. As I had told John Brise, this gave me an advantage over Albrecht, howsoever that he was my friend and comrade of many years. That meeting had been timely for, as Datini had guessed, the Pope had offered us much gold to go to Italy and free the Marquis of Monferrato from the unwelcome attentions of Bernabo, Duke of Milan, who was threatening to deprive him of his lands. Such thoughts were broken off as a rider hove into sight heading our way.

"Hallo, who is this in such a hurry?" John rumbled. "Looks like Hal Skelling, the way he's whipping that horse. I'll have to tell the Horsemaster about that. We can't have the poor beasts treated so. How now, Hal, why the pother?"

Hal came up and pulled his mount around so fiercely that the horse was almost on its back legs.

"The Almains are in camp about ten miles ahead, Sir John, but there's a party of three awaiting you at the next turn of the road."

Frank Payton

"Who are they?" asked John.

"One of Sterz's marshals, Hannes von Auerbach," replied the rider, a dark, wiry figure who paused and spat into the dust beneath us—from his manner it was difficult to tell whether this was to clear his throat or to express disdain of our Almain allies —"and two men-at-arms."

Auerbach was a name I did not recognise. I knew Albrecht had sent to Germany for more men to join his company, but little more than that. The man was clearly a newcomer.

"I don't know him," I said. "How far away are they?"

"About two miles, Sir John."

"Any sign of envoys yet from Monferrato? We are expected, and they should be on the lookout for us."

"I have not heard of any, Sir John, but perhaps Sterz will have word of them."

"Very well. We will meet up with Auerbach and let him guide us to their camp."

*****

The sun was high above the dark forest trees before we were established at Albrecht's camp. He had just come to see that we were settled when a commotion caught my attention and brought me to the entrance to my pavilion. The guards were lifting the barrier of young pine poles which served as a gate, and horsemen soon trotted through.

One, riding alone and leading a richly caparisoned white horse, came directly to where I stood with Albrecht at my side. I recognised him as Matt Sayers, a man-at-arms in John's company, reckoned to be a good soldier. Once a blacksmith, he hailed from the North Country.

"Here's one of the envoys, Sir John," he announced, "but he'll ne'er speak to you. He's as dead as a doornail!"

Hawkwood's Sword

I stepped forward and threw back a corner of the bloodstained cloak, which enwrapped a limp body hanging head-down across the saddle, and looked into the dead face of a once handsome youth. Now, besmirched with blood and soil, dark eyes staring lifelessly, it was both hideous and yet pathetic in death. Albrecht stood beside me, frowning.

"A noble youth, Jack. Cut down like a sapling. I wonder who he was."

A shadow fell across us both as a second horseman moved nearer. We looked up into the plump face of an exquisitely dressed Italian, whose dark eyes rested sadly on the dead envoy.

"Our fallen comrade was Giovanni di Francesco da Castellazzo, God rest his soul!" he said. "A noble youth indeed, now a sorry sight. His death is a great loss to us."

The speaker heaved a great sigh, but it seemed to me devoid of pity or sorrow.

"And who are you, Sir?" inquired Albrecht.

"I am Pietro Lamberti, envoy of the noble Marquis of Monferrato." He bowed slightly to us both from the saddle, then turned as another of his group joined us. Like Lamberti he was richly attired; to do him justice, he seemed truly upset at the sight of the dead youth before him.

Lamberti spoke again. "My young friend here is Filippo Sciatta, also an envoy of Monferrato. We are indebted to your marshal and his men, who found us in the wilderness. Some of our party are wounded." He paused uncertainly. "I wonder if...?"

"Of course, they will be attended by our healers," I called to Will.

"See to this directly, and arrange food and drink for the men-at-arms, as well as a place to rest." I turned to Lamberti and his companions. "Please dismount. Your horses will be taken to the lines, fed and watered. As for your good selves, follow me, an you will."

Albrecht and I led the three Italians into my pavilion, and we all took places at the table. Ralph had already set out a supply of

FRANK PAYTON

wine and a simple meal. Lamberti and Sciatta were accompanied by a third man, who was presented to us as Lorenzo Campagni of Pisa, also in the service of the Marquis.

I looked carefully at the three. Lamberti was a large, fleshy man of about forty, richly dressed in bright and, no doubt, fashionable clothes. Sciatta was younger, slim and dark, and like his elder, expensively attired. Neither was a fighting man, though they both bore swords, jewel-studded. 'Courtier' was writ large over the two of them.

Campagni was another matter. As old as myself, I judged, grey haired, hard faced. He wore plain armour which had seen some hard knocks. A plain, straight sword was at his side, and his visored helmet lay on the table nearby. He met my glance with a steady appraising gaze. He was, I knew, like myself—a free lance.

Whilst the three ate hungrily, Lamberti told us their story.

"We were attacked by a body of well-armed men who wore no marks of identity in any form. Our men fought bravely, but we were outnumbered and overwhelmed. We only escaped by fleeing for our lives. It is most unfortunate that young Giovanni was slain. He had carried himself nobly. His body will have to be returned to his family for proper burial."

"With your permission," said Albrecht, "I will arrange for a wooden coffin to be made in which to transport your dead comrade's body for the journey."

"Thank you, that is kind," said Sciatta. "His family will be most appreciative." He returned to the wine cup with a sigh and drank deeply.

"So you have no idea who your attackers were?" asked Albrecht, returning to the business in hand.

"We can only think that they were sent by the Visconti, or the Conte Verde," said Lamberti. "Apart from brigands of the forest—which is unlikely, as the men were too well armed and organised—there is little alternative."

Hawkwood's Sword

"You have several wounded, but only one killed. Was he singled out for any reason, do you think?" Albrecht persisted.

Sciatta pursed his lips. "Well, as to that, he was a kinsman of the Marquis, but not close, you understand."

"That should rule out brigands, unless they were hired to kill the one man, who would have been described to them," I said. "But there is little we can do now to pursue the matter. What does the Marquis require of us?"

At this, I saw Lamberti and Sciatta glance at each other, and a look akin to relief seemed to pass between them. Sciatta cleared his throat.

"The good Marquis wishes you to attack the Conte Verde with all your strength. It would please him if you were to lay waste the territories of Asti, and of Alessandria. We can provide you with a guide, as you will not be familiar with the country. The Holy Father in Avignon has paid you handsomely to undertake this campaign, knowing that, in addition, you would avail yourselves of opportunities to supplement your pay in the usual manner." He gave a sly smile.

Albrecht took the point. "Indeed. We have occasionally been able to assist people of substance to find a secure home for their valuables in return for the exercise of our good offices on their behalf."

"And now," I added, "I expect you will wish to rest. Suitable quarters have been prepared." I signalled to Ralph. "Please escort our guests to the small pavilion."

Lamberti and Sciatta bowed themselves out with courtly flourishes. Campagni stood up slowly, took up his helmet in his left hand and his wine cup in his right. He raised it in salutation, then drank the contents in one swallow. He looked hard at the two of us, nodded, and followed them out.

I turned to Albrecht. "What do you think?"

"I feel that all is not as it seems, my friend. Something, I think, is very wrong. Let you and I take a ride together, and discuss this out of the reach of prying eyes and ears."

Frank Payton

"I agree. If we were to speak to Campagni alone, I believe he would tell a very different tale."

*****

We went out into the sunlight, called for our horses, and shortly after passed through the gates of the camp to the salutes of the guards. Andrew Belmonte and a dozen men-at-arms followed us at a discreet distance.

The rough track slanted downwards through the forest trees, which clung in ever thickening numbers to the slopes of the mountain. As a countryman, I noted great chestnut trees and others familiar from my boyhood in Essex: oak, walnut, ash, and beech, with thickets of brambles, and small bushes between. The forest was still as we passed by, not even enough wind to ruffle the grasses. We rode as in a green aisle in a great cathedral, jogging along without speaking, each with his own thoughts. The only sound came from the horses' hooves, the creak of harness, the odd clink of metal on metal.

At length we came to a place where the way turned aside. The ground here fell away as though, in some time long past, part of the mountain had slid downwards in a confusion of large rocks. Only stunted, twisted trees grew there. The sky above now showed clear and blue, and it was possible to see over the tops of the lower trees to where the slopes of the mountain gave way to pasture and cultivated fields. Here Albrecht and I stopped and dismounted.

"What is in your mind?" he asked, seating himself on a large, flat rock and shifting his sword to lie across his knees.

"Like you, I think that the men we have just seen are not to be trusted. We do not know who they really are. After all is said, they have presented no proof of any kind."

"Just so. We might be misled by those two, and be trapped here in a strange country by a larger force. We could take heavy losses for no gain."

Hawkwood's Sword

I picked up a small stone and threw it far over the tumbled stones, and watched as it bounced from rock to rock, finally disappearing from sight. I repeated this several times. It was a habit left from boyhood, and in some way it helped me direct my thoughts.

"Well?" asked Albrecht impatiently, tapping his sword.

"What worries me is that only one member of their party was killed. In a melee of the kind which must have fallen out, I would have expected more—surely two or three at the very least—and some more serious wounding of the others. Lamberti and Sciatta don't have a scratch on them. They look as though they had been out for a morning's ride in the country."

He nodded. "Yes. I noticed that. As if they had not even been at the fight."

"There's the answer, then," I said. "They were not there—they arrived later, taking over after da Castellazzo had been killed. He was the envoy. The message he would have delivered could have been very different from the one we have heard."

Our discussion was broken by a stir amongst the still mounted escort. Their ranks parted to allow a solitary horseman to pass through. It was Campagni, and he was in a sorry state. His right arm hung limply at his side, his sword was clutched in the left hand, which also held the reins. Blood streamed from a great gash in his head, flowing down his neck and over his armour. Blood also ran down his thighs and over his saddle, from what was clearly a serious stomach wound.

I stepped forward and caught the horse's bridle. Campagni turned his head and stared at me from dulled eyes. He tried to speak and failed, sliding from the saddle in a faint. Two of the men dismounted and ran over, catching him as he fell. They laid him gently on the rough ground.

I bent over him. His eyes rolled wildly and finally fixed on my face.

"What has happened? Who has done this to you?" I asked.

Frank Payton

One of the men had fetched some wine, and now poured a little between his lips as we raised him into a sitting position.

"Lamberti and Sciatta, those thrice-damned traitors," he said, coughing. "They attacked me as I slept. Lamberti is dead. I slew him. He didn't know I slept dagger in hand. Sciatta I wounded, but he escaped me. I knew I had to find you, and tell you the truth of this matter. Your Signor Brise told me you had ridden this way."

His voice faded, and we gave him more wine. It could not have done him much good, but he was dying anyway, and we needed to hear what he had to say.

"It was those two who ordered the attack which killed da Castellazzo. Poor boy! They were not present, but came up later after word had been sent back to Monferrato, with the news of his death."

"Where are they from?" I asked.

"Oh, they are from the Marquis's court, but they side secretly with the Visconti, and would grow great in his shadow. You must not attack Asti and Alessandria. They lie in the Marquis's own lands. He wishes you to attack the lands of the Conte Verde, and the town of Lanzo."

He clutched at my arm, a dying man's grasp. "You must attack Lanzo, not the others."

His voice then trailed off, and his speech wandered. He called on several names, one of a woman, perhaps his wife. I placed his sword in his right hand, useless as it was. He died soon after, calling on God and St. Peter. We buried him there and then, under a cairn of stones, and left him to God and the silence of the mountains. It was a peaceful place for a warrior to rest. Maybe his spirit would protect the lonely traveller on the road.

"There lies a brave man and true," said Albrecht. Now we know what we wished to know, and what we must do. We must get back to camp and catch any traitors who remain."

I turned to De Belmonte. "Make all speed, Andrew. We will follow on. Leave five of your men with us. Off with you, now."

Hawkwood's Sword

As the main body of the escort turned and rode back up the track, Albrecht and I remounted to follow at a short distance. I drew my sword.

"Let us stand here, old friend," I said. "We may have to hold the trap closed."

He also drew his sword, as did the others, except an Almain who had a crossbow, which he spanned and loaded. We did not have long to wait.

Of a sudden there was a commotion ahead, shouts of anger, and the clash of steel on steel. Rounding a bend in the road we beheld six or seven horsemen fighting furiously with Andrew and his men. One broke through and spurred, yelling, towards us.

It was Sciatta, bloodied sword in hand. He was not lacking in courage, traitor though he was. He hit us like a whirlwind, slashing and stabbing. I parried a blow to my head and thrust at him as he passed me. The point of my sword raked his unarmoured side, but he was gone. Albrecht fared less well, and did not get in even one blow at him. He was through us and headed down the track. Then I heard the clack of a crossbow latch. The bolt streaked after him and struck his back with a thunk, like an axe hitting a block of wood. Sciatta screamed and arched back in his saddle, lost control, and fell sideways. The horse dragged him along with one foot still in the stirrup, and so out of sight. There came an awful cry. We raced down and found him dead, smashed against a huge rock. We found the horse later, cropping quietly.

"Strip this carrion, and get rid of the body," ordered Albrecht harshly. "Leave it for the beasts and birds of the forest."

The men scrambled off their horses, and were soon richer by a purse of gold coin, several jewelled rings, and a gold necklet and medallion. One came over and offered Sciatta's sword to me.

"I will not touch a traitor's sword," I said. "Throw it as far as you can amongst the trees." I watched as he did as he was bidden, albeit reluctantly, as it was worth much and well fashioned. We turned back and rejoined the others.

FRANK PAYTON

The fight was over. Four dead men lay face down in the dust and small stones, their bodies ransacked for anything of value. The other two we disarmed and sent off down the track. They were relieved to get away with their lives. We kept the horses. They were sturdy beasts and would be worth their keep.

It had been a sorry affair. Treachery usually is. Honest men had been led astray by evil ones, who only had an eye to their own greed for land and position. Luckily however, we had thwarted their designs and no doubt saved ourselves great loss. We had also gained some knowledge of the type of enemy that faced us in Italy: infinitely devious and treacherous.

I decided that the poor dead innocent envoy would have a fitting burial and monument. Before we finally left our camp in the mountains, I saw the body of Giovanni da Castellazzo properly buried, in a wooden coffin, at the foot of a tall tree. A large flat stone placed over the grave had his name chiselled deep into it. Underneath, one word only:

BETRAYED

Chapter 3
Revelations

The next day we broke camp and left to seek out the town of Lanzo. The Company streamed down the mountainside in a steel torrent, fully accoutred. We reached the open plain with all our panoply of bright banners and coloured pennons flying.

We met no resistance. The land was empty, the villages deserted, the livestock driven away by the fleeing people, warned of our approach by watchers in the high pastures who escaped unseen for the most part, except by the foreriders whom we had sent out ahead of our advance. We clattered down once busy streets in an eerie silence, through cobbled squares, past empty churches, their doors firmly shut against intruders.

I wondered in passing if the priests had deserted their places, or if, even as we went by, they were bent before altars shorn of the finery with which the Church was wont to adorn them to the wonder of superstitious peasants. I knew enough of priests and their hypocrisies from Nicholas, my brother, who despised the humbler members of his flock, the ones Our Lord said should be helped. My brother only gave them his attention when he wished to wring more pennies from their lean purses, supposedly to the Glory of God, pretending to save their miserable souls from Hellfire and Damnation.

Houses were shuttered, doors barred. But we made no stops and made no searches, neither for people nor anything of value. I had given orders that no one should break into houses or other

Hawkwood's Sword

buildings, on pain of severe punishment, since we were uncertain then as to whose lands we passed through. Until a reliable guide could be found it would have been the greatest folly to plunder our own patron's land and people.

We rode on through a golden autumn day. The country was well wooded on the lower slopes, with groves of walnut and chestnut trees. Here we lost the clean smell of the pine forest above and were met with warmer odours from the woodlands, mixed with the farmyard smells familiar to many. This was a land of rich pasture and cultivated fields, with many olive trees and vineyards.

John rode with me, and was visibly taken with all these sights.

"These peasants must be rich, Jack," he said in his deep voice. "Look at these crops! Much better than at home. Everything seems to be twice the size. God! I only scratched a bare living back in Essex!"

"So I see. I know little of these matters. My family were tanners, and we did not till our own land but rented it out to others; but I agree that this all looks very fine, better by far than many parts of France you and I have fought over."

It came to my mind then that it would be a fine thing to have a large holding of land here, and to be a seigneur with castle and moat. Perhaps, if Fortune smiled on me, I thought, I might achieve that. In addition, a wife would no doubt be useful and prestigious.

At noon the Company split into three columns. Albrecht led his Almains off to the right, John took half of our English to the left, and I remained in the centre with the rest. It was a familiar manoeuvre, often adopted in France. We maintained links between the columns by means of riders passing to and fro.

I occupied my mind by thinking back on recent events. I eventually realised that there were several areas where more detailed knowledge would be very useful. Therefore I sent Ralph back to fetch the lad Marco to ride with me. Soon they rode up, laughing and talking together as if they had been friends from boyhood, instead of adversaries only two days before.

Frank Payton

"Well, Master Marco Bandini," I greeted him, "how do we find you this morning?"

"In good health, I thank you, Signore. My foot is not broken, only sprained. So that is good." He eyed me anxiously. "But Ugo died in the night. Your men buried him, God rest his soul. What do you want of me?"

"I am sorry to hear that your comrade is dead, but he was sore wounded, as we know. What do I want of you? I think there is more to be known of Lanzo."

"So, if I tell you everything I know, then you will have me killed, yes?" He gave me a shrewd look.

I realised then that this was no ordinary youth. He had evidently pondered on the matter, and would use his knowledge to buy his freedom, perhaps. I tried again.

"Let us leave the matter of Lanzo for the present. Tell me about yourself. How did you come to be with the soldiers who attacked us?"

Marco was silent for while, apparently gathering his thoughts. "I was born in Genoa, and I am twenty years old. My father was a shipping agent in the port. We were not a rich family, but of good standing. My mother was the youngest daughter of a rich merchant, but he gave us little, the miser! When I was five years old the plague came to Genoa, and my parents died. I had been taken away to the country by my father's brother. We escaped death by travelling high into the mountains. The air was clean, and the sickness did not reach there."

He paused and looked away across the grassy countryside towards the far mountains. His dark face was solemn.

"And what then?" I asked. "When did you return to Genoa?"

"When I was eight. My uncle left me with a farming family who owed him service. They looked after me as one of their own and were kind to me, an orphan child. In Genoa I lived with my uncle and his wife, and they had no children of their own. On my seventeenth birthday he took me to the military barracks and

Hawkwood's Sword

enlisted me under the Captain Grimaldi. Thus I became a soldier and learned to use the crossbow. You will know, Signore, that the crossbowmen of Genoa are famed far and wide for their bravery and skills, and are sought after by many leaders of armies."

"Indeed they are," I said. "but they met their match at Crecy Field. Our longbows won the day then."

Marco laughed. "I was not there that day, Signore. Perhaps if I had been—?"

It was my turn to smile. I liked the lad. In the midst of an enemy host he could jest.

"At that battle, Marco, I was just one archer amongst six thousand others. We could shoot so fast that some men could have four shafts in the air at once. Your crossbowmen could not match that. In addition, the French were too rash and rode down to come at us. They were slaughtered for their impatience."

He looked at me wide-eyed. "So then it is true, as I have heard from the old ones? It seemed to them that the sky poured forth arrows like a storm."

"It must have appeared so. Perhaps if you were to stay with us you might see this for yourself." I did not look at him.

He was silent for a while. Then he said, "After we attacked your company the riders were supposed to take us on their horses when we withdrew. But most did not stay to help us, and your men-at-arms slew many of my company. Our horsemen broke their word."

I said nothing, and after a while he spoke again. "I could serve such a leader as you, Signore. It seems you are a man of honour."

"And what would you do for me, Marco? Why should I take you into my service? Not so long ago you were trying to kill my men."

"Ah, that was my duty, but my leaders abandoned me, and others who did not survive as I have done. To you I owe my life, but now I owe them nothing. In a strange land you need someone who knows the country, the people, the language; someone who can go about unnoticed, and find out what is of use and of interest to you. At need, I can pass where your men cannot. Besides, I hear

FRANK PAYTON

that you will fight against Milan. The tyrant Bernabo tries to extend his power, and sooner or later Genoa will have to fight for survival. I would help you in your fight."

"Very well, I accept your service, Marco, on one condition." I took off my right glove, and held out my hand to him. His face clouded.

"What would that be?" he asked.

"You shall teach me to speak Italian." I laughed at his relieved look.

He grasped my hand firmly and kissed it, and laughed in his turn.

"I am your man, Signore Gianni, to the death. And now there is something I should tell you, I think, about which I have as yet said nothing. At first I thought it of no importance."

I was curious. "What is that, Marco?"

"It concerns the Almain, as you call him, von Felsingen, the one who, as your servant warned me, would have killed me. I have seen his friend, the cold one, before, and heard his voice. It is so very quiet."

I could not believe what he was saying, and looked at him sharply. "What foolery is this? How can you have seen him before? When, and where?" My mind raced at the import of what he had said.

"Two weeks ago when we left Genoa, on our way to lay the ambush, we encamped one night at a village. I was told off with some of my companions to act as guards. Late at night some riders appeared, and one of them was von Felsingen's friend."

"You mean you saw Conrad Harzmann?" My mind was in a whirl. This news was almost beyond belief. "And?"

"He and one or two other Tedeschi—Almains, I mean—were accompanied by an Italian. He was very fat, and richly dressed, and he had an escort of several men-at-arms."

Hawkwood's Sword

"Indeed? This is all very interesting, Marco, and I thank you for telling me. It seems you understand well the importance of such information. I shall not forget. Be sure of that."

We rode on, and I tried to fit this news into the happenings of the past few days. One thing was sure. The fat Italian could only have been Lamberti.

*****

We continued our march towards Lanzo, helped now by Marco's knowledge of the country. He was able to say that we were then passing through the lands of the Conte Verde. And so we began to help ourselves to whatever presented itself in the way of plunder. Sweeping through the countryside, we garnered a rich harvest of cash and kind, and left smoking farms, villages, and small towns in our wake. Saddlebags bulged with gold and silver coins, crucifixes, chalices, plates and dishes, precious stones, costly tapestries, and silk stuffs from the East.

It wasn't all without cost, however. At times we were stoutly opposed by the local militias, well armed with sword, pike, and crossbow. Then we had to fight hard, and we took losses, and gained little. But that is a soldier's life. There was no respite for the wounded, who had to ride on or be left behind to be picked off by the peasants.

I had taken the opportunity at one of my meetings with Albrecht to put Marco forward as a valuable new recruit. Luckily Albrecht saw and appreciated the wisdom of my action. Of course von Felsingen looked down his long nose, but he could do nothing to change matters. It was clear even to him that the lad could be of great assistance to us.

As to the matter of who, if anyone, had informed Werner of the attack on our column, there was little satisfaction for me. Will Preston spoke to all the scouts, but not one admitted to telling the Almains they had met on patrol. This caused me grave concern, for clearly if one of our men had not told of the attack, then Werner

Frank Payton

must have either been informed afterwards by our enemy, or have known beforehand that the attack was to take place. When I took into account what Marco had told me about Harzmann and Lamberti, one or the other seemed likely. I pondered over whether to take Albrecht into my confidence, but decided in the end to say nothing, and to see how matters fell out.

*****

The Company resolved itself once more into one large column for the remainder of our progress. By now the local folk had warning of our approach and prudently fled. We marched through empty farmlands and towns, hastily abandoned. There was less valuable plunder, but plenty of provender left behind in the granaries. Our diet grew monotonous, but neither we nor the horses went hungry.

Finally, one August afternoon we came in sight of Lanzo. The town lies in a wide valley watered by several streams or small rivers, which spring from the mountain snows far away to the north on the borders of France. As soon as we were able, Albrecht and I, together with John Brise, von Felsingen, and a small escort of mounted men-at-arms and archers, set out towards the town to look over the approaches and what we might see of the defences. Marco rode with us to point out details which otherwise might have escaped us.

We drew rein about five hundred yards from the town walls, and it was easy to see that they had been repaired recently. The road led straight towards a heavily gated arch in the wall before us. There was a glitter of weapons above the gate. We were being watched.

Marco pointed. "This is the West Gate, Signori. There are three others in the walls. Over there you can see where the Count has built a new tower. The old one had fallen into decay and was taken down."

Hawkwood's Sword

We could see the squat tower in the centre of the town rising above the red-tiled roofs of the houses. It appeared to be strongly constructed and easily defensible. Arrow slits pierced the walls at regular intervals, and there was an overhang at the top to allow for stones and other missiles to be rained down on any attacker.

"What about water supplies?" I asked.

"One of these small rivers runs through the town, passing under the walls through two arched passages. Iron grilles bar the way in each one, but they are very old, I think."

"And well rusted away by now, I'll warrant, and mostly forgotten," added Albrecht, turning to Marco. "Isn't that so?"

"I don't know, Master Sterz, but come the dark, I will find out for you."

Albrecht looked across at me. I nodded in agreement. This would be an interesting test of Marco's new found loyalty, and I knew that the lad would recognize it as such.

As we continued with the inspection, it became evident that we had been expected. An air of watchfulness lay overall. There was none of the usual hum of activity to be expected from a town the size of Lanzo. We noted that although there was no moat, a deep ditch surrounded the town at a distance of twenty yards or so from the walls.

John pointed to this. "We'll need something to help us cross that in an attack. We can't all bunch together on the roads."

"You're right." I turned to Will Preston. "We'll need bundles of reeds or small tree branches, many hundreds of them. Set the men to work on this at first light tomorrow morning."

"Better to order each man to make his own, Jack. It will be much quicker that way," said Albrecht. "I will issue the same order to my people."

"A good plan. D'you hear that, Will?" I called to him.

"Aye, Sir John. I'll attend to it."

Frank Payton

"We'll need to block these roads as well, Jack," said John. "Then they'll be in trap of their own making. The ditch will keep them in, but won't keep us out."

"Well thought of, John," said Albrecht. "I'd suggest placing two hundred men on each road as a guard. Say a hundred and fifty men-at-arms, and fifty archers. That should stop any comings and goings. What do you say, Jack?"

I agreed this new plan, and we returned to camp to put it into effect. John Brise prevailed upon me to appoint the Yorkshire man-at-arms from his company, Matt Sayers, as one commander, and I took similar advice from Jack Onsloe when I decided the other would be Wat Ferrers. Both men had long experience in the field, and we knew they could be relied upon to carry out their duties properly.

As far as the archers were concerned I relied on Giles to make his own decisions, and he picked out Simon Bawdesley and Tom Edricson, both old comrades of mine from the Crecy days. All these men would choose their own companies.

All this being done, I threw myself down upon my pallet to rest before the evening meal.

*****

Next morning I arose and dressed with some care, and went to sit at the table in my pavilion where Ralph was preparing my breakfast. He brought food to me and bowed himself out, leaving me to my own thoughts. The cold morning air wrapped itself about me and I called to him for hot spiced wine, which he brought. After a spell he returned and laid my sword next to me upon the board.

"I've cleaned your sword, Sir John," he said, "and greased the blade against the damp." He paused. "I've polished the scabbard as well."

Lost in thought I thanked him and continued with my meal. It was not until he refilled my wine cup that I realised how overly attentive he was. I looked up at him and stared, astonished to see his dishevelled appearance. His clothes were damp and bedraggled, and he seemed unable to keep his eyes open for very long.

"What is it, boy? You look as though you have not slept, and you're wet and besmirched with mud."

He shook himself, and stood up a little straighter. A slow smile spread over his face. "Marco and I went into the town last night—under the walls. It's not hard, but the water is icy cold."

I gaped at him. This was startling news. "Where is Marco?"

"Fast asleep, I think, Sir John."

"Then wake him, and bring him here to me. I must hear what he has to say before anyone else. Do not speak a word of this to any other soul. Understand?"

Within a short space Marco stood before me, grinning broadly.

"*Buon giorno, Signore.* I hope you are well."

"Never mind how I am. What did you think you were doing in the night? The two of you could have been captured, perhaps killed. What made you go on such a mad escapade?" I spoke sharply.

He looked crestfallen. "I told Master Sterz I would find a way into the town."

"Yes, you did, and I agreed that you should. But why did you not tell me when you were going? Why take Ralph? He could not pass for an Italian like you."

"The town was all confusion. Many men were camped everywhere, in the streets, in the squares. It was dark. No one took any notice of us at all. What is yet one more page, one more soldier, in such a place?"

He made a sudden gesture of impatience. "Sir John, do you want to know what we found out, Ralph and I, or are we to be punished for helping your cause?"

I relented. "No, I suppose not. But in future, such ventures must be planned more carefully. You must learn to cover all

Frank Payton

possibilities. Leave word with me of what you intend. Ask me what I want to know, or you might miss something of importance. Go now and fetch something to eat and drink, and sit with me here at the table."

They obeyed with alacrity, and I proceeded to question them.

"Well, what did you discover? How did you enter the town, Marco?"

He gulped at his wine, and wiped his mouth on his sleeve. "We avoided our own people, who are encamped across each road as you know, went down into the ditch and out again until we were able to reach the walls. That was easy. Next we followed the wall around to where the stream runs underneath from the west. Luckily the level of the water was not so high as at the top of the arch, and we plunged in up to our waists. By all the Saints! It froze the blood in our legs so that we could scarce feel our feet. I have never been so cold! We pressed on under the wall. There was no light, so we had to feel our way. After about a spear's length in, we came up against the iron bars of the grille, which extends below the level of the water. We felt all over this ironwork for weaknesses, but there were none. Then we had to quickly retrace our steps, get out of the water, and recover the feeling in our legs."

"How were the iron bars held in place?" I asked.

"Oh, they were well set into the spaces between the stones, and held with mortar. We could not move them at all, even though we threw all our weight upon one which seemed thinner than the others, but all to no avail."

Ralph continued the tale. "We could then do naught else but to walk all the way around the walls to where the stream ran out from under. There we tried again, and this time we were lucky. One of the bars was rusted almost to nothing, and we broke it and thrust ourselves through. There however, the water was deeper, and we had difficulty in wading out and climbing up the bank."

Marco took up the story again. "We crept out of the water and into the shelter of a nearby house, to try and wring the water from our clothes. Then we went into the street, and just lost ourselves in

Hawkwood's Sword

the crowds of people and soldiers. Men were bivouacked everywhere, and occupied many houses as well. It seems most of the townspeople had been told to flee to the country for safety, especially young girls and women."

I laughed. "That will be a great disappointment for our people. We'll keep that to ourselves. But what do you think their strength is?"

"I can't be sure," said Marco. "There must be several thousands. There are crossbowmen and spearmen, and a goodly number of men-at-arms. We saw many horses stabled about the place, so they could ride out upon us if they chose. Some of the men were grumbling because the Count is safely lodged in the tower. At least we know where he is."

"What preparations seem to have been made to defend the town?" I asked.

"We saw constant patrols along the walls, and men stood to in readiness to rush forwards and man the fighting positions. Baskets of stones have been placed where they can be thrown down on any attacker. That is really all we can say about that, but there is more to tell. When we felt we could see no more we returned to the river, plunged through the water, and so out again under the wall. We decided to return by walking right around the town, and by doing so we found something which could be very important."

"Yes, well, and what is that?" I was impatient to know the full extent of their discoveries before we were interrupted. The knowledge had to be mine alone, at least to begin with. Marco was not to be hastened however, and only after finishing his wine did he continue.

"About halfway back we found ourselves climbing over a heap of large rocks, which have bushes growing amongst them. Between the stones and the wall, it is very narrow. Luckily we took that way, and we found that down there is a small door, partly covered by soil and rubble. It is in a corner where one of the buttresses stands out from the wall."

Frank Payton

I sat back in my chair, my imagination whirling. This was unbelievable luck, that two virtually untried lads should be giving us the town! Now we had three secret ways through the walls, although the door would have to be cleared, and the full extent of the entrance explored. It was possible, of course, that behind the actual door the whole thing could be blocked by new masonry, not easily removed.

"You've both done well, very well indeed, and you can expect to be well rewarded. Now go away, and when I next see you, I shall expect you to look more like soldiers than vagrants."

They grinned at each other, saluted me, and left. Moments later John Brise shouldered his way through the pavilion entrance and sat down at the board.

"What have those two been up to?" he rumbled. "No good, I'll be bound."

"Not so, John. In fact, they have done something very praiseworthy. But more of that later. What do you want of me?"

"Have you thought, Jack, that we can cut off the water supply to the town? We can dam the river to the east; let it flow into the moat and so away. They'll not like that, no water for men or horses. It would shorten the siege."

"Yes, I had thought of it, but now I think it would be useful to dam up the water for another reason. Again, more of that later, when we discuss tactics with Albrecht and the others. We must lay careful plans for this one, John. There'll be no stupid rushing in with frontal attacks, which only lose us men and equipment, all for naught."

He scratched his head. "So, what do we do now? Sit and wait, is that all?"

"For the present, yes. We have disposed our forces, made it clear that we intend to stay. When the Count looks out from his tower, what will he see?"

"Not many men, that's for sure. That might tempt him to sally out and try to break free. We would have to throw in more men to contain a general breakout, which would soon reveal our hand, and our true numbers. We could only keep that secret if we attacked at night."

"I agree, but you know, I think he will stay where he is. Besides, I should think he has a better idea of our true numbers than we imagine. It is fairly certain that we were watched on our approach here. No, I feel it is most likely that messengers have been sent to Milan, asking for assistance. For the present I think we can afford to await events. Do not relax patrols though, and some show of force about the countryside would not go amiss. Keep the men occupied, let them burn a few farms and villages. That should give the Count some reason for concern."

"Perhaps..."

I paused. "But enough of this. Pour yourself a cup of wine, and then we will go and seek out Albrecht. I have much to discuss with him. Do not, however, show any surprise at anything I have to say."

The discussions had to wait. We were interrupted by a messenger from Matt Sayers, who commanded the men on the road to the west of Lanzo. The messenger slid off his horse and came to the door of the pavilion, a bold, swanky lad with red hair under a close-fitting archer's steel cap. He stared at us. It was clear from his manner that he had not been in the presence of his leaders before, and was not sure how to address us, myself in particular. He looked uncertainly from one to another.

"I have a message for Sir John," he began awkwardly. "From Master Sayers."

"I am John Hawkwood. What have you to say to me? Take your time. I won't eat you."

"Master Sayers says to tell you that, shortly after we had roused ourselves this morning and changed the guard, the gates before us opened and two men rode out, a herald and a man-at-arms. The herald asked to speak to our chief men on behalf of the

Frank Payton

Count of Savoy, or some such person. That is all I know, sir. I have done as charged. May I say aught to Master Sayers for you?"

"You may tell him that I and Master Brise will join him directly, and we will bring the leaders of the Almains with us."

He saluted and made for his horse. I called after him for his name.

"It is Jenkin, Sir John—Jenkin Cope, out of Suffolk."

He mounted his horse and rode off as if the Devil were after him. John chuckled in his beard. "You certainly put the fear of God into that one, Jack. Good Lord preserve us, has all the wine gone? I suppose we had better arm ourselves. D'you want me to send a runner to Albrecht?"

"Yes, and send that rascal Ralph to me, will you, with my armour and my parade shield. Make sure he's cleaned himself up. Tell him to bring Marco as well."

*****

Later we rode out towards the town, where we were joined by Albrecht, von Felsingen and Harzmann.

"Good Day, Jack." Albrecht brought his horse alongside mine; von Felsingen dropped back next to John, who acknowledged him with a brief nod. "What can we expect, do you think?"

"Not much more than a curious look-over, and defiance, I'd say. They probably won't know what to make of us yet. But their spies will have been active, that's for sure."

"They might try to buy us off."

"Why should they? They're in a strong position. Walled tower, new fortress tower, and a goodly number of men, I should think. They'll guess we don't have siege engines. Mercenaries like us seldom do. No, they'll want to sit it out. With adequate supplies, and water, this could take weeks, as they see it."

Hawkwood's Sword

Albrecht glanced at me with raised eyebrows. "But not as you see it, I think, Jack. You have surely realised, as have I, that we control the water supply. The stream can be directed into the ditch, is that not so?"

"Yes, but if we do that we expose the water-gates, and those could be useful to us in an attack, a way to get into the town unseen. But you and I alone must discuss this later." I continued in a quieter voice. "I can tell you now, for your ear alone, that Ralph and Marco got into the town last night under one of the water-gates, and spied out the position. I will let you know more details later. Also, there is a small half-hidden door which must be explored somehow."

"*Du lieber Gott!* Those two boys?! You sent them on such a madcap prank? What were you thinking of?" He eyed me as if I were mad.

"I? I was fast asleep and knew naught about it until this morning. They told me all—and valuable information it is, too."

We had now drawn close to Matt Sayers' small command. He came out to meet us, together with Simon Bawdesley. Matt was my idea of a good soldier. He kept himself and his weapons and other equipment clean, and saw to it that the men under him did the same. The men also trusted and respected him, which is always a good sign amongst soldiers. He was tall, with short greying hair and beard. In England he had been a smith before taking to the life of a soldier. Old Simon I had known for many years, and we had been together at Crecy Field.

Matt saluted us both. "Good Day, Sir John, and also to you, Master Sterz. The Count's herald is still a-horseback and waiting on the road. I offered him hospitality, but he refused. His name is Oderigo Morelli."

"Thank you, Matt. We'll go to him straightway."

"I've stood the men to, Sir John, just in case this is a device to take us unawares."

"That was well done, Master Sayers," said Albrecht, unusually for him.

Frank Payton

I had noticed that he seldom addressed our English lower ranks directly, but I had also seen him glance around with approval at the neat guard camp straddling the road, and the men drawn up in ranks ready for action.

Our small party moved from the rear and approached the herald. We halted some twenty yards short, then Albrecht and I continued until we were face to face. Morelli was a small, dignified figure in semi-military dress. His sharp, dark eyes regarded us keenly. Behind him, also mounted, was a man-at-arms in full armour, who bore a light lance with a pennon bearing the device of a black eagle on a silver field. The herald wore a cap of black velvet with a white plume secured by a jewelled clasp. He swept the cap from his head with some elegance, bowed slightly and spoke.

"I am Oderigo Morelli, Herald to His Excellency the Count of Savoy, against whose town you come bearing arms," he said in heavily accented English. "I am required to ask who you are, and by whom you are so employed."

Albrecht bowed in his turn and answered for us. "I am Albrecht Sterz of Mecklenburg, and my companion is John Hawkwood, an English knight, lately serving in the army of Edward, King of England, whom I also had the honour to serve. Our service at present is to the noble Marquis of Monferrato, and we aid him against the Visconti of Milan."

"We are not aware that you have any dispute with my master," said the herald. "He demands that you pass on in peace, and cease from despoiling his lands."

"But you must know that your master is in open alliance with Milan, and he bears heavily on the lands belonging to Monferrato," responded Albrecht.

Morelli gave a slight shrug of his shoulders. "If that is so, and I do not say that it is, then it is not your concern. An you do not pass on in peace, we shall be obliged to come forth in attack. Your defeat is assured. I should warn you that we are strong in numbers, whereas you are too few. Even with your men at the

Hawkwood's Sword

other gate, you are too few. I repeat—this is not your land. Leave in peace."

"That is not possible," I replied, "until we bring a peace of our choosing and our making to the enemies of the Marquis."

The herald was silent for a moment, then spoke shortly. "I will give your reply to my master."

He replaced his bejewelled cap, bowed in salute, and turned his horse towards the town once more. We watched as the pair cantered off, and as the gates opened to receive them. Visible inside was a mass of armed men drawn up in ranks, probably as a show of strength. The gates closed with a dull boom.

We rode slowly back to the camp on the road. Matt Sayers met us, eager for information.

"What's to do, Sir John? Will they surrender the town to us, or do we have to fight for it?"

I laughed. "You'll have to earn your pennies with the sword, Matt. You would have been disappointed else, if I know you well. Stand the men down; they'll not be needed yet a while, but keep a close watch on those gates—beware."

"Well, you're right about the sword, Sir John. I'd liefer fight for my pay than take it easily, but there's those who wouldn't. I ought to tell you now that there are too many whisperings that this is a bad campaign. Too much action and too little to show for it."

Albrecht overheard this despite Matt's lowered voice. "Is this serious?" he asked. "If so, we had better look into the matter without delay. We can't be caught out here in a foreign land by a mutiny. What do you know about this, Master Sayers, or are you guessing?"

"What I know comes from your own man, Wilhelm Steiner. He and I talked when we came here on this detail, before he set up his own camp at the next gate." Matt waved an arm in the direction of the north side of the town. "He said there was word amongst your Almains that some wished to break off and join with the Count Landau, who serves the tyrant of Milan. He has a band of your countrymen, and some Hungarians under him. Wilhelm was thinking it was just campfire talk. You know how it is; but he was worried."

"Then he should have told me!" Albrecht stared at Matt, clearly aghast at this news. He turned to von Felsingen, who with Harzmann and Wolf, his page, sat their horses a little to our rear.

"Werner, and you Conrad, ride back to camp. I shall stay with Sir John and return later. Wolf, stay by me."

Thus dismissed, the two knights rode off, soon urging their mounts into a gallop, racing back to their camp. Albrecht saw this and shook his head at the levity. Wolf urged his horse to stand behind him. "Wolf, go to the North Gate, and tell Meister Steiner that I wish to see him here without delay. Do not wait for him but return immediately to me. *Verstehst Du?*"

"*Ja, mein Herr!*" and the boy saluted and cantered off on his errand.

We dismounted and stretched our legs, walking about the small camp. Albrecht had little to say; I think he was taken aback by the news. Wolf returned before too long and reported that Steiner was on his way.

When he did arrive, Albrecht took him a little to one side to hear his report of the matter. Since their speech was all in the Almain tongue, I had no idea what was said, but guessed that Steiner was receiving a severe dressing down from his leader. After dismissing him, Albrecht returned to where I waited by the horses.

"It is clear that I shall have to look further into this business, Jack, but I want to avoid involving Werner and his shadow. I'm never altogether happy with the pair of them. I shall take von Auerbach into my confidence on this. I know him to be totally reliable."

I nodded my approval. "And for my part, I shall have to find out if there are any like feelings amongst my men. Unfortunately they are not all English, as you know. The Bretons and Gascons are an unruly lot. If I am to have any defections it may well be from within their ranks, but one never knows for sure." At that, we

Hawkwood's Sword

parted for our own camps. First, however, I rejoined John Brise, Ralph and Marco, who had been waiting patiently whilst all this was going forward. Now we all set off for the main camp. I gave John the gist of what had happened. As I expected, he exploded indignantly.

"Any troublemakers amongst my lot with find themselves at the end of a rope! Too much action, is there? To my mind there's not enough to keep them occupied. We should attack this Lanzo as soon as possible, and get the men's minds on their work. Too much idling around campfires, if you ask me!"

I let him run on in this vein for a while, but listened with only one ear. I was trying to decide upon my own best course of action over this seemingly impending mutiny. I could not ignore such a threat.

On our return to camp I sent for Will Preston, William Turton, Andrew Belmonte, Jack Onsloe and Giles Ashurst. They trooped into my pavilion and joined John Brise and myself at the long table. Ralph and Marco put out wine, fruit and nuts, then stationed themselves at the door. Briefly I set out my reasons for the gathering, and added that Albrecht was holding a similar meeting at his own camp.

"Naturally you will all keep this to yourselves for the present. But I want you to tell me if there is anything for me to be concerned about amongst our men."

"There's nothing stirring in my company," said Jack. "They wouldn't dare, not after what happened at Lyons. I hanged six who lagged behind in the attack on the breach. That steadied any troublemakers." He shot a dark look around the table as if in triumph.

"You can rely on the archers, Sir John," said Giles. "They still look upon you as one of their own, despite your knighthood."

"I'm pleased to hear that, Giles, though it is long years since I drew bowstring in battle."

The two Williams also backed their men. No disloyalty there. The only exception was Andrew Belmonte, who hesitated, looked down, and unceasingly twisted the end of his sword belt this way and that.

"Well, Andrew," I said, "what about your Bretons and the like?"

"Er...well...hmm, Sir John, I can't really say for sure. They're a bit undisciplined, I know, but I don't think they would desert. I... I..." His voice trailed off uncertainly.

"Have you heard anything or not!" barked John Brise. "Well? Have you?"

Andrew sat up straight and took up his wine cup, which he drained in one gulp. "I think some of the Bretons want to go home to Brittany, and the Gascons feel they are too far from home here in Italy. They worry about their families, but I still don't think they would just desert to the other side." He sat back in his seat avoiding my eye. "I'll be more alert and see what I can find out."

Will Preston spoke up. "When are we going to attack the town?"

"Not just yet, Will. There are some preparations we have to make. We'll need all the scaling ladders assembled and brought forward, preferably under cover of night. Any main attack will also have to be made at night when there is a full moon."

"So there are to be some lesser actions? Diversionary attacks?" Will persisted. "To cover what, exactly?"

I could see that the time had come to tell all, and so I repeated what I had already told Albrecht and John Brise about the visit Ralph and Marco had paid to Lanzo during the night. I explained that the breach in the iron grille where the river passed under the walls had to be enlarged, and as quietly as possible. Also there was the hidden door to be properly explored, again on a moonlit night. Diversions were therefore to play an important part. My companions were frankly incredulous, and amazed that two young lads had had the nerve to undertake such an enterprise without any backing. Even Jack Onsloe was impressed by their bravery.

Hawkwood's Sword

After that revelation there was much speculation as to what could and should be done, but I was having none of it. The last thing I wanted was an inquisition into when, why and how, and so on. "No more questions, Will. My mind is not yet settled on this matter, and I have to speak to Master Sterz. You may all go about your duties. Patrols as usual. Everyone to keep their eyes open for any moves from the town. Most important of all, keep close what I have told you."

They heaved themselves off their backsides and passed out into the sunlight.

"Andrew! A moment if you please," I called to him.

"Yes, Sir John?" He turned back toward me, clearly ill at ease.

"I am surprised at you. I had expected better from you, of all people. You must get control of yourself, and also of your men. Work them harder. Slacking won't do. Give them more weapon practice, jousts, mock battles, anything to get them off their behinds and prepared for action."

"I'll try, Sir John. I'll try harder. I'm sorry to have let things come to this pass."

He was now painfully embarrassed. The only one amongst us of gentle birth, he had elected to follow me rather than return to England, in the hope of restoring his family name and fortune.

"Very well. Off with you now, and remember my words."

Thus I dismissed him, and turned to Ralph, who stood with Marco at the pavilion entrance.

"Fetch the horses over. We will go and wait on Master Sterz."

Chapter 4
Laying Siege

Albrecht's camp was ordered activity. Men-at-arms were practising armed combat, both on foot and on horseback. Two mounted squadrons wheeled and turned across the square, thundering towards each other with flying hooves, turning away only at the last moment before contact. It was a fine sight.

Mustered with the Almain infantry was a small company of crossbowmen occupied in shooting at butts set up at about one hundred yards. There appeared to be some fair marksmen amongst them. Marco surveyed them with a critical eye.

"They are good, Sir John, but they should learn to shoot in volleys as we were trained to do, not all together at once. To achieve an effective rate of shooting with crossbows, it is necessary to divide your men into three, or even four, groups. When the first group is shooting the second will just be taking aim. The third will be placing the bolt in the slot, and the fourth will be spanning the bow and drawing the string into the latch. Done in sequence by well-trained men, it is much more effective than each man shooting on his own account or a single mark."

I immediately grasped the principle. This was the only way that crossbowmen could come close to the rate of shooting with the longbow.

"That is very good, Marco. You shall explain this to Master Sterz at a suitable time. Be sure of that. Now, what have we here?"

Hawkwood's Sword

There seemed to be a general brawl amongst a large group of men-at-arms on foot. Armed with thick wooden cudgels and wooden shields, they hammered away at each other as if in full battle. It was well that they were not using sharpened swords, or there would have real wounding, even death. As it was, several men had been knocked down and lay unmoving on the ground. Even as we looked on, others stirred and began to crawl out of the melee. By now we had been seen, and Albrecht's page came forward to meet us.

"Meister Sterz has sent me to escort you, Sir John. You will follow me, please."

He bowed in his stiff Almain fashion, and set off with us in his train. Wolf was a well set-up, confident young fellow with a sturdy frame and a mop of thick yellow hair. I always had to smile inwardly at his serious manner.

Shortly afterwards we were received by Albrecht, and I was ushered to a chair of dark heavy wood, intricately carved. It looked as if it might once have stood in a monastery—an abbot's seat, perhaps. Ralph and Marco stood behind me. Wolf set a cup of wine in front of me and retired to stand behind his master, who raised his own cup to me. We drank to each other silently. I could sense that Albrecht was seriously worried. He ran his fingers through his dark hair and smoothed his short beard. Always, since I had first met him in Koblenz twenty-odd years before, these had been sure signs of his concern over events.

"What is it then, old friend?" I asked. "Have you too discovered some treachery?"

"I fear it may be so. Nothing upon which I can put my finger; it is as yet only a mere suspicion that all is not well—a whisper, a small wind which ripples the grass and is gone. But I feel it. And you?"

I shrugged my shoulders. "Not much more. One weak link, and the Bretons and Gascons are unhappy, I'm told. At this stage I fear we can but keep our eyes and ears open, and be ready for whatever may come."

FRANK PAYTON

Albrecht sipped his wine. "The most likely source of trouble would be from Count Landau, who might discreetly send agents to meet malcontents amongst my own Company in an attempt to turn them against the rest, and against your English. The siege of Lanzo could then be raised, and we would be under attack from two directions."

"But this is guesswork," I replied. "We should turn our attention to the discoveries made last night by Ralph and Marco. We must seek out this mysterious door, and also test the watergates again. If these are as reported, then we have the town at our feet. We need a diversion to allow these matters to be looked into. It demands a dark night, and a small force equipped with tools and darkened lanthorns."

"Why not field a strong force of mounted men to make a slow passage around the town?" Albrecht suggested. "They would be fully armed and have all warlike intent. They would hold the attention of the defenders, and at intervals your archers could send showers of fire arrows into the town. These might start a few fires and create even more of a diversion. The Conte Verde could be misled into thinking a general attack was about to be launched."

I agreed at once. "Yes! Put Werner in charge of your people and I will send John Brise with ours. Giles Ashurst can take a couple of hundred archers in addition."

The rest of the plan fell easily into place. Marco would go with Albrecht and a picked band of Almains to investigate the watergates. Ralph would accompany me and a similar party to try and clear the door.

*****

The progress around the town began as the sun was setting. There was still enough light for the defenders to see that a large force had been deployed. As the darkness thickened, trumpets

Hawkwood's Sword

shrilled and lights could be seen on the town walls as men took up their defensive positions. The torches carried by our men were bobbing swords of flame, and their effect was as we expected. All eyes were drawn to the spectacle before them. So far as we could tell, no one saw our small band cross the ditch and make its way up to the foot of the wall.

"Thus far, and all's well," muttered Will Preston in a hoarse whisper. "What now, Sir John?"

"We follow Ralph's lead. He's the one who found the way. Lead on, boy."

Our eyes now became better accustomed to the darkness, and although the way was not easy over the broken ground, we made steady progress.

At least we knew that, perhaps with some exceptions, the defenders were concentrated at the point where our riders were passing by. We would therefore be able to work unseen. We trudged on in file. Some of the men carried spades and iron crowbars, in addition to their weapons. There were not a few grumbles and stifled curses when one or another stumbled, or fell against some hidden stone or dip in the ground. Clad in full armour as we were, we sweated greatly.

At length Ralph stopped and whispered, "Here are the rocks in front of the door, Sir John. We will need some light to see clearly."

One of the men came forward with a small lanthorn. The shaded glow shone red on a wooden door set deep in the wall. No more than the height of a man, it was made of massy oak timbers and reinforced with iron bands. It was also half-buried in small stones and soil, and had an air of long disuse.

"Come then," said Will. "You Tom, and you Roger, break up this heap of soil, and you others shovel it back out of the way—but quietly. We don't want stones or worse about our ears."

Will and I stood back out of the way whilst the work went ahead. We were all intrigued by the door. Why was it there at all? Was it a lure for attackers? Was it in fact a trap? Or was it an escape route? There was clearly only one way to find out, and I was

Frank Payton

determined that we should do so. Work progressed, but slowly, and we had to take care that when the riders passed by there should be no noise, and no lights to be seen. To this end I posted a sentry twenty paces further on, to give us warning that work should stop and we must take cover.

As the horsemen went by we closed the lanthorns and crouched down amongst the rocks. On one of these occasions Giles' archers played their allotted part. Dismounting, they formed up and sent a storm of fire arrows high over the wall just above our heads. It was a fine thing to hear the hiss of the shafts arcing over, and to see their fiery trails. We could also hear shouts of dismay as the arrows took effect and fires were started in many of the houses. When the archers ceased shooting the whole cavalcade continued on its way. We waited a while longer, then unshuttered our lanthorns and got back to our business. At last the door lay open to view, and the question on all our minds was how to enter.

"We have no key," said Will, "but it does not matter, as there's no keyhole. The door is doubtless stoutly barred on the inner side. We could smash it open, but there would be too much clamour."

I agreed. "Too much now, but when we make a general attack there will be clamour enough to drown out the sound of such an attempt on the door."

"What we need is a man inside the wall," muttered Will in a low voice. "Remember, young Marco has been there already, if not at this point. If he could get to the other side of this door he might open it to us."

I knew well what he was saying, but how to achieve it was a riddle to think on. "We can do no more for now, save get away before we are discovered. The dawn cannot be far off, and we must not be caught here."

The men gathered up their weapons, tools, and other equipment, and we began to retrace our steps towards the camp on the road. After the show of strength by our riders, and the excitement caused by their passage, in the main the town lay quiet; but above our heads we could hear the clink of weapons and the

Hawkwood's Sword

fall of iron-shod feet as the sentries on the wall passed and repassed each other, and their calls of recognition. At some points there was more activity and noise where houses had been set alight by the fire arrows and efforts continued to put out the fires.

We reached Matt Sayers' camp as dawn was beginning to show in the eastern sky. The darkness faded from deep blue to a lighter shade. A thin line of gold appeared on the horizon, ever widening as I watched, and grew more intense until the Sun himself rose above the hills and fields. Away in the countryside a cock crowed.

Suddenly, for a few instants of time, I was at home in Sible Hedingham, waking in my bed in the chamber I shared with my elder brother John and young Nicholas. John would have already arisen and gone to his early duties in the tannery. My younger brother would get out of bed and fall to his knees in prayer. Already he was on his way to being a priest. He was so pious I would kick him in annoyance that he thought himself something of a saint at the age of eight. At two years older I couldn't have given a damn about the next world anyway. After my work in the tannery there would be the village girls to chase, and then practice with my bow and arrows under the watchful eye of old Walter, who had fought for the King in the Scottish wars. Full of hair-raising tales he was—of skirmishes, sieges and the great Battle of Boroughbridge in the North Country, where the King won the day over the House of Lancaster. Even then I looked forward to winning honour upon the field of battle.

The moment fled with the warning call of one of the guards, as we went in amongst the tents. Matt Sayers appeared before me, drawn sword in hand, flustered at our sudden appearance as if from nowhere.

"What's afoot, Sir John? Are we attacked? We had no warning. What-?"

I held up my hand to stop the flow of words. "Be easy, Matt," I laughed to see his worried face. "No, there is no attack. We have but spied out a little of the defences overnight. All we need now is sleep. But have no fear; when we make our attack, you shall not be left out!"

FRANK PAYTON

It was then his turn to laugh, though rather more grimly.

Before returning to the main camp I gathered the men about me and swore them to secrecy concerning the night's work. "For remember, only we know about this door, plus Marco the Italian, who is now one of my pages. Severe punishment awaits any who give away this secret. You were all chosen for your trustworthiness, and I will reward your silence well."

There was an immediate chorus as they fiercely affirmed their loyalty, after which I sent them off to break their fast and to get some sleep.

Followed by Ralph, I returned to my pavilion, where he helped me remove my armour. "Bring me a little to eat and drink, Ralph, and then take some rest," I said. "That was a good night's work, boy."

*****

Later I sat drinking and toying with the food, thinking of a plan of action. It seemed to me that the complete plan should be known only to Albrecht and myself. The main attacking forces would be commanded by John Brise and Werner von Felsingen, whilst the approaches through the watergates and possibly the hidden door would have to be made by Albrecht and myself, each with a body of picked men. As I sat thus, Marco returned from the Almain camp and came to report. He was flushed with excitement over the night's activities.

"We were able to break aside all the bars in the eastern watergate. Master Sterz's men had heavy hammers and steel chisels, which they used to remove the mortar holding the bars. They had files to cut the rusty metal. The way is now open. I am also to tell you that Master Sterz will come to see you after the noon meal. He will bring only Wolf."

Hawkwood's Sword

"Good! That is just what I had hoped. Perhaps he guesses my own intent. Now go and rest. You have done well. Say nothing of last night's work to anyone."

He smiled and bowed. "Trust me, Sir John. I shall not fail you."

*****

Albrecht arrived as the sun was beginning his long golden descent to evening. I watched him, straight-backed as ever, clad in black and silver, armed only with a short sword and dagger, riding a dove-grey palfrey rather than Wotan, his black destrier. He was followed by Wolf on his own white horse, very correct and upright. I noticed how Albrecht looked over at the gate guards, evidently inspecting their appearance, weapons, and their demeanour.

I had sent Andrew Belmonte on patrol to get him out of the way, and so the visitors were greeted at the gate by Will Preston and escorted over by him. Much to Will's disappointment, I merely thanked him and sent him off about his own duties again.

Ralph appeared, yawning from his sleep, and brought a flask of wine and a bowl of nuts, then took Wolf off to his own quarters. The pair always seemed to get on well together, although I thought that each must struggle to understand what the other said.

Albrecht and I sat in the shade of my pavilion, and I outlined my ideas and feeling about the attack on Lanzo. I told him about the door, and the likely problems of opening it. Together we discussed what Marco had told me.

"I agree with your general plan, Jack, and will send Werner, Conrad, and von Auerbach to lead our main assault. Then I will attempt an entry through the eastern watergate with, say, three hundred picked men. So far as the door is concerned I feel you should post a guard on it, and wait. As for yourself, if Brise, Preston, and Onsloe lead your main attack, I think you should take your men through the western gate. This the weakest anyway, as you'll recall. You should have little difficulty in breaking through."

Frank Payton

"Why not break in the door?" I persisted, but he shook his head impatiently.

"Think on it, Jack. We don't know what lies on the other side. It may be blocked with masonry—maybe not. That is why I say guard it and wait. My own feeling is that it could well be an escape route for someone. But we don't know, and it would be a waste of time to concentrate any force on it for too long. On the other hand, if you follow my suggestion you might make a useful catch."

In the end I had to agree that would be the best plan. The problem of opening the door was insurmountable. The attack, we decided, would be made that very night, at moonrise.

*****

The bustle of preparation was over, and our strength was now ranged against Lanzo in a steel ring encircling the town. As an angry red sun sank, the shadows deepened and darkness settled threateningly around the doomed defenders. The night sky was cloudless, dusted with a myriad of stars, an endless uncountable number of bright sparks of shimmering light.

The walls and towers of the town were blocks of deepest black. There was a murmur of voices from our men, a deep laugh here and there, a clinking of weapons and the whickering of the few horses amongst their number, for most of the men were on foot, apart from the commanders and the scouts who would bear messages back and forth as the attack proceeded.

As I had agreed with Albrecht, my men were assembled separate from the rest. All were men-at-arms, heavily armoured and weaponed. All had visored helmets. We wore white surcoats emblazoned with the red Cross of St. George back and front, with the same device on our shields. Most favoured, as I did, a plain straight sword, and carried in addition a rondel dagger or a ballock knife as a second weapon, or for giving the *coup de grace*. Others relied for their main weapon on either a double or single bladed axe, or a heavy mace. But some had been equipped with the heavy iron mallets used to pound in the stakes for the camp tents.

I explained our role to the men. Briefly, after breaking through the iron bars of the watergate, we would assemble on the river bank and then make for the nearest gate in the wall. Moving in a solid phalanx of three hundred, we should be able to crush our way through any opposition. I expected most of the defenders to be on the wall to repel the main attack anyway. On taking the gate, we would unbar and open it to our men on the outside.

"What about the water under the walls?" came a voice out of the darkness.

"There should be none, or very little. Even now the river is being dammed up, and the water diverted into the ditch around the town. It will be a shock to those inside to see their water supply disappear, I'll be bound."

This drew some grim laughter, and I continued. "But to clear the way we shall have to break the iron bars under the wall. Luckily, I'm told, the bars are badly rusted, so we should not have too much trouble. The Almains with Master Sterz will enter through the watergate on the other side of the town. We shall know them by their white surcoats." I looked around the men and noted the tension, how they waited like hunting dogs on the leash. "We move when the moon is in full sight above the town. Now, we wait."

We settled down in our position opposite the watergate. There was a bustle of activity on the walls. Our preparations had been watched. Indeed, the defenders could hardly have failed to notice. We had made no pretence of secrecy.

However, we had assumed too much. Perhaps we had been overconfident that the dice were heavily loaded in our favour, for as we watched, the huge gates nearest to us swung open. A torrent of horsemen flooded out and flung itself at the nearest attackers, who were completely taken aback and struggled to put up a defence. They were under John Brise's command, and even at the

Frank Payton

distance which we were from the action, I could hear his bull's bellow as he strove to rally his men.

Someone had planned well. Savoy knew that we could not attack the town on horseback, and he also knew that our men-at-arms were usually supported by archers. Night, however, is no time for accurate shooting, moonlight or not. We could not help them, and the uneven fight was not good to watch. But over many years I had found that when all seemed lost, the right course of action will somehow present itself. Suddenly, I knew what must be done. I called to Ralph.

"Get over to Master Brise. Tell him to fall back, but slowly. This should draw the horsemen out, further from the gate. They may not realise their peril until too late. Then they may be surrounded and cut off."

Ralph dashed off and was soon lost in the semi-darkness. I watched anxiously for some confirmation that my message had been received. It seemed a long time a-coming, but gradually the mass of footmen began to retreat, step by step. They had locked shields, and hacked and stabbed at the horses as their riders forced them up to the line in order reach down with their long lances. The poor beasts shied away, carrying their riders along the line, and soon all was confusion, and the shock of the charge was broken. Then the men-at-arms on each flank of the little battle began to lap around the horsemen like waves on a rock, and the tide of battle turned. Saddles emptied, and the battered riders sought to retreat. But few of them survived the flailing swords to ride back through the already closing gates, which boomed shut as the last survivor rode through at a gallop.

It was time for us to move. The attack had begun in earnest. With a roar, men flowed forward with the scaling ladders. As these were placed against the wall, the first men began to climb. Holding their shields above their heads, they sought to avoid the missiles raining down upon them. Those lucky enough to reach the top began to fight desperately in order to establish a foothold on the parapet. Those who were not so lucky were hit by stones and

Hawkwood's Sword

crossbow bolts and fell heavily upon those below, causing confusion and injury or death to themselves and others.

But we could not merely stand and watch, so I led my men off in the direction of the watergate. We were seen as we crossed the ditch, which by then was running with icy water from the diverted river. Crossbow bolts began to whip amongst us, and some found their mark. Men fell screaming with pain, the short stubby shafts sticking through their armour.

Matt Sayers' voice boomed from within his helmet. "Up with your shields, you fool rabble! Hold them high! Close ranks! Keep moving!"

Even so, some wavered under the attack from above. But I had foreseen this, and ordered Giles Ashurst to send archers to cover our close approach to the wall. Out of range of the crossbows, they now sent showers of arrows against the defenders. Cries of pain and dismay came down to us, and the rain of bolts slackened and almost ceased.

We tramped on, almost up the wall. Small stones and then larger ones fell upon us. Men were knocked unconscious and fell without a groan. These missiles could be pushed over the battlements without exposing the men above to the arrows, and since we had to enter the tunnel under the wall, we took some punishment. Twice I was knocked to my knees as large stones hit my shield full on. My arm ached, and I was dizzy with pain. Eventually I made it to the shelter of the watergate. I leaned against the side wall to recover myself as more and more of our men crowded in. The hammer men in the front went forward and began to pound at the iron bars.

As the two lads had discovered, the bars were badly rusted, and it was not long before the hammers broke through. We followed, Matt Sayers and I, with Ralph and Marco. The rest stumbled along in the pitch darkness behind us. There was much cursing and chattering.

"Quiet! Quiet! Goddamn you all back there!" I called. "No noise now, unless you wish a colder welcome at the other end."

Frank Payton

They fell into silence, and we carried on into the darkness. At long last a hoarse whisper came back from the front. "A light showing up front, Sir John. Could be a fire—it looks to be red and flickering."

"Good. Giles's men were to shoot fire arrows into the town. One of you go and see what lies ahead."

Against the glow I saw a single figure detach itself from the first group. Moving slowly, he went on—sword in hand, shield up. In the stone tunnel there was silence. No one moved. We held our breath as the dark figure turned.

"Clear ahead. No enemy in sight," came his muted call.

"Good! Let us get to it." I drew my sword and settled my shield securely on my left arm. "Forward! Form up on the left bank. Keep a sharp eye open for the enemy."

As quietly as was possible for a body of men so large, we moved out of the mouth of the watergate and grouped ourselves in a solid phalanx of steel—nigh three hundred of us. Ralph and Marco were on my left, Sayers to my right. The tall man-at-arms flourished a long-handled mace and grinned, showing white teeth. "This'll do for a few, Sir John, have no fear."

We closed our helmets and at my signal began to move towards the gate to our left, where defenders were clustered, peering over the wall, their backs to us. The first hundred yards was without incident. Then a shout went up from some Italian men-at-arms and foot-soldiers. They turned to face us and we were swept by a rain of bolts, while shouts of defiance reached our ears.

Fortunately they were too far away for the bolts to reach us with deadly force, and our raised shields intercepted the ones that did reach us. No one was killed or even wounded. Then, suddenly, came a change. I heard Marco's voice calling out a spate of Italian. What he was saying I could not even guess. Some voices came from behind me.

"The young whoreson's giving us away. Kill him!"

Hawkwood's Sword

There was a surge forward, and swords were raised at Marco, but he stood firm. "Tell them, Sir John, I have told Savoy's men we are friendly—that we have been sent to help." He turned. "See, they are breaking up and going on to the wall."

"Stop that, you fools! Marco has thrown them off balance. They think we are allies. Now is our chance, before they realise the truth."

I ran forward and the whole pack followed. The cry went up. "St. George! St. George! A-Hawkwood! A-Hawkwood!"

Too late the enemy turned to face us. We were amongst them, felling them like dumb oxen, but they rallied, and fought back with some vigour.

I threw myself forward, sword flailing, my shield arm jarring under blows from swords, maces, shortened lances. My shield clanged from more than one crossbow bolt. I slammed my mailed right fist, with the sword pommel, into the face of a man-at-arms with an open fronted helmet. He grunted as the blow shattered his nose and cheekbones, dropped and rolled away, clutching his face and head.

A mace was descending upon my own head, and I had to be quick to catch the blow on my shield. Turning it away, I clashed body to body with the wielder of the mace. We strained against each other for some moments like wrestlers. I passed my sword from right to left hand, and scrabbled for the dagger at my right hip. My opponent divined my purpose and grasped my hand like a vice, striving to turn it away. Stepping back suddenly, I threw him off balance, and his grip slackened and broke. At last I drew the dagger and plunged its keen point through the mail about his neck and throat. The dark blood flowed over his surcoat and he fell away with a gurgling scream.

I reeled on in the press, feeling faint after that encounter. Ralph, Marco and John were ahead of me, and the Italians were falling back on the wall. I knew we had to get to the gate. Struggling through clusters of embattled men, fending off and delivering blows as I went, I slowly regained my position at the

Frank Payton

front line. The opposition before us was beginning to fail. It seemed also that the fighting above us on the wall was turning in our favour, as more and more white coats appeared on the parapet.

"We must gain the gate, Matt," I gasped. "They're falling back."

"Aye, Sir John. Come on, you laggards!" he roared. "To the gate! Away with these knaves!" We swept on, over the last few men-at-arms who stood before us.

"Unbar the gates! Open them wide, and stand aside!" I shouted at the wearying men. They flung themselves, yelling, on the bars and winches, and worked like fiends. With a groaning and a creaking, the massy gates began to move. As they did so, eager hands on the outside lent their aid.

A press of steel-clad bodies pushed against the timbers, and anon the gates swung wide. We stood aside and allowed the torrent of our men to sweep in and engage the defenders. Behind us, the Italians had rallied and stiffened their ranks with fresh men. The town was by no means in our hands yet.

"How now, Jack?" John Brise appeared at my side, raising his visor. I had seen him come down from the wall. Never the one for the easy way, he had fought his way up a scaling ladder and over the wall. I imagined him raging along the parapet with swirling sword as one of the Northmen raiders of old, his men behind him like a pack of ravening wolves.

"Well enough," I said. "But they've made a tussle of it—and it isn't finished yet."

He grinned. "We'll see." With that he slammed down his visor and flung himself into the melee once more The noise was tremendous. Hemmed in by the town walls and the narrow streets, the clang of weapons, the yelling and shouting, screaming and groaning, seemed far worse than in an open battlefield.

I gathered our men together again and, with Matt Sayers, once more entered the fight. The resistance was stiff, and in the crowded streets it was scarcely possible for the dead to fall. But in the end the weight of our number of fresh men from outside the walls, all eager for their share in whatever spoils of war were to be had, began to tell. Slowly the defenders were pushed back towards the castle. I decided it was time for me to withdraw from fight and so dropped back. Ralph and Marco joined me.

"Are you wounded, Sir John?" Ralph sounded anxious, Marco looked worried. They were both breathing heavily and had dented shields and bloodied swords. Ralph limped.

"No, no. I am well, but it is now time for our latecomers to take over the work. We have played our part for a spell. You have both carried yourselves as men this night. I am proud of you."

I slapped them both on the shoulder, and they grinned at each other like schoolboys.

"We will look for Master Sterz and his men, and see how they have fared," I told them. "Look out for an inn or a wineshop, where we can take our rest and a cup of wine—if there is any left in this town."

*****

As the last few defenders, fighting furiously, were driven back into the keep, Albrecht and I met for the first time since the attack began. We leaned on our swords and looked at each other. A slow smile spread over his face.

"Well, my friend, we meet again in the midst of yet another stricken town," he said. "You are not hurt, I hope?"

"No, no. My luck still holds, though that fellow gave me a hard fight before I slew him." I pointed to where the body of a tall man-at-arms lay face down on the cobbles. His right hand still clutched the shaft of the great axe with which he had come near to killing me. Albrecht frowned and walked over to the body. He stooped and rolled the dead man over. "Hmm, a German by his armour." He looked around. "Where is his shield?"

I pointed to where it lay, a little to one side.

FRANK PAYTON

"This is a device I have seen before somewhere," he said, "but I cannot remember where." He beckoned to a nearby page, gave him the shield and some instructions in the Almain tongue, and sent him back to camp.

"We will see if Der Alte Helmut, our armourer, can tell us who the man was, or, at the very least, whose retainer." He drew a deep breath. "Now I feel I could drink a bucket of wine, for I am as dry as a desert."

Nearby, Ralph had found an inn—empty, but with a plentiful supply of wine. Others soon trooped in, John Brise full of noisy accounts of the action, and Giles Ashurst, jesting as usual with tall tales beloved of the archer kind. Matt Sayers sat silent, his surcoat smeared with the blood of enemies. Jack Onsloe slid morosely into a seat, drank two cups of wine in quick succession, and sank into his habitual gloom. The two Wills, Preston, and Turton, came in and took their wine off to another table and spoke quietly to each other.

John Brise nodded in their direction. "I wonder what those two are plotting?" he said. "How to hide some loot, I'll wager. They're always whispering together, after a fight. Up to no good I'd warrant."

I ignored him, having learned that this was just his way, to grumble about such things. Nothing ever came of these matters. He was not to be quietened however, on this occasion.

"I'll swear my back is broken, Jack. I fell down the last few steps from the wall and across a block of stone. I shall be a week before I can ride, I'll be bound." He looked so miserable that we all burst into laughter.

"Ride what?" said Giles with a grin, cocking an enquiring eyebrow.

Jack stared. "Ride what? Ride what? Why, a horse, you jack fool," he rumbled. Again we dissolved into laughter, except for Albrecht, who could never understand our rough English humour. He merely smiled politely, and shook his head in disbelief.

HAWKWOOD'S SWORD

Suddenly he stood up. "Where is Ritter von Felsingen?" he barked to one of his guards. "Go, find him. Bring him here!"

But it was Ralph who provided the answer to Albrecht's question, as he stumbled in through the tavern door. "Sir John! Master von Felsingen is trying to kill Marco," he gulped, "and there is a maid and a dead man. Will you come?" He rushed away. We drained our cups and clattered after the boy.

He led us down a narrow street and across a darkened square. The only light came from the fires started by our men and the full moon in the blue-black sky. The dead littered the cobbled ground. Here and there a stricken soul groaned or cried out in final agony. On one side of the square was set a large house, by the look of it the house of a man of some substance. A number of Albrecht's men-at-arms clustered around the door. They parted to let us through, and we rushed after Ralph up the wide stairs to the first floor.

The room we entered extended across the full width of the house. It was well lit by tall candles, and by the moonlight. I remember painted walls and hung tapestries. There was a long table of polished wood, and heavy wooden chairs stood about. In one corner was an iron-bound chest, broken open and the contents spilled out, showing the gleam of gold and silver.

Amongst all this stood Marco, backed into a corner. Behind him crouched a richly attired young girl with streaming black hair, wide-eyed with fear. Marco's crossbow was held in front of him, cocked, a bolt at the nut, ready to shoot. Von Felsingen stood in front, long sword held high to strike. I noticed that Conrad Harzmann half leaned, half sat on the end of the table, his sword swinging idly in his hand as he watched the scene, a slight smile on his lips. Behind von Felsingen lay an elderly man, unconscious. Blood from a head wound seeped on to the floor.

"What in Hell are you doing, Werner?" rapped Albrecht.

"I'll tell you, Master Sterz," declared Marco. "He wants the girl, and I'm in the way. If he moves, I shoot. At this distance the bolt will pass through him, armour or no."

Frank Payton

"My men will hew your head from your shoulders in the next breath, insolent puppy!" shouted von Felsingen.

"But by then you'll be dead," returned Marco, with a twisted grin. "It will avail *you* naught."

I stepped forward. "No one is to kill anyone. Put up your bow, Marco—and you, Werner, your sword. It is plain that this youth sees what you do not. The girl is clearly of gentle birth, and you as a knight are sworn to protect such as she, and the helpless. What of your oaths of chivalry now?"

"Do as Sir John says," added Albrecht. "I'll have no more of this nonsense over a girl. We are all comrades in arms here, not dogs fighting over a bone."

I made a sign to Giles and the half-dozen or so archers who had crowded into the room. They nocked arrow to string, and bent their bows to shoot. The Almain men-at-arms stirred uneasily. Von Felsingen slammed his sword back into its scabbard, spun on his heel and stalked from the room, and so down the stairs. Harzmann was the last to leave. His cold blue eyes met mine as he passed, though he was smiling.

"Good night to you, Sir John, and to you Albrecht. We will all be better for rest after this night's work. Perhaps we are a little over-wrought." He pointed to Marco. "Our young friend appears to be the victor for the present. To him the spoils." His glance passed briefly over the girl. He pushed through the knot of archers, and moved silently down the stairs. It felt easier to breathe when he had gone.

Marco helped the girl to her feet. She stood close to him, supported by his arm. "This is Genevra, Sir John, daughter of the merchant Paolo da Lucca, who lies there on the floor. I fear he may be dead," he said.

I started at the mention of the name, but said nothing.

"Let me have a look at him." Giles pushed forward, and knelt by the motionless body. He felt the man's chest, and held his polished vambrace near to his lips. "He yet lives. See, there is a

Hawkwood's Sword

faint mist on the steel. The young lady is in luck. With proper care, her father may yet recover."

He beckoned to two of his men and together they lifted da Lucca and placed him in a large chair near to the fireplace. Genevra hurried to kneel beside him, and chafed his hands between her own, and rubbed his cheeks until some colour returned. Taking a white scarf from her shoulders, she staunched the blood running from the cut upon his head. Giles fetched a cup of wine from the table, poured some over the cloth, and applied it to the cut. This helped to stem the flow, and the sharpness of the wine made da Lucca wince. His eyes opened, and he stared about the room. He whispered a few words to Genevra, then closed his eyes again.

"He recovers," said Albrecht. "I suggest we leave the girl to tend her father, together with Marco and Ralph. A few of the archers can stay for good measure. We will return to our own duties, and I shall have further words with Master Werner in the morning." He lowered his voice. "I shall also want to find out more concerning the German you slew out there."

So it was. Giles told off five of his men to stay and guard the house. I also told Marco I would send one of the healers from the camp, who would bring herbs and simples to help Genevra's father.

As we made to leave, Genevra came up to Albrecht and myself. I thought her to be about eighteen years old, dark and comely, with a mass of long black hair. She had long-lashed brown eyes, tawny skin, and full red lips. Shyly and gracefully, she put out a hand to each of us.

"Thank you, Sir Gianni, and you Messer Sterz. I am truly grateful to you both, and to your men for all you have done to save me from that dreadful man," she shuddered, "And from his companion. Marco and his friends will look after us now."

She raised our hands and kissed them lightly, her dark eyes looking at each of us in turn. The touch of her lips was no more than the settling of a summer butterfly, her fragrance was of Spring flowers. We both bowed and took our leave.

As we emerged into the square once more, Albrecht turned to me and said in his serious way, "You have a problem, Jack, or at least young Marco has. Your problem springs from his. That girl is smitten with him, and he with her. Will he follow you now?"

I shrugged. "We've all been young and impetuous in our time," I said. "We shall have to wait and see how things fall out. But now I'm for my bed. The guards are posted. There is naught else for us to do this night."

"You are right. As far as I am concerned Werner can wait until morning." He slapped my shoulder and smiled. "We can sleep soundly tonight, Jack, after this success."

I bade him goodnight, and took Boy's reins from the page who had brought him to me. As I rode back to camp with my guard, I marvelled how Fate had brought me to a position where I could call on da Lucca for assistance, for Genevra's father was one of the agents of Francisco Datini, with whom I had done so much business in Avignon. Datini was a shrewd and hard bargainer on his own side, but honourable in all things, and we had both known we could help each other. I had kept this knowledge from Albrecht, and indeed all others, except John Brise, who was worn to secrecy. There was no need to broadcast the matter, as I did not know how things might fall out in the future—whether the Company would remain as one, or not. It is the nature of mercenaries to shift allegiances, to split up and reform in search of more congenial employment, more pay for less effort. It was ever thus.

*****

The next morning I rode back into Lanzo. As I passed through the gate, now manned with our own guards, I was pleased to see that the fires started during the night had been put out and some

Hawkwood's Sword

semblance of order restored. The Italian dead were being gathered together, stripped of their armour, weapons, and anything else of value, and laid out in rows. The stench of death was everywhere. I had no desire to invite a pestilence to strike us, and looked around for Matt Sayers, who had been left in charge by John Brise. I sent one or two men to seek him out, and soon saw his tall figure striding towards me.

"Good Day, Sir John. I'm sorry I was not on hand when you arrived. Is there aught can I do?"

"Good morning, Matt. After last night's work, I am glad to see you unhurt. No one has yet reported any losses to me. There must have been some. Savoy's men made a warm fight of it in the end."

"I'll look into the matter when all the dead have been counted. Meanwhile, Master Turton is sending horse-loads of booty back to the main camp."

I laughed at that. "As is his way, Matt. He is ever the hoarder. It will all fetch a good price somewhere. No doubt the Almains are doing the same for their part. But go now to Master Preston, and say to him that I want all these dead Italians taken out and buried without delay. Our own can be dealt with separately, and Master Turton can return to his first calling and read something over them. It won't do them any good now, but it will look better for the rest."

"Shall I list our dead by name?" he asked, and I nodded in reply, my attention being taken by activity on the tower. He followed my gaze, then swiftly caught at Boy's bridle and pulled us both around a corner.

"Crossbows, Sir John!" As he spoke there came a whine of bolts from the tower. Several struck the house and quivered in the timbers. There was a cry and one of our men skidded round the corner with a bolt in his arm, cursing lustily. I recognized him as Jenkin Cope, out of Suffolk, as he had said when he brought the message the previous day.

"You goddamned fool, Jenkin! Can't you keep your eyes open for trouble?" railed Matt. "Get yourself over to the healers, and let them tend to that arm. Here, you!" he called to another of his men who had rounded the corner to avoid the bolts. "See to Jenkin, will you? This'll teach him to mind himself."

There were no more bolts from the tower, although the warning was there for all. I left Matt to his duties, ordering him to make a list of our dead for Will Turton. Turning Boy's head I made off in the direction of da Lucca's house. As I rode I wondered what his reaction would be when I showed him the letter I held from Datini. Would he trust me? Could I trust him? I shrugged off the thoughts of what might happen. Might was on my side, and I would use it if necessary.

A knot of men stood at the house door. Sim Costean, a gnarled old archer, stepped forward.

"Morning, Sir John. All's well. Your lads have been around all night. The healer is here as well. The old man's not much better yet." Sim's keen blue eyes, almost lost in the weather-seamed brown face, looked shrewdly into mine. We had known each other for many years. He lowered his voice. "This old Italian is of some value, is he? What about the maid?"

Holding his gaze in mine, I nodded slowly. "More gold in the pot for all of us, I hope. You know me, eh? The maid is gentle, and not for the likes of us, even freeborn English archers."

"Ah, but you'm a knight now, Jack. Well then?"

I laughed. "Too young for an old dog like me, you rogue."

He grinned and stood back from Boy's shoulder, taking the reins from me. I dismounted and went into the house. Ralph greeted me, a worried look on his face.

"Hal Peasgood says Master da Lucca is like to die."

Inwardly I cursed this mischance. Damn Werner's stupidity! Was this opportunity to be lost? I followed Ralph up the stairway. Marco stood at the top, his face set and glum. I passed him by and into the long room, thence into a small bedchamber. Paolo da Lucca lay pale and still upon the wide bed. It was canopied with rich hangings, replete with linen sheets and plump pillows against which the injured man lay propped up in a half-seated manner. Genevra sat by him, but as I approached she came forward to meet me.

"My father is very ill, Signore, and I fear for his life. What am I to do? We are only here by an ill chance on a journey to Milan."

I was at a loss, not knowing the ways of Italy, nor of a woman's mind. In the years during which I had risen in the world to be a captain of soldiers I had encountered many women, of high degree and low. One, now gone to another, I had loved. Others I had enjoyed for a brief space, but none had I stayed with long enough to learn their minds, if indeed a man were able to do that.

"Do not speak so," I spoke gently to her, "My healers are well skilled in their arts. With proper care your father will recover. You must try to be of good cheer, and help to nurse him. Now, is he conscious, can he speak to me?"

"Indeed yes," said Genevra eagerly. "He wishes to do just that, but he is so very weak." She led me to her father.

Hal Peasgood, one of Will Turton's band of healers, stepped out of my path. He was a small man, balding, with sharp grey eyes in a round face and a sharply projecting nose. I was reminded of a sparrow. He bobbed a little bow.

"This man is sore stricken, Sir John," he whispered in the manner of his brotherhood. "With your leave I will go back to camp and fetch more herbs from my store. Also, I will bring Simon Cheshunt for his opinion of this case."

I nodded my assent, and he slipped noiselessly away, twitching his worn brown robe about him.

Da Lucca's weak, hollow, voice greeted me. "So, you are that great Gianni Haccuud of whom I hear, who intervenes on my behalf whilst his army despoils poor Piedmont? What have you to do with me and mine?"

I sat on the stool which Marco brought me, and leaned nearer to him. "My main business is with Monferrato," I said, "And his cause against Milan. To you I come as the friend of a friend. I bring you this." I opened the purse at my belt and took from it the

FRANK PAYTON

sealed parchment given me by Datini. He took the letter from me and glanced at the seal before handing it to Genevra, who broke it open and read it over to him in a low voice. The effect of the contents seemed to buoy up his spirits, and he looked keenly at me. He spoke evenly, but his voice was weak.

"Now I understand the reason for your concern. My old and valued friend, Francesco of Prato, with whom you have done business, tells me that you are a man of honour and are to be trusted. With his recommendation you may ask me for anything, or for any service I can reasonably provide for you. At a fair price, of course," he added hastily, extending to me a rather shaky hand.

I grasped it firmly—and thus was formed a bond which was only to end years later with his death.

"You and Genevra shall stay in this house under my protection, guarded from all danger, for as long as it is necessary for you to regain your health. When you are able to leave, I will provide a suitable escort to see you safely to your home."

Genevra turned to him. "Is this not wonderful, Father? We are safe, and you will be made better."

He patted her hand. "So it seems, my child. But what does the Signore Haccuud want in return?"

"Naught, save to ask you to sell for me the arms and armour taken from the dead of yesterday's fighting. Datini deals in weapons. You may have the usual commission, of course. But all this can wait until you are returned to your place of business once more. Before then, I hope to see you and your daughter at my table as honoured guests."

He nodded his assent, and lay back on the pillows. The effort had tired him. As Genevra fussed over him, I took my leave. I sent Ralph on ahead to arrange a relief for the guards with Will Preston. I followed at a slower pace with Marco.

"Well, and what have you to tell me, Master Marco di Stoldo Bandini?" I asked him in a bantering tone.

Hawkwood's Sword

"That Paolo da Lucca is a rich man, Sir John. He is from Florence, and has a house of business there, and an estate, and farms in the countryside."

"And?" I pressed him.

"He trades through Venice to the East, and through Genoa to the West, and, of course, overland to Avignon where you met Datini—who I say is a rich man, but not as rich as he. He also trades with the Low Country and with your own England."

"Nothing else?" I was teasing him now.

"He has a beautiful daughter, Sir John, but I am only a poor crossbowman."

I laughed. "As I was a poor archer at sixpence a day. I told you, in this trade a man can rise in the world, especially by loyal service to the right leader."

"I will remember, Sir John. In any event, I shall not forget Genevra da Lucca. But here comes your man Peasgood, and another."

I reined in Boy as Hal Peasgood and Simon Cheshunt approached, and leaned down to them.

"Both of you must do your very best to heal the old man. Use all your craft. This is important. I will reward you well an you succeed. I will say no more."

The two men of medicine looked at each other. Cheshunt hesitated, then said in his careful way, "We can do no more than our best, Sir John, and of that you may be assured."

I smiled at the pair. "Your best will be good enough for me, Simon."

I shook Boy's reins to move him on, and looked across at Marco, who waited patiently. "Come then! To the camp with all haste."

We rode off, soon increasing our speed to a gallop, and so arrived at the gate in a flurry of dust and small stones, both horses snorting with the effort, and the gate guards shouting to urge us on.

Frank Payton

We dismounted at my pavilion. There was the usual knot of senior men at the entrance, all wanting my attention. I tossed Boy's reins to Marco.

"Take Boy and your own horse to the lines. Then get some rest. Find Ralph and tell him you are both relieved of duties until this evening, unless I am obliged to send for you." I clapped him on the shoulder. "That was good work last night."

He grinned at that. "Perhaps I will be a better swordsman than crossbowman, Sir John?"

"Perhaps, but for the present—off with you!" I turned aside to Will, who stood by impatiently, almost hopping from one foot to the other as would a small boy.

"Now, Will Preston, what ails you?"

"Naught, Sir John, naught. I've been waiting here upon your return. A word with you now, an you please."

"Very well, you first. The rest of you will have to wait. Come on inside, Will."

*****

We seated ourselves at the table, well away from the entrance. "Now then, what is the problem?"

"You will recall that after the ambush, when we left the mountains, you asked me to find out if any of our foreriders had told the Almains what had happened."

I nodded. "Keep your voice low. This must not be overheard. Go on."

"It was many days before I could come at the answer to your question. One of Belmonte's Flemings was the culprit, one Niklaas Kortrijk, or some such name. It seems that he and one of the Almains were old comrades, and often rode together."

I frowned. "You say 'were.' Why so?"

Hawkwood's Sword

"Someone took off his head last night. There is something else. Belmonte's division was next to the Almains at the last gate. It looks to me as if Kortrijk was singled out to be silenced." Will sat back with a satisfied air, and then. "There is yet more. We have a prisoner."

I sat up eagerly at that. This was becoming very interesting. We might discover more about our current situation with careful questioning.

"We posted a guard on the secret door in the town wall, hoping to catch anyone who tried to escape. We were lucky. I'm told that well into the fight, after we'd taken the gates, the door opened— just a crack, and it was possible to see the light from a lanthorn. Then the light disappeared, and the door must have opened wider, for after a moment a man slipped out. He was in black clothing, and difficult to see by all accounts. The guards took him as he was crossing the ditch. It was easy. He hadn't expected it to be full of water; it must have come as a bit of a shock. Anyway, he was brought here, and Will Turton has him under guard."

"Do we have any idea who he is?" I asked.

"No, I suppose him to be an Italian. You'll need Marco. We don't understand his speech."

"Let him stew a while longer. I've sent Marco off to sleep. Later will do." I took a swallow of wine from my cup to clear my mind.

After Will came a succession of claims upon my time, from Will Turton wanting more packhorses to my cooks complaining about lack of supplies. I told Will to ask himself where the horses were to be found, and the cooks to complain to him. In between these two, I dealt with petty quarrels, complaints about pay, the men's share of booty, and rations, until my head spun. In the end I lost patience, and sent them all packing, sitting alone at last to plan my next move. But before anything final could be decided, there was the matter of the as-yet-unknown prisoner to be resolved. To this end I sent a page to the Almain camp with a message.

Frank Payton

Thus, towards the end of the evening meal, Albrecht arrived, accompanied by Wolf and Hannes von Auerbach, the elder of his two principal lieutenants. von Felsingen was not present. I had asked that he should not be told of our meeting.

"Yours was a secretive sort of summons, Jack," said Albrecht, nodding to John Brise, Will Preston and Jack Onsloe, who were sitting with me over the wine.

"Indeed. A secret meeting for a secret matter. Our guards on that door we spoke about caught a fish in their net. You guessed aright in this affair."

"Who is he?" Albrecht leaned forward eagerly.

"We don't know. The men could not understand his speech. I have sent for him to be brought to us, and Marco may be able to get something out of him, if he is Italian."

We had not long to wait. The curtains at the entrance to the pavilion were thrust aside, and Will Turton entered. He was followed by Marco and Ralph, and then by a small, slim young man, dressed in plain black, who was urged along by two guards carrying drawn swords. He looked pale and frightened, as indeed he should have.

"Here's your fish, Sir John," said Will, sliding into a place at the table, and reaching for the wine, "And much good may he do you. I can't understand a word he says. Speaks a tongue I've never heard. He doesn't even understand Latin, although he looks as if he might have been well educated."

Will always set great store by education and the ability to speak Latin, having been both monk and priest in his time, before falling afoul of his superiors in the Church. He still retained a somewhat priestly look, with tonsured hair and a deceptively mild, round face, with a long delicate nose. As the Company's Quartermaster, Clerk of Accounts, and Treasurer, he was ideal, being of an acquisitive and orderly nature. His fighting abilities were not to be overlooked either.

Hawkwood's Sword

We all turned our attention to the captive where he stood between the guards.

"Speak to him, Marco," I said.

Marco asked his name, who and what he was, whom he served, and so on. At this level I understood all, having been tutored by Marco. The spate of questions continued, but it had no effect on the prisoner. He stood, ox-dumb, with a slight smile on his lips. At length Marco turned to me.

"He is clearly not Italian, Sir John. My words have no effect." He grinned. "I have insulted his mothers to the fifth generation, but it means nothing to him."

I looked at Albrecht, raising my eyebrows. "Try German." He did, but again, nothing. "What other languages do we have amongst our ranks?"

Albrecht stared into his wine cup. Raising himself he muttered aside to his lieutenant, von Auerbach, who drained his cup, stood up and beckoned to Wolf. They left the pavilion together.

"I have sent Hannes to find as many speakers of different tongues as he can in a short time," said Albrecht. "Maybe we will be lucky. If we are to get this man to talk to us, we must first know his speech."

"I'll get him to say something," Jack's harsh voice broke in. He stood up and, drawing a dagger from his belt, went along the table towards the captive.

"Hold his hands flat on the table," he ordered. The guards hurriedly sheathed their swords, grasped the man's hands and held them as Jack had directed. He placed the point of the blade on the back of the right hand. He pressed slightly. A tiny drop of blood appeared. The young man looked frightened. Jack lifted the dagger in his fist and raised it a foot or more. Swiftly it flashed down. The captive jerked back, trying in vain to free his hands. A babble of words in some strange tongue escaped his lips. The point of the blade buried itself an inch deep in the wood of the table between the outstretched fingers. Jack wrenched it out, and sauntered back to his seat, sheathing the dagger as he walked.

Frank Payton

"It always works," he said, picking up his wine cup.

Albrecht gazed at the prisoner. "*Ungarisch*," he breathed. "I don't understand it, but I recognise the tone. I should have known, Jack. I'll wager he was on his way to Conrad Landau. He has a following of Hungarians in his band. Savage swine they are, too. I hear they like to roast their prisoners over a slow fire. *Ach, du lieber Gott!*"

He had spoken in a low voice to me alone. Now he raised his voice. "Magyar?"

The youth nodded energetically, and spoke again in his tongue. Albrecht held up his hand to stem the flow. He turned to me.

"They call themselves the Magyar people and live far to the northeast of here. It is as I said. They're mercenaries as we are. I've met a few of them before."

*****

Waiting, we talked on, in the usual way of soldiers, sipping our wine, mulling over past exploits, future plans, ambitions, women, and the like.

Looking back to that time, when Italy was a new adventure for us all, I realise now how badly prepared we all were. Not in the way of military preparedness, of course; we'd all had far too much experience of war not to know our trade. No, we were not ready for the shifting nature of Italian city-states, which came together in alliances against each other, and just as easily broke apart and fought each other. The Church under the Popes tried to exert its age-old power. The cities just as energetically pulled away, and ran their own affairs with elected councils and rulers—which afforded more scope for alliance and re-alliance, coup and counter coup. We fell into the same habit, and so divided our forces.

If only we had held together, the combined power of all the Free Companies, we could have conquered the whole of Northern Italy, and as free rulers would have become kings or dukes.

Hawkwood's Sword

But it was not to be. I had to learn to survive by wiles and stratagems, by gathering secret information to further my own ends. By good fortune I have been successful, but affairs could have been much better. But I must return to my tale.

*****

Von Auerbach and Wolf returned within a short time with a group of Almain men-at-arms, all of whom, it seemed, had ranged widely over many areas of the Empire. Only one man had any skill with the Magyar tongue, and the rest were dismissed. The one chosen by Albrecht came close and leaned over the table to hear his instructions. Albrecht spoke rapidly and gestured towards the prisoner, who was by now beginning tremble with fear and had to be held upright. The Almain went up to him and spoke in that strange tongue we had heard before. There was question and answer, which Albrecht put into English for our benefit in his careful way.

"His name is Janos, and he was the bearer of a message to the Count of Savoy. Caught up in our siege, he was supposed to escape Lanzo by the secret door, steal a horse from us, and make his way to Count Landau. There he was to tell of our attack and the perilous state in which Savoy now finds himself. Savoy's hope is, of course, that Landau will move to raise the siege. We would then be caught between two foes." He frowned at the thought.

"So," I said. "What do you think is our best course of action?"

"At the moment, I don't know. On the one hand we could send him back to Savoy, who will then know without doubt that his cause is lost; or we can let him pass on to Landau with a warning that he attacks us at his peril. But I would rather leave the matter over to the morning."

I could only agree with him. In any event it was too late for anything to be done that night. I dismissed all my officers except John Brise, and Marco, who remained in attendance. Janos the Magyar was taken back to wherever it was that Will Turton was

Frank Payton

holding him. Albrecht sent away all his men-at-arms except von Auerbach and Wolf.

"Well, what is on your mind, Jack?" said Albrecht, leaning back in his chair and steepling his fingers.

"One of Andrew Belmonte's men, Niklaas Kortrijk, was killed during last night's assault on the walls."

"Jack," Albrecht broke in, "So were a good many of our men."

"Apart from the initial cavalry charge, which was unforeseen, none outside the walls, my friend. This man lost his head to one of your people, who I think were under Conrad Harzmann, and thus under the command of Werner von Felsingen."

"Well?" He raised an eyebrow.

I leaned my elbows on the table, and held his eyes with mine. "Are you aware that Werner and Conrad visited my camp the evening after we had been ambushed by the Italians? They knew about the skirmish. How? I asked myself."

Albrecht's brow furrowed, and he looked troubled. "And so?"

"I set one of my people to find out how the news had travelled. After some days he told me that this Kortrijk had a friend, a comrade from the past, amongst Werner's men. That is how the news leaked out." I sat back. "In addition, one of our foreriders was killed before the skirmish."

"I did not learn of the attack upon you until you told me yourself," said Albrecht.

"There is more to be said. Marco, tell Master Sterz what you told me soon after you joined my Company."

"As you know," said Marco, "I was one of the crossbowmen at the ambush. I was wounded and captured. Sir John saved me from death at the hands of your lieutenant, von Felsingen."

Albrecht nodded, clearly puzzled as to the direction of this account.

Marco continued. "When we marched to lay the ambush for Sir John's men, we were in camp one night and were visited by a group of men, mostly Italian, with a few of your countrymen.

Hawkwood's Sword

Later, when I was being questioned by Sir John, I realised that I had seen Master von Felsingen's companion before. I mean Master Harzmann. He was with the party I have just described to you."

"Marco also described to me an Italian in that group who could only have been Lamberti," I told him, "Lamberti, who posed as an emissary of Monferrato, and together with Sciatta was later killed by us. You know that story."

I picked up my wine cup and drained it. Albrecht sat, stunned by what he had just heard. He stood up slowly. "I will think on all this until our next meeting. Now I see the reason for your concern. And so, good night to all."

Upon that note we all parted, and I retired to my bed. It was long before I slept that night, and then but fitfully. I was well aware that Albrecht shared my concern. I was to find later that the seeds of our eventual undoing had been sown.

Chapter 5
Negotiations

Early evening in autumn, a red sun sinking, shadows lengthening, after a day which had held the feeling of summer, I was returning to Lanzo from hunting in the nearby countryside and forest. We rode easily in the warmth, pleasantly tired. I had left camp at sunrise with Will Preston, Giles Ashurst, Ralph and Marco, plus an assorted band of men-at-arms and archers. We had combed the hills and valleys for our prey. I had even taken bow in hand, after years without practice, and downed a prime stag just before its leap for freedom. Shouts of approval greeted this feat, turning to laughter as I tossed the bow back to Giles and grumbled "An old dog can sometimes perform old tricks."

Two weeks had passed since the taking of Lanzo and the capture of Janos, the Magyar. After lengthy consideration, Albrecht had agreed with me that our captive should be sent to Milan with a defiant message for Bernabo Visconti. The burden of this was that we would brook no interference in proceeding with the siege of the inner stronghold. Of course, we might consider alternative suggestions for a solution. Up to the day of the hunt no reply had been forthcoming.

There was little doubt that the position of Savoy and his garrison was serious. With the river dammed as it was, little water was to be had, even if, as we suspected, there were some wells which might go some way towards relieving the situation.

Hawkwood's Sword

There was also the question of food for the men and fodder for the horses, many of which had been taken into the stronghold. All in all, not an enviable position.

As we jogged on towards camp, we became aware of an armed party riding in roughly the same direction, having emerged from the country to our left. Smaller in numbers than ourselves, the group appeared to be comprised of a knight and a retinue of guards. That they had seen us was evident from the turned heads and arms waved in our direction. The riders did not halt their progress, but kept a converging course with our own route. We halted, and loosened swords in their scabbards. The archers strung their bows and shuffled arrows into a handier position.

I turned to Giles. "Tie a white cloth to a bow stave, go on forward, and find out who they are and where they are headed. Marco—go with him. Your Italian may be needed."

They rode off, knee to knee, a white scarf fluttering from Giles' bow. I noticed he hadn't unstrung the weapon, and that he carried two arrows in the same hand. I smiled to myself. Whoever they were, the riders would need to be quick if they wished to catch him unawares.

We waited. A pair of horsemen detached itself from the group, which had also halted—by the look of them, a squire or page and a man-at-arms. They rode to meet Giles and Marco.

We waited as the two pairs of riders stopped and faced each other. The distance made it impossible to hear anything, and I fretted impatiently upon our men's return. Eventually they rejoined us.

"Who are they?" I demanded.

Marco looked at me, opened his mouth to speak, then stopped and glanced at Giles, who shook his head, grinning. "No, no. Go on, lad—you tell him. I understood hardly a word spoken."

"Well then, Sir John," said Marco, "the knight is Sir William de Grandison, of the Order of the Annunciata. He is sent by the Pope to mediate between the Count of Savoy, yourself, and Master Sterz."

Frank Payton

"I see. And who does he intend to visit first?" I asked.

"He did not say, but he is the bearer of a letter to the Count. I do not know the contents, of course."

"Hmm. Go, tell him to bring his party alongside us. Not too near though, and to continue with his journey."

As Marco rode back to do my bidding, all pretence of a carefree ride now left us. We were all back on the alert. Sir William rode some twenty yards to my left. He was in full armour and carried a sword. His helmet was borne by a page who rode behind him with an older man, also fully accoutred, whom I took to be his squire.

In this fashion we rode on towards Lanzo and our encampment, which we reached just as the first stars began to show. I led the way past the sentries and up to my pavilion. Dismounting, I indicated that de Grandison should follow suit. Both parties dismounted, and our reluctant guests stood about uncertainly. I turned to Will Preston.

"You and Marco, put these men under guard," I said, indicating the rest of the entourage, and to de Grandison, "You, Sir, kindly follow me if you will. Ralph! Some wine!"

De Grandison followed me into the pavilion and gazed about him at the rich display, which was now customary. He was a burly sort of man, black bearded, with shrewd brown eyes. His armour was of the finest quality, and the sword at his side was not just for display.

"You live well, John Hawkwood. A far cry from the tannery at Hedingham." He had a heavy French accent, and laughed at my puzzled stare that he should know my origins. "Oh, yes, I know all about you, and how you have risen in the world. Of course you do not remember me. Why should you? I was a mere prisoner of you English at Poitiers. It was there you received your knight's spurs from the Prince Edward, I believe."

I showed him to a seat, and sank gratefully into my own high chair. Ralph appeared with a jug of wine and two silver cups. He poured the wine, set the jug on the table, bowed, and left. After a day in the saddle, I was ready both for the wine and a seat which didn't move about continuously. I raised my cup.

"Your health, Sir William. I expect you were ransomed. Is that the way of it? Yes, I received my spurs from Prince Edward, a knight of great renown and much honour."

"Yes, I was ransomed eventually by our Father, the Pope, in Avignon. In return, I was assigned to the Order of the Annunciata, and now travel on diplomatic missions for the Holy Father."

"My page tells me that you carry a letter to Savoy. Are you personally aware of its contents?" I asked, pouring more wine.

"I am aware of the essence only. The Holy Father wishes me to mediate between the parties in this dispute, now that it is clear that you and your Almain friends have the upper hand. He wishes Savoy to retire to his own territory. The Holy Father will then try to placate the Duke of Milan. As you are no doubt aware, efforts are being made to send armies to the Holy Land to recapture Jerusalem from the Saracens. It is not good that Christian rulers should war amongst themselves when there is a greater work to be attempted. Would you not join such an enterprise?"

I waved his suggestion aside. "There is no profit in such an undertaking. All previous attempts to save Jerusalem have eventually ended in failure. Leave Jerusalem to the Saracens, say I. Rome is enough. In any event, I could not persuade my men to that end. They are not fools, no more than I am."

De Grandison sighed, shrugged his shoulders, and drank his wine. "I am in your hands, Sir John. What would you have me do?"

"You shall stay here this night, and dine with me. I think you will find better fare here at my board than you will be offered by Savoy. In addition, I will bring in my comrade in arms, Albrecht Sterz of the Rhineland, with some of his principal officers. He will be eager to meet you when he hears of your presence. Of that I am sure."

"We are not your prisoners then?" he enquired, eyebrows lifting.

Frank Payton

"Most certainly not. If you wish for a bare table, and a stinking, crowded castle keep at the end of a long day's ride, you may go in peace, and we will meet again on some other day. But you will find discussions with us of greater use in your task as mediator. In the morning I will take you about the camp so that you can gain some idea of the problems faced by the defenders of Lanzo. When Savoy has heard your report he might decide that settlement would be best."

De Grandison gave a wry smile. "And at what cost? Savoy has his honour to consider."

"Harken, my friend," I said. "I too have my honour to consider. But I do not fight for no profit. War can be costly in men and equipment. My men must be paid, whether I fight or no. Possibly you can see my dilemma?"

"Yes, I can," he replied with another smile. "I can see also that the reports about you have not been wrong. I will accept your invitation gladly. May I have my squire and page with me, and my two senior men-at-arms?"

"Of course. It will be arranged. Go now, and select your party; the others will be looked after by my lieutenants."

I stood up and shook his hand. He had a firm grip and a steady eye, and I knew he would be a hard adversary in a fight if it should come to that pass.

*****

Towards noon next day, I sent John Brise and a suitably turned out guard of honour to accompany de Grandison and his party to Lanzo. I had taken care to inform the Count of Savoy of his arrival, sending Matt Sayers as herald, with a single man-at-arms bearing my knight's pennon, and Marco. They were met by Morelli, Savoy's herald, and the whole affair was conducted with the utmost attention to etiquette.

Hawkwood's Sword

The previous evening, Albrecht had eagerly accepted my invitation to dine, and had brought along von Felsingen, Harzmann, and von Auerbach. I had feared some friction between those present, but as matters were the meal had something of a festive air, a meeting of military men from the late wars, happy to exchange experiences and tales of past exploits over the table.

There was no rancour on anyone's part. Even von Felsingen showed a side of his character previously unknown to me. He had brought along a small stringed instrument, and to its accompaniment sang several songs in the Almain tongue, songs for soldiers to sing in just such circumstances. He soon had the rest of us roaring out the choruses in sound, if not in the exact words.

De Grandison, Albrecht and I finally settled down to a serious discussion of the situation. For our part, we left the Pope's envoy in no doubt as to the eventual outcome of the siege. As a military man of some experience, he was obliged to accept the truth of our words. We controlled Savoy's water supply, and there could by then have been little food for men or fodder for horses left in the stronghold. There was also virtually no chance of being relieved by a Milanese force against the Pope's wishes.

Thus, the following morning, after a tour of our encampment, de Grandison and his men were taken through the gates of Lanzo and were met by Morelli. Albrecht and I watched as they entered the fortress and the iron gates closed with a hollow clang.

"And now we wait, my friend," said Albrecht, turning his horse's head.

"Yes," I agreed, following suit. "And double the watch on the keep."

We rode out of the town side by side.

*****

Frank Payton

It was evening on the third day after de Grandison's arrival when Oderigo Morelli rode into the camp, accompanied by a man-at-arms and escorted by Matt Sayers.

Again we sat at table, this time in Albrecht's pavilion. It was a brave display, with the tapestry-hung walls and the silver vessels upon the table glowing in the golden candlelight. By chance, all those present were decked out in their best clothes, for that night we celebrated our host's birthday.

Morelli had been reluctant to enter the pavilion, but we refused to meet him elsewhere, and so perforce he found himself before the high table to deliver his message. He took off his black velvet cap with a flourish, and bowed deeply.

"I am come, my lords, on behalf of His Excellency the Count of Savoy. He has heard that you are willing to consider proposals from him which might cause you to lift the siege of Lanzo, and pass on about your business elsewhere. His Excellency therefore proposes that emissaries from both sides should meet at noon on the morrow to discuss matters of common interest. How say you?"

We all looked to Albrecht. After all, we were on his ground. Upon him fell the burden.

"Answer for us," I said. "It is your right."

He picked up his wine cup, peered into it, and then raised it to his lips. Morelli fidgeted, twisting his cap in his hands, and shifting from one foot to the other. The cup emptied, Albrecht replaced it upon the table. Wolf leaned over his shoulder with the silver jug and refilled it. Morelli waited.

"It might suit our purposes to stay here yet a while," said Albrecht. "We may do better to continue our exploration of your master's lands, more profitable, perhaps."

The herald's face fell, taken aback by this answer. He made a valiant attempt at recovery. "Perhaps," he gulped visibly, "your Lordships would accord the Count an opportunity to discuss these matters in person, at your pleasure."

Hawkwood's Sword

Albrecht allowed a faint smile to flicker across his face. "Are we to understand the Count is disposed to be generous?" he said softly.

"I think his Excellency would not wish to act dishonourably towards you. Indeed, I am certain that he would not." Morelli seemed eager to please.

Albrecht looked along the table from side to side. "Shall we meet this Count of Savoy, comrades? At noon tomorrow, perhaps? Jack, what do you say?"

I nodded my head slowly, and grinned back at him. Raising my cup I said, "Why not?" drained the last of the good red wine, and began to laugh. The others followed my lead, and of a sudden the whole group was consumed by mirth, tossing down the contents of the cups, and slapping each other on the back like schoolboys.

We had won! The siege of Lanzo was as good as over.

*****

Little remains to be said of the affair at Lanzo. The day after Morelli stood before Albrecht's table, we met Amadeus VI—'The Green Count'—before the doors of his castle in the middle of the town. Also present were de Grandison, Morelli, and sundry others of the court. There were few formalities and little discussion. Through the mouth of de Grandison we were offered 50,000 florins to go away. We were unmoved. The sum offered slowly crawled up to 90,000. I tired of this parsimony. Our horses shifted their hooves restively, jingling their harness.

"Tell the Count, Sir William, that we need 200,000 florins," I said, gathering Boy's reins as if to leave. "Deux cent mille florins," I repeated, and watched the Count's face turn pale. There was a hurried consultation in low voices before de Grandison again turned to face us.

"That is an enormous sum, Sir John," he said. "The Count would find such an imposition very difficult to bear. A reduction, perhaps?" he added, hopefully.

FRANK PAYTON

"Does the Count wish us to continue the siege?" inquired Albrecht.

"No, no. But, Sirs, this is a vast sum, " de Grandison repeated, clearly put about by the demand. "You are hard men to deal with, but there is a limit to the Count's purse. Please abate your figure by but a little and I will put certain proposals to his Excellency which may secure agreement."

"Well then," I said. "As a token of our goodwill we will take only 180,000 florins. No less, mind. Do not seek a further reduction, or your good offices will fail."

With great reluctance the Count agreed to our demand, and de Grandison undertook to arrange for the payment to be made within a month.

Just three weeks later Will Turton, as our Treasurer, had the enormous pleasure and task of stowing away the huge sum which we had exacted as the price of raising the siege of Lanzo. We also kept the train of packhorses which had borne the silver from Milan. Whether it had been paid from the treasuries of Milan and Pavia, or by the Lombardy bankers, I knew not—nor did I care once it was ours.

There remained only the matter of Paolo da Lucca and his daughter to be settled. As I had promised, the pair had been taken under my wing, and the old man had been given daily attention by our healers, as well as protection from unwanted advances. This last particularly applied to Genevra who, with her father, had been guests at my high table at a banquet to celebrate our success. Although she seemed only to have eyes for Marco, her saviour, as she called him, there were other young bloods amongst my junior officers who felt they had better claims upon her favours. She was in truth a lovely, sweet-natured creature, and I had some concern that she might be swayed by apparently earnest adoration.

With this in mind, and partly because I wished Marco to be able to compete for Genevra's favour on a more equal basis, I had advanced both him and Ralph to be my squires. To Ralph I gave more responsible duties under John Brise, who would bring him

Hawkwood's Sword

out of his boyishness to sterner manhood. Marco I kept with me for personal duties, and future missions of a special nature. Their advancement was also due to their bravery in entering Lanzo on the escapade which ultimately led to our success, and to the part they both played during and after the attack on the town.

It was to Marco that I eventually entrusted the safe conduct of the da Luccas when they completed their broken journey to Milan. I gave him a detail of twelve men-at-arms under Simon Bawdesley, and lectured them all on their behaviour on the journey. Privately, I explained to Marco that he should quietly ingratiate himself with da Lucca. At the same time he was to treat Genevra with all respect as a suitor for her hand, as I saw her father as a potentially valuable ally. I also pulled Simon aside and informed him that I myself held him personally responsible for the good conduct of the men-at-arms, and that his fortunes would be bleak indeed were anything untoward to happen.

For myself, I have always found women to be a hindrance on a campaign, taking men's thoughts from their duties, and slackening their resolve. If my men wished to waste their hard-won pay on the trulls and slatterns which follow every army like crows after the plough, that was their affair. Anything else I frowned on, as a rule. Women to wive are best found in good families and houses, where they have been brought up to wifely and motherly skills, not amongst the ranks of camp-followers.

So far as the weapons, armour and other equipment taken from the fallen enemy at Lanzo was concerned, this was despatched by pack train under a strong guard commanded by Wat Spykings, Will Turton's taciturn chief assistant. Da Lucca had given him details of how to proceed to his estate and place of business at Florence. The value of the hoard, when sold, was to be held by him on our account, and I expected some thousands of silver florins would be realised, for some of the equipment was of the finest quality.

Thus ended the affair at Lanzo, and we were able to look forward to the next stage of our campaign on behalf of Monferrato.

Frank Payton

*****

After Lanzo, we passed on to carry the campaign into the Milanese territory and made a great camp at Romagnano, near the town of Novara, thirty English miles to the west of the great city of Milan. Here ruled Bernabo Visconti, who coveted the lands of the Marquis of Monferrato.

This Bernabo had a brother, Galeazzo, as joint ruler. He, however, preferred to reside at Pavia, for him a much more pleasant city. Whilst Bernabo was notorious for his autocratic, dictatorial ways, and cruelly tortured his enemies, or indeed almost anyone he disliked, Galeazzo was altogether different, being a quiet, more studious man, although at need he could display the usual Visconti traits of ruthlessness and cruelty. He was also fond of walking and riding about the countryside.

We were opposed at this time by the Almain Count Conrad Landau, then in the service of Galeazzo. He attempted to deny us both loot and supplies by burning all before us, to the extent of a dozen or more castles and villages. Nevertheless, we were able to retake Castelnuovo and return it to the Marquis. Landau's efforts to contain us failed, as we moved swiftly to surround his smaller forces. In a number of skirmishing actions we drove him back. Thus we harried and burned, destroying all before us, until we had sacked all the lands up to the Ticino and Trebbia, which must have displeased Galeazzo.

*****

Late in September Marco returned to us, having had to learn of our whereabouts from fleeing peasants and from observing the retreating forces of Landau. He and Simon Bawdesley ducked into my pavilion one night just after sundown, during the evening meal. I was seated at table with Albrecht and John Brise, plus an assortment of other leading men, both English and Almain.

Hawkwood's Sword

I left my seat and went down the length of the pavilion to meet them. Marco looked pale and worn, and even old Simon appeared weary. I clasped both their hands in turn, and slapped them both heartily on the shoulder. Marco staggered a little at this, and there was some laughter from those gathered around the table.

"Welcome back," I told them. "It is good to see you both, safe and well. Sit down and rest. Pages! More food and wine."

I took my seat once more, and raised my wine cup. "A health to our brave comrades. *Waes Hael!*"

Shouts of "*Drinc Hael!*" and "*Zum Wohl!*" echoed around the board as the two took their places.

"It is good to be back safely, Sir John," said Marco. "We've had a hard time of it this past few days. Isn't that so, Simon?"

"Aye, lad. That it is. I tell you, Sir John, that but for your young squire we wouldn't be here at all. As it is, we haven't lost one man. We've ridden mostly at night and lain up by day. We wove and slid between stricken villages and Landau's fiends. I've seen sights no Christian man should see. He has devils on horseback with little bows you'd think were children's toys, 'til you see and hear the swish of their black arrows. I tell you, they're devils from Hell, the size of children when on foot, but as evil as Satan himself." He shuddered in disgust, and applied himself to his food as one starving.

"Who can these men be?" I asked, looking round the table.

Albrecht called down to one of his Almains, who rose to his feet. I knew him at once as the one who had spoken to the prisoner, Janos, whom we had captured at Lanzo. Albrecht repeated my question in their own tongue, and translated the reply for our benefit. "These small archers are from the Cuman tribes, out of the vast plains of Tartary. There are hordes of these horse people to the east of Constantinople, who press behind the Saracens for conquest. Some have settled amongst the Magyars, who buy their services. Walther here agrees with your man that they are as fiends from Hell. At least we know now that they are with Landau. What else can you tell us, Master Bandini?"

Frank Payton

Marco took a deep draught from his wine cup. "We counted many different bands of Landau's Almains and others. They were withdrawing before you, and were intent only on that, apart from sacking any village or farm in their path. I suppose they will lay the blame for that on our advance. They were well armed and did not ride as though defeated, only drawing back to fresh positions. I think they realise that we outnumber them, and so they will not stand against us."

"How many are there, do you think?" I asked.

Simon roused himself. "I reckon no more than three thousand, but it's hard to say, as they were broken up into small bands. Once, we were seen and hailed, but we rode off and lost them in the darkness. We had a brush with another group, but we took them unawares and were through them before they recovered. We hacked one or two from their horses, but lost none of our own, thank God."

There was more of such talk until it became clear that the pair were exhausted. Marco half lay across the board, his dark head on his folded arms, eyes closed. Even old Simon swayed in his seat, and at last I put an end to it all and let them go to their rest. I turned to Albrecht.

"Now that Marco is returned, I will tell you what is in my mind. You know I have long thought that we need crossbowmen. I intend to journey to Genoa and request the Doge to hire out to us several bands of these troops. We are going against castles and fortified towns, and this is where the crossbow comes into its own."

"I agree, they could be very useful to us. Besides which, it would give Genoa a chance to strike a blow at Milan on their own account. There is no love lost between those two cities. What will you do?"

"First, I shall leave John here in command, in my place."

At that, I saw my marshal look up, startled. Then a slow smile spread over his brown face. "Why, thank'ee, Jack. I warrant I'll not fail you. If you'll agree, I'll have Will Preston with me as second."

Hawkwood's Sword

"I do agree. I trust you and him, John, have no fear of that. Now then, Albrecht, secondly I'll take Giles Ashurst and fifty archers, plus Jack Onsloe and a hundred of his men. We should be more than a match for anyone we might meet on the road. Once in Genoa, I'll send in Marco as my emissary and request an audience. The rest should not be difficult to achieve."

Albrecht raised his cup. "Here's to your success, Jack. *Zum Wohl!*"

We all raised our cups and echoed his words, and with that we parted for the night.

*****

A day later saw us following the white dusty roads to Genoa through rich, rolling countryside. There had been no fighting here, and the farms and villages were untouched by the ravages of war. The sight of our armed band caused the people some concern, but we had shed our white surcoats with the device of the red cross of Saint George, and only my shield with its chevron and scallops, borne by Huw, my new page, was displayed. As occasion demanded, Marco would call out in Italian to those who would flee, and this usually allayed their fears. To be sure, the sight of a hundred and fifty or more well-armed men could be expected to cause some small stir in this hitherto peaceful countryside.

In truth we were a brave sight. With a visit to the ruler of a rich city in hand, I had ordered that all should put on as faultless a display as possible. Armour and weapons had been rigorously cleaned and refurbished. No dints in plate, no splits in mail were to be seen. Leather harnesses were polished, and the bridles, bits, and other steel fittings were burnished. Boy, my horse, wore his usual caparison of red and white, and his mane and flowing tail had been cleaned and combed. His chestnut coat shone bravely.

I sent out foreriders in front of us and to either side. I did not intend to be surprised by any hostile party, for Marco had explained that Genoa lay some seventy or so English miles to the

Frank Payton

South, and the further we went in that direction, the greater the dearth of friendly faces. The journey looked likely to take us three or four days of steady riding and, as a precaution, I had ordered twenty spare horses to be brought along. As it was, they were useful to carry items of baggage.

Our form of march was as follows. In front were twenty men-at-arms. I rode immediately behind these with Jack Onsloe, then came Giles Ashurst, Marco, and Huw, followed by twenty-five archers. Then came eighty men-at-arms, and finally the remainder of the archers. With matters so arranged, I felt content that if attacked, I had an instant line of battle, able to turn in any direction to meet a challenge.

We skirted the town of Mortara, riding out into the countryside, and at the end of the first day camped near a village named San Giorgio. This seemed fitting, as the Saint was our patron. There was a little rippling stream for water, and pasture for the horses. After the evening meal I sat by a small fire with my immediate companions to talk, tell tales, and drink the good red wine.

At the last, as darkness fell around us, the camp quieted and fell silent, save for the low calls of the patrolling guards, and the rustling and fluttering of the small birds and animals of the night. I lay wrapped in a cloak against the damp night air and gazed up at the glittering stars.

Before long I was hard asleep, and only awoke when the sun was up and the camp astir.

Huw brought me a morsel of bread with hard, yellow cheese and an apple for my usual breakfast.

"Did you sleep well, Sir John?"

"Well enough, boy. Though it's long since I slept on bare earth with only a cloak for padding. Have you tended my horse?"

"Yes, as soon as I was awake. He is cropping grass with Master Onsloe's and Master Bandini's mounts. I've made sure he has clean water to drink."

Hawkwood's Sword

He seemed eager to please, and I knew he put himself to his work with a will. Like most of the Welsh in our number he was usually silent when alone with us English, but with his fellows chattered away in their own tongue like churchyard jackdaws. Huw was dark, well-built, and seemingly very strong. I had noted him going forward with his companions at Lanzo, and he did not lack courage.

"Well, Sir John, how is it with you this morning?" came Jack Onsloe's harsh voice. His shadow fell across me as I sat on a low camp stool. "All the foreriders have been to me, and report no armed bands ahead of us. There is a small town about three miles ahead. They don't know its name."

"I do," said Marco, as he joined us. "Good day to you, Sir John, and to you also, Master Onsloe. The town is called Lomello, and since today is a Tuesday, it will be market day. You will be able to see peaceable Italians going about their business. Perhaps you have such markets in England?"

"So we do, though I cannot clearly remember when I last attended one. Can you, Jack?"

He grunted in the back of his throat, a usual sort of comment for him. "Markets? No I can't. That it usually rained all day I can recall. I wasn't a freeman like you, but was ordered about all the time by the lord's reeve. Meddling bastard!" He spat on the ground. "I did for him though... Broke his neck before I left England. I've no wish to see Shrewsbury market place again. Italy will do for me—at least for a while. We should go." He finished abruptly and strode off, calling to his senior men to get their men mounted and ready to set off on the day's march.

Marco looked at me with some concern clouding his usually cheerful face.

"He is a very melancholy man, Sir John—from some suffering in his past, perhaps?"

"Aye, I fear so, lad. Some day I will tell you his story. It is not good to hear. But now, as Jack has said, we should go. Huw! Fetch Boy here for me, if you please."

Frank Payton

Thus we set out on the second day of our journey to Genoa. Marco was right. Lomello buzzed like a hive of bees. Country people flocked to the market place; the roads and lanes were full of men, women, horses, and donkey carts. In the market, produce and wares were spread on wooden stalls, or on bright cloths that covered the cobbled streets. Hens, ducks, and geese clucked, quacked, and honked in endless chorus. There were butchers, whose stalls, piled high with meat and game, dripped blood onto the stones. Fish sellers there were, with tanks containing live splashing carp, and other fish which had been brought from the catchers at the seacoast. Bakers' shops, open to the street, sent forth rich smells of new bread, and there were all manner of cakes and sweetmeats, such as I had last seen in the streets of London, long ago.

I turned to Jack and Giles. "Pass the word to the men. If they want anything from the market they are to buy—not take. This is peaceful country here, for the present. I don't want any wine-guzzling either, at this time of day. We must be watchful."

The men broke ranks; some dismounted and began to fill their saddlebags with all manner of foods—and wine. One of Giles' archers approached us, bearing a handful of long white strands which he held out to Marco.

"What be these, Master Bandini? How can you eat them? They're too goddamned hard to chew!"

Marco threw back his head and laughed. "This is pasta, Tom. It is made from good white flour and eggs, then dried in the sun. But it must be softened in boiling water before you can eat it. We have it with all kinds of vegetables, meat and fish. It is very good."

"I have never heard of this before," I said, equally taken with this oddity.

"Pasta was brought to Italy many years ago by the Venetian, Marco Polo," Marco replied. "He had travelled East, to far Cathay, and spent many years with the yellow people. This is the sort of food they eat. This I was told."

Hawkwood's Sword

"We shall have to try this dish sometime, Marco. It will perhaps help us to become accustomed to the Italian ways. Now we should press on. Get the men moving again, Jack. They've had time to buy their wants." I gathered up Boy's reins and urged him on, and so we began our march again.

Many of the townspeople applauded us as we rode past, and I wondered if we might pass that way again in a different guise, and with different intent. At that time, the people saw us as a profitable diversion on market day; remembering such souls in England, I knew that our visit would be a subject for discussion and speculation for some time to come.

We proceeded on our journey south for two more days without incident. Mostly we followed roads which appeared to be relics from Roman times and were not always in a good state of repair. There were many wayfarers in both directions, and I gave orders for our lines to be opened up to make room for other people. I also agreed with Jack that we should skirt towns along the way to avoid confrontations. At night we camped in open countryside.

Only two more incidents arose during our journey. The first of these was on the third day. Marco had ridden to the front of the column with one of the foreriders, and after a lengthy space of time, he returned in some haste, but alone. He took up his place alongside me.

"Sir John, there is a band of armed men to our front about two miles away. They are fighting with a smaller but better-armed group who appear to be defending something in their midst which is not clear to me. Do you wish to see for yourself?"

The sudden excitement of impending action surged over me, and the old familiar rushing of blood in my veins. My scalp prickled, and I ran my fingers through my hair as if to calm the sensation.

"Yes, let us see what is happening. Jack! Twenty of your men, an you please, and Giles, ten of your archers. Huw, my helmet!"

As I spoke I drew on my armoured gauntlets, and then saw to it that my sword would run free from the scabbard. The whole

Frank Payton

company was stirring, but I ordered that they should keep to a steady jogging pace as they followed. Our smaller group formed up quickly, and we moved off at a rocking canter, gradually increasing to a gallop. The speed of our going made other travellers move hurriedly off the road, and many gazed after us, open mouthed. We soon came in sight of the skirmish which Marco had reported. I drew my sword and waved the men on.

The road ahead of us was a small battlefield. In the middle stood a litter with closed curtains. About it was a group of horsemen who fought furiously with a rabble of ragged figures, brigands they seemed. As we approached, one of the defenders of the litter was dragged from his mount and fell into the midst of a hacking, smiting group of attackers. Two of his fellows threw themselves off their horses, and plunged into the fray on foot, in a desperate attempt to save their comrade.

"Come on!" I yelled. "Follow me, White Company!"

We fanned out and hit the attackers from three sides. As we were on horseback and they were not, the issue was not long in debate. Few of the band wore armour of any sort, and most of their number were soon slain.

Some of the remainder threw down their weapons, but three, including the man who appeared to be their leader, ran off into the fields.

I called Giles to deploy his archers. This was a challenge they could not resist. They quickly dismounted and took up their shooting stand, flexing the long yellow bows before they each nocked arrow to string and drew to the ear. The ten arrows flew down the green meadow.

The fugitives had been forced by the presence of a small stream to run away in a diagonal direction and were some sixty yards away. They paused at some obstacle, unseen to us, and were almost immediately overtaken as the arrows converged on them. Two fell writhing in agony. Their leader, however, seemed to have escaped harm, for he turned back towards us waving his sword and crying out some defiance. He should have run on. Giles' second arrow took him in the chest, and he sank to his knees before falling sideways.

Giles turned to me and grinned, then faced his men. "Retrieve your arrows. Cut them out, if needs be—and Hal, bring mine as well. You know their marks."

"That were a fine shot, Master Giles," Hal replied.

"Was it then? I had aimed a foot lower! Be off with you. Sir John hasn't all day to listen to your prattling." Hal nodded and set off.

I removed my helmet and handed it to Huw. I dismounted, and in doing so turned and found myself confronted by a tall man, richly attired, who still held a bloodied sword—indeed leaned upon it for support. He had been wounded in the left arm; blood streamed down over his hand and dripped upon the ground. Beside and behind him stood a group of armed men; two others lay wounded on the ground. One other lay beside them, quite still, dead. I remember thinking that he was very young, perhaps not twenty years old, to die thus. About him was an aura of nobility. With his rich garments darkened by his own blood and besmirched with dust, he reminded me of nothing so much as a bright flower, cast down and trampled upon. The older man saw the direction of my glance.

"A tragedy, Signore. His mother's youngest son, dead in such a manner, and at the hands of brigands. This will not be well received in Genoa."

"Who was he?" I asked.

He looked at me with interest. Brown eyes glittered from a dark face, bearded by black streaked with grey. "But who are you? Whose are all these riders?"

I held out my hand which he grasped uncertainly, suddenly aware of the force at my back. "I am hight John Hawkwood, a knight of England. These men are of the White Company, which is now in the service of Monferrato. I journey to Genoa to seek an audience of the Doge. These men are my bodyguard."

FRANK PAYTON

"You are well served by such men as these," he replied. "And it is just possible that I may be able to assist you in return for your timely arrival, and for being our saviour from these rogues. I am Ludovico di Lucanti, and would be pleased to smooth your path to the Doge. I must not enquire of your business with him. That might be too forward on my part at the present time."

He turned as a woman's high clear voice rang out from the litter. At his signal the body of the dead youth was quickly concealed under a cloak as a woman approached.

"Ludovico! Am I to be ignored? Have you no thought for your poor sister, who has been terrified out of her wits, to say nothing of Taddea? Stay in the litter you said. Keep out of sight, you said. I heard a clamour of fighting, and the clang of swords, then nothing. What is happening? Who is this knight, and all these men? Are they our captors, or our saviours?"

I stepped forward. "Saviours, my lady. I am John Hawkwood, and these are my companions. Perhaps we may escort you and your brother on the road to Genoa, whither, it seems, we are all bound?"

"This harridan is my younger sister, Proserpina," said Ludovico, laughing, and placing his arm about her shoulders. "She was born making such a pother as this, and has never ceased."

The young woman was aged about twenty. She was tall, nearly as tall as myself, and, unlike most Italian women of my experience, had hair the colour of dark honey where it had escaped her headdress. Her eyes were grey, regarding me boldly and with much interest. Her gown and mantle were of fine rich stuffs, of silk and white linen. At that moment, as our eyes met, I knew that never before had I seen a woman of such beauty. As I held her eyes, her cheeks crimsoned, and her gaze faltered. She quickly composed herself.

"So! An Inglesi saviour. Are all your soldiers Inglesi?"

"Not all, my lady, but mostly. We fight best alongside our own kind. That is our trade."

Hawkwood's Sword

She nodded. "And all the world knows you are good at that trade. Ludovico, we should press on. I am anxious to return home to Savignone. I think we shall not have further trouble on the road, if we are under the Signore Haccud's protection."

She turned away to re-enter the litter, exclaiming "Oh God!" as Hal returned and handed Giles two bloodied arrows.

"Clean them, you fool!" rasped Giles, his usually pleasant face twisted with anger.

The curtains of the litter swished to. The bearers took up the carrying poles, and prepared to move off.

The spell was broken.

*****

Di Lucanti and his companions recovered their horses, and the whole entourage, including the litter occupied by the Lady Proserpina and the as yet unseen Taddea, was taken into the safety of our column.

The body of the young man slain in the fight was borne by one of the spare horses. There was little we could do in the circumstances to preserve any vestige of his dignity. The wound in di Lucanti's arm was dressed as well as was possible with what clean cloths we had to hand.

The three surviving brigands were roped each one to another behind a spare mount, and judging by their sorry appearance, they clearly expected to be executed on arrival in Genoa.

Upon our departure I asked di Lucanti to ride with me, and we attempted conversation by the use of his small knowledge of English and my equally poor Italian. Any problems were eased with the help of Marco, who rode close behind.

"We have heard of your success at Lanzo," di Lucanti began. "All Italy stands in awe of the English Company. Permit me to ask how Genoa would be able to assist you. You will no doubt already have been told by your squire that I am the Count Savignone, and close in the councils of the Doge."

"Quite right. Marco has proved to be a valuable addition to our Company, and is most useful to me on all matters Italian. The answer to your question is that I seek to employ some of your crossbowmen. We have very few, only a mere handful amongst our Almain friends."

Di Lucanti smiled. "Do you expect Genoa's crossbows to win your battles, Sir John? Some of the older men still harbour bad feelings over the great battle at Crecy, when they suffered so grievously under your long English arrows."

I shrugged. "Your men were ridden down by impatient French knights who have little love for arrows of any length."

"True," he admitted, "but I do not know if the Doge will accede to your request. However, in recognition of your service to my sister and myself, I am in honour bound to plead your case, and that I shall do."

"You might inform the Doge," I said, and this was pure invention upon my part, "that King Edward of England is anxious to further encourage the wool trade with Italy, and this can only be to the mutual advantage of both Doge and King."

I say this was an invention, but not entirely. I had remembered the gist of it from conversations with the merchant Datini, at the time the Great Company invested Avignon and threatened the Pope. I have found that information such as this often proves useful. Di Lucanti looked thoughtful. "I see. Well, we are a great trading people, we Genoese, and when I make your case to the Doge I shall take care to mention what you have told me."

We talked on this and similar subjects of mutual interest as we rode on, until it fell to me to raise the matter of our overnight camp, and the necessity of finding a suitable place.

"That will be no problem," said di Lucanti. "I have an estate within reach of here. Indeed, I ought now to send a messenger ahead to announce our coming. May I expect you and your lieutenants to dine with us this evening? Your men will be well looked after by my steward. I shall attend to that."

"Naturally, I accept. You are most kind."

He turned and called to one of his colourfully-clad retainers, who rode up alongside for instructions. A rapid exchange of Italian, and the young man departed with a clattering of hooves and much hand-waving to his companions. In later years, I became accustomed to the flamboyant ways of the Italians, but in the early days they came as something of a surprise to me.

Di Lucanti laughed at my evident disapproval. "Niccolo is very young, Sir John, and every day is a joyous adventure to him. He gave a good enough account of himself earlier. I shall inform his step-father that I am pleased with him."

"Is he then a kinsman?"

"No, no. Not of the blood. But his mother married a cousin of ours after the death of her first husband, when Niccolo was but a child. I took him into my service to see what he could make of himself."

*****

We reached the Savignone estate before nightfall. The house, a long double-storied building, painted white and tiled in red, like many another we had passed along the way, was approached by a paved road. We rode as far as a large ornate gateway, and there dismounted.

The Count was greeted with many deep bows by a small knot of estate servants, led by a man who could only be described as round from every aspect. He was nearly as broad as he was high, and possessed a round, genial face which perspired freely. In a modest brown robe which extended to his ankles, held in at his ample stomach by a straining leather belt, he was the very opposite of the gaily dressed group which now demanded his attention.

Frank Payton

"This is Gaetano, my steward," announced di Lucanti. "I have instructed him to see that your men have places to sleep, and to prepare their food. For you and your lieutenants he will arrange accommodation in the house."

Gaetano bowed deeply to me, and beamed. "I am honoured to serve your Excellency."

I beckoned to Marco. "I think it would be best if you explained to the Count's steward what the men will need. My Italian is not yet good enough."

"I will, Sir John." And off he strode, with Gaetano rolling alongside.

Jack and Giles also made to leave in order to oversee the arrangements, vowing to return as soon as possible.

"Before you go," I said, "Make sure the men understand there must be no mischief. I don't want any outraged fathers, husbands or betrotheds following us to Genoa."

Giles grinned in his usual way. "I'm sure I don't know what you mean, Sir John. Do you, Jack?"

"Hmph!" said Jack, and set off after his men.

I turned then to see the Lady Proserpina alighting from her litter. My heart leaped at the sight, I have to confess, she was so fair to behold. A servant ran to assist her, and they both helped an elderly figure dressed from head to toe in black to descend. This proved to be a small old lady of whom Proserpina seemed to be very fond. I felt myself being scrutinised by a pair of exceedingly sharp black eyes. She spoke rapidly in Italian to her young companion, who laughed, blushed and said, "Signore Giovanni, may I present my nurse Taddea, who has looked after us all since the day we were born."

I bowed gravely to this small person, and essayed a greeting in Italian which Marco had taught me to say on such occasions. "I am honoured to meet a lady of distinction," I said, adding, "Especially the nurse to the Lady Proserpina."

Hawkwood's Sword

Taddea bowed in her turn. There was another spate of Italian directed at her charge who translated with flaming cheeks. "Taddea says you are very handsome, and you appear to be the sort of man who could rein in my wild ways, and that you should take me to wife!"

This was boldness indeed, although I had to admit to myself that the prospect seemed very attractive on several counts.

"Well, my Lady, it is certainly something to be thought of, but perhaps the customs of your country would demand a more cautious approach. We would need to know considerably more about each other than we do at present."

"That is true," she conceded with a smile. "But as it appears we will be travelling to Genoa together, we shall have the opportunity —under Taddea's and my brother's eyes, of course."

"Of course," I said, wondering where all this would end.

At that point, Ludovico returned his attention to me. Laughing, he said, "Come, Sir John, leave this troublesome child to prattle to her nurse. We have much to discuss, and you will wish to rest and refresh yourself before the evening meal. Proserpina! To your room, please! Take Taddea with you. Do not be late at table."

To my surprise, Proserpina meekly obeyed, and preceded us into the house, followed by her small, black-clad shadow.

*****

That evening, seated in the place of honour at the Count's right hand, was, as I look back up on it after so may years, one of the happiest in my long life. The beautiful Proserpina sat to her brother's left, facing me across the table. She was in turn the meekly obedient child, the mischievous maid, and the young noblewoman very sure of her beauty and station in life. To Marco she was gracious. Of Jack she was rather fearful, but she could laugh merrily at Giles' japes and jests.

Towards me, Proserpina preserved much of her dignity, as if to show that she was indeed a young lady of both virtue and responsibility. Eventually, when the meal was eaten and our wine cups were refilled, she asked, "Do you have large estates in England, Sir John?" her grey eyes wide with enquiry.

"Unfortunately, none at all, my Lady. My elder brother inherited from our father what wealth we had. He is a man of business, and now a large landowner, due to his own efforts."

"But you are a knight, a nobleman," she persisted.

"Only for the past six years, since Poitiers. Prince Edward saw fit to raise me to knighthood after that little affair. Before then I was but a man-at-arms, though admittedly with a following of mine own!"

"I do not believe you!" she cried. "You make little of yourself. Even before Lanzo, all Italy had heard of your deeds, and those of your men against France—and now against Savoy. You have an army at your back!"

"Then that, my Lady, must serve as my estate. My wealth is in my men, and their devotion to the causes I espouse."

"And what are they?" Proserpina asked. "I am sure they are of the highest order."

"I could not even pretend to that. Like many another soldier, I fight for my pay. But if I take up a cause, I do not lay it down lightly until the final battle is won."

Ludovico intervened. "My dear sister, you must not subject Sir John to your interminable questions. I'm sure he does not thank you for your curiosity."

"Not so," I said. "I do not find them troublesome in the least. Indeed, I will say more to you. In England I have a daughter who I have not seen for eight years. Her mother died in the great plague which visited England. She scarcely knew me when I was last in England, but it is best perhaps that she is with her uncles and aunts, for mine is a hard life with no place for a child."

"But she needs a mother, surely?" Proserpina leaned forward and placed a long-fingered hand over mine. She looked at me, her

Hawkwood's Sword

eyes warm and bright. I turned to her brother, whom I sensed was watching me closely.

"The Lady Proserpina has a kindly heart," I said.

Ludovico sighed. "Yes, it is well known to me, and is a constant cause for concern. Her warm heart runs away with her head, I fear."

His sister pouted. "You are a miserable old man, Ludovico. God will not forgive you your hard heart. I shall pray for the Signore Giovanni's daughter this night. "Now I will bid you all good night."

She then rose imperiously from her seat, and sending a radiant smile winging over the whole company, swept from the hall. Old Taddea followed, bobbing a bow to Ludovico and one to me, before scurrying away like a small black bird.

Ludovico beckoned a servant to refill our cups. He shrugged his shoulders as if to dismiss his sister from his thoughts, and raised his cup to me.

"A health to you, Sir John. Now that my troublesome sister has removed herself from our presence, perhaps we grown men may talk together in peace."

"I do not find her troublesome," I replied. "Indeed, quite the opposite. Not every day does a man of my years and origin receive a proposal of marriage from a beautiful and personable young noblewoman. I return your good wishes." I raised my cup.

"You would be a very brave man to take that young vixen to wife," chuckled Ludovico. "She is very high-spirited, as I and others know to our cost. But enough of this talk. Let us discuss your business with Boccanera."

"We need smaller numbers to talk of this," muttered Jack. "Too many at table here."

"Yes, you are right, Messer Onsloe," said our host. He turned to the company lower down the table, and dismissed all save young Niccolo, his personal secretary Giuliano, and one other. This was an older man, soberly dressed, who had remained in the background of the afternoon's events. However, I had noticed him at the skirmish with the brigands, and he could well handle a sword. His name, as I learned later, was Orlando Scacci, and he was always in close attendance on the Count.

"Now then, you will wish to know why I desire to recruit crossbowmen," I said. "The answer is simple. I need such men, and I have none. Yes, I have many archers, but for siege work against castles and walled towns, where speed of shooting is not usually necessary, the crossbow comes into its own. It is less tiring to work over long periods. In an open battle, the weapon is less effective."

"But how will this avail Genoa?" asked Ludovico.

"I understand you are ever under pressure from Milan. It could only be to the Doge's advantage to assist us. At present, we fight to maintain Monferrato in his lands, but this will shortly come to a conclusion. We shall defeat the Visconti. That will relieve Genoa as well as Monferrato, I believe. Insofar as payment for the services of your crossbows is concerned, we have ample means to satisfy any reasonable demand. Also, at need Genoa could find us a strong ally."

"It is well said, but Grimaldi and Orsini will go against you. They still smart over the defeat at Crecy, and the loss of so many of their men."

"The French killed more Genoese than we did," Jack broke in. "I was there too. When your men retreated out of range of our archers, they were ridden down and slaughtered by the very people who had hired them, but who had neither sense nor patience to know how they could have been used to advantage. I felt sorry for the poor bastards, caught between the hammer and the anvil."

Ludovico looked at me. I told him that what Jack had said was true. "The King of France lost control of his knights. If he had held his men back, and waited until the following morning to give battle, there could have been a very different end to Crecy. No, I don't think we should be blamed entirely for the sad ending of your men."

Hawkwood's Sword

"I will mention all this, but I feel there will still be resentment."

"Maybe, we shall see. But remember this: Crecy was sixteen years ago. Many of the men who came home to Genoa will be too old for further service in the field. Your young men will be eager for adventure, and the chance to try out their skills in battle. The pay will be good."

"Do not mistake me," said Ludovico. "I seek only to point out problems which may arise. Because of the debt I owe you, I shall speak most strongly on your behalf. There are others who will wish to assist you when I explain how matters stand."

The evening proceeded with more such talk, turning from time to time to more general matters concerning the Italian cities, their alliances and feuds. I learned much from all this and committed to memory the names of many persons then wielding power in Northern Italy. I heard more of the tyrant Bernabo, Lord of Milan, who kept five thousand hunting dogs. He tortured unfortunate captives on alternate days with increasing cruelty until he achieved his purpose, or the wretched victim gave up his life before facing the next coming horror.

I listened with interest to accounts of the enmity between Pisa and Florence, and mused on the possibilities of future employment with one or the other. Also in this vein, I was intrigued to hear how the Church tried to extend its influence and power over cities and towns. Even the bishops were not averse to hiring soldiers to enforce their demands.

At the last, with the wine jugs emptied and the candles guttering low, sending their sweet scent of beeswax around the hall, we decided for bed, and, preceded by servants bearing lighted tapers, were led to our bedchambers. I saw myself to rest, bidding Huw sleep on a pallet outside the door. Shedding my clothes, I donned a sleeping robe left for me. I extinguished the taper and moved to the window looking down over the ornamental garden bathed in bright moonlight, which threw dark shadows where its rays could not pierce.

Frank Payton

As I watched, the figure of a man emerged into a moonlit patch, walking swiftly and with purpose. He moved out of my sight and away towards the front of the house. Waiting, I listened intently, and eventually heard the unmistakable sound of hooves on grass, quickening in pace as rider and horse left the house behind.

They were heading, I thought, towards Genoa. A little breeze stirred the night air, and brought the sweetness of late autumn roses. I turned from the window, and as I lay down I wondered briefly why Orlando Scacci was abroad so late in the night.

*****

I was shaken awake next morning by Huw. "Sir John! Sir John, wake up! The sun is already high, and Master Onsloe chafes to be away. The Count's man of letters has been to bid you break your fast with the family."

Slowly I came to my senses. A dream lingered in my head and would not be driven away by the daylight. In this vision I had seen Orlando, the Count's bodyguard, riding away with the Lady Proserpina across the front of his saddle. She had called out to me "Giovanni, Giovanni!", but however much I urged my own horse to greater effort, Orlando drew away from me. His mocking laughter seemed to ring in my ears. A feeling of great loss flooded over me.

I splashed my face and head with cold water from the ewer brought in by Huw. He handed me a fine linen cloth on which to dry myself. The cold water helped my awakening, and the dream faded, but a persistent foreboding had arisen in my mind, which did not leave me for many days.

Dressing quickly in my travelling clothes, I went down to the great hall, followed by Huw. Ludovico looked up as I entered and pushed some documents into Giuliano's hands, dismissing him to his place lower down the table with other members of his travelling party. He smiled, "Estate affairs, Sir John. Always I have papers to examine. Accounts to pay, debtors to press for payment; a heavy burden. But enough! Have you slept well? No disturbances?"

I wondered vaguely if he referred to the departure of Orlando in the night, but said nothing of it. I had noticed that he was not at the table. "Yes, passing well. I am fortunate to be able to sleep well almost anywhere, from an open field to a comfortable bedchamber."

"You have a clear conscience. I find it strange that a man of your calling can sleep so well. Are you never troubled by the faces of the men you have killed? How will you account to God at the last?" He laughed. "You think me a fool to ask such a question?"

"Not at all. I expect to be judged as one who did his duty by his liege lord, and without fear, as my opponents did in their turn. I have always fought fairly. I have never killed women or children, and would punish those who did. I have never forced a woman who would not be taken, and I never break a contract unless I judge myself to have been unfairly dealt with. Those are the reasons for my clear conscience."

"Hmm. I had not perceived the matter in such terms," he replied. "Perhaps you are right to think thus."

The arrival of Jack with Giles and Marco brought this talk to an end. Seating themselves at the table, they proceeded to break their fast with some enthusiasm, eating heartily of the various foods set before them. There was good white bread, and cheeses, with eggs cooked in their shells, olives, and figs. With all this I drank only watered wine, but the others drank the red wine from the silver jugs as usual.

At last Ludovico excused himself from the table and, beckoning to Giuliano, made to leave the hall with his retainers. "I shall gather my party together as soon as possible, Sir John. I know we are all anxious to reach Genoa before the end of today."

"And the Lady Proserpina.....?" I enquired.

"Will travel with her nurse in a horse-litter," he replied with a rolling of his eyes to the heavens. "To invite her to ride would be an invitation to trouble, and I have no intention of galloping all over the countryside to follow her mad pranks. No, the litter will be the best." With that he bowed and left.

I caught Giles looking at me. "Well, what ails you?"

"Naught, Sir John, but I'll venture that young lady would enjoy being chased around the countryside by one such as yourself. She looks a spirited lass to me."

"Enough of your impudence! You shall not speak thus about your betters. Away with you, and get your men ready to take the road. I'm not in the mood for your little jests."

"Perhaps not, Sir John," he answered, completely unabashed, "but I'll wager you have already thought it would be a pleasant pursuit." He stalked out of the hall laughing, and tossing an apple from hand to hand.

"One day he'll overstep himself," growled Jack. "My hand itches to take the silly grin off his face."

"Yes," I agreed, ruefully, "but he's often right, and it seems a pity for the girl to be denied her true self."

Jack looked at me grimly. "I'll go and gather my men together. Someone has to keep his eye on the mark."

*****

Before long, we were once more on the road to Genoa. It was a fine Autumn morning. There was something of a chilly mist in the air, soon to be driven away by a bright sun in a clear sky. Our formation was as before, scouts in front, a vanguard of men-at-arms, a ventaine of archers, followed by my own party—which now included the Count and his retainers—and, of course, the Lady Proserpina and her nurse in the horse-litter. After them came the main body of men-at-arms and archers, the small baggage train, and a final detail of men-at-arms. Thus I felt secure. The three brigand prisoners were also taken along, and were eventually handed over to the city authorities for trial and their later execution. There could be no other outcome for the wretches. It would have been better for them had they been slain in the skirmish, whether by sword or arrow. I had little doubt that the eventual method of their dying would not be so clean.

Luckily, there were no more incidents to halt our progress, and towards the late afternoon of the fifth day we sighted the towers, spires and red roofs of the great seaport of Genoa. Beyond lay the sea, a wide expanse of blue, glittering under an already setting sun. I had not seen such a sight for eight years, since I had last left England. I have heard it said that travellers overseas will often long for their homeland on arriving at a far away seacoast. However, this was no time for fruitless yearning, and I thrust the thought away, and turned to Ludovico.

"This is a wonderful sight to behold. Such a fine city set beside the sea."

"Genoa is the most beautiful city in the whole of Italy," he said, with no little pride. "We are a great seafaring and trading people, both to east and west. You can see for yourself the fine buildings, and the harbour always busy with ships of all nations."

He swept his arm around in a flamboyant gesture. "My house is one of the best in the whole city. It shall be yours and your principal officers' lodging whilst you are in Genoa. I will make arrangements for your other men outside the walls."

"You are most kind," I replied, "but I shall require a small bodyguard with me—of, say, twenty men. They could perhaps be housed within your compound and fed from your kitchens. We have plentiful supplies of food."

"Of course they could. But that is not the problem. Foreign soldiers are excluded from entering the city by order of the Doge. It might be possible to arrange for a slightly larger number in your personal following, but twenty would not be tolerated. But have no fear, I shall explain that yours is a peaceful mission—an embassy, even."

"Oh, I have no fear," I replied. "I do but take care. Of course, I have every trust in you personally."

FRANK PAYTON

So it was that the main body of the men set up camp on a military training ground outside the city walls. As for myself, I entered the city with Jack, Giles, Marco, and Huw. In addition there were three more archers and four men-at-arms, all chosen for skill and experience. The archers' bows and arrow cases were wrapped in cloths, and carried by two packhorses as secretly as possible.

I was not surprised to see Orlando, the Count's shadow, appear as we passed under the wide arch of the city's gates. He nodded to me and rode his mount alongside that of his patron. What passed between them I do not know, but all appeared to be well, at least for the present. I could afford to take no chances, and urged vigilance on all my companions.

*****

We were lodged in a separate wing of the Count's huge town house. This was convenient both for him and for me, as I could make arrangements to suit myself. Our rooms included a kitchen, with a small staff who would produce whatever was required in the way of food and drink for Huw, the archers, and men-at-arms. Jack and I, together with Giles and Marco, took the main meals of the day with the di Lucantis.

There was another matter upon which I felt myself content, and that was how we should appear before the Doge and his Council. Before leaving the Company I had sent for Will Turton and ordered him to produce the finest attire which had been taken into his care at Lanzo and other places, so as to enable us to make as good an impression as possible when we arrived in Genoa. Thus, our dusty and stained travelling clothes and armour were for the time being packed away, and we each arrayed ourselves from the store of clothes as we thought best. Will had also passed over certain items of men's jewellery—rings, chains, and medals of gold and silver—which would help serve to mark us out as persons of substance.

Hawkwood's Sword

Thus we four appeared at the evening meal in the Great Hall that first night in Genoa, well attired, but with not too much ostentation. I intended that we should keep our magnificence for the audience I hoped to have of the Doge.

As before, I was seated on Ludovico's right, with the Lady Proserpina to his left. The others took up their places, including Niccolo, Ludovico's nephew, and two elderly male members of the family. Grey haired and clad in dark robes, they joined in conversation very little, and by the way they regarded us, clearly felt us to be some kind of northern barbarians. They both ate little, drank little, and excused themselves early from the table.

Ludovico breathed a sigh of relief at their going. "Our Uncles, Domenico and Matteo, have no homes of their own, never having married, nor having left the family circle. They are both very bookish, and spend most of their time with their collections and in talking with like-minded souls. To me has fallen the responsibility of their care. Sometimes, however, it becomes irksome and akin to having a black crow on each shoulder."

"At all events," I said, "Your activities with regard to them do you great credit, and doubtless bring you a just reward in Heaven."

"Pah! A reward in Heaven?" cried Proserpina. "He is more like to burn in Hell! He regrets every soldi he expends on their care, a duty laid on him by our dear father. They have little enough income of their own from a few farms, and that they spend on books and a few comforts. He cannot wait to get his hands on their property!"

Her brother exploded with rage. "Proserpina! That is enough! You will go to your room. I will not have this infamous talk from you. You know nothing of which you speak. Go!"

"Certainly not, Ludovico!" she replied stoutly. "I am no child to be thus ordered. I have life and property of mine own, and I shall do as I please with either, and I know exactly of what I speak."

Her grey eyes met mine, flashing over the heightened colour of her cheeks, and once more I felt as if shot through by an archer's arrow. She was magnificent, with her dark blonde hair streaming

FRANK PAYTON

free, save for two heavy plaits, one over the front of each shoulder, framing the jewels of her bosom under the heavy blue silks of her gown. It was then that I told myself that by the God in Heaven above, I would have this woman to wife if I had to pass through the hosts of Hell to win her. I returned her glance, I hoped, as sympathetically and encouragingly as I could, but it was essential that I did not antagonise Ludovico. A slight smile adorned her lips, as if to say, "I know, I understand."

I picked up and drained my wine cup. "Signore di Lucanti, how shall you proceed with your approach to the Doge on our behalf?" I asked to change the subject.

Ludovico lifted his head from between his hands, and recovered his composure. "Thank you, Sir John, for bringing me back to reality and matters of moment. It will be necessary for me to make overtures on your behalf to those members of the Council who are likely to be sympathetic to your request. This may well take several days, and naturally you will understand that I have other business to which to attend. In the meantime, I suggest that I find you a guide to show you this great city of ours, and to direct you whilst in our midst."

"I will be your guide, Sir John," interrupted Proserpina, leaning forward eagerly. "No, Ludovico," she held up her hand to stem the flow of his protests. "I will brook no opposition to this!"

"Don't be a fool, girl!" he blustered. "You cannot go about the city in that way. It would not be seemly. It—"

"Dressed as I am, I agree. I shall put up my hair and go as a boy, a young man, and Niccolo shall attend me. Sir John will have Marco, his squire"—here she smiled sweetly at the two of them—"and I shall be quite safe. So, you see, it is all arranged. Now I shall retire. Taddea, it is late, and we should be abed. Good night, Sir John, Ludovico and all." Thus she swept regally from the hall, with Taddea in her wake.

Ludovico sat back in his chair, and placed a hand over his eyes. Our talk had died away, and we had ceased our eating. Now I reached out for a portion of the dish called ravioli, thin pastry that

Hawkwood's Sword

seemed to be enveloping a spicy meat filling. I had found this to be much to my liking. The others followed my lead, and so we resumed our meal and conversation.

Ludovico seemed momentarily to have forgotten us, and muttered to himself in Italian under his breath. Soon, however, he roused himself and took more wine. "You now see, Sir John, what a problem I have with my dear sister. She is beyond all reasonable control. I have even considered confining her to a nunnery, where she may be taught some humility and regard for others. She plays upon your good regard for her, and uses it against me, her brother." He tapped his chest with a bejewelled forefinger.

To my surprise it was Jack who spoke up. "To mew up a lady of your sister's spirit would be as if you were to put a falcon in a cage. You should make use of her in your affairs. She may well be of great help to you. As she is, she has no purpose, except to decorate your table. In any event, you can surely find for her a good husband from amongst the young men of your noble families."

Ludovico laughed. "You think so? She will have no one who has been put forward as a suitor. Her wildness turns them away. Our young men are scandalised by her pranks. They expect dutiful humility in the young women they are to marry, as well as some attention to religion, and to a wife's domestic responsibilities. Proserpina shows none of these. No, I fear she will end badly, or in a convent."

"I pray you will at least indulge her in her wish to show me your great city," I said. "She can come to no harm with such an escort as we can provide. One more good-looking youth on horseback can surely arouse no undue attention."

He smiled. "How can I refuse you, Sir John? But for you, she and I would be dead. Yes, I will relent, since you plead her case so well. But, I warn you, you know her not."

With that we rose from the table, and went to our sleeping quarters. I had arranged for one of the archers or a man-at-arms to stand guard on that part of the house, and I was glad to see that the man was still awake. Giles stayed to talk, since this one was

FRANK PAYTON

one of his own men, but we others passed in and went to our rooms.

Huw was already snoring on his pallet before the door of my chamber. I stepped over him and went inside. He did not stir. There was a single lamp burning which must have had some aromatic oil for fuel, as the air was heavy with the scent of it. I flung off the heavy robe I had worn earlier, and laid the jewelled neck-chain on a low carven table, together with the gold rings Will had given to me.

One of these I examined more closely. It was of thick heavy gold with the mask of a lion embossed upon the bezel. Tiny green gemstones formed the beast's eyes, which glinted in the lamplight. A fair thing, I thought, and although not caring much for frippery, resolved to keep it by me. It was nothing then, but later I came to prize it greatly.

Laying my boots and other garments aside, I put on a sleeping robe and went to the window. It was such a night as previously at Ludovico's country estate, and I thought again of Orlando's riding in the dead of night, and the dream I had had thereafter. It then came to me, as I gazed out over the rooftops of the great city, that this was the first time I had slept in such a place since leaving London for France eight years before.

I pondered on the wisdom of becoming close to the Lady Proserpina. It was clearly unwise to take her from her family home and its comforts, and fling her into a military encampment to such as I was accustomed. At first she would find the life exciting, free, and might revel in being the object of so much male admiration that would surely come her way. That in itself could cause many problems, such as I did not wish to encounter. In the end, no doubt, Proserpina would tire of the need to be constantly on the move and would begin to pine, perhaps, for her settled family life in Genoa, or at least for more feminine company. With these thoughts in mind, I went to my bed, where the effects of the day's journey, and plentiful food, and most especially wine, soon sent me into a mercifully dreamless sleep.

Chapter 6
Genoa

I awoke early the next morning and sent Huw to the kitchen for hot water with which to wash and shave my face of two days' growth of beard. Unlike many at that time, I never felt really comfortable unless I was clean-shaven. That done, I was dressed and ready for the day when Jack entered the room shortly after. He looked me up and down.

"Very fine, Sir John. Very fine. I suppose you to be bent on this ride about the city with the young mistress? For myself I shall go and see what the men are doing at the camp. By now, I'll wager, they'll be wanting to break out and visit a few wine shops, and go in search of some willing women."

"Yes, I am quite set on this ride, as you name it, and for more reasons than the Lady Proserpina." Jack's eyes widened at this, and I continued. "This ride is also an opportunity to see just what this city contains, and how it is laid out. I know we can't see into the future, but such knowledge might just be very useful sometime. Apart from pleasure, this ride will be for me something in the nature of a scouting expedition. So far as the men are concerned, you must ask the Count what rules apply to their entry to the city. I can't see the authorities allowing over a hundred well-armed foreign soldiers to roam around their city all at once. You may say from me that I will hang any man found to have been guilty of any crime, or to have been the cause of any trouble within the city walls."

Hawkwood's Sword

"As you wish, Sir John, but it seems very harsh. What if a man is provoked?"

"Come, Jack, you know full well that I do not wish for any pretext which might be used to turn these people against us. We need their assistance. There is already a faction opposed to our request for that assistance. No, I will not be gainsaid on this. You had better order that no swords are to be carried into the city, and tell the authorities beforehand."

He left me then with a long face, although I think he was happy to be going back to the camp and his command. He would feel more at home there. Jack was a fine soldier, and could be relied on to carry out whatever I required of him. But he was no courtier. He remained at heart a simple countryman. The loss of his family was something to which he did not refer, but it could never have been far from his thoughts. Indeed, I had thought from time to time that his reckless bravery and ferocity in the field was born of a desire to embrace Death as a final escape from his anguish, and mayhap in the hope that he might thus be reunited with those he had lost.

Musing in this way I made my way to the Hall where I was to break my fast. Marco and Giles, already seated, were companionably discussing the relative merits of the bow and the crossbow.

"I am explaining to Master Ashurst how we could obtain a faster rate of shooting with the crossbow, Sir John. If you recall, I spoke to you once before about this."

"Yes, I do remember your words, Marco, but as you know, Giles and I would still find the weapon too slow." His face fell, and I hastened to reassure him. "But be sure I shall find a use for the crossbow when we are at a siege, and elsewhere. I do not decry its power."

I reached out for my wine cup, which Huw had filled with watered wine, and drank deeply. As I replaced the cup, my glance passed along the table. Niccolo was seated a little way beyond Marco, and next to him sat a young man whom I had not seen

FRANK PAYTON

before. I called to him. "Who is your companion, Niccolo? Is he a new guest?"

"Ah, good morning, Sir John. This is my cousin Agnolo, who has been sent here with a special message for the Count."

The young man bowed his head and raised his wine cup to me, and then returned to his food. He was richly dressed in the bright colours affected by the young, and wore a cap of soft blue velvet. I noticed that he contrived to keep his face away from me, but there was something about the set of his head which seemed vaguely familiar. For myself, I took some bread and cut a piece of the fine white cheese which I had favoured since arriving in the country. On the table was also a basket of apples, pears and plums, of very good quality, and delicious to eat. There were some peaches too, large golden fruits which I had not seen before.

In the middle of each was a stone almost the size of a pigeon's egg. I found this fruit to be much to my liking, the flesh being sweet as honey, but in the centre of the stone was a flat, oval nut as bitter as gall.

Marco broke into my thoughts. "If you wish it, I shall go and see that the horses are made ready, Sir John. Do you wish aught else to be done?"

"No, there is nothing else, thank you. I shall stay and speak to Giles on certain matters."

Marco bowed and left the Hall. Giles moved into the seat opposite, and as he did so, Niccolo and Agnolo walked swiftly from the Hall. I stared after them.

"What is it, Sir John?" Giles asked with something of a grin upon his face.

"Why, that boy Agnolo reminds me of someone, but I can't say who. It is most annoying."

"I should think many of these young Italians look alike, and if he is a cousin of Niccolo's, well then, there's the answer."

"Yes, I suppose you to be right. Now, this ride about the city; I shall send Marco and Huw in front, and will follow with the Lady

Hawkwood's Sword

Proserpina. You will ride behind we two. Then, unbeknown to the others, I want two of the men who are with here to follow at a short distance, in the event that any trouble should befall us. Explain to them that they are to keep a close watch on the people about us. Also, I expect you and they to observe carefully the way in which this city is laid out. I have already told Jack that this knowledge may be useful to us at some time in the future."

He nodded. "I understand, for I have had the same thoughts. The militia here seems to be very strong, and even at a glance the city is seen to be well defended. These people live by the sea, and that is a great defence for them. They have many ships to fight off attackers from that direction. There are strong walls which face the land, too strong for us. They could sit behind those ramparts and shoot bolts at us all day."

"That may be so, but the strongest city will fall. You know it as well as I. For the present all we need to do is keep our eyes open, and remember what we see. Now let us away, or the Lady Proserpina will have cause to name us sluggard."

*****

Marco and Huw were already mounted and waiting as Giles and I stepped out into a street thronged with people hurrying by, both to left and to right. I took Boy's reins from Huw. The big horse sidled in alarm at the press of people, and neighed in greeting to other passing horses. I scratched his forehead, and stroked my fingers down his long silken nose. He threw up his head as a horse will do, and pawed at the cobblestones with heavy hooves.

One of the di Lucanti grooms had combed out his mane and tail, and brushed his chestnut coat until it shone. Boy was a good horse, and had carried me into many a skirmish and battle over the years. He had been taught to fight with his front hooves, and many men had gone down under those thrashing steel-shod hammers. I gave him an apple from the table, and he crunched it between strong teeth, and the sweet juice ran down onto the stones. He was thus content, and I swung up into the saddle and looked about me. As I did so Niccolo appeared before me, followed by the mysterious Agnolo, who urged his horse next to me and looked me full face for the first time, and spoke thus.

"Do I not make a handsome youth, Sir John?"

Then she laughed loud at my puzzlement. It was, of course, the Lady Proserpina. I joined in the merriment with a will, having been quite deceived by her disguise.

"I confess that you do, my Lady, but I would liefer see you as you were yestereve. But if you are to be our guide, let us away to see the delights of your fine city by the sea."

We two rode together behind Marco and Niccolo, who served as the heralds of our approach. As Marco was familiar with his home city, only a brief word or two from Proserpina was needed for him to lead us along the way in which she wished to proceed. Giles brought up the rear of our little group, followed at a distance of twenty or thirty yards by the two archers.

Our passing along the busy streets, and through the fine squares, or piazzi, as Marco had taught me to say, caused great excitement amongst the people. Heads turned, fingers pointed, and other individuals were fetched from shops and houses to witness our little cavalcade. In time, we passed into a quieter section of the city where venerable palaces lined the streets. The facades of these fine houses were built of white and black marble, which was most striking. Here also were churches with similar decoration, and overlooking the harbour area stood a vast cathedral.

"There! Sir John!" cried Proserpina. "Behold our wondrous Cathedral of San Lorenzo, guarding the city and the ships in the harbour. Is it not truly beautiful?"

"Yes, it is very fine indeed, as fine as I have ever seen in either England or France. But more beautiful to me is a certain lady, who, from what I am told, lacks a bold knight to tell her so."

Hawkwood's Sword

She struggled to answer this, perhaps being surprised by my blunt approach. Rose-red blushes chased across her cheeks, and, for a moment she hung her head. Then despite her confusion she looked up at me undaunted. "I have heard few such words from our young men. They flee my presence, and run home to their mothers when they witness my nature, and my behaviour." She sighed. "I confess, Ludovico is right. I am a harpy, and impatient with courtly dalliance. But now, from you, I have met that strength and directness for which I have pined in vain."

"I had hoped to hear you speak thus, Proserpina, for I too am blunt and direct by my nature. I was born into a large family, free, but in an estate below your own nobility. When young, I laboured in a stinking tannery owned by my father. On his death, my elder brother, also named John, took the inheritance. Since I did not wish to be his slave, I went for an archer in the King's army. Now, I am as you see me, raised to knighthood, and leader of an army in a foreign land. Despite this, I shall remain ever faithful to England and her King. Someday, I shall return there." I paused. "Would you follow me?"

She drew in her breath. "I have heard that England is a cold, dark land, where rain falls daily, and the sun is rarely seen. It would be hard for me to live without the sun." She looked at me from under long dark eyelashes. Any passerby seeing that glance would have known that here was no finely dressed youth.

I laughed at her feigned sadness. "We also have the sun in England, but we have much rain, it is true. Our countryside is wonderfully green because of it, and there are many rivers and small streams full of sound. The woods are thick and full of wild flowers, with many kinds of songbirds and animals. In winter we have snow and icy winds from the north and east. Even then the sun will shine forth from clear blue skies, and then there is no finer sight to be seen."

This had caught her imagination, for her eyes shone, and she looked eager to ride to England that very day.

Frank Payton

"I have only seen snow once, when we travelled north. Ludovico showed me the mountains of France, shining with snow, far away. Yes, I think I could follow you to England, my Giovanni."

There was then no more to be said.

*****

Four days passed during which Proserpina and I rode out alone, she still in her boy's disguise. After that first excursion I had deemed it safe enough for us to go without escort, and Ludovico seemed to accept that his sister would come to no harm. He revealed to me privately that she appeared to have changed greatly in her behaviour, especially towards himself.

"I confess myself amazed, nay, astounded at the change in her. Almost overnight, she has cast aside her childish ways. Perhaps Old Taddea was right from the very beginning. You are the right man to take her to wife."

I clapped my hand to his shoulder. "It is a pleasant prospect, and I do not deny that I am greatly attracted to her, but a wife needs a settled home, and that I cannot offer yet, not here in Italy. This Monferrato affair is but an opening campaign. When it is over, the Company will move on to further employment."

He nodded his understanding of the position. "Yes, and seemingly there will always be feuds between our cities to provide that work for you and your men. As to a home, there is an answer to that. You will recall that Proserpina spoke of property of her own?"

"I do."

"This is indeed the case. My sister inherited the tenure of an estate from her maternal grandfather. On her death the property itself must descend to me, or my descendants, unless she herself first has a husband and subsequent issue of her own. Another condition is that Proserpina may not take up her inheritance until she does marry. Up to that time, I hold the estate for her. So you see, Sir John, the problem of a home is solved. As I have said before, both I and Proserpina—whom I love most dearly, although at times it may not appear to be so—owe you our lives. I would welcome you as a brother, and a valuable ally to our family."

I was greatly moved by this declaration, and it was some little time before I could compose a suitable reply. There stood I, once a poor freeman and common archer of England, being offered entry to an ancient and noble family of one of the oldest city states in Italy.

"I am much affected by your words, Ludovico, and very grateful for your friendship and confidence in me, a stranger but newly come to your land. Let us say that when Monferrato can rest easy that his lands will not again be threatened by the Visconti, I shall return to Genoa and request the Lady Proserpina's hand in marriage.

"This I pledge you now, and I shall only be diverted from this by sword, lance, arrow, or plague. My word, once given, is not lightly cast aside. Further, so that there shall be no misunderstanding between us, I will myself acquaint the Lady Proserpina with my mind and intent." I thrust out my hand, and he took it in a firm grasp.

"I agree with all you that intend, and God preserve you safe until your return to us. But now, I have other tidings. On tomorrow's morn, you and I will have an audience of the Doge and his Council. He has spoken to me on this matter, and is aware of my debt to you. He is also anxious to further good relations between Genoa and England. I have hinted also that you are known to and trusted by your King Edward, and his son, the Prince of Wales."

"The King will most certainly be pleased to encourage trade between the merchants of Genoa, with its fine fleet of ships, and the ports of England. The wool trade is, I know, very important to him and to the country as a whole. Many goods from the East are traded by your people, and are much desired in my country."

Frank Payton

Ludovico smiled and continued. "Several friends of mine who are members of the Council have promised their support. As I told you, the Grimaldis and Orsinis still smart from their defeat at English hands, but I think they will not win the debate. It was a long time ago, and new matters have arisen which are of importance to both sides. I have little doubt that that we shall prevail. You will get your crossbowmen."

*****

That conversation took place in late afternoon, after Proserpina and I had returned from our daily ride. On that occasion we had forsaken the city and harbour, and had ridden away up steeper and yet steeper little streets which became tracks, and then mere paths. We rode our labouring horses past groves of lemons and oranges, passing by vineyards and olive groves, and little white painted and red-tiled cottages which seemed to have themselves grown from the soil.

At length we were prevented from going further by the precipitous mountain slopes, which loomed above the city. After tethering the horses to small trees, we turned to look out over the city, and the sea.

"Oh, Giovanni, how small Genoa appears from here," cried Proserpina. "The ships in the harbour and out at sea are tiny, like children's toys." She was disappointed that her great city had shrunk thus in her sight. "Our great Cathedral, the churches, and palaces have become no more than small pebbles on the shore, and we must be giants to see them so."

I laughed at her words. "Do not be so cast down. 'Tis but a trick of sight and distance. When we return, the city will be as great as before. From here we see as giants, but then we shall be smaller than the buildings. But come, we must find water for the horses. See how they hang their heads."

Hawkwood's Sword

She spoke in a small voice. "You think me foolish? As a small child? Perhaps I am. Unlike you, I have travelled little: to our estate, which you saw on the road here, perhaps to a farm or two which we own. Once only, when I was very small, we visited my mother's father at his castle far to the North. He was old and fierce, and had little patience with children. When he looked not, I drank all the wine in his cup. My mother was horrified, and would have sent me away with Taddea, but my grandfather roared with laughter, and pulled me on to his knee, and fed me with little cakes. I am afraid I was a trouble to all, even then."

"You are not a trouble to me, Proserpina, do not think it. But now, we must find water."

We began to cast about the area, looking for any kind of fall of water from above, or perhaps a spring. In that we were fortunate, for some little distance to our right we discovered a cleft in the rock-face. Out of this flowed a steady stream of crystal-clear water falling into a rocky bowl, probably carved out by its own action over many years. We brought the horses over, and let them drink their fill from the pool, then found them a patch of fresh green grass, hobbling them each with a length of leather strip.

"They will not stray far," I told Proserpina. "And now the pool has cleared again from their drinking we should help ourselves, I think." So saying, I flung myself down on the soft, springy, mountain grass, and, scooping up a double handful of the ice-cool water, doused my sweating head and face. After that I took up several more handfuls, and drank deeply. The water was fresh and sweet, being from the height of the mountain above.

As I began to rise, I felt a light touch upon my shoulder. Proserpina was kneeling by me. I turned and lay looking up at her. She smiled down at me.

"You looked like a small boy as you did that. I have seen village urchins do just the same."

"Aye, and as a country urchin I have done it many a time in England. This takes me back across the years to Essex, with its

Frank Payton

woods and small streams. It is a good way to catch fish too, if there be any in the stream worth eating."

We both fell silent. Waiting.

She reached up and pulled off her velvet cap. Her long hair cascaded down over her shoulders in a golden veil. Reaching up, I crooked my arm about her neck, and she came down to me, and for the first time our lips met and melted in a fragrant golden kiss.

*****

The Council Chamber of Simone Boccanera, Doge of Genoa, was high and lofty, hung about with bright banners and pennons. Sunlight streamed in from narrow windows set high up in the walls.

The Doge sat enthroned on an ornate chair raised on a low dais. About him were gathered senior councillors, greybeards for the most part. All were richly dressed in long robes trimmed with fur, turned with silk and velvet. Many wore jewelled chains and finger rings. As I strode into the hall at the head of my escort I was glad that we had taken considerable care over our own dress and could hold up our heads in such fine company. The chamber was filled on either side with other dignitaries and it was, all in all, a glittering concourse which marked our approach.

By this time I had acquired a reasonable grasp of day to day Italian, but on this occasion I ensured that Marco stood by my right shoulder as interpreter. I knew I could not afford to ruffle the feathers of some of these fine councillors by any misuse of their language.

Ludovico stepped forward from his place in the assembly.

"Your Excellency and Signori, may I present to you the illustrious English knight, Signore Giovanni Haccuud, Sir John, who is now in our midst to seek an alliance which will aid him in his exertions on behalf of Monferrato against the tyranny of Milan. Signore Giovanni is well known to Edward, King of England, and to his renowned son, Edward, Prince of Wales, who is acclaimed on all sides as the very flower of chivalry. I can humbly attest to the qualities of our guest, in that my beloved sister and I were rescued by him and his men from a band of foul brigands, and brought safe home to Genoa."

"Indeed, we have heard some account of this distressing episode, and thank the good God for your deliverance. The fame of our guest truly goes before him, and he is welcome here. What is the burden of his request to us?" The Doge had a deep, resonant voice which seemed to fill the hall. "We are of course mindful of the qualities of the English and their King, and of the value of trade between England and Genoa."

Ludovico would have answered here, but I put up my hand to stay him, and I replied through Marco.

"Your Excellency, it is an honour to be allowed to present myself before your Signori, and I thank you for your kind sentiments. In short, I need crossbowmen—the better for me and my Company to campaign against Milan. As you are doubtless aware, Monferrato petitioned the Pope for assistance, and it is he who laid it upon us to go to the aid of the Marquis. Genoa's crossbows are renowned, and I would hire a goodly company to add to our strength."

My words caused a rustle of conversation amongst the assembly, and already I could hear some dissenting voices raised in protest. I drew this to Ludovico's attention.

"That is the faction which looks to Milan," he whispered in my ear. "They defer to Bernabo in secret, and would favour closer alliance with him. Fortunately, they are in a minority. Although the Doge himself was reinstated in his office by the Viscontis, he values the freedom of the city."

Marco spoke on my other side. "The matter of our losses at Crecy has been mentioned."

"Who is it who now speaks to the Doge?" I asked, indicating one of the councillors.

Frank Payton

"It is Carlo Grimaldi, once a commander of the crossbows. He is old now, and he was at Crecy. He may oppose you strongly, but I know him to be a fair and just man. We must wait and see."

"I am placed in a quandary by your request, Signore Haccuud," the Doge spoke again. "On one hand I hear voices raised against you, and on the other hand voices in favour of you. There are some here today who were present at Crecy Field, where many of our men were lost. I do not say that it was entirely due to your archers, but whatever the reason, they still smart from the defeat. Then again, those in favour of you point to the need for employment of our men. Many of our young men chafe in idleness, their training rendered of no use in periods of lasting peace. How will your proposition advantage us?"

Again I replied through Marco. "Your Excellency, allow me to say that I too was at Crecy, and witnessed all on that long day of bloodshed. Your own military men will know well that the outcome of battles often turns on almost insignificant happenings. At Crecy there came a sudden heavy rainstorm, which rendered the strings of your crossbows next to useless. I know it can take some time to detach the string from the bow, and place it in a dry spot about the body. With a longbow the case is very different. Its waxed string can be put away safely within ten heartbeats. Thus, when the storm passed, your men had wet bowstrings which did not cast their bolts to the fullest range. I will not speak of the indiscipline of the French, who rode your men down, except to say that upon that day they proved to be your enemy no less than we, who only did our duty by our King and his cause."

The Doge turned to Grimaldi. "What have you to say to this, Messer? Is this the truth of the matter about which we have heard so much argument down the years?"

"Excellency," said the old soldier, "it grieves me to say so, but it is a truth I have long harboured in my own mind. Wet, slack bowstrings, of crossbow or otherwise, will not cast properly. There is no denying this."

"And the French?" asked the Doge.

Hawkwood's Sword

"Neither their King nor his marshals could exercise control over their mounted knights, nor the men-at-arms," said Grimaldi. "Thousands of them rode over us, hacking and stabbing, eager to rush upon their deaths into the hail of arrows. It has more than once been in my mind that we should have stood with the English that day, and shared in their victory over such caitiff allies."

Another elderly notable thrust forward, clearly enraged by his fellow councillor. "If your men had had the common sense to place their bows under their pavises, their bowstrings would not have failed. The remainder of your opinion is mere foolishness."

"If? If?" shouted the first. "If you had been at Crecy, if you had marched twenty miles in rain and mud to that benighted field! If you had been pushed about all day by arrogant French nobility encased in armour on their great horses! If you had been deprived of food, drink and rest before the battle, by our so-called allies, then I think you would have wished yourself on the same side as the English. But where *were* you, Messer? We all know you were here in Genoa, in your counting house, with your account books and your chests of gold and silver. You cared little for your fellow citizens of this great city, but greatly for the safety of your own skin!"

This drew the beginnings of a further outburst from the other man. Pale with rage, he commenced a torrent of words which I could not follow, but which stopped abruptly when the Doge held up his hand.

"That is enough! You forget yourself, and where you are. If you cannot carry yourself with dignity, you may withdraw."

Thus dismissed, my opponent drew his robe around his portly figure, and stalked out of the chamber. As he passed I received from him a look of pure hatred. In reply I bowed slightly, and bestowed upon him a faint smile. This could have done little to calm his anger.

I turned again to my front, and found that the old commander of the crossbows had left his position amongst the councillors and now stood before me. He held out his right hand.

Frank Payton

"Signore Haccuud, I greet you as a fellow soldier, one true to his cause, in the highest traditions of chivalry. I add my own welcome to our great city to that already voiced by His Excellency. You have my support in the matter for discussion before us today. I am sure you also have the support of many another."

Grasping his hand, I thanked him as best I could in his own tongue. Suddenly, our small party was surrounded by a throng of other councillors, anxious to show their support for us by handclasp and loud acclaim. Even dour Jack Onsloe found himself the recipient of the most voluble and high flown protestations of friendship and loyalty. The pity was that he understood not a word of it.

As this show of support slackened somewhat, the Doge's voice cut through the noise. "Signori, please now restrain yourselves. It seems that the popular vote accords with my own feelings. This being so, I propose to meet Signore Haccuud and his own staff, to arrange the terms of the contract to lend a suitable number of crossbowmen to assist the English Company against the Visconti."

With that declaration it appeared that the first hurdle in our negotiations had been successfully passed. Ludovico beamed at me.

"Well, Sir John, it appears that you have won the support of the Doge and the Signori by your own efforts. The blunt soldier triumphs over the diplomat. It remains now only to settle the details."

"It would seem so, but there could still be pitfalls ahead. There also remains a strong feeling against us from the other party. I would be foolish to ignore that."

"I agree. However, now that you have the majority with you, your opponents will not dare to go against the Captain General."

I had marked the approach of a tall figure in black as he made his way through the departing throng of councillors. He bowed in turn to Ludovico and myself.

Hawkwood's Sword

"Signore Giovanni, Count Ludovico, Signori: I am Pietro, Secretary to the Doge. If you will follow me please, his Excellency wishes to continue these discussions in private. He will also feel honoured if you will take some refreshment with him."

The talks continued over wine and an assortment of fruits and sweetmeats. The Doge was clearly a man of character. I had heard that his grandfather Guglielmo was more than half a pirate, a buccaneer. If true, then his blood had descended in a pure state to his grandson. The price for the hire of his men was very high. I despaired of success on that point alone. In addition there was the matter of clothes, weapons, items of armour, food, and much, much more. All these were items extra to the fee demanded and put forward by the councillors present.

It was in my mind that some of them sought to profit themselves from the supply of these items. After a lengthy period of argument, I came to a decision, and spoke more directly to Boccanera.

"Your Excellency, at this point I feel that it may be useful to have a short break in our talks. During that time I suggest that you and I together should walk in the very attractive garden which I see through yonder window. This will give us both an opportunity for informal conversation."

"That is an excellent idea, Signore Giovanni. We may clear our heads of wine, and perhaps come to know each others' minds rather better. You might also be interested to see the leopard which I keep there." To his councillors, the Doge said, "You hear, Signori; our meeting is now suspended, and Messer Pietro will inform you when shall meet again."

There were some dissenting voices, but it was clear to all that the matter was, for the present, closed. I spoke to my own people in similar vein, but on their side there were no protests.

"I'll be glad to get out of here for a spell," said Jack. "Too much talk I don't understand. Just warn this Doge that too high a price may have to be taken back, one way or another. Come, Giles lad, let you and I find a wineshop." And with that they disappeared,

FRANK PAYTON

together with Ludovico—who, however, was headed for his palazzo.

Marco stood uncertainly, and looked at me. I waved him towards me. "Stay with me, Marco. I shall need your assistance, I've little doubt."

"Come then, Signore Giovanni—and you, Messer Bandini." The Doge laughed at Marco's evident surprise that he should know his family name. "I was acquainted with your late father, and your mother's father. I have heard of your capture by Sir John's Company. You have certainly risen above your fellows, but in an army of foreigners. That is good, but remember always that you are Genoese."

Marco was in some confusion at this, but answered stoutly. "I shall not forget, Excellency, but I shall also remember that Sir John saved my life. I am honoured by your attention."

We had now emerged from the shadows of the residence and blinked in the bright sunlight. I recall the garden was very prettily arranged with paved walks between small trees and colourful flowers. At intervals stood graceful figures carven in stone, and several sparkling fountains played, their fine spray relieving the heat. I complimented the Doge on this very pleasant place.

"Thank you, Signore Giovanni. It is indeed a great solace to sit quietly and contemplate, away from the clamour of councillors, complainants, lawyers, and the like. No sound from the city can be heard here. But you must see my leopard. Come. You too, Messer Bandini."

We followed him to a shady corner of the garden where was placed a large cage of iron bars, inside which lay a huge spotted cat, far bigger than any hound I had ever seen. It gazed lazily at us from large green eyes and of a sudden yawned, showing shining white fangs and sharp teeth.

"A fine and no doubt murderous beast, Your Excellency. You must hope it does not slip its cage and look for food elsewhere in the city."

Hawkwood's Sword

The Doge smiled and replied, "It is chained as well as confined. But it is a quiet beast, having been born in captivity. It is possible to take it out on processions throughout the city, and if well fed beforehand it is content to walk along peaceably. The people love to see him."

We seated ourselves in a shaded arbor. A servant appeared with cool sherbet drinks, cold as ice. I commented on this wonder.

"We bring ice down from the mountains in winter and early Spring, to be stored in deep cellars, where it remains frozen for months on end. It can be used to keep meats and fruit for long periods. It is a practice begun in ancient times, I am told. But now we should discuss certain matters more closely, I think."

"Gladly. You will realise, I know, that your price is very high, and is made more so by the suggestion that the cost of equipment, clothing and horses and so on should be added." I paused.

"I must admit to you, Signore Giovanni, that was myself surprised by this. It has not been usual in the past," the Doge replied.

"Perhaps the old enmities still rankle in some quarters?"

"Perhaps, but we must rise above these paltry matters. I am anxious that Genoa should be able to increase trade with your country. Wool is an obvious commodity for you. In return, we can offer spices from the East, and many other rare and fine goods from as far afield as Cathay. Old enmities must fail before matters of moment such as these. Have you a proposal to which I can give consideration? It can then be presented to the Signori."

"I have, and it is this. You shall not ask for the extra payments, and in return I shall send word to people known to me in London, who will be eager and willing to work to increase trade between Genoa and England. This will expedite trade, and put profit in the hands of many merchants. Secondly, I shall pay but two thirds of the sum you demand, and in return I will undertake no hostilities on behalf of any other Italian power against Genoa and its possessions for the space of three years.

Frank Payton

"As one of my officers has observed, if we pay your full demands the excess will have to be taken back one way or another, at some time."

Boccanera looked at me gravely. "That is a hard bargain, Signore, and needs much thought. I see your mind more clearly now. We should meet again on the morrow, when I hope to be able to come to a suitable accommodation with you."

Upon that we clasped hands and departed, leaving the Doge seated in his sunlit garden, gazing across at the caged leopard. Pietro escorted us to the Palazzo entrance, where our horses were waiting for us in the care of liveried grooms. We each swung up into the saddle, and began to make our way back to the Palazzo Lucanti.

"Do you not wish to find Master Onsloe and Master Ashurst, Sir John?" asked Marco.

"In a wine shop after this length of time? I think that might be unwise. Let them find their own way back. Jack will be wanting to go on to the camp, and Giles is the better one to keep a clear head. I have no doubt they will return in time for the evening meal, as I have instructed."

*****

At the Palazzo Lucanti we found our host impatiently awaiting our arrival. Giulio, Ludovico's secretary, conducted us to his master's private salon, a fine chamber looking out over a garden in much the same fashion as that of Boccanera. This place was where much of family's business was conducted. The walls were lined with books, and several iron-bound chests stood about. A long table was littered with documents.

"I am glad to see you, Sir John. Have you concluded your talks with His Excellency? What is the outcome? Are you to get the men you require?" He rushed on, "I am very inhospitable. Please forgive me. Giulio! Some wine for Sir John, and for Messer Bandini."

I laughed at his eagerness. "No, no. Thank you. You are very kind, my friend." I looked across at Marco in query, but he shook his head. "I have put certain proposals to the Doge, which he has undertaken to consider, but he seems to have been taken aback by their content."

"Then let us hope that the Signori agree. When do you meet the Doge again?"

"As yet I know not, but I should think that if the Doge wishes to avail himself, and the city, of the benefits I have offered him, and can persuade his councillors to agree, then... perhaps on the morrow."

Ludovico sank back in his chair. "I am relieved to hear that, Sir John. It will surely be to the benefit of us all."

*****

The negotiations continued. We argued back and forth for two more days, until I despaired of ever reaching an end. At the last however, and due to the intervention of the Doge, it was agreed that the city would not ask for the extra payments, and would accept three fourths of their original demand in gold and silver. In return I agreed to undertake no hostilities for five years, if ever.

So it ended, and now, looking back over the years I see it was not such a poor bargain as I had at first thought. Thirty bands of crossbowmen marched out with us when we left Genoa. The service they later rendered us more than outweighed the cost.

Before we left the city, however, there was the matter of my growing attachment to the Lady Proserpina, which could not be left unresolved. In accordance with Italian custom, Taddea was nearby in the garden when I recounted to her what I had heard from Ludovico, and said to him, concerning my love for her.

"I am surprised that Ludovico has never told me that I must first be married in order to possess my inheritance," she said. I could see her colour begin to rise, and her dark eyes flashed in the first stages of anger. "Is this true Taddea? Do you know of this condition upon my grandfather's legacy?"

"Yes, it is true, my dear, just as the Signore Giovanni says. I was present at your grandfather's death, and heard his wishes, which were later set out in his will. He also said that you were a mischievous little mouse, but that he loved you dearly for it." The old nurse smiled fondly at her wayward charge.

Proserpina's eyes filled with tears, and her anger gave way to grief. "I loved him too," she whispered, "although he was so old and fierce."

I took both of her hands in mine. "My dearest girl! When this campaign is over, and the outcome cannot now be long delayed, I shall return as I have promised, and we shall be made man and wife."

"Gianni, my love, let it be now, before you leave. If you are slain I shall never see you more. That I could not bear."

I held her eyes with mine own, and saw her complete devotion in them. "I shall not be slain. It is not for nothing that I have fought over many battlefields in the past twenty years and more. One thing I have learnt is how to survive. You need have no fears, I shall return to you."

I opened the purse at my belt and took from it the gold ring with the lion's mask bezel, which I had had from Will Turton. I had set it aside for just this purpose.

"Take this ring as a token of my love, and also as a sign that I shall return."

She took the ring from me, and closed her long fingers over the massy gold of it. "I shall wear this as you say, my dear, but not on any of my fingers. It is too large even for my thumb. No, I shall wear it on a gold chain next to my heart, and think of you as it presses against my breast, as you did at our first embrace. It shall never leave me, my dear love. And now, kiss me before you leave, and I shall fly to my room and weep, as a foolish woman will do.

Hawkwood's Sword

But as you ride away, look back, and you will see me once more. Farewell!"

We kissed, a lovers' farewell kiss, which seemingly lingers into Eternity, and yet is as brief as life itself.

So I left her, but as we rode away I looked back at the Palazzo Lucanti, and she leaned out from a balcony laughing through tears. I caught the thrown silken scarf which drifted down from her hand, and swiftly bound it about my left arm. I raised my hand in a last salute, and then turned my face to the north, and duty.

Chapter 7
A Delayed Campaign

On a strange prompting I had chosen to ride ahead of the Company, with only a single forerider sent ahead to announce our immanent arrival to the camp. I wished to enjoy the quiet of the road as I pondered stratagems.

I came to a halt when the sound of drumming hoofbeats reached my ear. The forerider, Jenkin Cope, the lad out of Suffolk, was returning.

"Plague! Sir John, plague! Scores, hundreds, dead or dying!" he cried out as he drew close. His eyes stared, his lips were white, and he seemed on the verge of fleeing.

I caught his arm, nearly dragging him from his horse. It reared in alarm as the reins tightened the bit. The beast's eyes rolled wildly.

"Stand still, man. Control yourself. Speak low, and tell me what is happening at Romagnano. Quietly now, I don't want a panic."

Jenkin recovered his composure, and patted his horse's neck so that it stood quietly.

"I'm sorry, Sir John, but it is bad tidings. When I came near to the camp I felt that something was not right. There were men-at-arms on guard to prevent anyone approaching nearer than a hundred yards. Between each one was an archer, arrow on string, ready to shoot any who tried to leave! I called out my name, and said you were nearby on your return from Genoa."

Hawkwood's Sword

"And then? Did you speak to anyone in command? Who was there?"

"No one, save one of the healers—a little man in a brown robe, Hal something, I can't recall his other name."

"Peasgood," I muttered absently, my mind in a whirl, trying to take in the news. What to do, what to do? Where was John Brise, where were Albrecht and the others?

"Jenkin! Say no more now, to anyone. On pain of death, keep your mouth tight shut! Leave this to me."

He gulped at the threat. "I will, Sir John, never fear."

"Go back and fetch Master Onsloe, and Master Ashurst. Say that I wish them to halt the column and to join me here. Return with them, without delay."

Jenkin rode off at a gallop on the errand. I knew it was sheer luck that I had ridden ahead of the rest, accompanied only by Marco, who now came up alongside me.

"Plague?" he asked.

I nodded. "We will make camp here. I dare not advance further until I know more."

We two awaited the arrival of Jack and Giles. They rode up with Jenkin following. I told them what little we knew. Jack swore, Giles looked worried, and for once had nothing to say. They all agreed with me that we should make camp where we stood, and so it was done.

It was late afternoon, so it would not be thought unusual, and the men dropped gratefully from tired horses and turned them to graze. In a short time, the smoke from cooking fires began to drift upwards in the still air. Soon stews were bubbling in the pot, and the smell of meat roasting on the spit spread tempting invitations to the evening meal. On a cold autumn evening, hot stew would raise the men's spirits.

We gathered around the table in my pavilion and, as had become usual, were joined by Andrea da Varazzo, Captain of the Crossbows. He was a lean, dark young man then in his late twenties, hard-faced, but with a half-humourous glint in his eye.

Frank Payton

No crossbowman himself, he ranked as a junior knight. Marco had told me he was accounted an experienced officer. Seating himself at the table he looked around.

"I see worried faces. Something is wrong, yes?"

"Yes, Andrea, something is indeed wrong," I replied. "There is plague in our camp at Romagnano. At present we know no more than that. Tonight we stay here. For the time being say nothing to your men. Tomorrow I will try to find out more."

To my surprise Andrea made little comment, and began to eat heartily. "We have outbreaks of plague here and there, now and then," he said between mouthfuls. "Some die, most live. It is God's will." He shrugged his shoulders.

"What to you intend, Sir John?" asked Giles.

"Tomorrow I will take a small party of those who will, and seek out someone who can tell me more than we know at present. I will go alone if must be. I must remain hopeful that John Brise, Albrecht, and many others are safe. If Hal Peasgood is still alive with his companions, then there is still some hope."

*****

Early the next morning, with a heavy dew still on the ground, I rode out with Giles and Marco, leaving Jack Onsloe in command. There was a frosty bite in the air, which the early sun did little to chase away. Far to the north, the same sun twinkled on the snow-covered peaks of the mountains. We rode without speaking, and after a mile or two we espied a group of horsemen approaching us along the same track. We drew nearer to them, until their leader reined in his mount and raised his hand in a gesture for us to draw halt. I knew him by his yellow hair. It was Conrad Harzmann, Werner von Felsingen's shadow.

"Come no closer, Sir John. We have plague here. Albrecht, John Brise, Thornbury, and others of your Company are struck down. I am told they will recover. Many have died however, perhaps four hundred, English and Almain alike. Your boy Ralph is dead. We buried him yesterday. Our healers and yours have worked day and night. Fortunately, only two of their number have died."

These were grievous blows. Poor Ralph! If only I had taken him with me, as well as Huw, he would not have endured the agonies of the plague and death. I regretted this news deeply. Ralph had followed me for five years, and had grown from a boy to a man in our rough world. I knew I would miss his quiet, eager presence.

"What about the others?" I called. "Will Turton, Will Preston, Andrew Belmonte?"

"The pestilence has not touched them. They are well. Werner, and von Auerbach too, are well. Do you have supplies of food?"

"Yes, but not much. We shall have to forage. There are three hundred crossbowmen in our train now, so we shall be able to live off the land."

"You would be well advised not to approach any villages or farms too closely," said Conrad. We think we caught the plague from that source. Now we must return."

He swept off his velvet cap in salute, wheeled his horse, and rode off, the rest of his men clattering behind. I called after him.

"We should meet here again on the morrow, Conrad."

He half turned in the saddle and raised his hand in acknowledgement.

So it was. Our little camp became an outpost of the larger one. We organised defences and guards. Parties were sent out to forage for food and fuel. Water was a problem, but we were fortunate to find a stream which ran from a hillside towards Romagnano not far away, and we only took our supplies from its very source. This, I deemed, would ensure clean water both for men and horses.

It pleased me to have found such a spring, as it brought back to mind that enchanted day not so long past, when Proserpina and I first declared our love. When would I return to her, I wondered.

Frank Payton

The silk scarf she had thrown down to me at our parting was now worn constantly about my neck beneath my shirt. Our time together had been so short, it seemed then a beautiful fleeting dream. The scarf which carried her fading perfume was all I had.

We fell into a camp routine, foraging, hunting, and practicing our weapon skills. Importantly, Giles and Andrea devised contests of bowmanship between archers and crossbowmen. Apart from keeping the men from idling aimlessly, it brought about a mutual respect for each other's weapon. The young Italians were at first amazed by the speed at which our archers could loose showers of arrows. On the other hand, Giles and his small band had to admire the strength of the crossbow, and the accuracy with which the bowmen could place their bolts in the centre of the target.

Whilst all this was taking place, I spent much time meeting Conrad or some other to find out how matters were progressing at Romagnano.

"The number of deaths is falling daily, Sir John," Conrad said to me on the ninth day. "We are told that as the weather grows colder, the pestilence will itself die away."

Then, several days after that, Albrecht appeared with Conrad. We still remained a good distance apart, but I could see that my old friend was pale and drawn, and sat slackly in the saddle.

"It is good to see you again," I called across to him. "Are you recovered?"

"I am much better, but still weak. It would seem that I have been spared once more from death, this time by the grace of God and the healer's arts. We shall ride together once again, old friend. Conrad here has told me that there were no deaths yesterday, and the number sick of the plague has fallen. We look to have lost nigh on five hundred of our comrades, Jack—brave men all, taken by this pestilence." He shook his head sadly.

These were sorry tidings, and I turned back to our camp with a heavy heart.

Hawkwood's Sword

*****

Another month was to pass in this fashion, until Albrecht and I judged that the danger was over. It was then, with considerable relief, that on a fine day in early winter I and my small army passed between the gates of the main camp at Romagnano. The Company was once more complete. Our return was the occasion for great rejoicing and celebration. John Brise greeted me with John Thornbury at his side. Throwing his great arms about me like a huge bear, he thumped me on the back until I shook him off fearing I would never breathe again. He roared out his welcome.

"By the Rood, Jack, we thought never to see you and those you took with you ever again. John here was struck down with the foul pestilence before me, and was nigh to death before ever I caught the plague."

"Aye, and that's the truth, Sir John," said the other. "We lay side by side, and swallowed Hal Peasgood's stinking potions day after day. Hardly a crust of bread or a sup of wine passed our lips for weeks."

"But he rid you both of the plague," I felt I had to point out to them.

"Yes, and many another, thank God!" said John Brise. "He and Simon Cheshunt have earned themselves a place in Heaven, with their work for us all. Twas a pity, though, that young Ralph died. Simon told us he was just not strong enough to withstand the fever. He was a good lad. Will Turton has scriven a list of all the dead. Many a good man gone, Jack. Old Sim Costean was one. Mind you, he was older than most, but he'll draw the bowstring no more. God rest his soul!"

So Sim was gone to his Maker at last. He was a piece older than me, sixty years or more. I recalled what he told me years before about his training as an archer, when his grandfather, who had fought against the Scots with Edward the First, gave him a long stick to hold as if at were a bow. Sim had to stay with arm

FRANK PAYTON

outstretched for lengthy periods, day after day, until the old man was satisfied. Next, a string was attached to the stick to make a crude bow. The task then was to draw the string to the ear and hold, only releasing the string slowly from time to time, and then drawing it again. Next came the arrow: how to nock it to the string, how to draw and loose. Week after week, month after month, this was young Sim's exercise. With good food and rough play with the village boys, his body grew in strength. By the time he reached manhood, he had the barrel chest, the whipcord arm muscles, and the grace of a natural archer. In addition, he often carried off the golden prize for marksmanship at tournaments. Later, like many another, he took service under his lord, and fought for the King in nearly every campaign from Halidon Hill in Scotland to Crecy and Poitiers in France. His death was a great sorrow for me.

The two Johns babbled on, but I was hardly listening. At last I stopped the flow of words.

"Stop, stop! I've heard enough. We must look to the next part of this campaign. John, make sure our new recruits are settled in the camp. To begin with, give them a field of their own. In time I want to apportion them out to the different commands. Apart from that, for the present we should rest, eat and drink well, so that those who have been sick may recover their strength before we take the field again." I paused. "This young knight here is Andrea da Varazzo, who is Captain of the Crossbows. He is reported to be a good man, and luckily he speaks some English."

Andrea came out from the group about me, and solemnly clasped hands with John Brise and John Thornbury. They both towered over his slight figure, and he looked a little afeared, especially as John Brise slapped him on the back and bellowed one of his usual welcomes for newcomers. Andrea staggered, but recovered well, even managing a grin in return.

"I see that I would be foolish to anger you, Master Brise," he said. "You might have a sword in your hand on such an occasion."

Hawkwood's Sword

"Nay, lad, you've nought to fear from me, as long as you and your men are loyal to Sir John and the White Company. Any traitor had better take heed of me then."

*****

Albrecht settled back in his high chair and reached for the richly chased silver jug which stood on the table in front of him. He drew it towards him and slopped a generous amount into his silver wine cup. I noticed his hand shaking a little. Not a good sign, I thought. He held out the jug towards me, eyebrows raised in question. I shook my head, and he replaced it in front of him.

"You're still not yourself, old friend," I said.

He sipped the wine. "*Nein*, no, I am not, but I am much better than I was."

We two sat at the table in Albrecht's pavilion for one of our private meetings. Only Wolf, his page, stood by the entrance, ready either to prevent anyone entering or to minister to his master's needs.

"When you left for Genoa," Albrecht began, "I sent a strong probing force under Werner towards Pavia. Initially, he had some success, and confined Landau to Tortona, then continued his progress through the country as far as Pavia."

"What happened then?" I was eager for news after an absence of two months.

"A reverse. The Italian dal Verme appeared with a much stronger force. Werner, quite rightly to my mind, made a fighting withdrawal. To add to all this, Galeazzo Visconti sent over an envoy, in an effort to make peace." Albrecht paused, and took a long draught from his cup.

"And then?" I prompted.

"Then the plague struck us, and the envoy took to his heels in great haste." He laughed out loud at the memory. "He left at such speed that he lost his hat at the gate, and did not tarry to retrieve

Frank Payton

it, even though it had a great ruby set in a brooch upon it. About the plague, you have already heard enough. Many good men gone. How shall we replace them?"

"Send Werner on another visit to Germany," I suggested. "He came back with a company the last time. I will send word to certain persons in England who could raise more men for us. However, don't forget that I have just brought three hundred crossbows back from Genoa."

"I do not forget, Jack, but I had liefer have our own people with us." Albrecht stared moodily into space.

I realised then that the plague which had struck him, personally, had also hit him hard with the loss of so many of his comrades, some of whom had fought side by side with him over many years.

He continued. "I feel at times that I am become too old for this trade, and it is time to realise my fortune and return to Germany."

I scoffed at this. "To do what, Albrecht? Sit in a hilltop castle above the Rhine River and chew upon your nails, whilst your sword rusts upon the wall? Come, man, have some more wine. Be of good cheer. We have plans to make. We cannot kick our heels here much longer. Soon we must press forward to Milan and Pavia. Also, we must test this Galeazzo's resolve for making peace. There could be much to reap there, through war or peace."

"Of course you are right, Jack. I am a fool to lament so, but I suppose I am not yet fully recovered in mind. This feeling of melancholy sits on my shoulder and will not depart. I miss many of my former comrades. They were strong in battle, but had no strength against the pestilence, and many made a bad end. It is well that we cannot see our own end, Jack. For me, let it be by the sword, not some stinking plague which rots my body and soul at the last."

I reached out and touched his arm. "I will say Amen to that. Now let us leave the plague in the past, and look to the future. I have more news to share with you, at which may be in amaze. On the road to Genoa we rescued a Genoese nobleman, his sister, and their retainers from a band of brigands intent on robbery at the least, with murder and rape of the young woman at the worst."

"This is real knight errantry, as in old tales, Jack. I admire your selfless action. Now tell me what this availed you." He grinned mischievously at me, more like his old self.

"What else could I have done? Anyway, the nobleman is Ludovico, the Count Savignone, and his sister the very lovely Lady Proserpina di Lucanti. Apart from offering us hospitality, the Count was very influential in gathering support for our cause. All this in return for the rescue, which he saw as laying a duty upon him." I reached for the silver jug and poured more wine for myself. Albrecht placed his hand over his cup and shook his head.

"Hmm, and in return you fell for the flashing eyes and womanly wiles of the maid, I suppose?" said Albrecht with a knowing smile.

"In short, yes. She is a strong, high-spirited young woman, bold and wild, and a great beauty withal. Ludovico wishes her to be married and off his hands. I need and want a new wife, old friend. A wife to take back to England when the time is right. Also, she is not without means of her own, including an estate in Liguria."

Albrecht looked at me and shook his head in disbelief. "You are really resolved on this? You truly wish for a wife, after all this time? How many lovers have you had? Many women of both high degree and low have fallen to your lance. You even had the pleasure of that witch, Joan of Kent, I think."

It was my turn to laugh. "Who did not? Yes, Albrecht, I am resolved on this. With a wife, and an estate in England, one in Italy, and possibly more children, verily I shall be a successful soldier knight, and attract the King's eye."

"You are a sly fox, Jack. I wish you well of this ambition with all my heart. I have been wedded to the sword far too long to change my mistress. The Rhenish castle of which you speak was lost to my family many years ago. I am the last of my line. I chose the life of a soldier, and will doubtless die as one."

Frank Payton

I now deemed it timely to remind Albrecht of what Marco had told me of having seen Conrad Harzmann in the company of Pietro Lamberti, who had purported to be an envoy from Monferrato. As I had expected, my old comrade was reluctant to think ill of his companions.

"But, Jack, do you believe the lad's account? Could he be mistaken?"

"I doubt it. He is sharp-witted, and he described Lamberti to me in some detail. Also, he had noted the softness of Conrad's voice. You know well that usually he speaks almost in a whisper." I could see that Albrecht was sorely troubled by my words.

"But neither of them has yet done anything to give me reason to distrust them," he protested. "They were always by my side after their return from Germany, and..." he stopped and frowned. "How long before the ambush did Marco say he saw Conrad?"

"I can't be certain, but let us say seven days."

"You had not rejoined us by that time," Albrecht mused. "I told you that I had sent parties to the south as scouts. This would have been at about the same time. Now if Werner or Conrad, or both, had sent a messenger to Monferrato's court as they set out from Germany with intention of arranging a meeting, then the whole thing is possible."

"There is one other thing to remember," I pointed out. "Werner makes no secret of his dislike and mistrust of Marco, and indeed, on two occasions has tried to kill him. He may not know that Marco actually saw Conrad, but he has tried to guard against that chance, in the only way he can."

"But apart from the few instances of discontent told to me by Heinrich Steiner, and the killing of your man Kortrijk, nothing has happened." Albrecht was puzzled, I could see.

"That is true, but you know that when one looks at a river it may seem to flow very calmly on the surface. Underneath there are often currents which can sweep away an unwary swimmer. I think we deal here with very deep currents. Let us suppose that we bring

Hawkwood's Sword

Landau to a final pitched battle. Imagine: we have committed ourselves, deployed our men and the battle has begun. What, then, if a sizeable body of our own men turned against their comrades and fought for Landau? You and I, and the White Company, could be lost. Something we do not wish to see!"

"I suppose you to be right, Jack," said Albrecht. "I have always had doubts in my mind about Conrad. He is too silent and secretive for me, and besides, has too much of a hold on Werner. Werner at one time I would have trusted with my life, but now? How do we counter this?"

"Only by being vigilant, and by readying ourselves for the blow whenever it should come. We must each take some others into our confidence, but that itself is fraught with danger. For my part I am sure of John Brise, and of Jack and Giles, but will they be enough?"

Albrecht pursed his lips, and looked thoughtful. He spoke slowly, "I can certainly trust Hannes von Auerbach, Heinrich Steiner, and Klaus Wegener. Like you I think the fewer with knowledge is best.

"Woe betide the traitors, as and when their blow falls!" He yawned and stretched out his arms. "Now, Jack. I shall go to my bed. I am still weak from the plague, and must build up my strength once more."

I had noted how pale and tired he was, how his eyes were unnaturally bright. He came to the entrance of his pavilion with me, and briefly surveyed the night sky. I laid my hand on his shoulder and wished him well. He returned me a wan smile.

"*Bis morgen*, Jack, until morning. I shall feel better then."

I left him then and returned to my own pavilion, despite my former cheerfulness, with a grim foreboding.

*****

It was inevitable that at some time we would have to come to conclusions with Galeazzo Visconti. After my return from Genoa

Frank Payton

he tried to make a treaty of peace with us. However, we had information that our previous adversary at Lanzo, the Count of Savoy, had proposed just the opposite; in other words, he planned a major effort, an alliance with Galeazzo to drive us out of Lombardy for good and all. This news arrived by secret messenger from Paolo da Lucca, now fully recovered from his injuries at the hands of von Felsingen at Lanzo, and anxious to assist in any way as he had promised.

Gian Galeazzo's emissary arrived just after the messenger from da Lucca. He appeared in a flurry of excitement with an escort of gaily dressed retainers and a band of men-at-arms. Albrecht and I went out to meet him at the front of Albrecht's pavilion.

"Listen to this man," Albrecht murmured aside to me, as a richly attired rider slid down from his horse. "I would not trust him with a soldi, let alone with a mission such as this."

"Giovanni dei Pepoli at your service, Signores," said the emissary, with a sweeping bow. "I am delighted to see that you are fully recovered from the contagion, Signore Alberto. Perhaps you will present to me your distinguished comrade, who is unfortunately not known to me."

"This is my friend Sir John Hawkwood, an English knight, with whom I have had a long and and successful association."

Dei Pepoli swept off his hat and made an exaggerated bow in my direction. I inclined my head slightly.

"The Signore Giovanni H..H..Haccuud," he intoned, my name clearly being beyond his powers of speech, "I am honoured to meet you. All Italy marvels at your deeds."

"You are too kind, Signore," I managed to say, and bowed in turn. "Perhaps we can offer some refreshment to these fine gentles, Albrecht?"

"Yes, indeed. Signore dei Pepoli, will you bring your principal companions into the pavilion, where we can conduct our discussions in more comfort?"

Hawkwood's Sword

Albrecht and I seated ourselves at the head of the long table, and dei Pepoli and his half-dozen companions seated themselves in their order of rank. Wolf and the other pages poured wine for us all, and set out silver dishes of fruits and nuts together with sugared comfits for our refreshment. I had been observing our chief guest closely. He reminded me too much of Lamberti, although this man was slim where Lamberti had been fat, and had in addition a lofty air which he sought to conceal, for the time being, behind flowery phrases and gestures. I decided, as Albrecht had warned me, that he was not to be trusted.

"Well, what does your master, the Lord of Pavia, wish of us?" said Albrecht, cracking two walnuts between his strong fingers the while. "How may we please him?"

"My master hopes that good relationships may be established between us, and in token of that offers gifts of treasure, and other advantages which might persuade you to turn aside from your present course. It is most distressing to him, a peaceful, scholarly man, that this war should continue," dei Pepoli said with a smile, which served only to increase my distrust of him.

"The war is continuing because the forces of Count Landau will invade Monferrato if we do not deny him the way," said Albrecht. "He is aware, I hope, that our Father the Pope is equally distressed by the current state of affairs."

"Perhaps we may be able to come to some friendly agreement which will put the minds of both our patrons at rest?" came the silky reply from our foxy guest. He leaned back in his chair and steepled his fingers. "My master's settlement of your account would be most generous. You would then be free to offer your redoubtable services elsewhere."

Albrecht glanced at me and raised his eyebrows in question. I took up the point in question.

"We need to know what is being offered, before we can arrive at a decision," I said. "The sum offered must recognise our considerable expenses in conducting this campaign, and of course there is no guarantee that we will succeed in finding a new patron.

Frank Payton

In that event we would have little alternative but to levy contributions from the citizens of Milan and Pavia in order to maintain ourselves."

Dei Pepoli's face paled somewhat, and he took a quick gulp from his wine cup. "I am able to offer you six thousand silver florins per month for six months, and a payment of fifty thousand florins of gold to be paid at once. More I cannot, whether this suffices or no."

Albrecht spoke again. "I think we should be allowed time to consider your offer. We will send you our answer within the next few days. More we cannot do." He smiled slightly at this last, and stood up to signify that the meeting was over.

Dei Pepoli sprang to his feet, quickly followed by his group of companions. They departed from the camp with many protestations of friendship, bowings and scrapings, and handwaving. The escort of men-at-arms cantered after them a little more soberly.

As they were lost to our view, Albrecht's eyes met mine. I shook my head. He smiled and nodded his head in agreement.

*****

With all this in our minds Albrecht and I, and our lieutenants, sat late over the wine after an evening meal a few days later. We sat easily after the good food, warmed both by the wine and by several charcoal braziers placed around the interior of Albrecht's pavilion.

It was von Felsingen who began the serious discussion. "My friends, I think that we should regard our work for Monferrato at an end. After all, Savoy is in no state to make warlike noises against us, and Galeazzo would not make overtures of peace from a position of strength. We should state our price for ceasing operations in this Lombardy and move to fresh fields." He leaned back with a satisfied air, and took a deep draught from his cup.

Hawkwood's Sword

"You forget, Werner, the small matter of Conrad Landau," said Albrecht. "If we withdraw elsewhere, what employment would he have? His contract could be ended by the Visconti, and he might decide to attack Monferrato himself to keep his men occupied, or to seek booty, or be paid off. In that case, I feel that we would have failed in our duty to the Marquis."

"You care about that?" sneered Werner, a note of disbelief in his voice. "Well, I for one do not, and I am sure I am not the only one here in that mind. March off, say I, out of this Lombardy. There is nothing more for us here. There are the Pisan and Florentine lands to be exploited yet. Something easier. We have had a hard fight of it so far, not to mention the plague. The offer from Pavia should be accepted."

Oh, should it? I thought, and glanced covertly at Albrecht, but his face was impassive. I took up the discussion, saying, "Come now, Werner, you know that we cannot leave Landau in our rear. He is an active enemy even now. You do not turn your back on a charging bull, and that is what he would become, if only to exact revenge for our success against him in the past weeks. No, he and his army must be decisively beaten. There is no other sensible course of action for us."

Albrecht leaned forward. "Jack's intention is to launch further attacks now, when Landau and his master least expect them. War is not carried on in winter in Italy. I've been here before, and everyone goes home when the weather turns cold. But to us from the north this is not cold weather, so we can continue and press our advantage, perhaps conclusively."

Werner shrugged his shoulders and looked glum. He drummed fingers on the table impatiently, looking the while across at Harzmann, who appeared to ignore him, but who spoke for the first time in his quiet voice.

"When do you propose to set forth on this foray, Sir John? Are we in a good state of readiness for this? You know, many of the men are still suffering from the effects of the plague." As he spoke he toyed with a hazel nut, rolling it on the table from one side to the other between his cupped hands. When I began to answer his questions he slapped the heel of his hand sharply on the nut, crushing it to small pieces. He looked up, expressionless.

"We need only two-thirds of our strength for this, Conrad," I said. "It will be needful in any event to leave a strong garrison here. There is too much of value stored here to leave unguarded. For my part, I shall leave Will Turton in command here, with Andrew Belmonte and all the plague survivors not yet up to full fighting ability. Some of your archers will have to remain behind. Giles, I leave that matter to you. We shall travel fast and hit hard. We shall catch Landau unawares, and be up to the gates of Milan with luck. Then we will have the Visconti at our feet, and our rewards will be great enough to fill all our pockets! How say you, Albrecht?"

Albrecht's eyes gleamed as he looked around at the assembly. He raised his cup. "To a hard ride, a swift victory, and more booty that each man can carry."

There was a roar of assent at this, and all joined in the toast to success. A buzz of talk broke out, and I knew I had them wholly at my back in the venture.

"We ride on the second morn," I shouted. "Be ready!" and in an aside to Albrecht, "Keep a close watch on Werner and Conrad. No word of this must get to Landau." He nodded his assent.

John Brise had caught this last few words and leaned over me, his breath reeking of wine. "You suspect those two of some treachery, Jack?" he rumbled in my ear.

I moved away slightly. "Not only me, but Albrecht is aware that all is not as it should be. We do but take care."

"You've only to say the word, and I'll make them disappear."

"No, leave it," I said. "They are not our men, and there is no proof of treachery."

"Hmm. Why are you leaving Belmonte with Turton? It ought to be Will Preston."

I nodded. "If you think so, John, then let it be so. Will Preston shall stay here in command, and Belmonte can come with us."

Hawkwood's Sword

I pushed my chair back and stood up. Albrecht did likewise. We stood side by side and raised our cups, brimming with the good red wine.

"To success in the field, and gold for all!"

I remember the faces at that table, red and sweaty with much food and wine, the heady smell of it enough to stop a charge of French knights. The shouts of approval, the hammering of dagger-hafts upon the board resounded like rolling thunder.

"*Zum Wohl! Waes Hael! Drinc Hael!* Gold for all!"

I picked up my table knife and thrust it into the belt-sheath. I drew on my gloves as Albrecht walked with me to the pavilion entrance. Outside, the night air struck chill after the heat around the table. There was a steady wind from the west, which brought a smell of watch fires, and some of their fiery sparks hurried by. Huw was waiting with Boy. He handed me the reins, and I pulled myself up into the saddle. I leaned down to Albrecht, who stood wrapped in a cloak which Wolf had brought out to him.

"Good night, old friend," I said. "At the end, all will be well."

*****

The second morning after the dinner in Albrecht's pavilion broke clear and cloudless. A light frost dusted the grass, and the breath of both men and horses hung in the air. There was little wind. From the vantage point of Boy's saddle, I looked over the ranks of mounted men drawn up in divisions under their leaders. Jack Onsloe's black stallion was restless, and ready for the word to move off. Jack wrestled with the reins for control, and I could hear him cursing loudly. His men sat motionless; they were under his control at least, and dared not place a foot wrong. At my side John Brise chuckled into his beard.

"I'll wager Jack is furious. The horse lads must have given his mount some oats. I'd not be in their shoes for all the gold in Lombardy."

Frank Payton

Giles's archers looked as colourful as ever, yellow bows slung on their backs, the white fletching on the arrows showing atop the brown leather cases hanging at their belts. Giles was finding it hard to keep his composure as he looked across at Jack's discomfort.

"Yes, I suppose you to be right, but we must now begin this march, John, so let us get to it; no more delays. Jack will have to come along as best he can."

I shook the reins and urged Boy forward. At least he was a solid, biddable horse, and not inclined to tantrums such as Onsloe's destrier. The whole column began to move, Almains and English alongside each other. Albrecht was away to my left, with von Felsingen and Harzmann following at the head of their divisions.

We were fielding a force of two and a half thousand or so, including half the contingent from Genoa. They were led by Andrea da Varazzo, who rode with Giles. He had been careful to ensure that his men looked their best, and in his own appearance and demeanour I recognised the trained professional. I turned to John.

"You've sent the foreriders out in front in twos this time, John, as I ordered? We can't afford to be ambushed again without warning."

"Aye, Jack, there's no mistake this time. If the enemy is lying in wait, we'll hear about it. I've given clear orders what is to be done at the first glimmer of danger."

We passed through countryside already fought over twice. Ruined farms and villages marked our earlier actions against Landau, when we had driven him back to the Ticino and Trebbia rivers. Some life was stirring as the people crept back to shattered, roofless homes, and began to take up the threads of something like a normal existence again. In some of the villages makeshift markets had been set up, and farmers from outlying areas had begun to try and renew the supply of food to the population. Other

Hawkwood's Sword

traders from further afield appeared, anxious to resume normal commerce.

Under a leaden sky, everything about us seemed dark and not a little menacing. There was no sign of an enemy. For three days we rode steadily eastwards, making night camps in the open, and sleeping under rough and ready shelters. Foreriders came and went out, with little to report.

On the afternoon of the third day we came upon the ruins of a religious house. Hoping for a little better shelter from the poor weather, we halted and began to seek for places to rest amongst the remaining buildings. We dismounted, and I walked with John and Marco into a courtyard. In the middle of this stood an elderly monk at the head of a group of about thirty brown-clad brethren.

"For pity's sake, sirs," he called out in a quavery voice, "We have nothing left for you to take. Everything has been taken by raiders such as you. Leave us in peace! There is nothing for you here."

He made a feeble gesture of dismissal, and, in turning away from us fell heavily against two of the brothers, who struggled to hold him upright. They led him away to a place where he could sit and rest.

"Have no fear of us, old man," I said. "We do but seek refuge for the night, a place to sleep and prepare our food. I am John Hawkwood, a knight of England, and you have my word that no harm shall come to you from us."

At these words there was a stir amongst the brethren, and a young monk pushed his way to the fore.

"You are John Hawkwood from Essex? This is a miracle indeed! I am Brother Edmund, born Thomas of Halstead. I have heard of how you became a great man under the King, in the wars in France."

A miracle? It was certainly a great wonder to me also, that one born so near to my own village should appear before me in such a manner. The sound of his honest Essex voice carried my mind to England and home straightway.

Frank Payton

"I am pleased to hear your words, and in my own turn of speech, especially in this ruined place," I told him. "Tell me, who is this old man, and how comes your house to be in such state?"

I thrust out my hand which he took readily in his grasp. There were tears in his eyes which he hastily dashed away.

"He is the Abbot; Marcellinus is his religious name. He was badly used by the men who sacked this place. We are left with nothing now. Everything of value has been stolen."

I placed my hand on his shoulder, and painfully thin it felt too.

"At least you shall not want for food this night, and when we ride on we will leave you whatever we are able. But there are nigh on three thousand of us, so belike we shall disturb your prayers and orisons until we pass on. Tell the Abbot what I have said, and also that you and he shall eat at my table later. Your brethren shall be given food and drink from our store."

"Blessings on you, Sir John. We will accept the hospitality of your table with gratitude. I will go tell Father Marcellinus."

He turned away and went to speak to the abbot, who brightened visibly at his words. I noticed that Brother Edmund, or Thomas of Halstead, as with most religious folk, used Latin, and I wondered idly if he had any knowledge of the common speech of the country. I turned away from this scene to find Huw waiting at my side.

"Go to Wat Spikings, Huw, and say that he is to provide food and drink for these holy brothers, and also he is to contrive to leave some further supplies when we depart. After that, they will have to provide for themselves as before."

Huw saluted and left.

"It's good to hear the Essex speech again," said John Brise. "England seems very far away now."

"Aye, John, so it does. I often think so, and wonder what is passing there. It is long since any word came to us over the mountains. We know not if the King still sits upon his throne in

Hawkwood's Sword

London. There could be another war against France, and we would not to know of it. What has befallen the Prince of Wales in Spain?"

"And all the bold lads who went with him," echoed John. "We shall hear in time, Jack, I suppose. We have our own work to pursue here. That's enough for me, now."

He was right, of course, but even in the midst of the turmoil of our lives in the field, and in spite of my ambition, there were times when I longed for the quiet of the English woods and fields, little streams and slow moving rivers. Brother Edmund had brought it all to mind again. Perhaps in time I would be there with Proserpina.

We settled ourselves into such of the monastery buildings as could still be occupied, but the majority of the men had to sleep in their small tents. There had been a scramble for the better places, and not a few quarrels. Jack Onsloe had perforce to send in a few of his hardier followers to bring peace to a situation fast getting out of hand. As usual at such times, his tactics succeeded.

That night, as I had promised, the Abbot, Brother Edmund and two senior brothers sat in our company at table. They were all vastly grateful for what appeared to be their first proper meal for some time.

"What I do not understand, Signore Giovanni," said the Abbot, "Is why these various bodies of armed men are constantly raging back and forth across our once peaceful countryside."

"The answer, Reverend Father, is that Bernabo Visconti, ruler of Lombardy, is not content with the lands he has, and wishes to annex to them those of the Marquis of Monferrato," I replied. "The Marquis petitioned His Holiness the Pope in Avignon for aid, and for our sins we are that aid. We ride now on our way to engage once more the army of Conrad, Count Landau, who fights for the Visconti; and we shall win. Then, perhaps, peace will return."

Brother Edmund spoke for the first time since the meal began. "Perhaps, Father, we should tell Sir John who it was who sacked the Monastery. Usually we have been left in peace."

Frank Payton

The Abbot replaced his wine cup on the table with a shaky hand. He must, I reflected, have been a very handsome man in his youth. His face was now a time-assailed ruin: the bones visible under near transparent skin; the nose, once high and of noble aspect, a pitted relic; the eyes dull and lacklustre. He turned to me.

"Yes, you are right, my son. As you have heard, we have usually been left in peace, but on this last occasion we were attacked by raiders such as I have never seen before. They were small men, dark haired, having wide, flat faces with slanted eyes, clad in a fashion strange to us, with long padded coats and high boots. Their swords were curved, their bows of an unusual twisted shape. No one could make them understand that we are men of religion. Their speech was a gabble of unknowable words. They were merciless, killing for no reason, and taking away anything of value they could put their hand upon. Brother Lucian tried to prevent them taking the Crucifix and altar vessels, but he was transfixed by three arrows, and his head hewn off at a stroke. Only the Devil could have created such men. That God should have allowed us to be savaged thus must mean that we must have transgressed his laws in some way."

"I am sure that cannot be so," I told him. "We have had word of these men ere now. My Almain comrades name them as Cumans, wild horsemen from the wide plains of the east, beyond Constantinople. For myself, I have no other knowledge of them, but I expect to engage with them before long. They will find that we deal in harder knocks than peaceful monks."

"Let us hope so, Sir John. Let us hope so, and that God will help you and your men prevail against them," was the Abbot's reply.

"As a fellow countryman of Brother Edmund, I am curious as to how he comes to be so far from his own land and village. Are there not sinners enough in England for you, that he must wander so?"

The good brother laughed. "I have been on a pilgrimage to the birthplace of our founder, the Blessed Saint Francis, at Assisi, and paused here on my homeward journey. Thus am I caught up in this bloody conflict. I would seek a way out, possibly with your help, Sir John. I would be willing to render what service I am able." He sounded hopeful.

"Perhaps you could be of service to me, Brother Edmund, and in return I will set you on your way again. Do you know Sible Hedingham?"

"Aye, though I have been there but once. It is not so far from Halstead that I cannot go there again. For what purpose, if I might ask?"

"You may, and it is this. My elder brother, another John, has a tannery there, and I wish to know how he fares in health, and of his affairs. I would learn anything about my family which you might learn."

"But, Sir John, if I survive on the road to England and find your people, and learn their state, how shall I tell you of them?"

I smiled at his puzzlement. "It is quite simple. You shall have a horse to carry you, Brother Edmund, money in your scrip, and a small store of food. When you return to Halstead and find word of my family, you will write down the account of their affairs, and take the letter to a wool merchant in London, whose name I shall give to you. He will send it to a mutual friend in Avignon. He in turn will send the missive to one of his agents here in Lombardy, or Tuscany, who will bring it to me."

"I will do this for you, Sir John, to repay you for your help to these poor brothers, and to me." His eyes shone at my offer.

"It will be of great comfort to me to hear news of home. But for now, these men are as my brothers, and I must attend to them. I shall leave you all here to your own affairs, whilst I attend to mine."

With that I left with John Brise to make our rounds of this camp within a monastery. I found it not a little amusing that so many men of war should rest within a house of peace. The hour was late and mostly quiet. We had had a long ride and a fast one, but a few men still sat around the glowing, dying campfires. Only the silent guards moved about on their duties.

"Who comes?" came a hoarse whisper.

"Sir John and myself," growled John. "Is that you, Wat Ferrers? Is aught passing?"

"Aye 'tis me, John." No, nought save owls and small beasts. There's been some noise from the Almains, but they're quiet now."

"What sort of noise, roistering or fighting?" I asked him.

"Could have been a brawl of sorts. I know I heard the clang of swords." He seemed uninterested, and I didn't press him on the subject. Wat was a surly sort, and never said much, but was a good soldier all the same.

"Well, good night, Wat. Keep a good watch." I slapped his shoulder. He grunted some sort of reply, and faded noiselessly into the night.

We continued our rounds until I was satisfied with our positions. As we approached my quarters again, Marco appeared from the darkness.

"Sir John? Good. Have you heard the sound of horses? I think from the direction of the Almain camp."

"No, but Wat Ferrers has told of hearing a clang of swords. What do you think has happened?"

"I'm not sure, but one of the archers came over to report horses in the night, going away to the east."

"What in Hell is going on, Jack?" said John.

"I don't know, and I don't like the sound of it, but there has been no alarum. The morning will tell all. Now, I'm for my bed. You'd both better get some sleep too. It will be another long day tomorrow."

With a last glance at the night sky, I went to my sleeping quarters.

*****

Hawkwood's Sword

The next day a chill mist hung over the whole countryside with no sign of the sun. Brother Edmund met me as I emerged from my quarters. He held the reins of what was clearly one of the packhorses, sturdy enough I supposed, but Wat Spikings was evidently not giving too much away. How like his master, Will Turton, I thought.

Whether the beast would carry the good brother all the way to England I would not have liked to guess.

"I am leaving now, Sir John." It appeared that Brother Edmund was eager to be on the road. "And I thank you for the horse and the parcel of food. May God go with you and your men."

"A word or two of advice," I said. "Do not, at this time of year, attempt to cross into France over the great mountains to the north of here. You must go to the south, and pass by the coast roads. Have you been provided with money?"

"Yes, indeed. I am sorry I did not mention this. Your man Spikings gave me a small bag of silver florins. They will suffice for me. In any event, members of my order are not supposed to carry money, but have to depend on charity. I do not fear the journey."

"You have a stout heart, Sir Monk. Take with you this paper which I have had prepared. Show it to any English commander you may encounter on your journey, even in France. I am known to many, and they will help you for my sake. Here is another for you to give to Salvestro Mannini, a wool merchant, or his representative in London, to whom you will give your letter to be sent to me here in Italy. Now, fare you well, for we must be away!" We clasped hands, then he turned away and went to his horse. Huw, who had been waiting nearby, handed me Boy's reins. I swung up into his high saddle and turned his head towards the monastery gate. Brother Edmund then climbed clumsily into the saddle of his mount, and took up the reins. We rode out of the gate side by side, to a farewell and blessings from the old Abbot and his brown-clad flock.

Frank Payton

Once through the gate we parted company, as he made off to the west. I was joined by John Brise and Jack Onsloe, and we took up our places in the van of our column.

*****

"Master Sterz approaches," Marco said quietly, as he sat his horse next to mine.

I looked over to my left. Albrecht was already halfway between his column and mine, accompanied by Hannes von Auerbach and Wolf.

Behind them rode a man-at-arms who carried a bloodstained bundle across the front of his saddle.

"Good morning, Jack. I see you are ready for the day." Albrecht nodded to Marco, who dropped behind to stand next to von Auerbach. At a sign from his leader, the man-at-arms threw the bundle to the ground and jumped down to unroll the cloth. A body sprawled out, and the Almain placed a mailed foot underneath and turned it face upwards. I looked down into a dark face, framed by long, blood-matted black hair. The lips were drawn back in a grimace halfway between surprise and a snarl. I had seen that the back of the head had been smashed in, probably by a mace.

"Here's a Cuman warrior for you. One of the devils on horseback," said Albrecht. "We've kept his weapons for you as well." He handed me a curved sword, a twisted bow not much over three feet in length, and a quiver of black arrows. I examined them briefly.

"Ask Giles to come up here, Marco. He will wish to see these. There is good steel in this sword, Albrecht. This is very fine work."

"What's to do, Sir John?" came Giles's voice. "I've all my men chafing at the bit to be off. What's this then, a toy?" He took the little bow from me. It was still strung.

"It's a Cuman bow. There's the owner." I pointed to the dead man. "What do you think of his bow?"

Hawkwood's Sword

"A child's toy, surely." He took the bow in his left hand, hooking the fingers of the right around the string, and pulled on it. I watched as a puzzled look came over his face, and he had to use more strength, and yet more to get to full draw. He looked in some wonderment at the weapon.

"I'd never have thought it to be so stiff, to look at it. What is it made from? May I keep it?"

I smiled at his eagerness. I knew that anything to do with the bowyer's craft always held his attention. "Yes, of course. I know you will keep it safe."

Albrecht laughed. "One of my men says these bows are made from wood, horn, and the sinew from cattle or horses. I know not what else. But now, Jack, I expect you'll want the explanation for all this?"

"We knew something had happened in your camp last night. What was it?"

"A group of these devils fell on us out of the night, killed three men and stole a few horses. We turned out to fight but only cornered and killed this one. His friends fled away to the east, and we did not try to follow. It might have been a trap."

"That was wise. You could have lost more men. It's a warning, I'd guess. Our best course is to carry the fight to Landau. We should move now, my friend."

"I'll leave you then, Jack, and we shall see how the day fares. God speed. We will see each other this evening, at the latest."

With that Albrecht and his three comrades left us, and we began our day's march. I caused word to be passed down the line for all to be especially vigilant. To Giles and Andreas I gave instructions that the archers should ride with braced bows to hand, and the crossbowmen their weapons spanned and loaded.

As events turned out they were not needed, and by previous agreement the whole Company halted in the mid-afternoon for rest and an early meal. Our intention was to carry on into the evening and make a night attack on the outskirts of Milan. Such a

Frank Payton

thing would never be expected on a New Year's Eve, by the people of the city or of the outlying villages.

We crossed the River Ticino virtually unopposed by the pathetic guard at the bridges and fords, and left men to collect boats and barges against our return. Fanning out on the far bank we swept through the open countryside, firing farms and villages as we rode. We didn't stay for booty, as the richer prizes would come later.

*****

Resistance to our advance began as the night ended and the first flecks of light appeared in the east. I was riding with Jack Onsloe's men at the time. We were snatching a hasty breakfast of bread and wine when two scouts galloped in.

"To horse! To horse! They are on our heels! Sir John, Master Onsloe, to horse!"

"How many?" bawled Jack. "And what's amiss with Tom?"

One of the men was sagging over his horse's neck.

"Can't say, but a goodly company. A bolt in the shoulder, I think. They've some mounted crossbowmen amongst their number," he yelled. "I'll get him to the rear."

"Come on, Jack, or they'll be upon us." I swallowed a last morsel of bread, ran for Boy, and vaulted into the saddle. Huw tossed my helmet over, and I put it on and shook the mail aventail into position about my neck. Drawing my sword, I spurred Boy into movement. Jack followed with his men. We spread out in our usual three line formation and trotted forward.

"Here they come!" Jack yelled, his voice booming hollow inside his helmet. "Shields hup! Set on lads!"

Then we were at it. With a rolling clang, a double line of mailed horsemen crashed into us. I had secured my shield high on my left arm to protect that side. Swords and maces struck at me as I fought with whirling blade. I was glad that my sword had been newly secured to my breastplate with a long chain, which allowed me a full swing on all sides but guarded against losing the weapon. I carried a warhammer as well.

Jack was to my right, and Huw on my left. Beyond him Marco drove forward with a will, darting his sword like an adder's tongue.

All around us the noise was deafening, a great hammering of sword and mace on shield and armour. A knight—he could only have been such—in silvered armour, launched a great blow at my head with a long-handled mace. I ducked behind my high-held shield, dug my left spur into Boy's flank, and pulled on his bit on the left. The shock made him dance around, and the knight shot past me, bent over his horse's neck with the force of the blow—which missed. I straightened up and dealt a thrust into his neck and shoulder. The red blood flooded over his bright armour, and he fell away screaming in shock and agony. I did not see him again. Once down and rolled to and fro under the horses' flailing hooves, few lived through the ordeal. Here and there riderless horses, some trailing riders with one foot caught in a stirrup, bucked out of the press. We fought as men possessed by devils. Jack and I and our immediate companions carved a way into the ranks of the enemy. They began to shy away from us, but there was no escape, as our larger numbers wrapped around their flanks.

"This is goddamned hard work!" Jack's voice boomed from within his helmet.

I yelled back, "They're beginning to give way!"

There was a sudden caving in the ranks to the front of us, and a lessening of effort by the enemy. Gradually we made headway into their ranks, but still they fought on. Then into both their flanks came a drift of white-feathered English arrows, and that finally tipped the scale in our favour.

They began to wheel away, and soon were in full flight. I let Jack's men follow the rout, but the enemy were quick to disperse in all directions. The men-at-arms returned before too long. Many swayed in the saddle, and not a few slid to earth and lay exhausted.

Frank Payton

We removed our helmets and mailed gauntlets, and gulped in great gulps of cold fresh air. My face ran with sweat, and I pulled a cloth from my saddlebag and wiped it away.

"Goddamn me, Sir John, that was warm while it lasted." Jack handed me a leather bottle of wine. I drank thirstily, and gave it back. He passed it on to Marco with a quick nod to him.

"You've done well this morn, my lad. I thought that fellow with the mace had done for you, but not so. Your thrust as he raised his arm to strike was good to see. I saw him go down."

Marco smiled broadly with pleasure at the words. He knew that Jack's praise was not given lightly. He bowed and replaced his sword in it's sheath.

"Thank you, Master Onsloe, for your kind words. It was exciting work, but I was glad to see the arrows come in. They hadn't expected that."

"Nor had I," I said. I had left Giles with the main body of archers. I looked about me but there was no sign of him. A tall archer stood by, leaning on his bow.

"Master Giles sent us, Sir John. I am Alain Mawe, one of his ventainers. I hope all is well with you."

He was a tall, well set-up young lad, but with the hardness of battle experience written in his face, and a bold and forthright air.

"Yes, Alain, thanks to you and your men. We were hard pressed, but there's nothing like a gust of arrows to slow up the boldest horsemen. Give Master Ashurst our thanks for his thought. I'll make sure that in future there are two or three ventaines of archers with each company of men-at-arms."

He grinned, and saluted. "I'll tell Master Ashurst what you say, Sir John. Now I'd better get back to my lads." He turned on his heel and stalked away, very erect, yellow bow in his left hand. I watched him go, thinking back to my own days in his rank—standing in the harrow formation, bow in hand, arrow on string, more shafts stuck in the ground at my feet, left side to the advancing mailed tide, usually the French, waiting for the ventainer's shout. "Draw!" I'd swing the bow up, drawing the string with the arrow well nocked back to the ear. I'd see the arrrowhead against the blue sky. "Loose wholly together!" and the old familiar thrum of the string would resound from a thousand or more bows, followed by the hissing shriek as the white-feathered hail vanished into the distance, to fall with gathering speed, finally to smite the enemy like a huge fist.

We would repeat this time and time again as confusion spread amongst the oncoming ranks. Horses would go down, screaming and neighing in agony, throwing their riders to the ground. Other riders pressing behind would seek to leap over the fallen to come at us, their defiances booming from their helmets. Arrows would find their way through the mail-covered joints in armour, piercing the thinner plates as t'were paper. The knights and men-at-arms would fall to earth to be trampled by those behind. But still they would come on, and soon we would have to withdraw behind our own fighters, knights and men-at-arms, behind the spearmen who thrust the butts of their long weapons into the ground and raised the cruel points towards the fast approaching horsemen. And then...

"Jack! Jack! For God's sake where are you?"

I shook myself as John Brise's heavy hand descended upon my shoulder, bringing me back to reality.

"I'm sorry, John. I was lost in my own thoughts then. What's to do with you? Have we lost many men?"

"Don't know yet, I'll find out. More to the point, where now?"

"Carry on, straight ahead. I want to get up to the walls of Milan without delay, to give as little time as possible for any more resistance to be brought against us. Send a group with the wounded who'll live back to the river, and get them across to the far bank. We can take them with us on the road back to Romagnano. Recover anything useful from the dead. Let the men who take the wounded back do that."

"As you say, Jack. I'll see to it."

Frank Payton

We'd lost six men in that action, and took time to bury them with some sort of dignity before we rode on.

*****

We rode on fast, for once English and Almains together. I had Jack on one side and Albrecht upon the other, followed closely by our usual close companions. Stopping at mid-day for rest and a quick morsel of food, we found ourselves at the approaches to Milan. It was, I supposed, in peaceful times a pleasant region of villages, estates, vineyards, and farms. The population were celebrating the New Year, but scattered in alarm as we rode through.

Now we ignored the lesser people, and headed for the larger houses and small castles of the nobility and merchants. I had discussed strategy with Albrecht, and we had agreed that we should try to take hostages who could be held for substantial ransom.

I called to Jack. "Pass the word to the men. Gather up those who appear to be wealthy, anyone with an air of nobility, landowners, merchants, and the like. We want hostages."

He grinned, showing his teeth. "What about my lads, and their empty purses, eh?"

"If they want to fill their pockets they can, but we want ransom money, so tell them to get to it. And to leave the maids and the women alone. We have no time for pleasure."

He rode away, calling to his men, who hastened after him.

*****

I had a company of fifty with me, including Marco and Huw. We rode up to a large estate house where festivities were taking place. Many candles were burning in the house, and the light

Hawkwood's Sword

spilled out onto the paved terrace at the front through wide open shutters. The sound of stringed instruments followed it, and within the house a glittering throng of richly-dressed revellers paraded and danced in bejewelled costumes. The night air was heavy with perfume, and with tempting odours of wine and food. I suffered a fleeting moment of regret that all this pleasure would soon turn to grief. I also felt hungry. The men at my back murmured their own feelings in the matter of food and drink.

"I know, I know. You're all starving. You can fill your bellies as well as your pockets before we leave. But now I want half of you to go around the back of this house, and half to stay with me. Dismount, all of you, and let us get to this night's work."

As I spoke I slid down from Boy's saddle, and gave his reins to Huw. Marco followed suit, and Huw waited with the horses. "All of you, draw your swords, and follow me. When we're inside, form a line abreast behind me. Walk with me, Marco."

We both raised our visors, and I waited until half of my small force had slid silently into the shadows. An owl screeched from somewhere in the trees: the signal.

Marco walked alongside me into the light, and the men-at-arms lined up behind us. Suddenly, a woman screamed, and panic followed as the revellers realised what was happening. There was more screaming from the women, and their menfolk cursed their misfortune at being present at such a time. Panic reigned as the bright crowd surged about, looking for means of escape. Those who fled to the rear of the house found themselves herded back by grim men-at-arms with drawn swords.

I waited until the surging and jostling ceased. An uneasy silence fell, apart from the sound of sobs and curses. An old man stepped forward. He was white haired and bearded, richly attired in a black and gold fur-trimmed robe. Despite his obvious fear his voice was calm.

"Who are you, Sirs, to come into my house at this time with drawn swords? Do you seek to join our revels? If so, put up your swords and be welcome, at this New Year's Tide."

Frank Payton

I had schooled Marco as to his reply, and left him to speak for us. Marco began.

"We are Il Campagnia Bianca. This is the Signore Giovanni Haucuud. I am Marco, his squire. We come for hostages for the good behaviour of your Dukes, Bernabo and Galeazzo. You would be foolish to resist. There are thousands of us nearby. Your protectors have fled."

"This is an outrage!" spluttered the elder. "By what right...?"

A young gallant launched himself from amongst the revellers, tugging at a belted dagger. Suddenly Marco's sword was at his throat. The lad skidded to a halt and lifted his hands. Marco plucked the dagger from its sheath and threw it out of reach. He continued to speak in a quiet, calm voice.

"If there is no trouble, and the hostages surrender peacefully, the Signore Giovanni will guarantee that no harm will come to your ladies, wives and daughters. Otherwise..."

"We have no choice but to submit to you," cried the old man, "but before God, I curse you and all your kind. Take me as your first hostage."

He came towards me, but I put up my hand.

"No, old man. For your boldness, I absolve you from this indignity. Your young men, and others of lesser years than you, will suffice. Also, I tell you that your ruler Bernabo Visconti will pay before God for his injustices, both to his own people and to those whom he would enslave and bend to his will."

I reverted to English, and ordered my men forward. "Take them, and whatsoever you want, but mark this: I will hang any who harm the women." I waved the men forward, and walked out with Marco to where Huw was waiting with the horses. I was about to take Boy's reins when the old man appeared at my side. He clasped his hands before him in supplication. By now the tears were pouring down his face and into his beard.

"Signore, Signore, they have taken my only son. I implore you to release him now, for mine and his dead mother's sake."

Hawkwood's Sword

I looked at him for a long moment. "I have not seen mine own family for eight years now. I know not if they yet live, or are dead. Which one is your son?"

"He is the rash boy who tried to attack your squire, Signore. Please release him. He is all that I have now."

I placed my hand on his shoulder. "Have no fear, old man. He will not be harmed. However, you must ransom him. I can treat him no differently from the others, who will come to despise him if I release him now. Take heart: he is a brave lad, and will mayhap learn something of this hard world whilst he is with us at Romagnano. Tell your people we want two thousand florins for the return of each hostage, and no hostilities whilst they are in our care. Say that to your Duke Bernabo."

I put my foot into the stirrup, and thrust myself up into the saddle. I gathered the reins and touched my heels to Boy's flanks, and he started forth into into the moonlit night. Marco and Huw followed, and thus we began the retreat to the Ticino.

The sound of much weeping and cursing followed us into the night.

The hostages were hurried along, their hands bound together, and each one fastened again to a long rope which passed along our ranks to form a long train in the midst of our men.

The mansion had been plundered, but I had given orders that it should not be fired. All valuables had been gathered up, and the men's saddlebags bulged with the booty. At least they would be satisfied with their night's work. For our part Albrecht and I would have to wait to collect the ransom monies.

*****

My small squadron reached the Ticino without any further problems, just as a dull grey dawn was breaking. Albrecht met me at the crossing. "How have you fared Jack? We look to have made good haul of hostages. Some rich men are amongst them. We may have trouble getting them across the river, though."

Frank Payton

I dismounted and went to stand beside him. "We're not all here yet. Jack Onsloe is behind my lads. I guess we have about a hundred and fifty in our net."

The morning was cold with a bitter wind. The river was the colour of lead, and choppy with waves, save where the ford shoaled. The men who had been left to guard the boats sat about wrapped in cloaks against the weather, and were not too happy at having been kept behind, thus missing the chance of booty. I knew I would have to give them more than their usual pay or there would be trouble.

More and yet more of the Company arrived, English and Almain. Scores of hostages were dragged along by only one or two horsemen, and many looked the worse for wear; some older men were near to exhaustion.

"We must take care of these people, Albrecht; they're of no value to us dead." I called to Marco. "Tell the men to give some food and drink to the hostages. They'll take it if they hear you speak to them in Italian."

He set off with Huw, and they persuaded the men to give of their rations to the captives in their care. I knew that such a host of extra mouths to feed, and their very bodies to be given shelter, would cause problems. The question of providing guards would be simple beside that.

My thoughts were broken by shouts from the guards and lookouts. We had begun to push the hostages, who had been freed from their bonds, into the boats we had taken from up and down river.

"Sir John! Sir John! Attack! Attack! Herr Sterz! Herr Sterz! Angriff! Angriff!"

And so it was, as Albrecht had predicted. Several barge-like boats approached downriver. Others came upriver propelled by men with long oars. Volleys of crossbow bolts swept our ranks and for a short while all was confusion.

Hawkwood's Sword

"Get the hostages under cover!" I yelled. "Those in the boats must lie down. Up shields against those damned bolts!

Luckily our own archers soon sized up the position and began to shoot, not in volleys, but each man choosing his own target. Giles appeared at my side with Alain Mawe. They began to shoot, and I could but admire their skill. Man after man in the boats went down and over into the waters. They wore only light armour, and soon they were taking heavy losses as the tempered shafts found their marks. Their efforts slackened and almost ceased, and the men cowered under cover as best they could behind their pavises and shields.

Our main problem was with the mounted men-at-arms, and we had to engage them on both banks in the area of the ford. John Brise led some hundreds of our men across the river, which was churned into a muddy foam. I watched them fighting their way up, out onto the banks, heads down behind their shields, swords held straight out in front as a hedge of steel points. I shouted to Giles and pointed across the river.

"Shoot over our men's heads, and into the enemy ranks. Thin them down a bit." He waved his bow, and ran over to the main body of his men, who turned their bows where he pointed and began to shoot with dropping shafts into the Italian men-at-arms.

Jack Onsloe's men joined mine, and together with Albrecht's we turned our attention to our own side of the river. More men joined us under Will Preston and Andrew Belmont. Gradually their added weight gave us the superiority, and as the sun broke through our enemy gave way, broke, and fled. I forbade the chase, as there was no point. After such a night as we had had, I for one was glad to see them flee. I took off my helmet, and was joined by Albrecht and the others.

"Well, let us hope there will be no more interruptions," said Albrecht. He looked pale against his silver-and-black armour, and he swayed a little in the saddle. But he'd not been idle in the fight; his sword was bloody from point to pommel. I echoed his words. "Let us hope not."

Chapter 8
Reprisal

As matters fell out, it had to be left to Albrecht to receive the ransom monies for the hostages. When we returned to Romagnano, I found myself beset by events which proved to be as perilous as any I had met before.

The fifth day after our return was a cold day in early January. A chill wind swept down from the snow-bedecked mountains to the north. Icy puddles crackled underfoot as Giles Ashurst walked with me on my daily inspection of the camp. The two of us were wrapped in thick cloaks against the cold, but it still seeped through and chilled us to the bone. A pall of smoke from the men's cooking fires spread over the ground. The smell of food was good, but we had had to forage for the fuel with which to cook and to warm our bodies. Supplies were hard to get, whether by fair means or foul.

Tom Blount, the horsemaster, was worried too about the lack of fodder. "We're in a bad state, Sir John. The poor beasts have got to eat, and they've cropped the grass for miles around. We shall have to buy or take some from somewhere before long." His round red face was full of concern.

"I know, Tom. I know, but there is little else we can do at present. We cannot move from here until we rid ourselves of the hostages. This is a good defensible place for us, and that is of even more importance. I shall speak to Master Sterz on the matter and see what can be done."

Hawkwood's Sword

He grumbled on, but I had to leave him to his own affairs. In later years we were able to make better provision for our mounts, but in that first winter it was hard for both men and horses. We trudged on through the frozen mud, and found a warmer berth in the armourer's quarters.

"Tom's worried," said Giles, "And so am I. There's a lot of campfire talk, and it's not good. Many are complaining about food, lack of fuel, and no action. We should make a move before too long, before they take it out of our hands."

I sighed. "You heard what I told Tom. There's nowhere to go at present, and Marco tells me the local people are almost as badly affected as we are by this wild weather. I sent him out the other day to see what the position is between here and Milan. He can mix with the people, where we cannot. The farming folk are in a parlous state, worse in fact than we are, as our horses have eaten most of their grass and hay crop. I... But who comes here? What is it, Roger?"

"There's a horseman at the gate, Sir John: a well set-up lad on a black horse. He says ever, 'Signore Gianni, Signore Gianni'. Be that you?" His brow furrowed, and he shivered, holding his hands out to the armourer's forge-fire.

I laughed, "Yes, that's me, Roger. Send him over. Is he armed?"

"He has a sword and a dagger, but he doesn't look a match for any of us." He said no more, but turned on his heel and walked swiftly away.

Despite Roger's words I loosened my sword in its scabbard as I awaited the stranger's arrival. I looked across to the gate, where the guards were having a fight to restrain the black horse, which reared, plunged, and curvetted. Whoever he was, the rider sat his mount like a centaur. Roger called out to the guards, who set the beast free, accompanied by a suitable curse or two. The horse cantered towards us and was pulled up with a rearing flourish. Its rider slid to the ground and bowed low before me, sweeping off his black velvet cap at the same time. He straightened and looked at me full face.

Frank Payton

"Signore Gianni, it is I, Niccolo della Sera, of Genoa, Ludovico's nephew. Do you remember me?" He seemed to be nervous at our meeting, and only gave me a faint smile.

I released my sword hilt, and reached out my hand to him in welcome. "But of course I remember you, Niccolo. How should I not? You are to me a reminder of some happier days than I have had of late. You may also remember Giles, the Captain of our Archers, who was with me at Genoa."

Niccolo smiled and swept Giles a bow, a courtesy which quite amused him. "I am glad to see you again, Signore Giles."

I waved our visitor in the direction of my pavilion. "Let us not stay here in this cold wind, Niccolo. I am sure you would be glad of a cup of hot spiced wine, and something to eat."

As I said this a bolt of some unknown, unlooked-for fear passed through my heart. Why had he sought me out here, in the dead of winter?

I guided him to my pavilion, followed by Giles, who was no doubt as curious as I was to discover the reason for Niccolo's visit. We seated ourselves at the table, I in my high chair, and the others on either side of me. At least inside, with several braziers glowing, we could talk in comfort. Huw brought us hot spiced wine and retired silently.

"You are very welcome, Niccolo," I began, "but this is a bad time of the year to be travelling the roads from Genoa. Are you seeking adventure with us, perhaps?"

"No, Signore," he said with a sigh. "If only it were that simple, but I am the bearer of ill news. Ludovico has sent me to tell you that the Lady Proserpina has been abducted, taken away we know not where, nor by whom."

His dark eyes filled with tears, and he gulped at his wine to cover the emotion. My feeling at first seeing him had been right. I stared at him unbelieving, and then at Giles, who had a serious look on his face.

Hawkwood's Sword

"We must gather a small company together, Sir John, to go and seek the maid. Ten of my best archers under Alain Mawe, and some of Jack Onsloe's trustier spirits should go."

"Thank you, Giles. I can do no better, but first we must learn more of this matter." We had spoken in English, which I knew Niccolo did not understand. I began in his own tongue as well as I could, but knew I needed Marco's help. I called for Huw.

"Go and find Master Bandini, Huw, and say I need his help, but say no more." He left at a run on the errand, and I turned my attention back to our guest.

"Now, tell me, Niccolo, how did this happen, and when?"

"It is five days, Signore, since the Lady Proserpina was taken. She and her brother, the Count, were riding in the country near the estate; you remember, where you stayed overnight with your men on your journey to Genoa. A band of armed men, wearing plain jupons over their armour and helmets with closed visors, surrounded the group which was the Count, the Lady Proserpina, and some of the estate stewards. Swords were drawn, and my uncle tried to defend his sister. The stewards were armed only with wooden staves, but fought as well as they could. Lady Proserpina reared her horse over one of the attackers, and the hooves felled him. She tried to ride off, but was overtaken, surrounded by the men and carried off. One of the stewards was killed, the other injured, and the Count received a thrust from a sword in his side, and still lies sore stricken in his bed. The healers attend him, but his condition is very poor."

"Great God in Heaven!" I exclaimed. "Giles! We must lose no time. Go and fetch Jack here to me, and tell Hal Peasgood, the healer, to attend me also." He rose to his feet and made to leave. "Wait! Send for John Brise as well. Huw! Huw! Come here!"

"I'm here, Sir John. What shall I do?" He stood uncertainly, shifting from one foot to the other.

"Ride to the Almain camp and say to Master Sterz that I shall be coming to see him directly. With all haste, now!"

Frank Payton

When they had gone I slumped down in my chair and buried my head in my hands. My Proserpina, lost to me! My love! My hope for the future taken away! After all we had just gone through, to lose her! Niccolo's voice broke into my thoughts.

"Signore Gianni! Signore! This was found half-buried in the mud, at the place where the fight took place."

I looked up. He was holding out his hand. Dangling from his fingers was the golden chain bearing the signet ring with the lion's head carved upon it, the token of my love which I had given to Proserpina! I took it from him, pressed it to my lips and placed the chain about my neck under my tunic.

"Thank you, Niccolo. Now I have this token returned to me in this manner, I shall not rest until it reposes once more in my lady's bosom. Is there anything else you can tell me of this affair, however small? You say one of the men was struck down by my lady's horse? Was he killed?" I rose to my feet, waving him to remain seated, and walked along the length of the table, sliding my left hand along it, but not seeing the smooth brown wood of which it was made. I heard Niccolo's voice as if from afar. My thoughts were still on a sunny hillside above Genoa on that golden afternoon, which seemed very long ago.

"They must have thought so, Signore. They left him there where he fell. But he was not dead, and I left him unconscious in a locked room at the estate house, under strong guard."

"So. If you have him safe, we can make him tell us who is responsible for this outrage. Is there more?"

"Signore, it is known that Orlando Scacci was approached by a group of men in a tavern in Genoa. I am told they bore swords but were not wearing armour at the time. Orlando left the tavern with these men, and they rode away together. He did not return to the Palazzo Lucanti until very late, and that was the evening before the Lady Proserpina was taken."

Whilst I was trying to make sense of this Marco entered in a state of excitement. I didn't know what Huw had said to him, but he seemed to have some idea of what was happening.

Hawkwood's Sword

"Sir John, good morning. What has happened in Genoa? I see Niccolo is here, and I guess he must the bearer of bad news. If it is of concern to you, then the Lady Proserpina must be involved for him to be riding here at this time of the year. Am I right?"

"You guess only too well, Marco, I am afraid. Know that my Lady has been taken by some persons at present unknown, and the Count her brother is sorely wounded. Only one of the band has been captured, and he is wounded also. The Lady Proserpina laid him low with her horse's hooves."

He smiled. "That seems very much like the Lady Proserpina as we remember her, Sir John. These unknown men may find they have trapped a wild cat who scratches, and is not easily daunted by them."

"Thank you, Marco. I am sure you are right, and that reassures me when I most need reassurance. But we need also to take horse and ride swiftly to Genoa, or at least to the Count's estate, and there take up the chase."

Now Jack Onsloe ducked into the pavilion. He was followed closely by Hal Peasgood, still attired in his shabby brown robe, and flustered at being dragged from his usual surroundings in the healers' quarters, where he and Simon Cheshunt, and others of their calling, muttered to themselves over bubbling pots of stinking herbs, or pounded the dried leaves with pestle and mortar. Overawed by the rich interior of my pavilion he sat timorously on a chair like a small brown mouse. Huw set a cup of wine before him at which he stared, as if to drink it might poison him. Jack sat down with something approaching relief and gratefully accepted another cup of spiced wine from Huw. He took a huge gulp, swallowed it, wiped his mouth with the back of his hand, and looked darkly around the table.

"What's to do, Sir John? Why the gathering? What's he doing here, so far from home?" He nodded towards Niccolo.

"My Lady Proserpina has been taken, Jack, and I need your help, and that of some of your men, to bring her home."

"Do we know who has taken her?" he asked.

Frank Payton

"Not yet, but one of the miscreants was wounded and is under strong guard at the Count's estate. Also, Orlando Scacci might be involved."

Jack smiled in his crooked way. "I'll talk to the prisoner, Sir John. He'll tell me what we want to know. I'll be off and get some of my best men together, about twenty should be enough. They've been asking for action; now they'll get it." He finished his wine and stood up, nodded to me and left of the pavilion.

I returned my attention to Marco, who sat disconsolately gazing into his wine cup. His obvious concern was touching.

"Marco, before we leave I want you to resume your traveller's guise and seek out our friend in Milan. Tell him what has befallen my Lady Proserpina, and say I pray him to give me a letter to his agent in Genoa, which will allow of his aid in my search for the poor girl. Then follow me to Genoa with all speed."

He finished his wine and rose to his feet. "I will do this with all haste, Signore, but it is possible that our friend will by now have returned to Florence. If he has, I shall have to ride there. Whatever happens, I shall meet you at the estate, or at the Palazzo Lucanti in the city. I..." He paused uncertainly.

"Well, what is it boy?" I asked.

"If I am to go to Milan, and possibly to Florence after that, I will not be able to take my weapons and armour, nor my best horse. As a mere traveller, it will not look well for me to have such a good mount, but I shall need La Fiamma when I arrive in Genoa."

"Do not worry about the mare, Marco. We will take her and your war gear along with us. I will see that Huw takes good care of her."

"Thank you, Sir John. I will be away as soon as I can be ready."

He took his leave then, and as he slipped out of the pavilion, I felt a pang of anxiety about him. Such a mission was not easy, as he would be in enemy territory once across the Ticino. I could only offer up a silent prayer for his safety. I knew he was resourceful,

Hawkwood's Sword

but this might prove too difficult a test of his abilities. As for his horse, which he had acquired after one our skirmishes, I knew he was very fond of the red chestnut mare, and they had taken to each other as if he had always been her master. I realised also that I would miss his dignified but always cheerful presence at my side, but I knew there was no one else to send in his place. At last I turned my attention to Hal Peasgood.

"Now, Hal, I want you to ride with us to Genoa. There are wounded men there, two in fact—one who must live; he is the Count Savignone. The second man must be kept alive long enough to tell me where the Lady Proserpina has been taken by his fellows, who wish to thwart my plans in Italy. I will pay you well for your aid, Hal, so I need your craft. Bring your best herbs and simples with you, whatever you need. And this must go no further. Do you understand, not even Simon can be told?"

"I understand you, Sir John, and to the best of my poor craft I will gladly help you as I may."

I thanked him, and he scuttled away to begin his preparations to leave with the rest of us. As for me, I sent Huw to fetch Boy, and with a heavy heart made ready to pay my visit to Albrecht.

As I waited, John Brise arrived, thrusting his heavy way into the pavilion. He slumped down in a nearby chair and came straight to the point.

"I hear from Jack that your Lady has been captured, and that you are off to Genoa to rescue her. Is that the way of it?"

"Yes, I fear so, and I will have to ask you to look after our affairs here whilst I am away. I know I can trust you, John. Keep close to Albrecht. He is not himself lately, since the plague struck him. He is not fully recovered, and he is having problems with Werner and Conrad, so keep an eye on them too."

John had helped himself to a cup of spiced wine and was sipping it reflectively. "You know you can trust me, Jack. Just get the maid back to where she should be. So far as Albrecht's two problems are concerned, I've thought for a long time now that he would be well rid of them. I'll do it if you like. Quietly, and without any pother." He took a another sip of wine, and his eyes met mine. He raised an eyebrow.

"I'll give it some thought, John. But now I have to go and see Albrecht and acquaint him with what has happened. I'll see you when I return. I can hear Huw bringing Boy for me."

I left him sitting at the table, and went outside.

*****

As I rode to the Almain camp I turned to thoughts of the possible identities of Proserpina's abductors. The first name, of course, was that of Orlando Scacci. I had never quite lost my fears about the man since I had seen him leave the Lucanti estate late that night, before we finally arrived at Genoa. My waking dream at the dawn of day had seemed then only to have been a nightmare. I had been anxious that I might lose the lady I had just met, who appeared to be the wife I had sought, almost without knowing it, or so I had told myself. But now? Had the dream been a true warning?

I drew nearer to Albrecht's pavilion, when a sudden vision of a face swam into my mind's eye from the day when we were in Boccanera's hall. An enraged noble or merchant had been ordered by the Doge to leave on account of his outburst against us.

I didn't remember hearing his name spoken, but his appearance and the look he gave me as he left remained with me. I had seldom witnessed such venom in a glance. Could he be the man behind the abduction? I wondered. Mayhap Ludovico would remember his name.

Albrecht met me at the entrance to his pavilion. With him were von Felsingen and Conrad Harzmann, who themselves appeared to have just arrived. This would not do, I thought. I had too many suspicions of the pair to require their presence at a meeting such as I had in mind. I thought back to what John Brise had been saying.

Hawkwood's Sword

Albrecht was not attired even in half armour and was wrapped in a thick cloak which he did not remove when we all moved into the warm interior of the pavilion. As ever, I was taken by the lavish furnishings of the place. It was, perhaps, for Albrecht a reminder of the grand castle in the Rhineland of which he spoke from time to time with such with such faraway longing in his eyes. This had become even more evident since his near brush with death by the plague.

We all seated ourselves at the table, and I seethed inwardly as Werner and Conrad settled themselves down for what they anticipated would be a long discussion. Wolf appeared and poured wine for us all. Healths were proposed and drunk. I fidgeted as the talk pursued well-worn paths, none of which could be followed in the winter months. Time slipped by, and my contributions became less and less. Eventually I fell silent, but raged in my mind. Mercifully, and fortuitously, I was saved by the reappearance of Wolf. He went to Albrecht and whispered a few words in his ear.

Albrecht frowned, then nodded and turned to Werner. His voice was harsh.

"You must get back to your commands. A brawl has broken out amongst your men. Settle the matter and give them something useful to do. Send out patrols towards Milan, but they should not seek action, only take note of what is passing, and make our presence known."

Werner made a gesture of impatience. "Cannot Steiner do this? We have much to discuss."

"No!" shouted Albrecht. "Get about your duties. These matters are for your attention. The men grow lax enough without encouragement from you. Be off, both of you!"

I sipped my wine thoughtfully through this and their departure. It seemed that Werner was reluctant to go outside again, and sought an excuse to stay where he was and drink wine in comfort. I looked at Albrecht and raised my eyebrows. He met my eyes and spread his hands upwards as if in despair.

FRANK PAYTON

"I tire of them, Jack. They are becoming worse than useless. I have to hound them daily. It is most unsatisfactory. As you know, we can do little at this time of year, but they chafe and grumble constantly."

I put out my hand and touched his shoulder, which felt painfully thin. "Do not worry, old friend; your other commanders are loyal, as are the majority of your men. Those two can do little to harm you. We discussed this once before, and it might not be such a bad thing if they did desert to Landau. I am sure they will have pondered on this. They need employment." I withdrew my hand.

"You are right, it might be a good thing if they did leave us. It would cleanse the air. But enough of that; it is my problem, not yours. What has brought you here today? Your Welshman seemed in some agitation when he came to announce your intention to come here. Is aught amiss?"

"I fear so. The Lady Proserpina has been abducted—by whom, I know not. I ride to Genoa without delay. Jack Onsloe and Giles will accompany me, each with some of their men. John Brise will command whilst I am away. You know him well, and he you, so there should be no problems. I have advised him of your position with regard to Werner and Conrad. He will help if called upon."

"That is kind, Jack, but only in an extreme case would I call on him in this matter. Now you must make all haste to Genoa to rescue your lady. From what you have told me of her, she seems to be a spirited young woman who will not be easily cowed by her captors. You go with my blessing, Jack, and may Good Fortune attend you."

He stood up, and we clasped hands and embraced, and so I left him. He seated himself again, and on leaving his pavilion I glanced back—to see him a sad, lone figure.

Wolf brought Boy to me, and as I swung up into the saddle, I knew I had to get Marco away from our camp before Werner's patrols set out towards Milan.

Hawkwood's Sword

*****

I made all haste back to camp, and was told by the gate guards that a traveller had left shortly before my arrival. Roger Capsey, to whom I had spoken earlier, came up as I turned away. He moved to Boy's side away from the other guards, and looked up at me.

"That traveller was your squire, I reckon, Sir John. The others don't know, but I knew by the way he sat his horse. It weren't his usual horse neither, and was right sorry-looking nag. I don't know what Tom Blount thought of letting him go out on that animal."

I leaned down and affected to adjust the stirrup and its leather.

"Thank you, Roger. I'll ride after him. Which way?"

"He went straight ahead out of the gate, to the east, more or less."

"And now I shall be on my way. When I've left here and you can get to him, tell Master Brise where I have gone, but no one else." I gathered up the reins, and urged Boy forward, and out of the gate.

I cantered away in a leisurely fashion, but at a turn in the track which took me into the trees, I kicked Boy into a gallop. Marco had clearly done something of the sort, because I had gone only about two miles before I espied a solitary horseman away in front of me.

Little by little I overhauled the horseman, who had by then slowed to an amble. As I drew nearer the rider took a quick look behind him, and straightway pulled up his mount. It was indeed Marco. He faced me, clearly alarmed by my sudden appearance.

"Sir John! What do you here? Why have you ridden after me? I had not thought to see you again this side of Genoa. Have you changed your mind on this matter?"

I would not have known him from from his sorry attire. Usually neat and carefully dressed, he was in patched dark green hose, a brown padded tunic, with a soiled white shirt beneath, and a long, torn, hooded cloak overall. On his feet were much-worn tall leather boots. His hair was awry, and his face had been mired in the mud of the road.

Frank Payton

"No. I have ridden after you to warn that von Felsingen and his familiar, Harzmann, have been sent out on patrols by Master Sterz, order to keep them occupied, and they are none too happy at the task. This could cause you trouble if they catch up with you and you are recognised."

He frowned at this news. "Then I must make all speed to put a good distance between us, Sir John. This horse does not look much, but in truth is quite strong. I will not delay any further, and will bid you farewell."

I reached across and placed my hand on his shoulder. "Take great care, my lad; you are fast becoming as a son to me. Keep well out of the reach of von Felsingen and his kind."

Marco's eyes gleamed strangely. "I will not fail you, nor your Lady, Sir John. I shall see you at Genoa."

He shook his horse's reins and set off at a canter, increasing to a gallop. I watched him for a little while, then turned Boy's head back along the way I had come.

*****

We took but four days to cover the country between Romagnano and Ludovico's estate near Genoa. Niccolo, Jack Onsloe, Giles Ashurst, Huw and Alain Mawe accompanied me, with forty archers and thirty men-at-arms. The men had been handpicked for their known skills and daring. They were willing volunteers, and I had promised extra pay and rewards. All had sworn their fealty to the mission. Hal Peasgood made up the party, bumping along uncomfortably on his horse, which was festooned with bundles and packages of herbs and whatever else was bound up with his craft as a healer.

We had ridden swiftly, spurring the horses to greater efforts than was fair to the beasts, but I wished to lose no time in getting to Genoa. Country people and other travellers were pushed aside by our thundering progress, and many were the curses hurled in our wake. The weather was cold and unkind, with ice-cold rain lashing our tired bodies, soaking us to the skin, turning our mounts into gleaming metal in the pale-sunned daylight. It was with great relief that at last I saw the white walls and red roofs of Ludovico's estate house. I slid to the ground and stretched to ease my aching body and legs, stiff from the day's ride. It seemed to me that I had eaten and slept in the saddle.

Gaetano, Ludovico's steward, greeted us with deep bows and flowery words, and I was shown into the house with Niccolo, Jack, and Giles. As my page, Huw would also sleep in the house, whilst the men moved on to a suitable area where they could pitch their own camp.

The portly steward was deeply troubled by his master's state of health and fluttered around in an excited state.

"He takes little food and drink, Signore Giovanni, and sleeps a great deal. He has scarcely spoken since that dreadful day, and Father Pietro has twice given him the last rites, and he prays mightily for him."

"I have brought one of our most cunning healers with me, Gaetano. Let us see what he can do. He will see your master directly. Now, what about the prisoner? Where is he? I must see him as soon as I am able, and our meeting will not be pleasant."

"He is locked in a deep cellar under the house, Signore. Do you wish me to have him brought up? He is quite recovered from the kick which the Signora Proserpina's horse gave him. Much of his time is spent in prayer."

Jack laughed. "He'll need more than prayer if he doesn't tell us what we want to know, and that quickly. Let me see him now, Sir John, and I'll give him something to think about which will frighten him so much that by the time we ask him questions, he will want to tell us all about this abduction."

"Very well. Gaetano, please take Messer Onsloe to the prisoner. You go with him, Niccolo, to translate. I will go and see the Count, with Hal."

Frank Payton

"Lead on then, lad. Let us go and speak to this wretch. Mayhap he is ready to tell all he knows, even now." Jack followed Niccolo out towards of the house, his burly form towering over the slim Italian boy.

As they left together, a servant conducted me to Ludovico's room, which was large and airy, and faced the afternoon sun. The Count lay upon a low bed well provided with white linen and plump pillows. He did not open his eyes as we entered, and he was as pale as death, seeming hardly to take breath. As I entered, a priest rose from his knees where he had knelt by the side of the bed and held out his hand.

"I am Father Pietro, sent by my Bishop to pray for the recovery of our good Count. So far Our Lady has not seen fit to bless my efforts."

He was tall and spare and, to my eye, had the look of a man-at-arms in the guise of a priest. Shrewd brown eyes were set in a gaunt face above a thin long nose, and his tonsure was grey. His robe was of good thick brown cloth, held in at the waist by a rope belt, from which hung a black leather scrip. On his feet were leather sandals. As he turned his face to the side, a long scar down the cheek showed itself, clearly made by a slash from knife or sword. I knew then that I had been right: yet another soldier turned to the Church, perhaps after years fighting the Saracens or the heathen Slavs of the northeast. I took his hand, which was dry and sinewy, and from it I felt a restrained strength.

"You will know from Gaetano that I am John Hawkwood from England. Let us see what Hal can do by way of giving some assistance to Our Lord's Mother." The priest's eyes narrowed. This might be taken for blasphemy by some, but I was past caring about religious sensibilities, so long as I gleaned what I wanted to know, both from the prisoner in the cellar and the wounded nobleman lying before us on his bed.

"What think you, Hal? Is my Lady's brother lost to us?"

Hal pulled a face, and looked serious, shuffling his feet nervously.

Hawkwood's Sword

"He faces the dying sun, Sir John, and should be moved to a chamber on the other side of the house, where he may face the sun's rising each morn. Its rays will strengthen him each day, and will help my medicines in their work."

I began to translate this for Father Pietro, but he raised his hand to stop the words. For the first time he smiled, and spoke in accented English. "I understand what your healer says, and doubtless he is right. I have heard it said before by the doctors in the East. Pagans they may be, but they have great knowledge of medicine. I am sure now that Count Ludovico is safe in your man's care." He inclined his head slightly towards me, and walked from the room.

"Giovanni?" A weak voice came from the bed. I leaned over Ludovico, the better hear his faint words.

"Yes, it is John Hawkwood. I arrived only a short time ago, bringing one with me who is cunning in leechcraft. He has said you must be moved to another chamber, where you will see the sunrise each day."

"Thank God you are here. Perhaps now I can have some hope for the return of Proserpina." He had tried to raise himself but now fell back with the effort. I took his hand.

"Do not fret, Ludovico. Save yourself. I will send Gaetano with others to move you." And to Hal, "Wait here, follow your patient to his new quarters, and begin your work." He nodded and sat down on the small stool at the bedside.

"I will see you again early on the morrow, when Hal will have had time to work his craft upon you." With that I left the stricken Count.

Once Gaetano had been set to work, I went in search of Jack and Niccolo, and met them as they emerged through a side door which evidently led from the cellar. Jack seemed to be his usual grim self, and, muttering something about seeing to the men, went off without a word. For his part Niccolo looked pale, and leaned against the wall for support.

"What ails you, boy." I asked.

Frank Payton

Niccolo had difficulty in answering, and shuddered uncontrollably. "Y...your Messer Onsloe is a fiend from Hell!" he stammered at last. "He has so terrified the prisoner that he is even now praying for Death to strike him before tomorrow's dawn."

"What has Messer Onsloe said?"

"He...he... has said that at dawn he will return with two of his men, to question him as to the whereabouts of the Lady Proserpina, and who is to blame for taking her away. If he does not speak quickly, said Messer Onsloe, he will first lose his manhood, then his guts, which he can watch spill out on to the floor, before his eyes are put out. And there were other things of which I cannot speak for horror, but which will require red-hot irons."

"Ah," I said, stifling a smile. "Well, Jack is a hard man, as you say, but mayhap such things will not come to pass." I clapped the boy on his shoulder and said, more kindly, "Now I think it is time for the evening meal. Let us go and prepare ourselves. I feel very hungry after the day's long ride."

"Then I will see you at table, Sir John. But first I must take the fresh air."

I watched the poor lad stagger away and heard him retching outside the door. I smiled to myself. If Jack had put half the terror into the prisoner as he had into Niccolo, there would be less trouble finding out what was necessary. I went to my room to find that Huw had laid out clean clothes from my saddle bags, and placed water and towels on a small side table for my use. I took great care over my appearance; finally satisfied, I made my way to the great hall, where several persons were already assembled, including the Count's secretary and Father Pietro. Taking my seat, I was served with wine by one of the servants. I raised my cup to the priest.

"Your health, Father. Have you anything to tell me, perhaps about the disappearance of Lady Proserpina? Have you heard any whispers about the affair?"

He drank to me in his turn. "Unfortunately not, Sir John, but it would not be difficult for me to ask about for such information.

Hawkwood's Sword

There is a certain person of my acquaintance who might be helpful."

"You must know that I would be prepared to be very grateful for any aid you may be able to give me, and very generous to the source of any information." I leaned nearer, and spoke in a low voice, although as I spoke in English it was unlikely that the Count's secretary would understand. "I would be particularly interested to learn of the whereabouts of one hight Orlando Scacci."

Father Pietro sipped his wine. "A very dangerous man to meddle with, but I will see what I can do. Now I see that more of our company are arriving. We will speak of this again, Sir John."

Jack and Giles entered the hall, made their way to the table, and took their places opposite Father Pietro and myself. Jack glowered at the priest, who returned his gaze steadily. I noticed this, and as I knew my grim lieutenant was not fond of priests, I sought to nip any trouble in the bud.

"Jack, this is Father Pietro, who has been sent here by his Bishop to minister to the Count. Fortunately, if I guess rightly, the good Father has some experience in our trade, and therefore some sympathy with our mission. He also understands our English speech."

Jack grunted something which might have been a grudging approval and thrust out his hand. Father Pietro grasped it firmly, and found a vice had closed about his own hand. He raised his eyebrows and exerted more pressure, and the thing became a matter of strengths and wills. Suddenly Jack released the priest's hand, lifted his own in a mock salute, and I thought—to my surprise, that just for one instant—I saw the ghost of a smile on that grim visage.

"Well, I reckon he is more of a soldier than a priest still, Sir John. That hand has held sword or mace at some time past. I can trust him, which is more than I can say for many of his calling."

At that I relaxed and began to help myself to the food which had been brought to the table, and once again relished the delights

FRANK PAYTON

produced in the Count's kitchens. I seemed to recall Proserpina's voice speaking to me, saying, "You must know, Sir Giovanni, that we have in our household some of the finest cooks in the whole of Liguria." It seemed to me that I saw her smiling at me from across the table, but the illusion faded as quickly as it had appeared, and I found my gaze had been fixed on the face of an angel woven into a tapestry which hung upon the opposite wall.

A servant refilled my cup. I took another mouthful of wine to clear my head, and then reached out for food, taking a portion of chicken stew, rich with the smell of herbs. I ate this with ravenous enjoyment, and soon went on to lasagne stuffed with minced lamb, crushed nuts and spices.

"By God, Sir John, this is a welcome change from camp food," said Jack, chewing mightily. "We should recruit some of these cooks to our own service. What do you say, Giles?"

Giles grinned, and winked at me. "Why, I reckon that after a week or two on this fare, you wouldn't be able to lift your sword, and I'd be unable to draw a bowstring. It's all a little too rich for me. No wonder these Italians hire us to fight their battles. Look at Gaetano. He's so fat he must roll out of bed each morning to get on his feet."

Jack grunted, swallowed his food, and took a gulp of wine. "You'll hang with your own bowstring one of these days for jesting with me, young jackanapes. We'll take a turn together come the morning, then you'll see how I lift my sword."

"Now, Jack," I said, knowing full well that given the chance Jack would beat Giles into the ground. "He means no harm, and I cannot afford to have my Captain of Archers treated so. His skills and yours are equal but different. I forbid you both to quarrel over nothing, and you, Giles, hold your tongue. It runs away with your head at times."

Giles subsided with a grimace and, muttering under his breath, applied himself to his food. He was always a merry sort, but some of his jests were out of place. I returned my attention to Father Pietro, who ate sparingly, yet contrived to taste almost every dish on the table—and without any seeming effect emptied his cups of wine, which were promptly refilled by one of the servants.

"I was right then, Father, to think that you had carried the sword at some time in your life? Was this perhaps against the Saracen hordes?"

He gave me a brief smile. "You were quick to see the soldier in me, Sir John. Yes, I confess that in my youth, as a member of an ancient house, I entered the military service against the heathen, as we term them. What I found, however, was that in many respects they were more civilised than we. Oh, they were hard fighters for their cause, and cruel enemies, but in their way quite chivalrous. I was taken prisoner near Jerusalem, and far from being badly treated, I was most kindly received by one of their Emirs or great lords."

"But this is not what we have heard in the in England. We believe them to be barbarous and grossly cruel," I replied, quite startled to hear such words.

"I've never heard much good of these people, either," grunted Jack, whilst downing yet another cup of wine.

Father Pietro continued with his account of the Saracens. "My captor was a most cultured person. He had studied in Byzantium, and apart from his own tongue he was conversant with English and French, and he had read some of the ancient Greek and Latin authors who had been translated into Arabic. Apart from all this, he had studied, as do others of his kind, astrology and the movement of the heavenly bodies, and all manner of sciences about which we know almost nothing."

I confessed myself stunned by these revelations, having seen few of these Saracens, and then only captives who had been made servants by some of our own lords who had seen service in the East.

"I see, and were you ransomed from this Emir?"

"No. I was released after a year with all manner of kind words and gifts. I rejoined my former companions. It was then that I resolved never again to soldier against the Saracen. I left the army

FRANK PAYTON

in the Holy Land and returned here, where I entered the Church, and so you see me now. Sometimes I wonder about the Emir, my captor, what happened to him, and where he might be, but these are fruitless thoughts which lead me nowhere."

"You were lucky not to lose your head," said Jack, with his usual bluntness.

"Yes, you are right, Messer Onsloe, and every day I pray for the souls of those who did." He paused and sipped his wine. "But to other matters, Sir John. I was called earlier to give some comfort to the prisoner. He has been threatened with dire consequences should he not divulge information concerning the Lady Proserpina's capture and abduction. He is terrified of the return of your worthy lieutenant here, and his intentions."

I stopped in the middle of dividing a succulent peach with my knife. "So he should be. He was a party to a caitiff act in the taking of a young woman of noble blood. I want information, and I want it quickly. God alone knows how my Lady is being treated. I would have her back here in safety as soon as possible."

The good priest drained his cup, and rose to his feet. "I have told the prisoner that he must help you, as God will be his judge. Also that, as an honourable knight, you will not allow him to be questioned under horrible tortures. I have further said that you will no doubt reward him for any useful information he can give you. If you will not agree to these things, then I cannot help you either. Until the morning, I wish you all Good Night."

With those words he left the hall, his long robe swirling about him as he walked. I looked across at Jack, who grumbled in his beard. "One look and a touch of a cold knife would have been enough."

I shook my head. "I need Father Pietro's help as well. He has other sources of which I can take advantage. So, no knife, Jack, unless all else fails. Now I am for my bed." I stood up, and would have fallen if Giles had not leapt up caught my arm and held me upright.

Hawkwood's Sword

"You've drunk too much, Sir John, after the long day's ride. Here, I will help you." He lifted one of my arms about his shoulder, and with me leaning upon him, helped me to my chamber. Huw had also seen my state, and run on ahead. Between them they helped me onto the bed, and I lay down fully dressed, falling asleep in a moment.

Chapter 9
Pursuit

Next morning, I awoke with a thick ache in my head, and a sickness in my belly. Swinging my legs over the side of the bed, I sought to stand, but staggered and would have fallen had not Huw, who had entered the chamber on hearing my movements, caught me and helped me to sit again and recover myself.

"Shall I run to Hal Peasgood and ask him to tend you, Sir John?"

"No, I thank you. Leave me and go to break your fast, but first fetch hot water and towels, and a razor. Also, bring me fresh clothes, watered wine, a crust of bread, some of the white cheese which I like, and an apple."

He left me then, and I began to try and gather together the threads of the last evening's talk with Father Pietro and the others. I knew I would have to give the prisoner the chance to tell us what he could of the abduction if I was to retain the help and respect of the priest. Also, I hoped against hope that Hal's ministrations through the night had had a good effect on Ludovico. He must be cured of his of his wounds and the fever which had resulted from them if I was to hear his account of events, and get from him the name of the enemy I had made in Simone Boccanera's Council Chamber.

Huw returned with my clothes, followed by a servant carrying the food I had asked for. I dismissed them both, sending Huw to break his own fast in the hall.

Hawkwood's Sword

"Give my duty to Master Onsloe and Master Ashurst, and Father Pietro, if he is present, and say that I will see them later."

I took a cup of the watered wine and drank it down. I then ate some of the bread and cheese, and a bit of the apple. Straightway I felt much better. Throwing off my crumpled clothes of the last evening, I washed and shaved off four days' growth of beard, then sluiced myself down from the ewer of water. I dried myself on the towels, donned fresh clothes, and buckled my sword belt around my waist. Huw returned with clean boots into which I thrust my feet. I felt my old self once more, ready to face the day, and my comrades.

"Master Onsloe is on his way to see you, Sir John, and has two of his men outside the house."

"Very well, Huw, I'll await him here."

I sat at the table and carried on with my breakfast. Shortly afterwards, Jack lumbered into the room and stood looking out of the window.

"This is a good house, Sir John, well built with many rooms, and a fair estate withal. I would end my days as a rich man in a place such as this."

"If you stay alive long enough. Our trade has few old men. You know that."

I wondered to hear Jack speak so. It was not like him to share such thoughts with others.

"Perhaps I dream. But what about this prisoner? Are you ready to see him?"

I drank the rest of the watered wine and stood up. "Yes. We should go now and find out what we can. For the present, you can leave your men outside. Where is the priest?"

"I don't know now. He was in the hall earlier, but left as I entered."

I said nothing, but suspected that Father Pietro had gone to the prisoner. Jack led the way, and we descended dark stone steps into the undercroft of the house. There were numerous storerooms leading off a central passage. Light was provided by oil lamps set in niches in the walls. The air was fresh, but damp and cold. As I had thought, Father Pietro was there before us, seated comfortably on a wooden stool outside one of the doors. Two lanthorns burned brightly where they stood on the stone floor.

Father Pietro rose to his feet. "Good morning to you, Sir John, and to you also, Messer Onsloe." He handed me a key and pointed to the door.

I thrust the key into its hole and turned the lock. There was a cry from the inside as we entered, and a dishevelled figure backed to the far wall away from the light of our lanthorns. Clad only in braies and a torn shirt, the prisoner was a sorry figure. He was a youngish man, longhaired, and with a beard several weeks old. His eyes stared wildly, and he trembled constantly.

"He is a sorry sight, Father," I said. "Has he been badly treated already?"

"He was beaten by the Count's servants when he was first brought here, and Gaetano locked him in this dark hole with no food and little water for a week. I prevailed upon him to feed the man when I came here. Let me speak to him. I know his name is Alessandro."

Jack and I stood back as the priest went to the man. They spoke together in rapid Italian, from which I learnt little, its quickness and subtleties being too much for my knowledge of the language at that time.

"Alessandro tells me that he was recruited in a tavern by one he did not know. He was given several pieces of armour and a helmet, also a sword. On the day of the abduction, he was lent the use of a horse. He is a seaman from the ships which carry cargo between Genoa and foreign parts."

"What was he told?" I asked.

"Very little it seems, except that a gentleman of blood wished to rescue his daughter from the clutches of a nobleman who had carried her away in order to force himself upon her." He gave a wry smile. "The very reverse of the truth, it would appear."

Hawkwood's Sword

"What can he tell us of the man who approached him, and how much was he paid?"

There was another exchange of Italian, and Father Pietro continued.

"It is difficult. The man was heavily cloaked and sat in the tavern with his face in the shadow of a deep hood. As for pay, he was given five silver florins to begin with, plus the promise of a further fifteen. He is a poor man, and could not refuse such a sum."

This would not do. I could see Jack was impatient to vent his anger against the wretch. He drew a ballock knife from his belt and tapped the blade upon his left thumb. The prisoner's eyes bulged with fear.

"Does he know how the hooded man arrived at and left the tavern? Was he on foot or a-horseback? Does he remember anything of that?"

Father Pietro translated the answers to these questions. "He had a horse, which was dark brown with a white blaze down the nose."

"Anything else? Does he recall anything else about the horse, Father?" My heart had begun to pound within my breast.

Again the question, again the reply.

"Most of the left ear was shorn away," Said Father Pietro.

Startled, I looked at Jack. "Orlando Scacci!"

He nodded his head slowly. "I recall his horse from our first time here. You suspected him from the beginning; it seems that you were right. How do we get at him? Where can he be found?"

I turned to the priest. "Well, Father. Can you help me here? Can we together find Scacci? I would speak to...the source about whom you told me yesterday."

He looked me squarely in the face. "And if I do, what about Alessandro here? Will you still punish him, a poor man, who thought he was only doing right by helping a daughter be reunited with her father?"

Frank Payton

"I will keep him here, but in a better place, and with more food, drink and comforts. If all is well, and my Lady is saved, then I will free him and give him a rich reward. But he had better die now than later, if he has told me lies."

I was as blunt as I dared, as things stood.

Father Pietro nodded and touched the plain wooden cross which hung from a leather thong about his neck, as if he would draw some guidance from the holy object.

"So be it. I agree, but if you come with me, you must trust me without question. We shall go amongst the lowest of the low in Genoa, where thieves and murderers abound, and a man's life may hang upon a glance."

"I understand. I have been in dangerous places ere now. You'll have to find me suitable clothes, Father."

The priest laughed. "It seems you do know the sort of place I have in mind. Very well, I accept your judgement. Alessandro must be told before we leave."

He spoke again to the ragged seaman, who cowered against the wall. The sailor's face brightened and then took on an aspect of wonderment. I knew that must have been at the promise of the rich reward I had made. He went down on his knees in front of me spluttering out a torrent of thanks. He would have kissed the tips of my boots, but I drew back.

Jack slammed his knife back into its sheath, and snarling "Carrion!" sent the wretch sprawling with a vicious kick before stalking from the chamber.

Father Pietro's eyes met mine. "You have a cruel and hard lieutenant, Sir John."

"He has had a hard life which has treated him cruelly, Sir Priest. If you knew his tale you might think otherwise of him. Now, let us get to our own affairs without further delay."

I locked Alessandro in his underground cell, and with Father Pietro went in search of Gaetano.

Hawkwood's Sword

*****

The fat steward was seated in his chamber of business, listening to one of the servants read out details of the last grape harvest and the wine produced since the autumn. He silenced and dismissed the man, and, lumbering to his feet, bowed low to us both as we approached.

"Good morning, Signores. Have you spoken to the prisoner?"

"We have, Gaetano, and I wish you to move him now to a secure chamber on this the ground floor. It must be a very strong place, as he must not escape. If all goes well I will free him myself. In the meantime he is to be given better food and drink, plus clean water. Find him some work which he can perform in his cell. I will go to see the Count directly. Have you visited him this morning?"

Yes, indeed, Signore. He seems unchanged, but your healer may tell you more than I."

I left him then, and together with Father Pietro went up to Ludovico's chamber, which looked out to the east and was flooded with light. Hal Peasgood was busy at a small side table covered with fragrant bunches of dried herbs, and jars of God knows what. He was pounding some mixture in a mortar, and its bitter, aromatic odour assailed our nostrils.

"How is the Count in health this morning, Hal? Has he slept easily?"

"I will answer that myself, Giovanni."

I turned towards the bed to see Ludovico struggling to sit up. Hal rushed to help him; and, once laid back on the pillows, the wounded Count gave us a weak smile. "I am still very tired, but I have slept well for the first time since that dreadful day. Your Hal has achieved that, at least. It is good to see the sun, and in this chamber I can look out over part of the estate. Tell me now what you have discovered."

Thus I sat and recounted what Alessandro, the prisoner had told us. I also spoke of my early suspicion of Orlando Scacci. In addition to all this, I asked Ludovico if he recalled the name of the irate merchant who had been ordered to leave the Council Chamber by the Doge. He shook his head after a moment.

"I cannot remember, my friend. My mind and memory are not yet clear, and I find it impossible even to say what happened when we were attacked and Proserpina was taken away. Perhaps later, when the medicines have had more time to do their work, I shall remember."

"Then we must leave the matter be for the present. I am going now with Father Pietro, to see a likely source of information. Until I return, Messer Onsloe will be in command of my men here. Ask of him what you will; he will help you. He is loyal to me. For the present then I must bid you farewell." I laid my hand briefly upon his shoulder, then turned and left. He gave a wan smile, and closed his eyes once more.

*****

Father Pietro led me into a warren of mean streets in Genoa, where it seemed just as possible to get a knife between the shoulder blades as a 'Good morning' greeting. I was dressed as poorly as we could contrive, and I slouched along beside the good priest in manner suited to the rest of the population of the area.

It was a far cry from the stately palazzi and elegant squares through which I had ridden on my excursions with Proserpina, so long ago, it felt as if it had been a dream.

I had taken care to wear a mail shirt under my other clothes, and an iron skullcap was concealed by my hood. My sword I had to leave, but I carried in its stead, under my cloak, as long a dagger as I could find amongst the men who had accompanied me on the venture.

"This not a good place to be, my friend," said my guide. "Even though I am a man of the Church, I carry a stout stick as some form of defence. Many of these are just poor people, not thieves or murderers, although it is difficult to say which are which on occasion. We turn in here."

'Here' was a low sort of tavern frequented by the lower orders of Genoese people, the kind of place I had not entered for many a year. Villainous faces were on all sides, or so it seemed. Slatternly serving women moved between the rough tables, bearing jugs of wine and bowls of stew and other food, which I had to admit smelled reasonably appetising. We found a clear space at the end of one of the tables and seated ourselves.

"God save you, Father, and help your good works amongst us poor sinners," a fawning voice spoke at our side. Its owner bowed and scraped before us, but I noticed his sharp eyes slide over me like a snake over a stone.

"May I send some wine to you and your friend, Father? You know it will be of the best."

"Indeed you may, Benito. The best is your trade, is it not? Is the wine honestly bought, though? That is a another matter, I think."

Benito's thin lips twisted in what might well have been either a smile or a grimace.

"We poor sinners must make shift to look after ourselves as best we can, Father. I will send the wine."

He slipped away between the tables, and I felt the air, foul as was, a little cleaner for his going.

The wine, when it came, was good; indeed it was better than much that I had tasted since arriving in Italy. I remarked on this to Father Pietro.

He sighed. "Yes, I know. Stolen of course, and probably lives lost in the taking. But that is the way of things at this level of society."

"Bless me, Father," the serving maid had said when she brought the wine and a dish of sweetmeats. Her grimy face, rat-tailed hair and filthy garments repelled me, but her voice had been soft and low, and I wondered at this but said naught. I had begun to grasp that much at this tavern was not as it appeared at first

FRANK PAYTON

sight. The maid had knelt to receive the blessing, and despite her lowered gaze I felt her questing, appraising glance when she rose to her feet and gave us an innocent smile. She moved off to clear away cups and dishes from a nearby table, and as she disappeared behind a screen she looked back directly at me.

"Well Father, where, pray, is your informant?"

He smiled. "You have just met him, and shortly will do so again. Be patient. You must be patient. These matters take time, and money."

"I see. I fear I have little enough of the one, but am well provided with the other. As the matter now lies in your hands, I must be guided by you."

Some little time passed, during which I chafed and fretted. We sipped our wine. The affairs of the tavern went on about us, but I noticed that the fawning man did not reappear, neither did the maid. Eventually, my patience gave out.

"Enough of this waiting. This man, whoever he is, plays with me, and that I will not endure. I will bring men and tear this hovel to shreds, and teach this informant a lesson in manners. I will not be trifled with in this way." I stood up and turned for the door.

"If you go now, you will lose all. Now sit, for here comes a messenger, if I mistake me not." Father Pietro pulled at my sleeve and so, raging inwardly, I seated myself once more. In later years I became used to the slowness with which the Italians dealt with matters, even those of importance, but at first it caused me much frustration.

A boy was moving towards us between the crowded tables. He was small and dark, and to my great wonder in that place, clean of face and neatly dressed.

He passed us by and in passing said, "My name is Carlo. Please come with me."

We both finished our wine and started after him. Across the main room of the tavern we followed him. Then on to a door set in the far wall, which the boy unlocked, then relocked after we had passed through. Before us was a narrow passage, poorly lit by slits in the outer wall. Carlo hurried on ahead, and turning a corner we found ourselves at yet another door. A knock, and the door was opened from within. I grasped the hilt of my dagger as we stepped inside, and the door closed silently behind us.

"Welcome, Father Pietro. You, Signore Giovanni Haucuud, are especially welcome."

Before us, seated behind a long table littered with books of account and documents, was a man richly dressed in clothes of gold-stitched velvet. I was startled to find myself looking at the fawning tavern host who had greeted us in a most servile manner on our first arrival.

"You are surprised to see me in another guise, Signore. Behind you is your serving maid." He laughed at my confusion as I whirled about. Sitting demurely in a sunlit corner was a young lady, or so she seemed by her rich attire and jewels. She inclined her head graciously towards me, then carried on with her work upon a piece of embroidery with lowered eyes.

"My daughter, Caecilia, Signore, who is the light of my poor life. Please seat yourselves. Will you take some more wine, Father?"

I shook my head, as did the priest. I had need of a clear head and sharp wits. "I would fain know your name," I said, "so that I might commit it to memory for the future."

"Many wish to know my name, Signore, some for ill purpose. I must therefore decline to accede to your request, but if in Genoa you ask the right people for the 'Innkeeper', they will know who you mean. But now to your business, Signore Haucuud. The good Father here has spoken to me of your concern for the Lady Proserpina di Lucanti, stolen away by...but who knows who?"

"I am more than merely concerned," I said. "She is my love, my betrothed, and I would wrest her from whoever it may be who has taken her, and see them brought to punishment."

My nameless host sipped his wine. "I have asked some questions already, of those who might have heard something of the affair, but as yet I have received no replies. If is often difficult and costly to gain access to such information."

I took his meaning. "You must know that cost to me is of no consequence, but I will not be cozened. I have behind me a veritable army, which I would bring to bear if I felt that any advantage was taken of my good nature."

I took a leather bag from the wallet at my belt, and slid it across the table. The 'Innkeeper' picked it up and hefted it in his hand. His eyes met mine.

"This is a large sum, Signore. I have no cause to insult you by examining the contents of the purse. You may rely on my intense interest in this affair." He placed the bag carefully on one side. "I shall send a messenger to you at the Palazzo Lucanti as soon as I am able, with whatever I have been able to discover."

We took our leave then, and the boy Carlo took us through a maze of passages and rooms and showed us out into a street which was not the one from which we had first entered the tavern. Thence we made our way back to the Lucanti residence, where Huw awaited us with the horses.

"I note you did not say that you were not at the Palazzo," said my priestly companion, as we set off for the countryside.

I laughed. "It would not have been wise. The 'Innkeeper' is not the only one who can be secretive."

*****

Upon our return to the estate, I had all the four servants who had survived the abduction attack brought before myself and Father Pietro. They were stalwart young men, dressed alike in the di Lucanti livery of gold and green.

"What can you tell me of the attack?" I began.

They looked at each other, and at the floor. They shuffled their feet and one coughed nervously.

"Well?" I asked.

Hawkwood's Sword

"We are sorry we could not save your Lady, Signore Haccuud. Wooden staves are of little use against swords and men clad in armour."

"I do not blame you. It was not your fault, and I am told that you all fought bravely. One of your number was slain, another wounded. It is in my mind to give you all a reward, but first I must ask you some questions."

"Anything, Signore, ask us what you will," they chorused, doubtless with an eye to having my florins in their purses.

There was a great difference of opinion as to the number of attackers. There were six, or eight, perhaps, or even a dozen, or more. The men all rode black horses, no, there were three brown ones, and a grey. There was certainly no dappled one. As for the weapons, well, they all had swords, but no, perhaps there were two each armed with a mace. All this was delivered in a babble of Italian, some of which I understood, but most of which Father Pietro had to translate for me. Finally, I held up my hand for silence. Peace reigned at last.

"Think now, what colour horse did the leader have? Only one of you answer."

"A brown one, Signore, with a white blaze upon its nose. Oh, and only one ear. Its rider was the one who fought with our master, the Count. He wounded him with a thrust of his sword that caused our master to fall off his horse. The same man also snatched the reins of Lady Proserpina's mount and dragged her away."

"In which direction? This is important."

"To the north, Signore. To the north, like the wind. We looked for them no more, but attended to the Count and our wounded comrade. We also had to carry the body of poor Fabrizio back to his house, to his widow and children. He did his best, Signore, but lost his life in the Count's service."

"You also brought the prisoner Alessandro here." I added, "And gave him a good beating into the bargain."

Frank Payton

"Yes, Signore," he said shamefacedly. "Perhaps we should not have done that, but we were so angry."

"I understand, but it is good that you did not kill him in your anger, for he has told me much that I wished to know. He is only a poor seaman, not a man-at-arms."

I dismissed them then, and later gave Gaetano a purse of silver florins to share amongst them all, making sure that the widow of the dead Fabrizio received a double share. I sat back in my chair and took a sip of wine which Huw had poured for me. I pulled a face at its sourness. Father Pietro smiled.

"Your Innkeeper's wine is better than this," I said. "What do you make of all we have just heard? They are not used to the field of battle, which I think explains the confused account."

"I agree, but one thing stands out, and that is the description of the horse. Its rider would certainly appear to be Scacci. Alessandro's account is thus confirmed."

"Yes. I feel I should now seek a private audience of Simone Boccanera. He at least should remember the incident in his Council Chamber on the occasion of my first visit here. I will arrange for a letter to be sent to him without delay."

******

My letter to Boccanera was carried by Niccolo, who relished that kind of duty. I found him to be a good lad, willing to help wherever and whenever needed. As a kinsman of Ludovico and Proserpina he had entry to places where it would have been difficult for me, a foreigner, to go. He was fond of dashing about on his black mare, and loved a measure of military display, but as Roger Capsey had said when Niccolo arrived at Romagnano, he would be no match for any of us at swordplay. Later, I was able to get one of Jack Onsloe's men-at-arms to teach him a few points and tricks of fighting with the sword. It saved his life, I know, on more than one occasion.

Hawkwood's Sword

He left for Genoa in a flurry of excitement, accompanied by one of the house servants, armed this time with a sword, and I had perforce to contain my impatience until his return.

*****

To ease the passage of time, I asked Giles to ride out with me into the countryside in order to explore what lay to the northwards, where Scacci and his men had fled taking Proserpina with them. Alain Mawe came with us, and another of his ventaine, an archer from Cheshire by the name of Tom Nurley. He was a silent sort, dark and serious of face, dressed in the green and white of his kind. Giles told me that Tom had been at Poitiers, and there took captive a high born French noble, for which deed he had received a purse of gold from the Prince's own hand.

"I chose him from amongst the others, as he is said to have the long sight," Alain said. "It could be useful. He was one of our foreriders."

In addition I summoned Tesoro, the servant spokesman who had been present at the abduction, to accompany me. "For I wish to see the place where the attack took place, Tesoro."

"I will show you gladly, Signore, though my heart fears to return to such a place of sorrow."

Thus we five rode out of the walled courtyard, and through the well-ordered fields and vineyards of Ludovico's estate. It was a fine morning, and in other times I would have enjoyed the excursion, but as it was I felt myself bound by a serious intent. We came at last to a place of open grass fields, where cattle grazed under the sharp eyes of several herdsmen. I had seen Tesoro looking carefully at the ground as we passed, and so was not surprised when he suddenly reined in his horse.

"Here, Signore, is the place," he announced. "You can see where the ground is still churned up by horses' hooves." He pointed downwards.

Frank Payton

I dismounted and gave Boy's reins over to him. Giles joined me and we walked over the area, looking about us.

"Not much to be seen here," Giles said. "There has been a light rain since, and the cattle have wandered over here as well."

"As I can see, but let us see what we may find, anyway." I called to the others, "Dismount and search this area. Keep your eyes open for anything which may help."

Thus we searched about on the ground, but apart from the cut and broken pieces of the servants' staves with which they had sought to repel Orlando Scacci and his men, there was nothing. At the last, I fetched Tesoro to point out the direction in which the attackers had fled.

"As I said, Signore, to the north, over there." He pointed towards the blue shadow of low hills, which overtopped a wooded area some distance off. "That was their way. The last I saw of them was when they passed under the trees. They were riding fast until then."

"Very well, we will go the same way."

We all took to horse again and headed for the woods, which were about three miles away, by my reckoning. Gradually the trees grew in our sight until we were right under the apron of the woods. The trees were dark and old, a tangle of chestnut, walnut and oak, with an undergrowth of young trees and bushes. We paused at this barrier, and Giles spoke up.

"Now then, Tom, you're a forester, I'm told. Find us a way through these woods, if there be one."

Tom pushed his archer's helmet back from his forehead and scratched his brow. "I'll have to ride along a bit, Master Ashurst, there's no way here." He set off, first to our right, ambling along and looking at both the ground and the trees, disappearing from our sight at intervals, either in folds in the earth, or amongst the trees. At about a half-mile away he turned back, and eventually rejoined us.

Hawkwood's Sword

"There's naught that way, Sir John," he reported, as he passed us, going to our left.

I slid from Boy's saddle and let him wander off a little to graze. The others followed suit, and we threw ourselves on the lush springy grass to rest. I pulled a stalk of grass from its leafy sheath and sucked at its sweet wetness, and thought of Proserpina and when we found our love, high on the sunlit hills above Genoa. The sun was warm on my face, and I began to slide into a dreaming sleep that was abruptly interrupted.

A hoarse call from Tom, away to our left by some hundreds of yards, made us spring to our feet. We swiftly recovered the horses and swung up once more into the saddle. A quick canter, and we clustered around the dour archer who wordlessly handed me a scrap of green silk surely rent from a woman's apparel.

I held it to my face and smelled again the perfume which, although faded, I knew to be the one favoured by Proserpina.

"I found that caught on a bush over there, Sir John. It be from a lady's dress I reckon, and there's an opening in the trees, and the tracks of about eight or nine horses, I'd say."

"That was well done, Tom. I'll not forget it. Let us see where this path leads us. Keep a sharp lookout for any more traces of their passage. Tesoro, is this the colour my Lady wore that day?"

He nodded silently, with a sad face.

I tucked the piece of silk into the scrip at my belt, and urged Boy forward, following Tom into the cool, green shade. The wood was quiet; any birds which had been singing had fallen silent at our approach. There was an earthy, mouldy smell of last year's decaying leaves.

"This path was used, not long ago," Tom said. "There's hoof marks going back as well as forward. I'll wager this is the way your lady was brought, Sir John."

"We shall see. Can you see through to the other side of this wood?"

"Not yet. It's thick grown, and has not been tended for years. The path is still good though."

Frank Payton

We carried on in silence for at least another mile before the tangle of trees and bushes thinned out a little. I reined in and held up my hand to stop the others, then sent Tom forward on foot to see what he might.

After a short time he turned and beckoned me to join him. I dismounted and followed. Still keeping within the shelter of the trees, we stood looking out over rolling open countryside. Tom pointed away to a range of low hills, a little to the right.

"There, Sir John: a big house, or a small castle. See that tower? To the left is a village, I reckon. See, there are red roofs."

"You have eyes like an eagle, Tom, but yes, I can just make out where you mean. Now, if there is a tower, a lookout should be able to see any approach in daylight. That is, if there lies the place we are seeking—and we don't know that yet. We'll go back now."

We returned to the others and remounted our horses. Then we retraced our way through the woods. As we did I wondered if I was riding away from Proserpina, but I had no other course. It would be folly to take armed men against an innocent household and village. I had to await the outcome of my talks with Boccanera, and I needed word of Scacci from the Innkeeper.

*****

I dismounted at the door of Ludovico's estate house. Rummaging in my small saddlebag, I took out an apple which I had saved and offered it to Boy, holding it on the flat of my hand. He took it, crunching the fruit in his large teeth with enjoyment. I stroked my hand down his nose, and he threw up his head as a horse will, and suffered Huw to lead him off to the stables. Giles went off with the two archers, and the servants returned to their duties under Gaetano's sharp eyes.

"He is a very big horse, Signore," said Niccolo, who had been awaiting my return.

HAWKWOOD'S SWORD

I laughed at his admiration. "And a very brave one. He has never failed me in a charge into battle, and has killed men with his hooves. More than once he has passed through fire for me, which is something most of his kind will not do. Once we had to swim a raging river to escape pursuers, but he did it for me. Now, what word do you have for me from the Doge? First, however, come into the Great Hall, as there may be those out here with large ears for what they should not hear."

I took off my helmet as I spoke and gave it to Niccolo to carry for me; I unbuckled my sword-belt and carried it slung over my shoulder. My face felt hot, and I wiped the sweat away with a corner of my jupon, and several times ran my fingers through my hair, which felt as though harvest mice were running about in it.

There was no one in the Great Hall, and I sat down in a carven wooden chair near a window which looked out over the ornamental garden. The thought came to me that it was there that I saw the dark shadow of Orlando Scacci on the moonlit night of soft hoofbeats, and my later dream of the carrying off of Proserpina. These thoughts were interrupted by a servant who ran into the Hall to ask what I required. I waved him way, not wanting to begin wine drinking so early, and certainly not before taking some food. Niccolo stood waiting.

"Now then, what sayeth the Doge?"

"His Excellency invites you to a small reception at his residence on the morrow, Signore."

"Is the Doge aware of why I am here once more in Liguria?"

"I... I think so, Signore," stammered the boy, clearly somewhat embarrassed.

"I see, and had he enquired of you concerning the matter?"

"Yes, Signore. I said merely that it involved your intended marriage to the Lady Proserpina. He seemed satisfied with my reply."

An idea was forming in my mind. It might be that Boccanera had deduced the real reason for my visit, knew something of the matter and had issued the invitation to divert the curious.

Frank Payton

"Was the Doge's Secretary present at your interview with Messer Boccanera?"

"No, Signore."

That was something worthy of note, I thought. "Thank you, Niccolo. You have done very well, and I shall not forget this service. There is, however, one more thing which you can do for me, if you are willing."

He brightened, as if at first he had feared dismissal. "Of course, Signore, anything."

"On the morrow, I wish you to ride out on the road towards Milan, and keep a look out for a traveller on a grey horse. If you find the right man, it will be Marco Bandini, though he will be poorly dressed, and mayhap dirty and muddy. Do you remember him?"

"Your squire, Signore? Yes, I remember him. I will do as you wish, early in the morning. When I meet him, what shall I say?"

"Tell him to come here, clean himself and change into his best apparel. He must then ride to the Doge's residence. I will need him there."

"And if I do not find him, Signore? What then? Shall I seek you in Genoa?"

"In either event, come to the Doge's residence, with Marco or without him. Be off with you swiftly now. I shall visit the Count."

I thrust myself away from the comfort of the chair and made my way to Ludovico's room, where I knew I would also find Father Pietro. I arrived to find the Count sitting in a chair, and was greeted with a smile. His face was still pale and haggard. The sword wound had woefully sapped his strength, and the red velvet robe which wrapped about him showed his much reduced frame. Grey hairs showed above his brow, and he was certainly very ill, but he tried manfully to make his voice strong and clear.

"Giovanni! It is good to see you. You find me in better point than of late, but I am still very tired. What have you to say to me today? I hear you have been out and about in my countryside. Have you found anything of use or interest?"

"I am pleased to find you in good spirits," I said. "And, yes, I think our ride today has renewed my hopes. If it does not tire you, I will tell of our discoveries."

Thus I gave him and Father Pietro a good account of the day, but before I had finished Ludovico had fallen into sleep. I looked at the priest. He laughed quietly.

"I am afraid your talk has sent our friend to sleep. It will do no harm, and you can repeat the details tomorrow. I will fetch Hal Peasegood to him, and between us we will put Ludovico back in his bed. Do not worry: I shall look in from time to time, and your healer is very attentive to his duties."

"It is well I brought him here," I said. "I will leave Ludovico in your care for the night. Shall you be at the evening meal? Yes? Then I shall see you there."

I left Ludovico's chamber with a heavy heart, hoping that Proserpina would be found and brought home before an even greater tragedy visited her family.

*****

Simone Boccanera received his guests in the private garden with its sun-sparkled fountains, bright flowers and fragrant herbs, where a few short months before we had met to discuss the business of recruiting crossbowmen for the Company. The captive leopard still lounged lazily in his cage and gazed listlessly at the onlookers who had gathered to view the unusual beast at close quarters. Several unhooded falcons were also displayed, shifting uneasily on their perches, stretching out their wings and flexing their razored talons. Unlike many, I have a dislike for these birds, since as a boy I had seen a hawk stoop on to a man's head and tear out one of his eyes.

I had left Savignone early that morning together with Giles, Huw and Alain Mawe, together with four archers from his

FRANK PAYTON

ventaine. Jack Onsloe remained behind in command. As before, Giles and I had arrayed ourselves in rich attire with gold chains and other jewellery in an effort to match the brilliance of the Genoese. Huw was also dressed as befitted the page to a knight of my standing. The three of us were met by the Doge's Secretary, Antonio Certaldo. He greeted us gravely, clad in sombre black, although I noted that his attire was of the finest quality. His sole concession to decoration was an engraved signet ring worn on the fourth finger of his right hand. He bowed low.

"It is an honour and a pleasure to welcome you once more, Signore Haccuud. His Excellency had heard that you were nearby at the Savignone estate, and hastened to renew his acquaintance with you. Perhaps you will take some refreshment?"

He crooked a finger at a passing servant who bore a tray of silver cups which brimmed with red wine. We each took one and inclined our heads in thanks. I raised my cup.

"Thank you for your greetings, Messer Certaldo. We drink to the health of His Excellency, to your good self, and to the continued prosperity of the city of Genoa."

"That is most kind, and similarly I wish you good fortune," he replied, and bowing, melted away into the throng.

"Black crow!" muttered Giles, tossing down the contents of his cup and looking around for more. "These people make my blood run cold, with their black clothes and fawning manners. I wouldn't trust him with a farthing of mine. Give me a plain spoken archer or man-at-arms, say I."

"So say we all, Giles, but these are the people we need to help us for the nonce. We must perforce play the game on the board of their choosing, and in their fashion. Now, come with me over to the corner there, and I promise you will see a rare sight."

We moved towards where I knew the Doge's leopard was held and jostled with the crowd to see the beast. Giles gazed round-eyed at the sight of the huge spotted cat as it lay with one large paw placed to hold down a large piece of meat, at which it tore with bloodied ivory teeth.

Hawkwood's Sword

"God's Blood, Sir John, I'd not like to meet that demon without my sword to hand. It would be fine to hunt it down with bow in hand and arrow on string, though." He turned to me bright-eyed at the thought, and then touched my arm. "Here comes one who seeks you, I think."

I looked over to where he pointed, and saw the richly clad figure of Simone Boccanera walking towards me through the throng, which parted respectfully at his passage.

"Yes, Giles, he does. It is the Doge, the most powerful man in Genoa, so mind your manners."

"Signore Giovanni! It is good to see you in our midst again, so soon after your last visit." He extended his hand in welcome, and lowered his voice. "It is a sorrowful errand on which you come amongst us again, and we shall talk later upon the matter." Raising his voice, he spoke again. "I see you have a different companion, am I to make his acquaintance?"

Thus I presented Giles, who took the Doge's hand and bowed low.

"Master Ashurst is our Captain of Archers, Your Excellency. He has been comparing methods with Messer Andreas Varazzo, who leads your crossbowmen presently in our service."

"Ah yes, our Messer Varazzo. I am sure he and his men will acquit themselves with honour. Now, Signore, my master cook has prepared a simple repast for all, and I should be pleased if you would accompany me at the table. Also there is with us this day an English merchant, new come to Genoa, and I am sure he and Messer Ashurst will find much to discuss."

At that the whole company moved in the wake of the Doge to take their places at the horseshoe of tables which had been arranged in the shaded part of the garden. I had time only for a hurried word with Giles before we separated, and told him to discover as much as he could of what was passing in England, which might be of interest and use.

The "simple repast" proved to be a rich collation of savoury lasagnes, raviolis and pastries, the latter wonderful in their shapes and presentation, as were the sweetmeats which followed them. Pastry and sugar had been moulded into the forms of birds, small beasts and flowers, all coloured with culinary dyes and glazed with honey. Placed about the table were wondrous arrangements of many types of fruit, most of which we English had never seen before. One caught my eye: a yellow, tough-skinned fruit in the shape of a strung bow, which was joined to its fellows in the form of a hand. I ate one, and found its interior rich and creamy, like new butter. I never learned its name, and have seen few others since. All this food was accompanied by the finest wines, both red and white, the latter chilled in silver pails filled with iced water.

The meal also reminded me that Huw was standing obediently, and foodless, behind my chair, also that I had forgotten the presence of Alain Mawe and his men. Concerned, I spoke of this matter to the Doge. He laughed and assured me that food and drink had been taken to them. I sent Huw off to take his own meal in their company forthwith.

I was anxious to raise the matter of Proserpina's abduction, but was prevented by the company at the table. Furthermore, I wondered if Marco had been found. Eventually, to my great relief, a servant approached the Doge and, leaning down, whispered some message which I did not hear. The Doge's reply however, was heartening.

"Bring them in, and find places at the table for Signore Giovanni's squire and Messer Niccolo della Sera." Boccanera turned to me with a smile. "Your squire Bandini is here, accompanied by Niccolo, Count Savignone's nephew. Perhaps we will be able, shortly, to turn our attention to the matter which has brought you here."

"I am relieved to see them, Your Excellency. Messer Bandini is a most valuable aide to me, and before my departure from Romagnano he was despatched on an errand of great importance. I eagerly await his news."

"And am I right in thinking that young Niccolo is now also a member of your Company?"

Hawkwood's Sword

It was my turn to laugh at such a suggestion. "He has proved to be very useful to me at times, but I fear that his youth and inexperience do not fit him for the sterner work of campaigning. Perhaps in time he may make a soldier, but now..."

I left the rest unsaid. I did not say also that it was in my mind for the future to make more use of Niccolo's eagerness to serve, but in the role of a secret agent. Privately, I had long seen it as essential for future success to build up a web of such people. Niccolo had useful connections, and entry through many doors closed to me at the time, and by using these advantages I sought to make gains denied to others.

The meal proceeded with much talk on many matters of mutual interest to the Doge and his intimate circle, and of course myself. I looked down the length of the table to see Marco and Niccolo talking animatedly as they ate and drank with great relish, as young men will when bound up with great enterprises. They were good companions for each other, and I could see that Marco's seniority of experience was a great attraction for the younger lad. My instructions to Marco, to clean himself up and array himself as befitted my squire, had been carefully carried out. All traces of the dusty traveller I had seen, only days before, had vanished. In their place was a sturdy young man of somewhat serious mien in red and black velvet, with some small show of heavy gold here and there. His sword would have been left with Alain Mawe, but I had seen a plain serviceable dagger at his right hip when he entered the garden. Niccolo's youth, bright clothes of the latest fashion, jewelled dagger, and general air of scarcely subdued excitement was in complete contrast. I could see however, that beneath this exterior show he was beginning to acquire a little of the manner of his companion, and this pleased me greatly.

The meal concluded, the guests began to depart, and at last the Doge summoned me and the others to his private rooms, where we could talk without fear of interruption. Of the Doge's staff, only Messer Certaldo was present. As we followed Boccanera, Marco plucked at my sleeve.

Frank Payton

"A moment, Sir John. There is something I must tell you, one thing only; the rest can be told later. Von Felsingen and Harzmann are in the pay of Milan! They will sell you and Sterz as prisoners to Bernabo, and take as many of the Company as will go with them into his service!"

I was not surprised at this news, but at the confirmation of my suspicions my mind whirled in furious confusion, and I had but little time to compose myself before we were ushered into the Doge's withdrawing room. Boccanera seated himself upon a carved wooden chair and waved me to another. Certaldo stood by his master, and my people ranged themselves beside and behind me.

"How can I help you, Signore Giovanni?" Boccanera asked.

"By giving me the name of the person who caused the uproar in your Council Chamber, when I first visited Genoa. As I recall, he quarrelled with Messer Grimani, who had been present at Crecy Field. He was against me hiring Genoese crossbowmen for the White Company, and made his feelings towards me, personally, very plain."

"And what will this avail you? Do you suspect this man of some wrong doing?"

"I do. I believe him to be the person behind the abduction of the Lady Proserpina di Lucanti, but what he intends now, I know not. I have had no approaches from him, nor anyone on his behalf. My Lady has simply disappeared."

"I understand your reasoning, Signore, but I cannot agree with it. There would be no point to an abduction by that man. His life is bound up with trade and commerce. It is extremely unlikely that he would venture into such an activity, even to spite you. No, I think we must look elsewhere for the culprit. Is the man Orlando Scacci known to you?"

"Yes he is, and I know that he was involved from information given me by the di Lucanti servants who were present. On my first visit he appeared to be very close to the Count, but for some reason has turned against him."

Hawkwood's Sword

The Doge laughed. "You are quite right in this, but you seem not to realise that you are the reason. He is a member of the minor nobility, a landowner in his own right, and had high hopes of taking Proserpina to wife himself. Until your arrival this was almost an accomplished fact, though Proserpina herself was not in favour. If nothing else she saw in you an escape from, to her, an unsuitable marriage. You will know her feelings for yourself better then anyone."

"You are right, we are resolved to be man and wife, and I should tell you we have the blessing of the Count, her brother. Now, where does Scacci's land lie? I do not intend to delay further before freeing my Lady from her prison."

"I understand your concern, but I council you not to rush into action before taking advice. I believe you to be acquainted with a person known only as the Innkeeper. Is that correct?"

I nodded my head, and wondered where all this was leading. I chafed to be told where Proserpina was being held. At the same time I realised that I needed as much information as could be gathered to give me the advantage over my enemies in this affair. Patience had to be my watchword.

"Yes, though I have met him but once only. He offered his help —at a price."

The Doge gave me a thin smile. "I can imagine. Do you trust him?"

"I trust none who deal in secret matters for money, not when a young woman's honour and life are at stake."

"Then I should tell you that he came to me after your visit in the company of Father Pietro, and told me of your search for the Lady Proserpina. I have dealt with him before, and I am familiar with his methods. It was he who told me that Scacci is the villain you seek. He had discovered that Lady Proserpina was taken to Scacci's estate, which is to the north of Savignone. In addition, he now tells me that she was moved from there two weeks ago. He does not know where, and has tried but failed to discover her present whereabouts. What he asked of me is my support in his acquisition of Scacci's property when he is brought to justice. I said that I would seek your opinion on the matter. A criminal forfeits property when found guilty. It could be yours, if you desired it, or the Lady Proserpina's."

"I care not for Scacci's property; my sole concern is to recover my Lady and restore her to her family. With your permission, or without it, I shall take my men and attack the estate village. Once having prevailed, I shall extract from Scacci, or whoever remained behind, the whereabouts of Proserpina. Then I shall march on that place."

As I spoke these words, the door to the chamber swung open to admit a servant, who bowed to us all. The Doge's Secretary hurried over to him and there followed a short whispered exchange. The servant left and Certaldo returned to stand by his master, leaning down to deliver a message *sotto voce*.

Boccanera looked startled, then frowned, and spoke to Certaldo behind his hand. Finally, he turned to me.

"It seems we are to hear more from your mysterious friend, Signore Haccuud. He has arrived at the Palazzo, and is now being brought to us here. We may hope perhaps that he has heard something more of the whereabouts of Lady Proserpina."

At this the door reopened, and through it stepped the man I had met at the tavern. He was neatly dressed in black, wore a costly gold chain about his neck, and there was a sparkle of jewelled rings upon his hands. He gave no sign of awe or emotion at the imposing surroundings, and merely advanced to a point before us all, and bowed.

"Good day, Your Excellency, Signore Haccuud, gentles. I see that I am in most distinguished company."

"You are, Innkeeper," said Boccanera, "And your arrival is most timely. I am discussing the unfortunate affair of the Lady Proserpina di Lucanti with Signore Haccuud, who will no doubt be eager to hear what further knowledge you have been able glean, if any."

Hawkwood's Sword

The Innkeeper bowed once more. "I have discovered that the unfortunate lady has been moved yet again, only yesterday. I was not able to ascertain the destination, but there was some rumour that it may have been to a convent. More I cannot say. As you are well aware, Excellency, there are several in this area. It would be a task beyond my resources to discover which is the right one."

I rose to my feet. "Innkeeper, I thank you for your efforts on my behalf. Now it seems that I shall have to follow my own instincts in the matter. The direct course of action is sometimes the best. I bid you good day, Your Excellency, and thank you for your help and hospitality. To you, Innkeeper, again my thanks. I shall ensure that you are amply rewarded when this affair is over."

Boccanera stood and extended his hand to me. "Good fortune attend you, Signore. I hope that you will find your lady unharmed." And in a lower voice, "It would be advisable to have the blessing of Mother Church on this venture, since a house of religion is involved, however innocently, in this sorry affair."

We clasped hands in farewell, and I resolved to seek the good offices of Father Pietro on my behalf. With that we left the Doge's Palace and took horse for the Savignone estate. Before we left, however, I spoke to Alain Mawe, leaning down from Boy's saddle.

"Alain, there is with the Doge a man known as the Innkeeper. Stay here, and when he leaves, as he doubtless will in a short time, follow him with two of your men. At a suitable point and time, I want you to accost him and say that he is to come to the Count's estate, and that you will be his escort. Make sure that he does not escape you, but do not harm him. Say only that I wish to speak to him further."

Alain nodded. "How shall I know this man, Sir John?"

"He is small of stature, dressed in black. His hair is black and curling, and presently he wears a gold chain about his neck."

"It shall be done, even as you say," said Alain, stepping back and raising his hand in as salute.

As we rode away, I told Giles what I had asked Alain to do.

Frank Payton

"Then the Innkeeper is as good as at Savignone already. Alain is a good man. There are not many better."

We rode on, my mind awhirl with plans.

*****

On arrival at the estate, I hastened to my quarters to exchange my finery for more sober dress. Apart from other matters, I needed to hear from Marco what had happened, both on his journey to Milan and thence south to Genoa.

As a consequence of his news, it would now be necessary to send a rider to Romagnano to warn John Brise and Albrecht of the coming storm, for a storm it would be if von Felsingen caused actual strife within the Company. I was assailed on two fronts, and great care was needed if I was not to fail on either, or both.

I sent Huw to fetch Marco, and he alone, to me. I wanted to hear his news and keep to myself what I deemed needful for only me to know, and broadcast only what others needed to know in order to carry out their part in these affairs.

When Marco entered the chamber I noted that, like myself, he had resumed his usual attire. We clasped hands, and I embraced him as a father does his son.

"It is good to see you again, Marco. I have had fears for your safety ever since we parted on your road to Milan."

"It is good to be back, Sir John. Even I had doubts at times. However, once at da Lucca's house, I knew I was safe. The old man sends you his good wishes in all that you do."

"Sit down with me, my lad, and tell me of your adventures. But first, what of Genevra?"

"She appears to me more beautiful than before, even more so than I remember. She also sends you her warmest greetings."

"And...?" I asked with raised eyebrows.

Hawkwood's Sword

"She... she seemed pleased to see me again, and I her. But I am still only a humble soldier, Sir John, whereas she has a rich father, and lives in a fine house, with servants to attend her."

"Know, Marco, that you are now squire to a belted knight of England. It also lies within my power to raise you to knighthood at the proper and appropriate time, according to the laws of chivalry. Even now you may hold up your head in any fine company."

"Is this true?" he cried, leaping to his feet. "Is this really so? Then I owe you an even greater debt than I thought. If I can attain high rank, then I may aspire to Genevra's hand in marriage. Sir John, you would make me very happy, and eternally grateful."

"We must hope that nothing happens to spoil this dream. Now sit, and take some wine, which Huw has brought for us, and let me hear of the time after we parted in the north, until you arrived in Genoa today."

*****

We passed through the night-silent forest and reformed on its northern edge, dividing into two main groups, one commanded by Jack and the other by Giles. I kept Marco, Huw, Father Pietro, three men-at-arms and two archers with me. Ludovico rode by my side. He was scarcely recovered from his woulds, but he insisted upon riding, for he said, finding his sister would do more than any medicine to restore him. I had spoken with Father Pietro at length, telling him all that the Innkeeper had told us. It was in Pietro's mind that the convent of the Holy Mother would be where Orlando Scacci might have taken Lady Proserpina; it was secluded, and dark rumours were told of it. But I needed confirmation and hoped to find it from Scacci's men, for I could not go about blindly raiding convents.

Jack's group set off to the left, Giles' to the right, to encircle the hamlet. They rode off at a canter and were swallowed up in the gloom. I intended to ride for Scacci's manor house straight across

Frank Payton

the open meadows. There would be little noise from the horses' hooves, as we would be on grass.

"When shall we go, Giovanni?" Ludovico was anxious to be off.

"Calm yourself. We will wait for a little longer," I replied. "The others must be in place before us, and they have a longer ride. Don't be too concerned, my friend. I am as anxious as you to begin this action."

We waited for what seemed an age. Marco was the first to speak. "Sir John, there is a faint lightening of the sky in the east."

I looked away to my right. "So I see. Good, we will leave now," I said, and shook Boy's reins, urging the horse forward. Ludovico was on my right, Marco to my left. Huw followed, carrying my pennon on a light lance in his stirrup. The men-at-arms and archers brought up the rear.

I rode with a mind full of anxiety, and an eye to the east. The faint but growing light of dawn was spreading up the sky, putting out the stars as if unseen fingers poked them out of being, one by one. How long until the sunrise, I wondered. How far to the hamlet? Who or what would we find there? We cantered on over the thick grass sodden with the dew of morning. Its fresh smell brought memories of English fields.

Of a sudden the golden rays of the sun struck across the meadows, and at last we had a clear view of the hamlet and the tower, not two hundred paces away. Even as I looked, a figure appeared on the parapet. Placing his hands on the stonework, he looked towards the sun—and then slowly his gaze turned towards us. He leaned forward and stared. For a moment too long, he stared at our approach. As he began to turn away, a solitary archer on horseback near the foot of the tower raised his bow, drew, and loosed.

The arrow struck the watcher under the jaw and passed on into his brain. I knew he would be dead before his body slid to the ground. By this time we had reined in at the foot of the tower, to be greeted by a grinning Giles.

Hawkwood's Sword

"A good shot," I told him. "Is all well?"

"Aye, Sir John. We are all around the house, and there are others guarding the village. I've seen Jack. He's over by the main door, at the other side."

"Do you know this place, Ludovico?" I asked him.

"Not well, but I have been here once or twice. The main door leads directly into the Great Hall. There are other doors leading out of the kitchens and storerooms."

"We've men at all the doors," said Giles. "Jack wants to break in now."

We all dismounted, and Huw took Boy's reins. I drew my sword, closed my visor and settled my shield on my left arm. The others followed suit.

"Giles," I said. "Go around to Jack and tell him to raise a clamour at the main door, as if breaking in. We'll unbar the door ourselves once inside. Now let's get to it."

He rode off, and we started for the rear doors. As I had half expected, some servants were already at their duties and the doors were open. I strode into the kitchen. An empty iron cooking pot clanged on to the stone floor as one of the cooks turned and saw me. He stood as if turned to stone, eyes starting from his head. I placed the point of my sword at his throat. His eyes bulged with fear. Another servant entered.

"*Silenzio!*" hissed Marco's voice behind me. The two men froze.

"Stay and keep these two quiet," I ordered Wat, one of the men-at-arms.

I left the kitchen, followed by the rest, through a buttery and into the Great Hall. It was lofty, with windows giving on to a paved area which faced the sunrise. To one side was a stair which I surmised led to sleeping quarters. At the far end a railed gallery extended from side to side. Also in that wall was another door.

"Marco, go forward and unbar the main door. Dickon, Roger, you go with him. Tell Jack and three more to enter. We'll see who we have caught in this fine net. Follow me, and keep your shields up." I sprang for the stairway. The others surged after me.

Frank Payton

Halfway up I heard the rattle of a door latch. A man emerged from a chamber at the end of the gallery. He was clad only in braies and a shirt, but carried a drawn sword. Behind him came another with a crossbow, spanned and loaded. He sighted briefly and pulled the lever. The bolt glanced off my raised shield, and I rushed forward. The bowman retreated into the chamber to reload. The swordsman came to meet me, his weapon raised. I beat it down with my shield, and smashed him on side of his head with the flat of my sword. He staggered and fell to the floor. "*Basta*! Stop!" I yelled through the open door. The bowman still struggled to reload, but on seeing me in the room, dropped his weapon and backed away. Ludovico came behind me and kicked the bow out the door.

I went to the door and called to the others. "See if the other rooms are occupied. Mind, they may be armed."

A groan returned my attention to the swordsman. He was trying to pick himself up off the floor, and reaching for his sword. The effort was too much, and he slumped against the wall, hands to his head.

"Rafaello!" said Ludovico, stooping over him. He looked up at me. "This is Orlando's younger brother. I know him well."

"Ask him where Orlando is, and Proserpina," I said.

Father Pietro came along the gallery. "There is only one elderly lady and her maid in the end room. The others are empty."

Ludovico stood up. "He knows nothing. He arrived with his cousin Lorenzo two days ago. Orlando had gone from here before then. I have told him who you are and why you are here. He is horrified at what Orlando has done."

I slammed my sword back into the sheath and raised my visor. "We must find one who knows," I said. "Who is the old lady, Father?"

"Her maid tells me that she is the Signora Margherita, Orlando's grandmother. She says also that her mistress is very old and frail, but that her mind is clear."

Hawkwood's Sword

"If so, she can tell us where Orlando is. Tell her I wish to see her."

By this time Jack was running up the stairway. He took in the scene at one glance. Rafaello had regained his feet and leaned unsteadily against the wall. Lorenzo stood in the doorway of the bedchamber, looking dejected.

"It looks as though we're too late," said Jack. He turned to Dickon. "Go down to Master Ashurst and tell him to stand the men down. They are to keep alert, mind. So, Sir John, what now?"

Father Pietro returned. "The Signora will see you shortly, and will send her maid when she is ready. In the meantime, I suggest we all repair to the Hall."

I was not ready for that, and said so. "No. We will search about up here, to see what may be found, if anything, which can help us. Then we will speak to the servants. The promise of gold might loosen their tongues."

This further setback served only to increase the feeling of anger and helplessness which boiled and seethed in my breast. Was there to be no end to this purgatory? I longed only to find, and beat this goddamned Orlando into a bloody pulp. Then I could take Proserpina into my arms once more. We would be married as soon as possible thereafter.

The search of the upper floor revealed nothing, and we descended the stairway to the Hall. I threw my shield on the long table, took off my helmet and dropped it on top.

"Fetch the servants from the kitchen, Marco. Go with him, Huw, and you two as well," I indicated the men-at-arms. "Find out if there are others, and bring them all here."

They soon returned, pushing the servants before them: two cooks, a scullion, and a young boy who was clearly terrified.

"These are only the kitchen servants, Sir John," said Marco. "There must be others. We'll search about for them. Come on, Niccolo."

Eventually we gathered over a dozen more: ostlers, gardeners, labourers and the like—but none who ranked any higher; no steward, secretary nor similar person. Rafaello and Lorenzo were also brought down into the Hall, where we could keep a watchful eye on them.

"It looks as though Scacci moved away in the nick if time," said Jack, frowning. "Perhaps he had word of your intentions."

"It's very likely," I agreed, "but how? We did not meet the Innkeeper again until yesterday. If Scacci left two days ago that would be when my Lady was removed from here. The Innkeeper would not have known so soon that we would come here today. No, that cannot be the answer. But now we need to know where Scacci has gone—"

I broke off as a woman began to descend the stair from the upper floor. She stopped and called out when halfway down. "The Lady Margherita will see the Count Savignone, and the Inglesi Signore. None other."

"Come, Ludovico, let us go up," I said. "Jack, whilst we are gone, you and Marco take these servants severally into another place and find out what they know of their master's movements. See if they can give us any idea of the direction in which he went. Most importantly, I want to know how the Lady Proserpina fared here. Don't let the servants speak to the others after you have spoken to them. Keep them separate."

We ascended the stair. Her Ladyship's maid waited at the top, a pleasant-faced middle-aged woman in plain dark blue. Her dark hair was partly covered by a folded white cloth. "Please follow me, signores," she said, bobbing a brief courtesy.

The Lady Margherita Scacci received us seated in a carven wooden armchair. Although of great age, she retained a remarkable dignity and bearing. Dressed in black with her face framed in an elaborately folded snow-white wimple, she sat with her fine hands folded in her lap. Above an aquiline nose and high cheekbones, keen black eyes regarded us. I was reminded of Taddea, Proserpina's elderly companion and childhood nurse, but whilst Taddea was a small black sparrow, this woman was a she-eagle. She ignored me.

Hawkwood's Sword

"So, Ludovico di Lucanti, you come seeking your sister in the company of an Inglesi ruffian, whose army is notorious for the rapine and plunder of defenceless people. He would presume to take Proserpina to wife, I hear. This upstart would rise above a noble of Roman lineage?"

Ludovico was enraged by this barb, and showed it. "My Lady Margherita! You insult the Signore Haccuud, who is a noble knight of England. He has the approval of his King, and the favour of the Prince of Wales, who is renowned throughout the world as the very flower of chivalry. You do him a discourtesy, and whilst his command of our tongue is yet imperfect, he will no doubt have understood enough to feel insulted by your words."

The black eyes turned towards me. "Is this true, Signore?"

"Quite true, Signora," I replied. "My lineage may not be noble, but my family has been honest far longer than many members of noble families have been rogues."

"A bold answer, Signore. If your sword is as sharp as your tongue, you will go far." The shadow of a smile lay upon her pale lips. "If I am honest, I will say that I do not approve of Orlando's actions of late—but I am only an old woman. No longer can I guide him in the right ways. He heeds me not."

"I will be bolder, My Lady," I said. "Will you tell me where your grandson has taken Proserpina? A lady such a she should not be dragged about the countryside like a captive."

"If you can tell us, please do so," pleaded Ludovico. "I fear for her safety."

"I cannot tell you. I do not know," she said. "Orlando came to me two, or perhaps three, days ago. I cannot remember now. He told me he would not be far away, that I could call him at need, but he would not say where he would be. Arnaldo, the steward, will know. Find him."

"Thank you, my Lady," I said. "Proserpina will be grateful."

I bowed to the old dame and left her chamber, followed by Ludovico. As we began to descend the stair, the maid came out and called to us.

Frank Payton

"Signores, my Lady would have you send Rafaello and Lorenzo to her."

We gained the ground once more, and found the two young men sitting at the end of the long table. They both had glum faces. Since they had been disarmed, and the upper floor searched for any other weapons, I had no reason to keep them from their grandmother, and so sent them off.

Jack had not been idle. All the servants had been taken off one by one and questioned by him, with Marco and Niccolo acting as translators. Not much detail had been forthcoming, beyond the fact that Proserpina been taken away. Orlando had no more than five men, all his friends or their personal henchmen. Proserpina had ridden her own horse, but her hands had been tied to the saddle-bow and the reins held by one of her captors. One of the female servants had volunteered the information that "Lady Proserpina appeared very downcast and sad."

Telling me this, Marco added, "I have kept this woman away from the others, as she seemed to be sympathetic to your Lady."

"Good lad. Take me to her. Perhaps she will have more to say." I called Jack over. "Take some men and search this place. I believe the steward was left here. His name is Arnaldo. Take Niccolo with you. He can call out Arnaldo's name; the man might give himself away."

"This woman's name is Clara, Sir John," said Marco, as we walked towards a small room set off at the side of the main kitchen.

Clara was a kindly middle-aged woman in a peasant's plain brown dress. She wore a white barmcloth about her ample waist, and a linen kerchief over her greying hair. On seeing me enter, she backed away to the opposite wall and stood clasping her hands anxiously. Her wooden clogs scraped on the stone floor.

"She's frightened, Sir John," said Marco, at my shoulder. "Though I've told her no harm will come to her."

Hawkwood's Sword

"Tell her, again," I said, smiling at her. She responded with a slight twist of her lips.

"Does she have any idea where Proserpina has been taken?" I asked.

After a brief exchange in Italian which I could scarce understand, he said, "She is a very simple woman, and does not really know what all this is about. She thinks the Lady Proserpina guilty of a crime, and that she was being taken away to be punished." He shrugged his shoulders in dismissal and turned up the palms of his hands.

"God's Blood, Marco!" I shouted. "Is the woman mad? Find out what she heard, for I guess she heard something or we would not be here with her now."

Another question, answered in a faint voice.

"Clara says that the day before Lady Proserpina was taken away, she was cleaning the floors in the house. Scacci and two of his friends were sitting in the Hall, drinking. She had not realised that her sweeping was taking her closer and closer to them, until she was startled when one of the men shouted angrily for her to leave the Hall immediately. All the drinkers glared at her, and she was so frightened that she dropped her broom and ran away in tears."

"What then?" I asked, impatient to get to the details.

"When she recovered herself she recalled that her master had said, 'We will take her to the Mother, and lodge her there. She will not be able to escape, and no one will dare to invade such a place for fear of Holy Church.' That is what Clara wished to say to no one but yourself."

I breathed a sigh of relief. At last I had what I needed. Father Pietro had been right in his choice of the probable hiding place for Proserpina. I went forward, and laid my left hand on the poor woman's shoulder, which trembled at the touch. I smiled down at her.

"I thank you Clara. I count you as a good friend to my Lady, and I shall reward you well."

Frank Payton

She did me a clumsy courtesy, and fled from the room in tears—of relief, I supposed.

"So now we know, Sir John," said Marco quietly.

"So now we know," I echoed. "I will come down on Orlando Scacci like the Hound of Hell. Come, lad, let's to it."

*****

We found Father Pietro in the Hall, with Jack and the others. There was food on the table: bread, cheese, cold meats, fruits and wine. The first meal of the day had begun. As we sat down, Giles joined us and reported that lookouts had been posted, and the men withdrawn to positions around the house. They too were breaking their fast. I sat at the head of the table and set to with a will; I had realised that I was very hungry. At length I spoke to Jack.

"Well, have you found the steward?"

"Aye, dead of a knife thrust, by the look of him," he remarked in his morose way. "What do we do now?"

"It's lucky, then, that I have learned of the whereabouts of my Lady from another source. I'll tell you once we are on our way; I've no wish for curious ears to hear what they should not."

As I spoke, I heard footsteps on the stair and looked up. The two Scacci cousins were making their way down to the Hall. They came over to me.

"May we speak to you, Signore Gianni?" asked Rafaello.

They stood before me, Rafaello, the elder, striving for a proud bearing as would befit his present position as the head of the household in the absence of Orlando, but more than a little unsure of himself. Lorenzo stood by, nervously shifting from one foot to the other.

"Well?" I said, and paused, wine cup halfway to my lips.

"I—We are ashamed," stammered Rafaello.

Hawkwood's Sword

I ignored his words. "Have you yet broken your fast?" I enquired.

"No, Signore," they said, looking at each other.

"Then do so; we can talk later." I waved them to places at the table.

Marco and Niccolo made way for them, and they gratefully attacked the food spread out before them. I continued talking to Jack and Giles, but secretly watched the two Scaccis. Before long their natural youthful spirits took hold, and the food eased their tongues, so that Marco was able to engage them more closely in talk. He looked along the table when reaching for more cheese, and sought my eye, raising an eyebrow in question. I divined his intent, and gave a quick nod in agreement. I knew he would work to allay their fears, and to glean what information he could.

"Somebody knifed the steward," said Jack through a mouthful of bread and meat. He swallowed hard. "Someone we haven't found yet, for that was no work of ours."

"Oh, aye," Marco agreed. "We bore arrows, swords, and a few maces. No, this was done by someone inside the house."

"What about the watcher on the tower?" said Giles. "If it was he, then he must have killed the steward before I shot him. But if he didn't do it, there must be someone who is still in hiding or who escaped unnoticed when we arrived."

"Very good," said Jack, full of mock admiration. "I'd never have thought of that. What do you think, Sir John?"

I had finished my wine, and now took up an apple. "Are all the servants still about the house? If so, take those two lads"—I pointed to the two Scaccis—"and ask them if anybody who should still be here is missing. Show them the dead man who was on the tower. Is the body still up there, Giles?"

"No, Sir John. I had it brought down. I suppose we'll have to bury him."

"Good. See to it, will you? Jack, take Marco with you as well."

Frank Payton

He rose from his seat, finished his wine, and sheathed his eating knife. "Come on then, young Marco, and bring those two as well. Let us see what we can find."

It didn't take long. Rafaello was soon able to say that one Guido, a groom, was absent.

"He looks after Orlando's two horses, Signore Giovanni, and helped my brother in other ways. He would have killed Arnaldo if Orlando had asked it of him."

"So," I said. "He would have seen our approach, realised what was happening, silenced the only man who knew with certainty what we would want to know, and slipped away unnoticed. Orlando will know now we are here, and will act accordingly."

I called Ludovico and Father Pietro to me and told them the news. Ludovico groaned,"We will lose them again."

"Not if we are quick," I said. "How far now to this convent, Father?"

"Not very far, so Guido will certainly be there by now if he took a fast horse," said Rafaello. "Signore Gianni, I tried to tell you. Lorenzo and I are ashamed. Orlando has fouled the honour of our family. We wish to restore it. If you can agree, we will help you. Will you trust us?"

I was touched by his earnest appeal, and held out my hand. "Fetch your swords, and any armour you have. We ride now to the Convent of the Holy Mother." *Or to the shrine of some ancient pagan goddess and unnamed horrors,* I told myself.

Chapter 10
Rescue

The last crust of bread was swallowed, and the wine cups drained. The men were fetched in from their posts and ready mounted for our next foray. We set off, guided by Father Pietro, and with the two Scaccis in my leading group. They bestrode fine horses, and their war gear was good. Lorenzo's crossbow and a quiver of bolts was slung at his back. Both had mail shirts over padded leather aketons, some leg armour and an open-faced bascinet. They both carried plain, useful-looking swords.

The countryside became less cultivated, and was given over to woods and thickets of scrubby bushes. The land tilted up into rolling hills, and our path wound through narrow valleys which I did not like overmuch.

"We are ducks on the water here, Sir John," said Jack, who rode alongside me. "I have an itch between my shoulder blades. It usually means that eyes are watching."

"I know," I replied. "I feel the same. Pass the word back for the men to keep a watch on both sides."

We rode on and, towards mid-morning by the sun, found ourselves on the brow of a saddle between two hills. Below us lay a green and pleasant valley. To one side lay an ancient stone-walled enclosure about a number of low, red-roofed buildings, centered with a squat-towered church. Nothing moved save the wind in the grasses. High and far off, a large bird hung black against the cloud-strewn sky.

Hawkwood's Sword

"There it lies, Sir John: the Convent of the Holy Mother," said Father Pietro. "It has not changed since my visit twenty years ago, so far as I can tell. What will you do now?"

For answer I turned to Giles. "Where is Tom Nurley? I want him up here with me."

The word went back down the line of horsemen. I looked back and soon saw the burly archer riding towards me. He drew up alongside me and touched the rim of his helmet in salute.

"You wants me, Sir John? What be I to do?"

"I need your eyes again, Tom. Go forward a little and tell me what you see over by yon convent buildings."

That said, I withdrew the whole company back below the brow of the hills. Following Tom's example, Giles and I took off our helmets and went forward again, throwing ourselves down amongst the grasses and shrubs to lessen the chance of being seen. Tom had disappeared. There was no movement from the convent buildings.

"It is a good fortress," whispered Giles. "Open ground all around, and many walls."

"We'll wait here for Tom's return," I said. "He may tell of something which we cannot see from here."

I had counted thrice to five hundred before Tom slid in beside us, breathless from the exertion of crawling back up the slope. "Steep hill, that, Sir John," he gasped.

"Rest easy a while," I said. "Then you can tell us what you've seen."

"I'm well enough, I thank you. There could be a way in from the back." He pointed away to our right. "Send some men over there under cover of the hills, and they might be able to get in from the other side."

"Whilst we show our strength at the main entrance. Yes, we will do that," I decided, and the three of us rejoined the company. I gave Ludovico and Jack the details of the plan, and left it to Jack to choose the men for the group to circle round to the rear of the convent. They were about a dozen, and just as they were about to leave, a thought came to me.

"Wait, Jack. I'll lead this group, and the one I replace can pose as me. That way, I will be one of the first into the convent."

He called to one of the men. "Here, Rob: you can act the knight for a while. Don't get above your proper station, though."

The man Rob grinned sheepishly as we exchanged surcoats and shields. He then took up my place while I joined the men-at arms. We were already carrying ropes and grappling hooks for scaling walls, so I had no worry on that score. I stripped Boy of his caparison, and Huw folded it away in its leather case strapped behind his own saddle. He went with the main party, carrying my pennon as was usual, to keep up the pretence.

"Keep a good watch on the hillside behind the convent," I told Jack and Giles. "When we're in place, we'll raise a signal. Then you go forward to the main gate and demand entrance in my name."

"Have no fear, Sir John, we'll play our part," growled Jack. Giles made some jesting answer, such as I had come to expect from him, but I knew I could rely upon him.

I mounted Rob's horse—a sorry looking nag compared with Boy, but strong withal—and joined Marco and the chosen men. We rode off in single file to seek some way around the hillside. We were lucky, as the hills there had a gentler slope on the sides hidden from the valley, and we were able to make good progress. After a scrambling ride of a mile or more over rough, tussocky grass, I judged us to be at the back of the ridge overlooking the convent.

"We'll halt here," I said, and dismounted. "We shall have to go on foot now, so hobble the horses, and bring the ropes and hooks."

Whilst the men bustled to do this, Marco accompanied me to the top of the ridge. We peered over cautiously and saw the convent almost directly below.

Hawkwood's Sword

"It's not too steep a slope, Sir John," said Marco. "We could scramble down easily. I used to do this when I was a boy in the mountains."

I laughed at his youthful eagerness. "There no hills like this where I hail from, but I think I could do likewise. What can we see? Is there anyone about down there?"

At first there seemed to be no life at all. Then, from a building in the outer courtyard came a figure leading a horse and carrying what looked to be a saddle over one arm. Another man appeared and stood watching whilst the groom, or whoever he was, prepared the horse for riding. The watcher mounted and walked the horse in our direction, preceded by the groom. They disappeared from my view, but as I looked I realised that they were heading for a door which I could then see set in the courtyard wall, leading to the outside. I knew then that the horseman was going to emerge from that doorway, and if he could get out, we could get in.

Marco had seized on the same thing, and stood up.

"I'll give the signal," he said, and waved his white shield in the direction of our main party.

I called softly to the waiting men-at-arms, "Follow me, but quietly, and quickly."

We threw ourselves over the top, and slid, scrambled, and all but fell down the slope. Marco, being the youngest and most agile, was the first down. He ran, fast as he could, across the open ground, followed by the rest of us. We were nearly all in place along the wall as the door opened and the rider trotted his mount under the arch. A mail-clad arm reached up, pulled him out of the saddle, and a swift blow to the head laid him unconscious upon the ground. The groom was seized and also knocked senseless. Another man-at-arms caught the horse, a fine beast which neighed once and trembled with fright, quieting it with a few soothing words. The gateway was ours, and the convent lay open to us.

Frank Payton

"Inside, and close the door," I ordered. "There will be people here who will wonder what is happening. Bring that horse inside and stable it again."

We fastened the double doors and began to look about us.

"Which way now, Sir John?" asked Marco.

"To the church. It's the strongest building here, and my Lady will be there, I'll warrant."

We ran towards the ancient stone church, but before we reached the shelter of the doorway a roar of voices fell upon our ears, and suddenly we were assailed on all sides and fighting for our very lives. *So much for Orlando's five companions*, I thought, as I dashed a shield aside and darted my sword-point at the open helmet before me. Its wearer jerked his head back. I lowered the point and thrust him through the throat. He melted away away before me, but immediately I was engaged by another with a mace. Fending off the hammer blows with my shield, I backed away, drawing him forward. I feigned to slip over, and he raised the mace high above to strike me down. As the blow fell I rolled aside and thrust upwards at his overbalanced body. The sword-point entered his body just above the buckle of his belt, at the join of his brigandine, and he was spitted like a rabbit. I wrenched the weapon from his writhing form and looked for my next opponent.

Away to my left Marco fought furiously with a tall man-at-arms, but as I watched the sword was struck from his hand. I lunged toward him, shouting in horror, but he drew a long dagger from his belt, and, ducking behind his shield, he closed with the man. I saw his arm sweep upward. The keen point entered the man's throat despite the protection of the camail. He screamed as blood gushed out over his armour, and casting his weapons aside, reeled out of the melee. Three of our men were down, but still lived, I thought.

"Keep together! Close ranks!" I yelled, my voice booming from my helmet. "Who has a horn?"

"I have, Sir John," panted a figure beside me.

Hawkwood's Sword

"Then sound it! Sound it, man!" I gasped. "Maybe the others will hear."

The deep rallying call of the horn rang out, spurring our men to fight on, harder still. A short moment, and seemingly far away came an answering call, the call of the hunter when the quarry is sighted in the faraway forests of England.

And the hunters came: Jack, Giles, Ludovico and the rest, helter-skelter around the side of the church. They flung themselves upon our opponents, who quailed before their onslaught. They fought on bravely for a space, but the odds were too great, and they began to throw down their weapons and cry "Quarter!" Father Pietro strode between the ranks and struck up the swords with his iron-shod staff, else my men would have killed all. So it ended.

*****

The defeated men who still lived were led off and secured in an empty stable building, whence they could not escape to do us more harm. The dead were stripped of anything of value or use, and laid out for for later burial. Only one of our men had been slain, Hal Waltham, and later he was buried. As was the custom, his weapons, armour and any other effects were shared out amongst his former comrades.

As we now held the upper hand, I exchanged shield and surcoat with Rob, and stood forth in my true colours. The problem then remained of the whereabouts of Proserpina and her captors, especially Orlando Scacci.

"Search about," I ordered. "We must ferret out all the people of this place, and find my Lady Proserpina. Leave no door unopened, no nook or corner unexplored. But 'ware treachery, and go in pairs. Let us get to it."

We all scattered and began the search. I entered the church with Ludovico, Marco and Father Pietro behind me.

FRANK PAYTON

"It is as I told you," said the priest. "This place is built over an ancient temple. See the columns which support the roof; they are far older than the remainder of the building."

"Where is the Abbess and her flock?" I said, looking about me. "This place is empty."

The church was barely furnished, the altar plain and covered only with a green cloth. Upon it stood a carved wooden crucifix, and next to it an ornate figure of Our Lady, the Mother of Christ. Some undecorated vessels of silver, an ewer and three platters, were placed before the figure. Behind the altar screen was deep shadow. Within this darkness a figure moved and slowly emerged into the dim green light: a woman, aged almost beyond life itself, it seemed to me. Her eyes were black against the pallor of her face. When she spoke her voice was cracked and thin, but had a strange strength.

"What do you in this holy place, armed with sharp swords? Do you come to the Mother for guidance, or to destroy? We have been here many ages, we who serve her."

Father Pietro broke in, "Do you then serve the Mother of Christ?"

"We serve The Mother, of The Christ, if you will." She shrugged her shoulders. "The Mother of all men, from time so old you cannot know it. She has had many names, but she is The Great Mother." The thin voice died away.

I moved forward until I towered over her. The black eyes stared up at me unflinchingly. Her breath in my nostrils was old and rank, laden with strange herbs.

"I seek a young woman, brought here against her will by evil men. We are betrothed, she and I."

The thin lips twitched in what might once have been a smile. "One such came here with her betrothed, of her own free will. She is beyond you now. Now go hence! Leave this sacred place."

"Where is she?" I thundered. "Where? Tell me, or die!" I raised my sword, but she remained unmoved.

Hawkwood's Sword

"No! This is not the way, Sir John." Father Pietro forced himself between us. "You cannot kill this woman. She is not at fault."

I lowered my sword. "Very well, let us hear what she will tell you." I sheathed the sword, the sudden rage leaving me.

"I know you, priest," came the thin cracked voice. "You were here once before, long years ago. You were young then."

"Aye, so I was. Then for the sake of that previous peaceful meeting, please tell where the Lady Proserpina di Lucanti has been hidden away. Further, where is Orlando Scacci, who took the lady away from her brother and family? Come, for the sake of Christ's Mother, I beg it of you."

"Orlando Scacci you can have, and any such as still cleave to him," said the Abbess. "The fool! He sought to force a marriage upon the lady, and so lay claim to all that is hers by law. But she is now of the sisterhood, of her free will. The lady is lost to you. She shall not leave this place. "

"What do you mean?" I asked, scarce believing my ears. "Has she taken the vows of a nun?"

"This is wrong," said Father Pietro. "You cannot take her into the convent so. She knows not what she does. I know what you have done!"

The Abbess snapped her mouth shut, and her eyes widened.

He turned to me and spoke in a low voice. "I'll wager the lady Proserpina has been given some potion to turn her mind. This the work of that devil Scacci. He must have given a large sum of money to the convent, to persuade the Abbess, only to be cheated of the prize he thought to take for himself. We must find her and Scacci, and get her to your healer, who may be able to rid her of this curse."

He turned back to the Abbess. "You have wrought evil, Woman, and have betrayed your vows. Mother Church cannot protect you from the retribution these noble men will wreak here."

The Abbess turned and scurried away, with a speed remarkable for one of her age.

Frank Payton

We scattered about the church and began to search for secret doors or hidden ways. Behind the altar and its screen, a narrow stair led down into an undercroft. It was dimly lit by daylight which seeped in by way of slits in the lower walls. There were also oil lamps set at intervals in niches cut into the stones. Here and there lay pieces of carven stone, pieces of ancient figures, they appeared. There were beings half men and half horse, others as of men with bulls' heads. Stone slabs carved with scenes from ancient battles stood against the walls, or lay broken on the floor. It was a forbidding place, and Ludovico showed his horror at all these things. He crossed himself fervently.

"Abominable! Surely Proserpina cannot be down here. God preserve her soul, and ours as well, in such a place."

A large iron-banded door in a square arch confronted us. We battered it down, the booming sound echoing hollow along the passage. A stair led upwards from there, a spiral of stone steps.

"This must be the tower," said Marco, pressing behind me. "See, there are landings, with chambers off them."

"Up then, and let us see who is here," I said, springing upwards.

There were few inhabitants of these chambers. Mostly they were women of middle to old age, but with a sprinkling of younger ones. They shrank away from us into the far corners of the chambers. After ensuring that Proserpina was not amongst them, we let them be.

Finally we beat down the door of the topmost chamber. Confronting us were three men-at-arms with drawn swords. Behind them stood Orlando Scacci, and cowering in a corner upon the floor was Proserpina, ill-clad in dark robes, besmirched with dust and grime from the masonry. Her hair hung in rat-tails about her face, which was dirty and streaked with dried tears. I was enraged to see her thus. She stared at us unknowing, her once lovely eyes dull and lifeless. I called to her.

"Proserpina, my sweeting, it is Giovanni—with Ludovico and Marco, come to take you home."

But it was useless. There was no sign of recognition in those eyes.

We went for the guards then, and beat them down, one by one. One died quickly, the other two choked out their lives bloodily over long moments.

Scacci leaped back, and pulled Proserpina to her feet. Setting her by the sill of the window, he stood before her, sword at the ready, a grim smile on his lips.

"You shall not have her, Inglesi bastard!" he spat. "Attack me, and she goes down to Hell—by way of this window, and this blade."

I was momentarily taken aback, and hesitated. Scacci laughed —then his eyes widened in horror as a bolt from Lorenzo's crossbow whickered from behind me and took him in the chest. He wavered, clutching at the short thick arrow with his left hand is if to tug it away. He stumbled and gradually sank to his knees. Blood poured from his mouth, his sword clattered upon the floor, and so he died.

I turned. Lorenzo stood trembling, white with horror at his own act. Rafaello put his arm about his shoulders.

"I could not do it, cousin," he said. "I could not kill my own brother, evil as he was."

"No, it was for me, of all the family, to restore our honour," quavered Lorenzo.

I laid my hand on his shoulder. "I thank you," I said. "You have acquitted yourselves with honour. Now I must tend to my Lady."

*****

We left that place of death, of old and evil mysteries and its deluded sisterhood. I would have put the convent to the flame, but Father Pietro stopped me and swore he would bring down the full power of Mother Church upon the Abbess and her flock. As we

FRANK PAYTON

prepared to leave, the Abbess stood and watched us. I looked down from Boy's saddle.

"Farewell, old mother. You should get to your knees and pray for forgiveness for your part in this affair. Retribution will follow, in this world if not in the next."

"Get you gone, Sir Knight," she wheezed. "Enjoy your Lady whilst you can, for you will have little joy and much sorrow from her. Oh, she will bear you children, but she will not see them full-grown in the time left to her. You will rise in the affairs of men, but you will never see your own land again."

A chill went through me at her words, and I was angry enough to draw my sword to strike her down, but once more Father Pietro's hand stopped me.

"No, Sir John, no. She will be dealt with by the good Lord, at her appointed hour."

"And you, Sir Priest, are not long for this world," hissed the Abbess. "The Great Mother awaits you, not two moons hence. Get you gone!"

*****

Proserpina's poor wilting body was passed up to me, and I placed her in front of me upon Boy's broad back. Wrapping her in my cloak, I held her with my left arm about her slender waist. Boy's reins I managed with my right arm and left hand. Accompanied only by Ludovico and Marco, and leaving the rest to follow under Jack's command, I set as fast a pace as I dared with such a precious burden. The attentions of both Taddea and Hal Peasegood were needed as soon as possible, if Proserpina was to be returned to health.

The ride became a nightmare. It was endless. The impression of every blade of grass, every twig of tree and rocky stone stayed with me for days and restless nights afterwards. The Scacci stronghold passed almost unseen, as did the deep gloomy paths of the forest. As we cleared this last obstacle, Marco brought Fiamma alongside Boy.

"An you will, Sir John, I will ride on ahead," he murmured, "And warn the people at Savignone to make ready."

"Good lad. Do that," I said, and he put his spurs to the mare, which flew ahead of us in an instant.

We finally clattered into the courtyard at Ludovico's estate house to be met by Gaetano the Steward, with a group of manservants. At first the fat steward beamed with pleasure, and he seemed to have no idea of the travail and danger we had encountered, greeting us as returning heroes.

His face and demeanour changed as I lowered Proserpina into the arms of two of the servants, who placed her upon a simple litter and carried her off into the house and towards her chamber.

After dismounting I gave Boy's reins to one of the waiting stable boys, who led him away, together with Fiamma. I removed my helmet and stretched to relieve my aching back and legs, cramped by being in the saddle for so long a time and holding Proserpina safe in my arms.

"Now, Giovanni," said Ludovico, dismounting from his own horse, "let us pray that the effects of any noxious potions, given to Proserpina by that old harridan at the Convent, lift of themselves—or are removed by Hal's skill, and Taddea's loving care."

We entered the house and hurried after Proserpina, and I was with her when she was lifted onto her own bed. Taddea hurried in, tears upon her cheeks. She gave a cry, almost a scream, at the sight, and threw herself down on her knees beside her beloved charge.

"Oh, my dear," she sobbed. "My dear, dear child," and placed her arms about Proserpina, resting her head upon her breast.

Hal Peasegood appeared shortly after, resplendent in new garments given to him by Ludovico. Despite the finery, in which he looked the very figure of a prosperous Italian doctor, Hal had still not lost his sparrow-like appearance and general air of woe.

FRANK PAYTON

Taddea rose to her feet and stood sobbing, holding on to one of Proserpina's hands.

"The Lady Proserpina has been given potions to send her into deep sleep, and to take away her mind and will," I told him. "Can you rid her of these things, and return her to her former self?"

He did not answer at first but bent over the still form on the bed, taking Proserpina's hand in his own. "She is cold, Sir John, and must be bathed with hot water." He placed his hand upon her brow, then bent and, opening her mouth, sniffed at her breath. He straightened, and looked at me, saying, "The Lady has been given a very strong draught, of poppy juice and the ground dried root of setwale—probably more than once, if she has has been in the hands of someone determined to subject her mind to theirs."

"Can you rid her of this? Completely?"

"I can try, Sir John," he said in his cautious way. "If Master Bandini will translate for me, I will tell Mistress Taddea what must be done."

"Do that for me, will you, Marco?" I said to him. I leaned over Proserpina and kissed her icy lips, then left, sick to the depths of my soul.

*****

I was met outside by Alain Malwe, who was concerned over the matter of the Innkeeper.

"He is ever a trouble, Sir John," he said, brow furrowing. "We have treated him well and fairly as you ordered, but he shrieks and screams the day long for his freedom, and will not be quieted. Some days he will not be still, nor eat nor drink; also he swears revenge on you."

"His troubles are at an end," I said. "We have brought my Lady home, so he may be released. Bring him to me, in my chamber—at sword point if necessary—and tell him he is to be quiet, or I will hold him in a cellar underground for another month."

Hawkwood's Sword

Alain grinned and set off for the stables. I called to Marco, "Fetch me the money chest to my chamber."

I went to my quarters, and shortly after Marco came up with the chest. He set it upon a table, which we dragged across the chamber to a point in front of the window.

"What will you do?" Marco asked with a smile.

"Blind him with gold!" I laughed. "That will close his mouth. Off with you now, and bring him here to me."

Taking the key from its chain about my neck, I opened the chest. From it I took six bags of gold coins, and spilled the contents of three of them onto the table and into a patch of sunlight. They gleamed there like a pool of bright yellow water. On top of this I scattered several jewelled rings and brooches, and a heavy chain of solid gold.

I turned away from the table at a hubbub of noise in the passage outside the chamber. There was a scuffling, dragging of something heavy along the floor. The door banged open. Marco and Alain entered with a still resisting figure in black between them: the Innkeeper. They released him to fall in a heap upon the floor. He scrambled to his feet.

"I will not be treated thus!" he screamed. "I am a free citizen of Genoa! The Doge shall hear of this affront, this scandalous treatment meted out to me, who only wished to help. He will...he will... I will..."

His rantings faltered to to silence as his eyes fell on the sight of the riches upon the table. "I will... What is this?" His mouth gaped open for a long moment. Then he closed it with a snap. "Signore?"

"Well, Innkeeper. What do you have to say now? Now that you see your promised reward before you?"

He gulped, and stammered. "I...I did not believe you, Signore." His eyes strayed back to the table. "There is so much, so much...I apologise. I apologise most profoundly for my behaviour." He fell on his knees before me. "Forgive me?"

Frank Payton

I pulled him to his feet. "Take it. I keep my word; remember that. Never seek to betray me—never—or I promise you will live to regret it, but not for very long."

"I will never betray you, Signore. Never, on the honour of my family. I will be true to you always."

Or as long as the gold keeps coming, I thought to myself. I watched as, with trembling hands, he scraped the gold back into the bags and filled his scrip with the rings. Placing the gold chain about his neck, he bowed to me.

"I hope that your Lady recovers from the ill-usage meted out to her, and that you have happiness and good fortune together. I will leave now, if I may."

I held out my hand to him, and he took it eagerly and kissed it after the Italian custom, bowing low the while.

"See the Innkeeper safely to his home, Alain," I said, "but do not dally in the city. We have work to do here."

He saluted and left, shepherding the Innkeeper before him. A short time after, I heard him calling to his men. I drew a deep breath, and sighed.

"What next, I wonder?" I asked, more of myself than of anyone present. Marco, however, thought that I had addressed him.

"He will not betray you, Sir John. Not now that he has kissed your hand. To an Italian, it is a sacred bond. He is bound to you for life."

I muttered some sort of reply, and asked, "What else is there?"

"Gaetano has asked me to remind you that Alessandro the seaman is still in his custody. What is he to do with him?"

"Ah, yes, Alessandro," I said. "Send him away, with a purse of silver and my thanks. Will you do that for me? I have other matters to occupy me. Take the silver from the chest, then lock it and give me the key later. Do not delay. We must all talk about the danger in the North. For the present, I will sit here and await the others."

Hawkwood's Sword

I had not long to wait. The sound of hooves and raised voices roused me from my tumbling thoughts. I left my chamber and went down to the Great Hall. Ludovico was already there, and we were soon joined by Jack and Giles. Gaetano waddled in behind them, and Ludovico asked for wine and food to be brought in.

"How fares the maid, Sir John?" asked Jack, tossing back a cup of wine.

"She is not in good health. She has been given strong potions to turn her mind and will. Hal Peasegood is hoping to rid her of these evil effects with no lasting harm, so we must wait and pray that he will be successful."

"And now, what do we do?" he asked.

"Now we have serious talks about something which Marco discovered on his way to Milan. You will know that I sent him there to see Paolo da Lucca. He will tell you of the problem we now face in Romagnano."

Marco went over the details once more of his encounter with Landau's men, and the officers at the tavern on the way to Milan. When he had finished, Jack exploded.

"I should have killed that bastard when I had him at swordpoint, the night after the fight on the way to Lanzo. You stopped me. I have never trusted von Felsingen, or that cold shadow of his," he finished accusingly.

"We knew nothing of his intentions then, Jack. Marco is the one who pointed us to the source of treachery, and has also brought proof to me now. What we must do now is to act upon this news." I paused.

"We need to return to the North without delay," said Giles. "We'll be needed."

"A messenger must go ahead of us, to warn Sterz," added Jack.

"That is so," I said. "I will send Niccolo, with an escort of three —two men-at-arms and an archer. Find them three good mounts, Jack. Niccolo has his gelding, and he knows the road."

"And what do we do?" said Jack. "The maid is safe now, surely?"

Frank Payton

"Yes, she is, but in all conscience I cannot leave here just yet. When I can see that her eyes are open, that she knows me and her family, and also when she knows that we rescued her, I will leave then."

"You'll need an escort, Sir John," said Giles.

"Yes. Jack, leave five men-at-arms. And you, Giles, leave Alain Malwe and two archers. Marco and Huw will stay with me as usual. But you should leave tomorrow morning."

Marco rose to his feet. "I'll go and find Niccolo, Sir John," he said, "and get him prepared for the journey. I'll bring him to you here."

Jack and Giles then left to go to their commands. Niccolo and his escort I wanted on the road as soon as possible. Ludovico left to deal with Gaetano, the affairs of the estate and the family.

Marco soon returned with Niccolo, and I waved them to seats next to me. I asked if Niccolo were willing to accept the task of riding to Romagnano.

"I want to help you in any way I am able, Signore Gianni, but I must have a fresh horse. Il Nero is lame. Otherwise, when you will."

"Very well. Go to the Count and ask him to find you one of his best and fleetest mounts. He will know why."

I then explained that I knew that certain of Albrecht Sterz's men were planning to desert to our enemy. In addition they intended to take Sterz and myself prisoners, and deliver us to the Duke Bernabo of Milan.

"Tell no one else of this matter, Niccolo, on pain of death. Too many lives hang on this matter. I am giving you an escort so that you will be safe from roadside brigands. You can leave later this afternoon, and get a good start on the way. Master Onsloe and Master Ashurst will follow behind you in the morning. Rest awhile now, and your escort will be ready to leave with you."

*****

Hawkwood's Sword

Niccolo left Savignone in mid-afternoon with his escort of four.

"I've put Simon Bawdesley in charge of this escort," Jack said. "You'll mind he was with young Marco on his scouting ride some time ago. He's one I can trust."

I remembered Bawdesley, and was glad to know what Jack had told me. Niccolo was very willing, but he was then young and needed a steady sort of man beside him. Giles had sent along Rob Allsebrook—one of his best men, who hailed from Nottingham—for the same reason, and also that he was a good marksman. So I was content as they rode off at a good pace and were soon lost to sight along the road.

As for myself, I went again to visit Proserpina. Taddea and two of the maids had wrought wonders with her, but she still lay supine on her bed, seemingly bereft of life. Only the rise and fall of her bosom spoke of the life still within. She had been bathed and cleansed of all the foulness from that accursed convent, and her skin glowed against the white of her gown. Her dark-honey hair had been washed and groomed, and lay spread upon the pillow in a shining mass. The familiar fragrance of her favourite perfume filled the chamber. I kissed her cheeks, which felt soft and warm. The ice had left her.

"Has she opened her eyes yet?" I asked the old nurse.

She shook her head, the tears starting again in her eyes. "Messer Hal has looked in her eyes, but as yet there are no signs of recognition. She has taken a little food, some soup, though."

I patted her shoulder. "You are doing well for her. Your love will help her. Where is Hal now?" I asked.

"Gone to his own chamber I believe, Signore, to prepare healing draughts."

I left her then and went in search of Hal, and found him as Taddea had said. He was pounding dried herbs and I know not what else in a mortar. He looked up, startled at my appearance.

"Sir John! You surprised me, I was so intent upon my task. I am preparing a purging draught for the young lady. It will not be

Frank Payton

pleasant for her, but this mixture is most efficacious, so I have found."

"How long will this cure take?" I asked him, wrinkling my nose at the smell.

"Days, weeks even—I do not know, Sir John. These things have a course to run, and it can be ill to hurry the healing process too much."

"Thank you, Hal," I replied, my heart heavy within me. "I know you will do your utmost."

There was nothing I could do but wait. The evening meal that day was a glum affair. Ludovico and I were too worried about Proserpina to be good company. Jack ate too much, drank too much, and also quarrelled with Giles over his habit of trying to laugh his way out of gloom, and was at last carried off by two of his men whom Marco had to fetch in from the encampment. The rest of us sought our beds early.

On the next day I visited Proserpina again, but found little change in her. Ludovico was there.

"Shall I send for doctors from Genoa?" he asked. "I have much confidence in your man, but two or more heads may be better than one. The medicine which cures the English may not be wholly suitable for we Italians."

I heaved a sigh. "Do whatever think best, my friend; she is your sister, and you are responsible for her. As for myself, I shall go riding in the countryside, after I have seen Jack's departure."

I went over to the men's camp, which had been broken up after the morning meal. All equipment had been packed on the horses, and Jack was preparing to leave. He was more morose than usual this morning. I had heard him cursing the men as I approached with Marco at my side.

"A poor night's sleep, Jack?" I enquired.

"Too much wine, and a thick head," he admitted ruefully, turning bloodshot eyes upon me. "You should have stopped me."

Hawkwood's Sword

I laughed at this. "I'd liefer have tried to stop a herd of wild horses. The ride and the morning air will clear your head. Niccolo is about half a day ahead of you, at a guess. I've told him to try and get to Romagnano in four days, if he can. You can be a little slower. When you arrive, go and see John Brise, then the two of you together go and report to Albrecht. See him alone, no one else present, and act on his orders."

"He's bound to ask when you will return. What am I tell him?"

"I shall return when I can see that my Lady has at least started on the path to recovery. Our enemies in the Company will not act until I do return, I am sure of that. They aim to take me prisoner, a prize for their new master."

With that we parted, and I watched them all ride out to pick up the road to the north. Huw had brought our horses, and Marco and I took to the saddle and set off into the country.

*****

There followed anxious days of waiting for Proserpina to show signs of recovery. Ludovico's Genoese doctors exercised their skills, came and went, but to little better effect than had our good Hal Peasegood. I visited her chamber several times each day, but there seemed to be little change from one visit to the next.

Marco and I rode about the countryside with a few of our escort, sometimes accompanied by Ludovico when he could spare time from the management of his estate. We took the archers' spare bows with us, and Marco's crossbow, to try our hand at hunting, shooting at whatever was started up from under our feet or the horses' hooves. I was pleased to find that I could recover the trick of shooting without thinking or seeming to aim. As the old saying had it, 'the eye to the mark and the arrow to follow.' Sometimes we came back at the end of the day with something for the pot, a rabbit or two, a hare, a duck or goose, which Marco pronounced to be good eating. I sought a deer or a wild boar, but none such were forthcoming.

Frank Payton

Then, on a Spring day when the sun was sinking fast to its rest, we arrived back at Savignone to be greeted with much excitement by Gaetano and a knot of servants. From their babblings we gathered that Proserpina had at last opened her eyes and had spoken a few words.

I threw myself from Boy's saddle, and, followed by closely by Ludovico and at some little distance by Marco, I ran towards my Lady's room. We were met at the door by Hal.

"God be thanked, Sir John, and you, my Lord; your lady has at last opened her eyes and spoken to us," he said, and stood aside for us to enter.

We two pressed on into the chamber and placed ourselves one on each side of the bed. Proserpina lay propped against a heap of pillows. Her lovely eyes were bright, and filled with tears, of gladness I thought, and her colour was restored. She held out a hand to each of us. They were warm and alive, not icy cold as they had been.

"I have woken from an awful dream," she said. "One of darkness and strange imaginings, full of horror." She shuddered at the recollection.

Ludovico reached out and took her in his arms. "My dearest sister, I know not what to say, or how I can express my joy at seeing you returned to us. Now you must thank Giovanni here, for all his help in freeing you from that brigand Scacci."

Then at last I embraced my love, after what had seemed an eternity. I was unable to speak, being overcome with a mixture of love and relief at her recovery.

"Oh, Gianni," she said, "I thought never to see you again, nor go riding in the hills with you."

"My dear, dear love. I am able to say little now, but in time all shall be told, and until then know that you have my undying love."

At this she buried her face against me and wept such tears of joy that I thought they would never cease. We were lost in each other, and when we came to ourselves once more, we were alone. The sun had set, but our love for each other had been rekindled.

*****

The days then passed swiftly towards Proserpina's full recovery, and on a bright day we rode out of the estate with a gaily dressed throng, towards Genoa and the great Cathedral of San Lorenzo. We were to be formally betrothed, and a Mass celebrated in thanks to God for my Lady's deliverance. The two young Scaccis, Rafaello and Lorenzo, had been invited to be with us. We were as anxious as they that their family should be reinstated in society. Their help in freeing Proserpina from the Convent of the Holy Mother had been made known to all, for which they were very grateful.

In the matter of the convent itself, Father Pietro had told the story of the whole affair to his Bishop, who had lost no time in sending envoys to investigate. It was to be many months before I heard of the matter again and was told that the convent had been closed, the sisters disposed of amongst more conventional houses of religion. To the Bishop's annoyance, the Abbess had disappeared, never to be seen again. After being cleansed and deconsecrated the buildings of the convent were de-roofed and left to fall into ruin. Few travellers had ever passed that way, and that was a fit end to it.

Chapter 11
Confrontation

After the Mass and our betrothal, the whole glittering company celebrated the occasion at dinner in the Great Hall at Savignone. Relations and friends of the di Lucanti family were gathered there, even the ancient uncles Domenico and Matteo, clad for once in clothes more befitting their position than the threadbare robes they habitually wore.

I had fitted out with new clothes all the men who had remained with me. Alain Malwe was resplendent in the latest fashion from Genoa, whilst the men had new white tunics with the Cross of Saint George in red upon them, together with new quilted aketons, hose and leather shoes. I had also presented all eight with new daggers, or knives, and belts according to their fancy. Proserpina and Ludovico sat at the centre of the high table. I was placed to my Lady's left, and on either side were various members of the di Lucanti family. Marco and Alain were immediately below on the side table to my left, whilst the men were lower down with Gaetano the Steward, and Giuliano the Count's Secretary.

We tasted course after course, each one seemingly more delicious and of more splendid appearance than the last. The good red wine of Liguria flowed as from a river, and there were many who over-indulged and were carried from the table before the evening was over. I had ordered my people to be on their guard, to drink but to remain sober.

Hawkwood's Sword

One other guest was there at the table that night, and at my request. Father Pietro sat with us. I had told Proserpina of the part which the good priest had played in her release, and she gave him her heartfelt thanks in no small measure.

At that time we were not to know that the Abbess's prophecy was to come to pass, all too soon. Within the two moons foretold by her, Father Pietro was dead—thrown from his horse, frightened by a cat which leapt from a tree on to its head, clawing and biting. On falling, Pietro struck his head upon a stone and died instantly. On the evening of the banquet however, he was his usual gravely kind, slightly humorous self.

I was not to know of his death for some time, being away on campaign, but I was sorely saddened by the news.

Into the midst of this joyous evening Fate sent the news I was expecting, dreading almost, for it was to tear me from my Lady's side and place me once more in mortal danger. The door at the end of the hall was flung open and through it came the slight, black clad figure of Niccolo, dwarfed by Simon Bawdesley and Rob Allsebrook.

The noise of voices and music died as the trio passed between the two tables. Niccolo was pale and would have stumbled but for the strong arms of his companions. They halted before the high table. Niccolo drew himself up, stepped forward a pace and bowed.

"Signore Conte mio, Signore Giovanni, Madonna Proserpina, I bring word from the north."

I rose to my feet, and turned to Ludovico. "It would be better if we heard this in private, I think. Proserpina, you will forgive me, I hope, for a short while."

She bowed her head in assent, and I turned to leave. The Count followed, and we made our way to the private chamber where he conducted his business affairs. As I left the table I looked at Marco, caught his eye and nodded imperceptibly. He left his place and followed us.

*****

Frank Payton

"Well, Niccolo, what do you have to tell us?" I asked when we all were seated.

He drew a deep breath. "It is not good news, Signore. Messer Brise went with me to see Albrecht Sterz, as you instructed. I told him your intention. He did not take it well, and swore that you were bewitched away from your duty to the Company by the Lady Proserpina."

"What?" I cried, half rising from my chair. "Albrecht said that!"

"Yes," said Niccolo, unhappily. "But, Signore, he looked very ill, not himself. Messer Brise told me he had been drinking too much wine of late."

"I see. What else is there?" I asked.

"Messer Sterz said that the Company had suffered several reverses. Attacks towards Milan had been thrown back by the soldiers of Count Landau. These failed attacks had involved your English as well the Almains."

"I shall have to return," I told the others. Albrecht is clearly not himself. He has been ill since the plague struck us. He never really did recover. Anything else?"

"Yes, Signore. Messer Brise told me that there is a rumour that Milan has approached von Felsingen, with offers of gold, to defect and join the forces of the Count Conrad Landau. Nothing has happened as yet, though."

"I cannot say I am surprised. You have done well, all of you. Go now and take your rest, but eat and drink first. Sit with Marco, Niccolo, and you, Simon and Rob, with Alain Malwe. I will see you again on the morrow."

After they had left for the Hall, I turned to Ludovico.

"You heard? Now you know the difficulties before me. I have to leave, but I will speak to Proserpina myself, if you agree."

He laid a hand upon my arm. "I am concerned for you, my friend. Your troubles exceed mine own, indeed, compared with you I am carefree. If in any way I can help you, you have only to ask."

"Whilst I am away, look after Proserpina for me. I shall try to explain everything to her in the morning, but it will be difficult for her, I know."

*****

"I knew you could not stay long, Gianni," said Proserpina, as we walked in the garden after breaking our fast. "When Niccolo and his escort came into the Hall at dinner last night, I knew that the news they brought would take you away from me. It has been so short a time. Are we fated not to be together?"

"Mine is the life a of a soldier, my love," I replied. "When matters arise that mean I must return to my duty, then I must go. Albrecht Sterz is ill, and there may have been desertions to Milan on the part of one of his marshals and some hundreds of his men. Also, I am told that the Company has been driven back several times. If this continues, more men will drift away, and that I cannot afford. I must return to rally them again and restore their spirits."

She took my hand and drew me into the shelter of an arbor. "Let us sit here a while, Gianni, where we cannot be seen. I feel that eyes watch us, even when we are alone."

So we sat together and I took her in my arms and kissed her, not once but many times, and we whispered those sweetnesses to each other which lovers will do. Then she wept, but after a while she looked up and smiled through her tears.

"I weep because you are going away, and doubtless shall weep again when you return, as I know you will."

I laughed, and comforted her. "Yes, I shall return, and we shall be wed. My time is not yet come. We shall have many years together, and one day perhaps we will go to England together."

Frank Payton

As I spoke my heart lurched as the prophecy of the black priestess at the convent came back to me. I held Proserpina closer, and swore to myself that she must never know the Abbess's dread words.

"We must go, my love," I said. "It is time to begin the preparations for my departure. Come!"

We returned to the house hand in hand, and were met at the door by Taddea. "Signore Giovanni! There you are—and you, Proserpina, where have you been? I apologise, Signore; this naughty child has been leading you astray, and your men seek you. Messer Marco wishes to see you, and Messer Peasegood has medicine for you, child. There, I am now quite out of breath, and must sit." So saying, the old nurse dropped onto a nearby stone seat and closed her eyes.

"There now, Taddea dear, you have worn yourself out for nothing." Proserpina laughed and seated herself by the small black-clad figure, putting her arms about her fondly. "I will look after you now, and Gianni may go to find Marco."

I left them there, and went to the men's quarters.

"Good morning, Sir John," Alain Malwe greeted me. "What are the orders for today? Marco has been seeking you, and is in the stables with La Fiamma."

"We shall leave here today, Alain," I told him. "There are urgent matters to attend at Romagnano. Gather the others, and tell them to pack their equipment. They need not arm themselves fully; there should be no need for that today at least. Mail and helmets only, I think, and bows. I'll find Marco myself."

My squire was indeed in the stall with his mare, La Fiamma, brushing her coat until it shone darkly red. She was a fine mare, and willing, having little fear in a fight. I had thought to breed from her and Boy, but no opportunity had yet arisen. A horse from their union would be a fine beast to train for war.

"Good morning, Sir John." Marco appeared agitated. "I have looked for you without any success. Have you slept well?"

Hawkwood's Sword

"Well enough, boy. I was but walking in the garden with my Lady, whom I must leave yet again. Now, I have given Alain orders to make ready for departure, so we must prepare ourselves too. Tell Huw to pack, will you? Half armour today will do. We should not have trouble on the way, yet. We will leave at midday."

"What shall I say to Niccolo?" he asked. "He fears he will be left behind."

"I will see him myself. He will be disappointed, but he shall stay here for the time being. I need his eyes and ears in Genoa."

*****

As I expected, Niccolo was full of protests. "But Signore, have I not served you well? Have I done aught to offend you in any way?"

I took him aside, placing an arm about his shoulders. "No, you have not offended me at all," I said. "I place a high value on your efforts on my behalf, but I need you to stay here to keep an eye on matters in Genoa. I have had introductions prepared for you, to certain merchants here who will give you news for me from England, as well as from other parts of Italy. Any information you hear which you think will be useful to me, remember it well."

"What if there is something which you ought to be told quickly or urgently?" he asked.

"Then you must ask Messer Guiliano to write it down in a letter, and Ludovico will find a fast rider to bring it north."

"But when shall I see you, Signore? You may be away for a long time. Shall I seek you out?"

"I shall return here before too long, as I am to marry the Lady Proserpina, as you know. Matters in the north are coming to a head and a conclusion will soon be reached, one way or another, between the White Company and Milan. Remember, you are well connected here, and will be rendering me great service. I do not forget those who help me."

Frank Payton

"Very well, Signore. I accept your service, and I will do all I can to assist you." He spoke bravely, but I knew he was sad at heart at being left behind.

*****

At last all was ready for our departure. Proserpina and I had said our farewells in private, and I had spoken to Ludovico on certain matters, such as the need to encourage Niccolo.

"I will watch over his progress, Giovanni, and guide him where I can. He is devoted to you, but he is young. I realise, if he does not, why he is not going with you. Now, farewell. God go with you"

Proserpina put up her face for a final kiss and whispered, "I love you, Gianni. Come back to me safe and sound. See, I weep as I said, but I am happy. May God keep you safe."

I swung up into Boy's saddle and caught up the reins. Taking off my velvet cap I waved to the small crowd of onlookers.

"Farewell! God save you all!" and to my escort, "To the north with all speed."

We rode out of the gates, on to the white, dusty road to Romagnano, and away.

*****

"So," said Albrecht, "You have finally tired of your leman, and have returned to your duty. It is not before time. Your men have grown idle, and do not obey my instructions." He sat hunched in his fine carved oaken chair, wrapped in a cloak over his other clothes. He was thin and drawn, with unkempt hair and untrimmed beard. His usually bright eyes were dull and red-rimmed. When he reached out for his wine cup his hand shook. I recognised the illness as described by Niccolo. It was a malady born of too much wine, taken to drown his loneliness, I thought.

Hawkwood's Sword

I was angered, but contained my annoyance with my old comrade, shaking my head sadly. "Albrecht, Albrecht, old friend, you are not yourself, so I will forgive you your harsh words. The effects of the plague are still with you, and are not made better by the wine, or we would be at sword strokes by now. The Lady Proserpina is a worthy and beautiful young noblewoman, who loves me, and I her. She will become my wife."

"So you say, John, but first there are other matters to consider."

"Such as Werner?" I asked. "How could you let that happen, Albrecht? We knew he could not be trusted. I told you, after Lanzo, what that false knave Harzmann had done. Did that mean nothing to you? Is this rumour of desertion I hear true?"

"I don't know. He and Conrad are away, supposedly on patrol duty. Of course I took notice of what you said, but so many things have happened since: the plague, with the loss of hundreds of men, and mine own illness." He sounded tired and defeated, a shrunken shadow of his former bounding and immaculate self. "You were not here. There was no one else I could trust."

"Hannes was here. John Brise was here. Why didn't you take them into your confidence?" I pressed on relentlessly. "Why? Why not?"

He raised his hand to stop me. "I need your help now," he said. "Blaming me will not help us. We must think what to do to gain the upper hand."

"Very well. Then we must attack again, and win. If Milan thinks we are defeated, we must prove them wrong. Where can we hurt Landau most, in his own purse?"

Albrecht poured more wine from his silver jug, seeming not to have heard what I had said. He gazed at his cup fixedly. "I drink too much, Jack," he said at last. "Perhaps now you are returned I need no drink to drown my sorrows." Nevertheless he lifted the cup and drank deeply.

FRANK PAYTON

"Where can we hurt Landau most?" I repeated. He made no answer. I lost patience. It was like speaking to a child. "For God's sake, Albrecht! Leave the goddamned wine alone!"

I reached out and knocked the cup from his hand. It spun across the table spilling its rich red contents around as it careered away to fall off the edge and roll to rest upon the floor.

"You should not have done that, John," he slurred. His eyes blazed briefly, and he scrabbled for the hilt of his sword which lay along the table before him. I reached out and slid the weapon away from his grasp.

He lunged forward after it, and collapsed helpless over the table.

"Wolf! Wolf!" I called to his page, who ran in straightway.

"What is it, Herr Johann?" he looked at the still figure of Albrecht. "What ails my master?"

"Drunk, Wolf. Too much wine taken," I said.

"I will get him to his bed, but I must have help." He turned to leave.

"No, I will help you. No one else should see him like this. Come."

Together we lifted Albrecht and half carried, half dragged, him to his private quarters, and so on to his bed.

"Leave him there, Wolf, and fetch Meister von Auerbach to me here. I wish to speak to him. Say nothing about Herr Sterz to anyone else."

The boy slipped away, and I returned to the table where Albrecht's sword still lay. I straightened it to lie neatly along the board. I also picked up the cup and replaced it in front of Albrecht's chair.

No sooner had I done this and returned to my own seat then the burly figure of von Auerbach ducked through the flaps of the pavilion. On his seeing me, a wide smile spread itself over his scarred face.

Hawkwood's Sword

"Herr Hawkwood! It is a pleasure and a relief to see you here again. You have been sorely missed. Wolf tells me Albrecht is ill."

"Apart from that, he's drunk, Hannes." I held out my hands in greeting. He grasped them firmly and looked squarely into my eyes.

"Yes, I am used to hearing this," he said, and sighed. "The plague affected him greatly, and the rumoured desertion of Werner, Conrad and their men do nothing to help his misery. I could do little but await your return."

He sat down heavily in one of the carven chairs. I began carefully.

"Whilst Albrecht is, er, ill, Hannes, I want you to act for him. I will answer for you when he is recovered. It is now needful for us strike back at Landau. Where can we hurt the Count in his own pride and person to tempt him to battle?"

Von Auerbach frowned. "I believe he has a castle and a village at Briona, to which he is very attached. That would be a good place to begin with."

"Good. When Albrecht is sober, I will get him to approve. In the meantime, we had better make some preparations. Come to my pavilion for the evening meal, and bring those with you in whom you repose most trust. Our plans must be kept secret from any likely turncoats."

Hannes stood up and we shook hands once more. "I understand, and I thank you. Perhaps we can now begin to weather this storm together." With that he left, and I spoke to Wolf again.

"You heard what Herr Auerbach and I spoke about?" He nodded. "You will say nothing of these matters to anyone. Understand?"

"*Ja*, I understand, Herr Hawkwood. Also I will tell you when my master has recovered."

I left then and returned to my own quarters, and called for Huw.

Frank Payton

"Go around to all my chief men and say that we shall meet some of the Almain officers here at table over the evening meal tonight. Tell Will Turton that I want the best wine and food." He turned to leave. "Oh, and send Marco to me."

When Marco arrived I was at my usual place at the long table trying to put together a plan of attack upon Briona. He slid into a nearby chair. "Yes, Sir John. What may I do for you?" he offered.

"I want you to play the innocent traveller again, and ride to Briona. It lies to the south of here, on small river, so I am told. Become my eyes and ears once more, and explore the way and the place itself. Count Landau holds a castle there, and we intend to sack the village and the castle."

"I will speak to Tom Steyne, and ask if the horse I took before is still with us. It's just the sort of sorry nag for a poor traveller."

"Do that. I want you there and back as soon as possible, but take great care of yourself. I leave it to you when you shall depart, so farewell for the present." We clasped hands in farewell and so he left.

*****

As luck would have it, in the early evening, as a heavy mist was settling, I was out near the main entrance to the camp when a grey shape riding a grey horse trotted silently past me and out into the open country.

"Who was that?" The guard with me spun around and peered into the gloom.

"No one, Roger. No one is there," I replied, but I knew that Marco was on the road to Briona.

John Brise was the first to arrive for the evening meal. He shouldered his way in and strode up to the top of the board. He sat down and reached for the wine, poured a cupful and swallowed half the contents before sinking back in his seat. He wiped the palm of his hand across his mouth and down over his beard.

Hawkwood's Sword

"So what is really amiss with the Almain, then?" he growled, then belched softly.

"Drunk, and sleeping it off," I said. "But make sure it doesn't get about. For anyone else, he is ill and tired from the leftover effects of the plague."

"You're too late," he scoffed. "Even our men know what happened. That thrice-damned von Felsingen quarrelled with Sterz, and they came to sword strokes. Sterz lost. Then von Felsingen said that we might do better to fight for Milan. That was a week before Niccolo came up here on your orders."

"Any trouble with our men?" I asked.

"Not a lot. I think they were content to await your return, although Belmonte's Flemings are a bit restless."

We were interrupted by the arrival of the Almains, von Auerbach leading his men into the pavilion. There was Heinrich Steiner, whom I already knew, plus Klaus Wegener, Hans Ullmann and Otto Kornfeld, whom I hadn't met before. They were closely followed by Jack Onsloe and my other lieutenants.

"Where's Andrew?" I asked.

"Off with some woman in the town, I hear," said Jack. "She's the wife of a merchant. He's old, she's young. Andrew can't leave her alone, some say."

"Oh, do they? Then I'll see him on the morrow. But now we'll see what the cooks have sent us."

Huw directed the lads who brought the food to table. It was rougher and much simpler than I had eaten of late, but it was wholesome fare. There was a great stew of rabbit, hare, quail and partridge, with beans and turnips, and flavoured with wild herbs. It was followed by half a sheep roasted, and several chickens in another stew. There was fresh barley bread, cheese and fruit. With all this and jugs of the good red wine, we were well contented.

Afterwards we settled down to the business of our next course of action. I told the others that Albrecht on his 'sickbed' (there were one or two smiles at that) and I had decided to attack the village of Briona and its castle. As this was a fief granted to Count

Frank Payton

Landau by the Visconti, it would be the cause of great annoyance to him if we sacked the place. He would want to revenge himself upon us, and so could be brought to battle.

"If we throw all our forces into this foray, we shall prevail," I told them. "I hear there have been differences between you whilst I have been away, but for this we must come together again, or we shall not defeat Milan."

"We're not so strong as we were, Sir John," said John Brise. "Five hundred and more men were lost to the plague. Werner might take away another few hundred. Add to that the men lost in all the other actions since we came into Italy, and we are now down to fewer than four thousand men fit to stand in a battle line."

Von Auerbach added his voice. "He speaks truth. We are weaker as well because Werner will take many of our best men, if he goes, and he is a bold leader, whatever his faults."

"We still have archers aplenty," Giles spoke up. "And we now have Varazzo's crossbows. Together they will outnumber any such under Landau. However, I know he has a few of those Tatar horse archers."

"I know," I said, "And Landau has seen a massed arrow storm, and he'll know to guard against the worst effects. On the other hand, most of his men have not met us before, so will not know what to expect."

"We need them to attack us," said Jack, "Not the other way around. You know what the King's tactics were, Sir John, and they stood us in good stead at Brignais."

"That is so," said Steiner, "but Landau is not a mad Frenchman puffed up with chivalry and vainglory. He is more like us, and sees things as we do."

"If we conduct this affair properly, we can draw them on to us," I said. "Are we all agreed on the need for this attack on Briona? Those in agreement, place their right hand on the table." I slapped mine down as I spoke.

Hawkwood's Sword

My men's hands followed in quick succession, with von Auerbach next. Then came Ullmann and Wegener, and finally Steiner and Kornfeld. I knew that Albrecht would be broadly in agreement, and so the thing was settled.

"Good. Now you've all got two days to prepare your men. Get all repairs to armour, weapons and other equipments done. Sort out the best horses, get them shod, check all their trappings and their condition. Those with a lame horse will have to walk to Briona, and I'll see that they do. One other thing: I don't want anybody out of this camp until we move, on the third day from now. There are too many eyes and ears in the town, and elsewhere. You all know what is needful, so from tomorrow morn let us get to it."

They all rose to go, but I waved for my men to remain. I needed further words with them.

"What then is your plan, Sir John?" began Jack Onsloe, refilling his wine cup.

"Before we come to that," I answered, "Let me say that I have sent Marco south to Briona. He left earlier this evening, and should be back, God willing, by tomorrow's afternoon. Until he returns, my plan must wait. It will stand on what he discovers."

"This Briona is not far then?" asked Will Preston.

"Not far, but that is not important now," I said. "What I want to make sure is that we do not fail in this enterprise. If we do, the campaign will drag on and we shall lose men. They will drift away in search of more profitable employment. By waiting for us to attack him, Bernabo Visconti can wear us down. We've lost men in fruitless general forays to no effect or profit. But if we hurt Landau enough, he will lose his head and come seeking revenge."

John Brise pushed back his chair and stood up. "If there's nought else, Sir John, I'm for bed. It's late." He yawned hugely and stretched out his arms.

I sat back. "No, that will do for this night; but remember, all of you, when Marco returns and tells me of what he has seen, then I shall have some idea of what action to take. There must be no

Frank Payton

leaks of information which could get back to Landau. We know not yet if any Almains will defect, so we must keep our intention secret."

With that, they all filed out of the pavilion. I finished my wine and, replacing the cup upon the table, walked to the entrance and stood looking out at the night sky. The camp was quiet. Only a few voices could be heard here and there, and there was a smell of woodsmoke borne on the night wind. Somewhere amongst the nearby trees an owl screeched. I hoped the bird had caught its prey, as I wished to catch mine.

*****

The late afternoon air began to strike chill as I walked back from a tour of inspection, both of the men and the camp, which I had made to reassure myself of our readiness to meet the challenge ahead. The sun was setting, turning the sky and clouds to a richness of reds and golds by the time I reached the entrance to my pavilion. As I ducked through the door flaps, I called to Huw to bring out candles that I might see in the dimness of the interior. A voice came out of the darkness, and being startled by the sound, I had laid my hand on the hilt of my sword before I realised that Marco must have returned, unseen by me, and likely enough not by anyone else.

"The candles are here, Sir John," said Huw, as he entered. He grinned mischievously as he set them on the table. "Marco asked me to keep a watch for you, and then to bring them directly. I will return with more." He bowed, and left the two of us alone.

"It is good to be back, Sir John," said Marco, as we clasped hands in greeting. I noted he was still wrapped in the grey cloak which he was wearing when he had left the day before.

"It is good to have you back safely," I said. "Sit you down, and we will have some wine to celebrate your return. Have you eaten?"

Hawkwood's Sword

He shrugged himself out of the cloak, tossed it onto the back of a chair and sat down. "Thank you, yes, but not since the morning. I have had enough, I think, to sustain me until the evening meal."

Huw came in with more candles, and I asked him to bring a jug of wine and cups for us. He brought them, and left again to supervise the cooks who would be preparing our meal. I poured the wine and pushed a cup over to Marco. We each took a cup and drank to the other. As we did so, I looked at Marco over the rim of my cup. Since joining the Company before Lanzo, he had grown. In a matter of months, he had gone from boyishness to manhood. He was taller, and had a seriousness about him which belied his years. His clothes were now more of our English pattern, and he wore them with an air of confidence born of the experience he had gained with us. As an observer and a spy, he was proving to be invaluable. We set our cups upon the table. It was time for his report.

"Well now, what have you discovered?" I asked, eager to hear his news.

"Briona is but a small village set between two streams," he said. "To one side is a castle which houses a garrison of Landau's men. It lies between the meeting of the streams. Otherwise, it is a quiet area of farmland and forest."

"How many men are there at the castle, do you think?" This was something I especially needed to know.

Marco shrugged. "I did not have the chance to see inside the castle for myself, but there were half a dozen or so in the tavern where I ate, slept and watered my horse. They were all Almains. It seemed that they were newly returned from Milan, with a string of fifteen pack horses, and were going to the castle with supplies. If most of what they had was food and drink for a month or so, then I would say that there might be thirty to forty men all told."

"I take it that there was no sign of urgency then," I said. "No hurried preparations, no sign of an impending visit from Landau?"

"No," he answered. "I talked to some of the people in the tavern in a general way, but directed their thoughts towards the castle and the soldiers. They told me that Il Conti Lando, as they called him, visited the village often and stayed sometimes for weeks on end, hunting and holding banquets for his chief men and others. The villagers to whom I spoke seemed to think kindly of him."

"Hmmm, perhaps he treats them well, and they feel that they are protected," I said. "How much of a barrier against attack are the two streams?"

"They are small rivers, but are shallow and and can be crossed easily unless there is rain or flooding. They meet just to the south of Briona, and spring from a low range of hills to the north." He finished his wine, set down the cup and looked at me, and said in a quiet voice, "It will not be a difficult place to take, Sir John."

I laughed. "Ha, I will send you and a dozen more then." We both laughed.

"Five hundred will be enough for both the village and the castle. The people will flee, and the garrison cannot hold out against a determined attack. They will surrender the castle, claim their right to march out under a flag of truce, and return to Milan."

"You know my mind, Marco, almost as well as I know it myself," I told him, for it was true that his words could have been mine own. "That is what I want to bait the trap. Landau will not be able to resist coming out against us in strength. He will be blinded by a desire for revenge, and we shall be ready."

Our talk was interrupted by the appearance of Wolf, Albrecht's page, who stepped carefully into the pavilion and bowed.

"Yes, Wolf?" I said. "What says my old friend, Albrecht? I suppose him to be recovered from from his illness now, and wishing to see me?"

"That is true, Sir John. He would be grateful if you would attend him directly, before the evening meal. May I say that you will?" He waited anxiously.

Hawkwood's Sword

"I will be along to see him as soon as Master Bandini and I have finished our talk. Tell Albrecht that I am pleased to hear that he is recovered."

"I shall do that," said the boy, and bowed himself out—in his usual stiffly correct fashion, which never failed to amuse me.

"Accompany me, will you?" I asked Marco. "Your presence might avoid an unseemly quarrel between the two of us."

"Are things so bad between you then?" he asked.

"Albrecht appears to have taken against me. How much of this is due to the effects of the plague, and too much wine, I know not. But we shall have to await the outcome."

We left the pavilion then and went out to the horses. Huw had brought Boy from the lines, and Marco remounted the strong but sorry-looking rouncey which had carried him to Briona and back.

Albrecht was seated in his usual chair when Marco and I entered his pavilion. When he rose to greet us, I noted a great change in his appearance from the day before. Something of his old look had returned, and he stood tall and straight. He was properly shaven, except for his small beard, and his greying black hair was neatly arranged. His clothes were in his favourite colours of black and silver, and he no longer shivered under a heavy cloak as with fever. He rose and came towards us with outstretched hand.

"Jack, I am pleased to see you here. It is well for me that you are returned. I regret my hasty words of yesterday, and hope that you will forgive them." We shook hands, and of course I forgave him, though I wondered secretly at the sudden change in his manner.

He turned to Marco. "You, Master Bandini, are also welcome. Will you both have wine? Wolf! Some wine for my guests."

I think Marco was also taken aback by this effusive welcome. He well knew that Albrecht was not given to such displays, and he caught my eye, raising an eyebrow in question. I lifted my shoulders to show my own uncertainty.

Frank Payton

"*Waes Hael*, Albrecht!" I raised my cup as did Marco. "You are not drinking?"

"Thank you, no. I have decided that too much wine is not good for in our present situation. So, only at mealtimes will I drink wine. Now, Jack, Hannes tells me that you have devised a stratagem to bring Landau to open battle." He smiled at my obvious surprise, and raised a hand against any protest. "The thing has gone no further. My lesser officers have no knowledge of this, and so the men do not know either, which is as it should be at present."

"I am glad to hear you say so," I replied. "I had hoped to tell you myself, but clearly Hannes has forestalled me. I cannot say that I am at all pleased by this."

"Do not blame him, Jack. I had recovered before they all returned yesterday evening, and was told that my commanders were at your table. Poor Hannes was obliged to tell me of your plan as a duty to me, his superior. Have no fear: I do not disagree, and I take no offence. On the contrary, I am pleased. The news shook me out of the lethargy and despair into which I had allowed myself to sink."

I concealed my rising anger. "Very well, I will tell you of my plan," I said, "And you may judge for yourself as to its likelihood of success. It is my feeling that our main thrust should be made at Briona, although in one sense it will be a feint. I sent Marco there yesterday to look over the place. The village itself is not large, but with its surrounding land is a fief held of Bernabo Visconti by Conrad Landau. From what Marco has told me, it is a pleasant country estate to which the Count can retire from time to time when not in arms in the field."

"I believe there is a castle," said Albrecht. "Is it strongly held and fortified, Master Bandini?" His keen glance rested on Marco.

"It appears to be quite strong, but as I have told Sir John, I calculate that there are only about forty men at the most in the garrison, though the place could hold many more at at need. In addition, the streams give it some protection."

Hawkwood's Sword

Albrecht nodded. "You are a very careful young man, Marco. You do not make too much of the castle, but then you do not underestimate the problems facing an attacking force."

He turned his attention back to me. "So, Jack, we have some slight knowledge of Briona. It should not be difficult to take the place. How do you propose to entice Landau into your trap?"

"We shall approach," I said. "Once there, we shall sack the village and take the castle. As Marco has suggested to me, two hundred men will be enough, and that number is all we shall use. The main body will be kept out of sight. It is certain that the garrison, after making a token resistance, will sue for a stop to the fighting. We shall offer to let them ride out under a flag of truce, with all their weapons, to return to Milan.

"We will prick them forward, with patrols to help them well on their way. Then our main force will swing in behind and follow at a good distance." I paused.

"I begin to see your strategy," said Albrecht. "Go on, please."

"Behind our patrols we will send forward, say, a thousand mounted men-at-arms and mounted archers. These will appear to Landau to be his enemy, for I am certain that he will not be able to resist the chance to beat us in open battle."

Albrecht followed this well. "Presumably our forward force will then fall back before his advance, and lead him on until he suddenly faces our total strength well set in a prepared position. He must come on, since to withdraw would lead to a rout. Am I correct?"

"You are right, and that is my plan, old friend," I said, and picked up my wine cup and drained it of its contents. "With God's help we shall win the day."

Our eyes met, and Albrecht allowed himself another slow smile. "Yes," he said in his careful way, "I think we shall." He began to rise from his chair to say farewell, but I forestalled him.

"There is one other thing," I said, and he sank back. "You remember what I told you after we had taken Lanzo, about Werner and Conrad?"

Frank Payton

Albrecht looked startled. "I do, but surely that book is closed? They have given me no real reason for our suspicions to be aroused since that time."

"Have they not? Albrecht, how many men have you lost from amongst your Almains on forays against Landau? How many have not returned? How many wounded have you seen return? I ask this because we have lost above two hundred dead, and near enough the same number have returned wounded in some way. Luckily, most of these have recovered and are now fit to ride and fight. This has been told to me by my officers." I deemed it impolitic to remind him of what John had told me of his quarrel with Werner.

I could see Albrecht's assurance begin to waver. His face paled, and he suddenly looked haggard. He spoke quietly. "Werner has reported losses after each action, and I have seen men return swaying in the saddle, and with bloodied cloths about their heads and limbs. Do you tell me this has all been deceit, a trick to blind my eyes to desertions on the part of some hundreds of my men?"

"It has been a thought in my mind for some time now," I said. "Since the plague struck us last winter you have been ill, not yourself. Despite Hannes' support, things have not gone well with your command. I believe your men are being leeched away from under your nose, my old friend. Let us be realistic. Werner and Conrad cannot declare themselves to be siding with Milan, and then send armed men against Landau's outposts. We must put an end to their treachery, at the very least drive it into the open, and deal with it harshly."

Albrecht sat hunched in his chair, his hands covering his face. There followed a long silence. Finally, he sat up and faced me. "I agree, but how? What do you suggest?"

I sat forward. "In two days' time, two hundred of my English will leave camp under Onsloe and Sayers," I told him. "They will ride south, to the sack of Briona and the capture of the castle. Riders will be sent back to me here, to report their success. Upon that news, the whole Company will prepare itself to move south to carry out the next part of our plan. Only then should Werner and Conrad be acquainted with our destination."

"And what do you expect them to do then?" said Albrecht.

"They will then have a choice of only two courses of action," I replied. "Either they spirit their men away in the night, and haste to warn Landau that something is afoot, or they go along with us and even onto the field of battle—and then desert. I would prefer them to take the first way."

Albrecht frowned. "Why so?"

"Because I think the first way will lose us less men, and I would be rid of them sooner rather than later. In addition, if they go with us even onto the field of battle, and then desert when we have deployed, it will cause us more upset. Worse, they might attack men who trust them."

"Word of our long-term intentions must not be noised abroad," said Albrecht. "I will be careful to advise only my most senior men."

"Good. Then we are agreed," I said. "I shall go now. It is time for the evening meal, and I grow hungry. Come, Marco, you have eaten since early morning, I know."

So we parted, and the two of us remounted our horses and made our way back to our own camp. As we left the Almain camp to the salutes of the guard, Marco asked, "Are you now content, Sir John?"

I glanced across at him, at the knowing smile on his face. "No Marco, my lad, I am not, as it seems you well understand. We can only wait now, keep our wits sharp and our eyes open, and see how matters fall out."

We arrived at my pavilion as the tempting smells of roasting meat had begun to spread from the cooks' quarters. There was a blaze of light from dozens of wax candles, which was given back from the silver wine jugs, platters and cups set along the table. Huw and the cook's boys were busily bringing our food to the table My hunger increased with the sight of it all, and I admitted as much to Marco. He laughed.

Frank Payton

"I agree, Sir John. I feel now as though I have not eaten for a week."

It was not long before the usual crowd of my lieutenants and other senior men began to flood in. Soon there was a buzz of talk and laughter, as the cares of the day began to recede with the first cup of wine. I took my place at the head of the table—the general signal for the meal to begin. John Brise was on my right, with Jack Onsloe to my left.

"How has it gone with Sterz?" asked John, through a mouthful of roast lamb.

"Good enough," I replied. "I believe us to be of one mind again, which is well for us all."

"Does he agree to your plan, then?" said Jack.

"He has agreed. There is no real alternative," I said. "We must put an end to this campaign. We need to defeat Landau decisively to make the Visconti sue for peace."

"So. How do we go about this?"

"Not now, Jack," I cautioned him. "We will talk later, when all but we few here have departed. Keep Matt Sayers back, though; I need him for the first part of my plan."

I applied myself to my food and joined in the usual soldier talk —tall tales of daring deeds against great odds, of riches won and lost, women won and lost. Some present still lamented wives and children lost, to death or otherwise. I secretly observed Jack when this latter subject arose, but his face remained impassive.

At last the others drifted away in ones and twos, perhaps to drink elsewhere or to seek a woman in the town. I was left with John Brise, Jack Onsloe, Matt Sayers, Giles Ashurst, and Marco. The table had been cleared, and the cook's boys sent away. Huw stood guard for us at the entrance, but I did not expect visitors so late in the evening.

Jack returned to his earlier question. "How do we go about this thing?"

Hawkwood's Sword

"Very carefully," I replied. "No loose tongues. I want two hundred of the best we have, and that includes fifty archers, Giles. They must prepare to leave on the morning of the day after tomorrow. Marco will guide you to the village of Briona, six or seven miles to the south. There Conrad Landau holds a castle from Bernabo Visconti."

Sayers cut in. "How many men at the castle?"

"About forty," said Marco. "That is my guess. It is not a large stronghold."

"Hm!" snorted Jack in contempt. "Then what? We take the castle?"

"Yes, and no," I replied. His eyebrows rose. "Sack the village first. Then attack the castle. Put on great show of strength, but after a spell withdraw and offer a truce."

"A truce?" Jack's eyebrows rose even higher. "What sort of game are we playing?"

"A deep one, I hope, Jack," I said. "Likely as not, they'll ask for one. After all, there's no profit in dying for nothing, and I expect they are only there to guard the place, not fight off two hundred or more. Let them ride out with their weapons, and whatever else they want. Set them on the road to Milan."

Jack shook his head in disbelief, but Matt said, "Do we take over the castle?"

"Sack the place, and burn anything which will burn. But more important than that, send two or three patrols after the garrison to prick them on to Milan. Marco, you and two men will return here with the news of your success."

"What happens then?" said John Brise.

"By the time Marco returns, the whole Company will be ready to march south to Briona, Almains and all. When we arrive there, I'll tell you where we go from there. From now on, no one leaves our camp to go into the town or anywhere else, except on patrol duties, and then only under the eye of a trusted commander. That is all I have to say for now, so get to your beds. Tomorrow will be a full day."

Frank Payton

I was left sitting alone, toying with the silver wine-jug. It was a fine piece which I had had a for a long time, since before Poitiers. Its design showed a battle between warrior women and beasts which were half man, half horse. I had always thought it a strange thing. Huw was snuffing out the candles, and at the last only the two before me were left. I rose and, taking one of the candles, I bade him good night and sought my own quarters.

I did not fall asleep straightway, but lay puzzling over something, I knew not what, but something that lurked in my brain and would not go away. A little wind ruffled and rattled the canvas and ropes of the pavilion over and over again.

An owl hooted nearby, and I awoke suddenly. It was still the dark of night, but at last I knew what had kept me awake.

Chapter 12
Battle Joined

I rose and broke my fast early the next morning. In the night I had become aware that the day would be more important to the success of my strategy than I had first thought. It was imperative that I speak with Albrecht without delay. To that end I had despatched Huw with a message. Albrecht returned directly with Huw, strode up to the high table and sat down opposite me.

"Good morning, John," he began. "See, I have saved you the trouble of another journey to my camp. We will be able to speak more freely here. I shall join you at breakfast, if I may."

"I am pleased to see you, my friend," I said. "Huw! Bring more food, and somewhat to drink for Herr Sterz. Then guard the door please."

We exchanged small talk until Albrecht had his food and drink before him, and Huw had gone to stand by the pavilion entrance. We ate in silence for a while longer, and then I deemed it a suitable time to say what was on my mind.

"Albrecht, what have you to occupy Werner and Conrad today, and for the next few days?" I began.

He looked up sharply. "What is in your mind? Is something wrong?"

"I was awoken in the night by the cry of an owl," I told him. "And I thought straightway of something which had escaped me yesterday evening when we last spoke."

Hawkwood's Sword

"And that is?" he asked.

"Why, that Werner and Conrad and their men must be sent out of the way, preferably towards Milan, whilst my men set off for Briona. Their curiosity must not be aroused."

"Of course. For them to see the departure would not be a good thing," he said. "I usually send out patrols and light probing attacks, so it should not be difficult to send them off for a couple of days."

"I will do the same," I said. "I'll send patrols out as if to the south, but they can turn west when out of sight and return before nightfall."

Straightway, Albrecht left for his own camp. Later, looking across, I saw a hundred and more Almains ride out to the northeast. At their head were Werner and Conrad, behind them their pennon bearers with the fluttering strips of coloured cloth: chequey of or and sable for von Felsingen, paley of azure and rouge for Harzmann. As they passed out of my line of sight, I turned away and began my own preparations for the coming conflict.

Work had already begun and proceeded apace all that day. We kept all our efforts to arm and provision the advance party out of sight from the Almain camp, behind a screen of large tents and pavilions. Farriers worked hard, checking over the horses and re-shoeing where they deemed it necessary. Tom Steyne, the horsemaster, had picked his men carefully, and they were all good craftsmen. Similarly, the armourers under Nick Peyton laboured like demons at their forges, repairing mail and plate. Amongst Giles' archers, bowyers and fletchers were in high demand. Sheaves of arrows were issued to each man from the store, together with spare hempen or linen strings.

Will Turton opened his food stores and issued marching rations to all, enough for several days. For their horses, every man also received a bag of grain to add to whatever grazing might be found around Briona.

Frank Payton

At the same time, but at a slightly easier pace, similar preparations were also being made for the rest of the English half of the Company. After all, there would be perhaps three days before we would hear any news from Briona. I knew that Albrecht would be putting similar measures into effect. On his part, however, he would tell his people that it was a general exercise to keep the men up to the mark.

The evening meal that night was a much more subdued affair than before, at least at the top end of the table. Jack Onsloe and Sayers, his junior, were talking quietly throughout the meal, and it pleased me to see that they each seemed to have the measure of the other, and were confident in the others abilities. From the lower end of the table there was the occasional outbreak of laughter. Giles was his usual jesting self, his way of hiding any fears of the next battle.

The evening wore on to its close. Marco was sitting in his place near me, and I told him to remain there as the others began to drift away after the meal. The lower end went first, as some of the senior men-at-arms amongst them were going to the attack on Briona. At the last we had the place to ourselves, and I began to speak of the morrow to Marco.

"I've told Jack that I want everyone away by dawn," I said. "He'll pick two trustworthy men from his command, to accompany you on your return here. Which horse will you be riding tomorrow?"

"I'll take La Fiamma, Sir John," he said. "I'll need a fast mount for this work. Need I arm myself fully?"

"No, I think not. Half armour will be enough for your mare to carry on a fast ride. I don't want you caught up in any conflict which may take place. I need you back here in good point to report on what will have passed at Briona. I have told Jack of the the part you are to play, so he will give you all the help he can."

I picked up my near-empty wine cup and drained its contents. Marco followed suit, and we parted for the night and went our

Hawkwood's Sword

ways to bed—where I slept well, without interruption, until roused by Huw.

"Sir John, Sir John!" he called. "Marco is waiting. Master Onsloe reports that all are ready to depart for Briona."

I dressed quickly and went out into the still-dark early morning. There was a warm smell of Spring in the air. Looking to the east, I could just make out a faint brightness in the sky. There was the remainder of a waning moon, and still a multitude of stars. Jack and Marco loomed up front of me.

"All's well, Sir John," said Jack. "The men are already mounted, and we can leave now." He nodded at Marco standing by. "I'll look after the lad. He'll be back safe with the good news, never fear."

"Very good, Jack," I replied. "No more delays, then. Leave now with all my good wishes."

I watched them as they disappeared into the twilight, and shortly afterward the whole two hundred rode past me and passed out of the camp by a temporary gate which we had broken through the defences on the southern side. As the last man rode out, the tree trunks and uprooted bushes were quickly dragged back into position by some of Will Turton's men. I turned and went back to lie upon my pallet, until it should be time for the general call for all to awake and be about their daily duties.

*****

It was on the evening of the fourth day that Marco returned with his escort. They rode off to their own quarters, and he shouldered his way into my pavilion. I looked up to see him take off his helmet and shake it free of the rain which I had heard pattering upon the canvas roof. He shrugged off his heavy woollen cloak, from which the water also streamed, before stepping on to the wooden boards which formed the floor.

"I see that you have returned in good time for the evening meal," I said, taunting him, "but we expected you before now."

Frank Payton

He laughed. "I deemed it a good time to to get here, Sir John. Will Turton's rations were good, but not as good as the cook's dinners. My belly cries out for hot stew, and a draught of good red wine. Where does he get the poor stuff he sent us out with?"

"Now you know at least one of the advantages of being my squire, my lad," I told him. "Here, try this; it is hot and spiced." I handed him a cup from the jug which Huw had brought in for me.

I was glad to hear him in good spirits, although truly that was his usual manner. The events of the last few days had clearly tired him, for he cast himself down in in a nearby chair and gratefully took the cup I offered him. He drank thirstily before setting down the cup.

"Aah! That was good, Sir John," he said, and took another gulp of the steaming wine.

I let him take his time before questioning him as to the result of the raid on Briona, but before long he was leaning forward with his elbows on the table to tell me.

"It was not so easy as we had at first expected," he began. "The commander of the castle was a very determined man, prepared to withstand a full-scale attack. I'm sorry to say that my guess at the strength of the garrison was not correct. There were well over forty men there."

"What did Jack do?" I asked.

"At first he talked of an all-out attack, but we had no scaling ladders, nor in truth enough men for such a course of action. A few men, including the commander, appeared on the wall above the gate in full armour, and with large wooden pavises such a crossbowmen use. The archers would not shoot at them, saying it would be a waste of arrows."

"Hmm, a problem," I said. "What then? Did they ask for a parley?"

"They only asked who we were, and Jack told them we were men of the White Company. They were all Almains, so far as could judge," said Marco. "Jack withdrew us all out of crossbow range, and we set up camp. When darkness fell, Matt Sayers and two others went up to the gates to gain some measure of their strength, but decided they were too strong to assault directly."

"We need some of the blasting powder, such a the king used in his cannons at Crecy, and at some other places," I told him. "That would open any castle gate, I think."

"Perhaps, Sir John. Perhaps, but we had none, so we had to resort to a night attack over the walls. Jack had taken rope and grappling hooks. He had noticed when we rode around the castle that the battlements were of such shape that they would hold the hooks."

"How high are the walls?" I wanted to know.

"Not as high as some I have seen; about six or seven times the height of a man, I should think."

"So, not too high to throw a hook to the top," I said. "But what about the noise?" I remembered that sort of attack, always difficult unless there were large numbers of men involved and a commotion elsewhere to distract the defenders.

"Alain Malwe had a better notion than to throw the hook," said Marco. "He told Jack he could shoot an arrow, trailing a string, over one of the towers which stood out from the wall. The string would be attached to a rope. When pulled, the string would take the rope up and over the battlements, and down to the ground again, where it could be secured. One man could climb up and secure it to the battlements, allowing others to follow. Once inside, they would surprise and overpower any guards, then open the castle gates and let the rest of us in."

"Did it work as Alain thought?" I was amazed even to think that it would.

"Luckily, it did, although I was very doubtful," he said. "We scoured the village, what was left of it, for twine—and were fortunate enough to find a quantity in an outbuilding. Jack let everything die down to quiet for the night, and waited even longer, almost until dawn began to break."

Frank Payton

I chuckled at that. "Jack knows full well that that is the time when even the best guards begin to go off to sleep. He has made many dawn raids in his time."

Marco continued. "A chosen group went forward with Alain, up to the walls by the tower and overpowered the guards. The rest of us gathered by the main gates, some on horseback. From then on, the whole affair went so quickly and quietly that we were surprised when we heard the doors being opened to us. We flooded in, and those guards who did realise the danger, and ran up with their weapons at the ready, soon gave up on seeing our numbers. An alarm was sounded, but it was far too late by then; the castle was ours. The Almain commander forbade any resistance, to save his men."

"So, then Jack allowed then to take with them whatever they wanted, including weapons, and sent them off to Milan?" I said.

"Just as you said, Sir John. Then we ransacked the castle, but it was bare of anything worth carrying away, so we put it to the flame and watched it burn. It will take a lot of work to restore it and make it habitable again. All the woodwork and roofs are gone, and the great gates too. It is down to the bare stones."

"Did you sack the village?" I asked.

"Yes. We took away anything of value which could be found, but in truth there was very little. The people fled at our first approach, taking their animals and anything they could carry with them. Everything else was put to the torch."

"Good," I said, and rose to my feet. "Come, we will go and tell Albrecht your news. It is important that we move now without delay."

*****

The whole Company was put on alert to move on to the offensive early the next morning. The advance battle of one thousand men needed to be placed in the field, to follow the

Hawkwood's Sword

retreating garrison from Briona. It was made up of seven hundred men-at-arms, half of which were English and half Almains, two hundred archers and one hundred crossbowmen. The commanders were John Brise, Heinrich Steiner, Giles Ashurst and Andrea da Varazzo.

The time for any other than thoughts of battle was now over, and all now began to ready themselves for the following day. We posted two screens of guards around the camp, and I urged all night vigilance on all the men involved. Albrecht also undertook to have a check made on all the guard posts throughout the night.

That done, with Huw's help I laid out all the weapons which I customarily carried into battle, in order to check them over. Huw also fetched out the padded clothes which I would wear under my armour, to protect my flesh from the chafe of the cold metal. I bade him go off then, so that he might make his own preparations for the following day.

When he had departed, I took up the old sword from Crecy and checked that the armourer had put a sharp edge upon it and had rewound the twisted silver wire which covered the wood of the handgrip. I hefted it in my hand, and swung it about to get the feel of the weapon again. It felt good. Satisfied, I laid it aside in its scabbard and took up the warhammer, which I carried slung from Boy's saddle, ready to be snatched up should my sword be struck from my hand. It went next to the sword.

I usually carried two daggers on my right side into a fight. One was a slim-bladed misericord, the other a ballock-knife with a broader blade. They had been sharpened well, and I placed them by the sword.

By the time all these tasks were complete, I felt myself ready for sleep. I knew the call would come at dawn, and there would then be no time for sluggards. I lay down on my pallet, and before falling asleep I let my thoughts slip back to Proserpina, threescore and more miles away in Savignone. I hoped that she was fully restored to her usual self. I silently renewed my promise to return safely, and, having commended my soul to God, composed myself for sleep.

Frank Payton

*****

We rode out into the Spring dawn, English and Almain together, fully accoutred for battle that day. In our rear we left camp, baggage train and stores. Will Turton and Klaus Wegener, Albrecht's Quartermaster, each retained a strong force for defence, including riders of swift horses to fetch help if needed.

The seven miles to Briona were covered before noon, and we straightway set up a field camp around the castle area. The thousand men of the advance battle assembled, and John Brise and his fellow commanders placed themselves at the head of the column. I rode over with Albrecht.

"Is all well, John?" I asked. "You know the plan. Send out foreriders in twos as usual, and move fast to throw your force across the way that Landau will travel."

"Yes, I know, Jack. We've been over it time and again," was his gruff reply. "Don't worry. When I find a suitable place for the main battle, I'll send word back. You'll need to move fast. We'll be falling back, remember. Don't be too far behind us; Landau may come on faster than we expect, and they'll have their own spies out in front."

"Good luck, then, John," I said, and we clasped hands in farewell. I thought then, as I had thought many times before and have done since, that sometimes it is in the nature of the soldier's trade for such leave taking to be for Eternity, but we go ever forward in hope, not in fear and despair.

Albrecht no doubt had had similar words with Steiner. We both sat our horses, side by side, and watched as they rode off on the road which led to Milan.

Albrecht sat and stared at the departing horsemen, his face set and grim. I waited, saying nothing. Eventually he heaved a sigh and turned his face towards me. He looked haggard, and seemed to shrink into himself. Suddenly, I knew the cause.

Hawkwood's Sword

"Where are Werner and Conrad?" I asked, in a low voice. "Have they sent word of their whereabouts?"

He shook his head. "No, my friend, they have not. I fear it is as you said; they have deserted us for Landau. Steiner told me this morning that they did not return last night, nor early this morning. Indeed, another hundred men had melted away in the night to add to the one hundred and fifty which went with Werner on patrol. Add that to those falsely reported as killed, and we have lost something like four hundred or more of our Company." He shook his head. "I would not have believed that they would desert me."

"Then they may all go to Hell and Eternal Damnation, and they surely will during the battle to come," I said as I wheeled Boy around. "Come, let us return to those who keep faith, and prepare ourselves for the battle. We shall prevail, never fear, but now we must send a rider after those who have just departed, for they must be warned of Werner's treachery."

*****

The Company now assembled for the march. On that day, English and Almain men-at-arms were mustered together. As the archers were all English or Welsh, and the crossbowmen Italian, they rode with their own kind under their own leaders. There was a strong vanguard of men-at-arms, followed by myself and Albrecht with our own personal guards. The rest came behind, company by company, under their own constables. We proceeded in three columns, some four hundred yards between each column.

Albrecht and I rode side by side, our pennon bearers following. The pennons would form a rallying point in the ensuing battle. There are times in the press of conflict when men need to look around to see if their leaders are still in the fight, and that the standard still flies. That sight will bear them up knowing that they are not alone.

FRANK PAYTON

"I hope that we are not too far behind the advance guard," said Albrecht, his face anxious and pale. I had never seen him in such a state before a battle. I spoke as cheerily as I was able.

"No, we are not, my friend. John and Heinrich know that we will come to their aid at the right time, when it is needed. It is we who are setting the trap, remember, not Landau."

"But Werner and Conrad are with him now," he answered. "They will be able to warn him of the possible danger. Do not forget that more men deserted last night."

"I have not forgotten, but they did not know our intention," I told him. "For God's sake, man, I cannot hear the Albrecht I know speaking. You will have us defeated before the battle even begins."

"I'm sorry, Jack, to be so cast down, but my dreams of late have been sorely troubled by visions of bloody defeat, and terrors unknown. I fear my end is near."

I did not answer, but rode on in silence. If Albrecht had made up his mind to die, there was nothing I could do to stop him.

The sun was now at its height, and we sweated freely in our padded clothing and heavy armour. I took a mouthful of mixed water and wine from the leather bottle I carried, hanging from Boy's saddle. It eased the dryness of my mouth, but I coughed as its tartness hit the back of my throat.

As the early afternoon wore on, I began to look out more and more for signs of the advance guard. We had splashed through a small stream, and I had stopped to allow Boy to take a drink from it, when there came a shout from the vanguard. "Sir John! Sir John! Foreriders!"

I spurred Boy to a quick canter, Albrecht followed, and we raced to the front. Jack Onsloe was waving to me. Next to him were two riders on light, fast mounts.

"Is aught amiss, Jack?" I called to him as we drew near.

"A message from John, up ahead," he said as we halted. He nodded to one of the riders. It was that same Hal Skelling who had

Hawkwood's Sword

brought the message to me that Hannes von Auerbach was waiting for us, on that mountain road on our first day in Italy.

"Master Brise has sighted the enemy," he said, "And there has already been a skirmish between advance parties. There are horse archers. Master Brise says to tell you he has stopped his advance and taken up a battle position. He asks that you come up to him quickly, as he is badly outnumbered. What shall I say to him for you?"

"Tell him, Hal, that we shall make all speed to be with him as soon as possible. That is all you can say, so be off with you, now."

As he saluted and turned to leave with his comrade, I turned to Albrecht. "See, my friend? The plan is working. John has done what we asked of him, and is awaiting Landau's main army. We must hasten now."

As I said this, I was pleased to see him straighten in the saddle. He turned to me with something of his old fire in his eyes and a quickening of his whole being.

"Yes, Jack, now that the conflict approaches, I can perhaps throw off the effects of these vile dreams. Let us make all speed to the field."

We both stood up in our stirrups and waved the whole Company on, and as we now led from the very front, our guards came clustering about us from their former position at the rear of the vanguard.

*****

John and Heinrich had chosen the ground well. They were halted along the brow of a low ridge, from which they looked down on an expanse of open fields. To their front a shallow stream ran from side to side, ensuring an obstacle to an advancing foe. Away to the left was dense woodland, and I could see there the glint of weapons. John had sent a strong body of mounted men-at-arms to hold that flank. His right flank rested on an area of wetland, a

Frank Payton

boggy place which would be difficult to pass for both men and horses. There were archers there, and mounted men-at-arms.

We met in the middle of the battle line. The two marshals had done well. Archers were dispersed along the whole front, and I could see Giles walking amongst his men, doubtless giving them words of advice and encouragement. Knowing his nature as I did, there would also be a jest or two thrown in as well. Here and there along the line, the ventainers were engaged in plucking tufts of grass and tossing them in the air to test the direction and the strength of the wind.

Andrea da Varrazzo and his crossbows were in three open ranks, with their pavises set up before them. This would be an opportunity for us to see their volley shooting and how effective it would be, I told myself.

The rest of the Company now moved into position, swelling the ranks already there. As was our custom, most of the men-at-arms dismounted and their horses sent back to the rear, to held by the horseboys and pages until needed. Albrecht and I had decided to hold back a reserve of mounted men on each of the flanks, one for Albrecht and another for myself, to command when needed. At the beginning of the battle, though, we remained in the centre of the high ground with our horses and our own bodyguards. Marco was at my left side on La Fiamma, the red mare, which pranced and curvetted about, unused to the clamour.

He turned to me, eyes shining with excitement. "This is my first proper battle, Sir John," he said. "I hope to survive and do deeds of valour."

I laughed. "Just stay alive, boy. Leave the valour to the warriors."

I sat and looked out over the country. Following upon the heels of the foreriders came John Brise's skirmishing party. Around and amongst them swirled the black-clad Cuman riders. Some shot with their crooked bows, and I saw the long arrows thrumming into our men. Others attacked with their curved swords, and the hand-to-hand fighting swayed from side to side, but slowly nearer

HAWKWOOD'S SWORD

our own lines, which stirred as trees in a wind with the desire to get at the enemy. At last the Cuman horse archers drew off and grouped in a body, doubtless fearing to come closer.

I stood up in my stirrups, and called out, "Giles! Rid me the field of that rabble of horsemen!" He raised his bow in answer, and passed the order on to the ventainers.

The horsemen were distant some two hundred yards or so. I saw our archers raise their bent bows to shoot. Giles' arm flashed down, and hundreds of arrows arced up into the blue sky, their white fletchings seeming a flock of small birds, but their going was heralded by a hollow whistling howl.

If the black horsemen had thought themselves safe, they soon learned of their mistake. The white storm fell from the sky as a steel-tipped hail, which pierced men and horses, mail and padded leather, as if they were parchment. Horses went down bucking and screaming in pain. Men fell to the ground, shot through and through with the ashen shafts. There came to our ears a wailing and a moaning, and out of perhaps two hundred horsemen barely a hundred limped away, leaving the field littered with dead or sorely wounded men and horses.

"They'll not be back again," Jack's harsh voice broke into my thoughts. "They've not been bitten like that before, I wager."

"No, that is true, Jack," came Albrecht's voice. "Now Landau has seen what awaits him, he will be very cautious in attack."

"They must attack us, though," I said. "He cannot turn and run now, or it will be a rout. We can afford to wait for them on this ground."

We could now see the full extent of Landau's army. Apart from the remaining horse archers, in the front there were several companies of crossbowmen at intervals between his men-at-arms, who were still mounted. On each flank there was a strong contingent of men-at-arms, and in the centre the Count's standard moved sluggishly in the light airs. Around him stood his personal bodyguards. They would be knights and picked veterans, I thought.

Frank Payton

As I looked over the field, a small bird rose from the meadowland to my right. It soared up and ever up, and when at the peak of its flight, began to pour a liquid trilling song to the earth below. It could be nought else but a lark, such as I remembered last seeing in English fields. Its sweet song recked little of the death which lay beneath its small wings, and only welcomed the springtime of the year. Looking about me I saw that more than my eyes had followed the little bird's ascent to the heavens. Did those men also think back to their homeland as I did, I wondered?

"They are massing horsemen for the charge, Sir John," said Marco, from my left. "See the horses being brought forward from the rear." He pointed with a gauntleted hand.

"Aye, I see it, Marco. Landau has decided to brave the storm. He can do no other. The die is cast for him and his men." I turned to Albrecht. "How many do you think they muster against us?"

"I have just asked Heinrich the same question," he replied. "He reckons about three thousand or so. He also says that one of his foreriders has seen Werner's and Conrad's pennons on Landau's right flank."

I followed his pointing finger and could see the gold and black, red and blue of the traitor Almains. I could also see that they still wore the white surcoats of the Company, as if in defiance of their former leaders.

"Goddamned traitors!" I heard Jack Onsloe's snarl behind me, and twisted around in my saddle. "Go and command the left," I told him. "Make sure our men know whom they are facing. Drive them off the field, Jack. No quarter!"

"Aye, no quarter it is then," he replied, grinning—and spurring his black destrier into movement, he thundered away. His chosen companions streamed after him, to take position on our left flank.

*****

Hawkwood's Sword

"We should ride along our front, Jack," said Albrecht. "The men need to see us before onset. I'll take the right flank if you take the left."

"Willingly, my friend," I said, and held out my hand to him. He shook it firmly, and so we parted. I watched him go, and wondered if I should see him again. "Ride with me, Marco, and you, Huw."

We threaded our way through the ranks of men-at-arms and spearmen, to the accompaniment of a mixture of coarse jests and acclaim. "Where's the gold, Sir John?" came a voice I knew.

I looked down at a tall dark-faced figure in well-worn armour, who leaned on a shortened lance. He grinned up at me.

"In your purse a week ago, Nick," I said. "You asked Will Turton for an advance of pay, he gave it to you, and now you will have to earn it. Don't try to avoid paying by getting killed; I've a feeling Will might ask the Devil to send you back."

His comrades laughed at his downcast face. Nick's greed for money was as much a thirst as for women and wine.

I raised my voice so more of the men around could hear me. "All of you will earn your pennies today, when we defeat this Count. I've little doubt there'll be some rich pickings on the field afterwards."

"There's more of us from Essex here, Sir John," came another voice.

"Then if you men of Essex want to see your homes again sometime, fight well today," I called back, and passed on through to our front, to be met by Giles and Will Preston on the open ground in front of the archers.

"We saw those black devils off, Sir John," Giles crowed, leaning on his bow. "Now we're ready for the others. My lads are waiting."

"Aye, and you'll be ready to scuttle behind the spears when they get too near, as well, my lad," grumbled Will. "Us poor souls'll have to take the brunt, as ever."

"And we'll pick off a few more for you whilst you're pushing and shoving," said Giles, laughing.

Frank Payton

"Don't let them through. That's all," I told them both. We can't afford a broken line. It is their numbers against our position. Just do your best to keep them out, all of you."

It was good to see the men in high spirits. We passed on down the line to where Jack Onsloe and Matt Sayers sat their horses, amongst the men of the left flank. John held his sword across the back of his horse, the blade resting upon his forearm behind his shield.

"Hold this flank, Jack—and you, John. I see there are some crossbows as well as archers in the woods."

"Yes, Sir John. I'm glad they are there," said Jack. "Giles sent them before you arrived. They'll help break up any charge on this side."

"Good, and I know there are others on the right," I said. "So, we can only wait now."

"I see we're facing that forsworn bastard, von Felsingen." Jack waved his arm towards the enemy opposite.

"Yes," I told him. "You can finish him for good, and his Shadow, if you can catch them." He grunted a reply, and I turned away. "God save all here," I called out as we left.

The men raised a gruff cheer as we rode away. We soon regained our place a few ranks back of the centre of the line. From the height of Boy's saddle and the ridge upon which we rested, I could see across to Landau's position. As I watched there came a blare of trumpets, and the distant horsemen began their advance.

They came on bravely with pennons flying, trumpets blaring, and at a steadily increasing pace. As they drew nearer and nearer, their lances swung down to the level position. In front of me I could hear Giles yelling orders at the top of his voice, and the shouts of the ventainers as they passed the message along the line.

At two hundred-odd yards the shrieking white arrow-storm burst upon the front ranks, and was repeated again and again. The horsemen went down, their mounts kicking and screaming, the riders thrown off and struggling to rise, or dying. The second line rode over and through the wreck of the first, yelling their defiance.

The attack slowed at the stream, and the riders took more punishment from the bowmen's shafts, added to which, the crossbowmen began their volleys. The short, stubby quarrels flashed across the open space and fetched down more of the enemy cavalry. Slowly, reluctantly, they began to fall back to reform. In the rear, I could see the bulk of Landau's army, and at its centre was the Count's standard. They began to move forward.

*****

Albrecht joined me again at the centre, and together we awaited Landau's advance. This time it was a steady rolling forward of his entire strength. There seemed to be no reserves.

"He's risking all on one last throw of the dice!" said Albrecht.

"Aye," I replied, "and there'll be no turning them back at the stream this time. Huw," I called to him, "Go down quickly, and tell Master Ashurst to withdraw his archers and crossbowmen to here on the heights. They can shoot from here over the heads of the front lines."

"Very good, Sir John!" he said, and slid off his horse. I watched him as he ran down between the ranks of the men-at-arms and spearmen, carrying my message. Only a lad, I thought, scarce older than I was when I went into my first battle. Would he survive the day? Perhaps. It would rest on his own bravery and agility, besides any skill with arms. Moments later I saw him speaking to Giles, who raised his bow to me, and the word was passed down the line.

As usual, there was some coarse banter between the retreating bowmen and the others, as they hurried back towards me. Before long, however, they were in position ranged in front of Albrecht and myself, busily making their preparation for the next stage of the battle. From the stock in his arrow case, each man took several shafts and stuck them point-first in the earth beside him within

FRANK PAYTON

handy reach, and nocked yet another to the string. Then they waited, talking quietly to each other. Once an archer myself, I knew their thoughts then.

Again I took up my watch on the field before me. Landau and his men had reached the stream and crossed it—but with some break in their lines. They sought to regain the line, but lost the original rhythm of their advance. It was time to strike again. Giles also knew this, and was looking towards me. I drew and raised my sword on high, then swept it down in a flashing arc.

Once again the song of bowstring and fleeting arrow was heard, but this time there was no break in the tune. Scores of men and horses went down to ruin. Their comrades pushed on over them, on foot or still on horseback, and closed with our front line, where the cruel spear butts jammed firmly into the earth were held against them. Horse after horse carried its rider skittering along the line, to go down wounded, dying, or dead. It was now hand-to-hand with sword, mace, or shortened lance. The lines swayed back and forth, the clang of metal was deafening: sword on sword, mace on armour, lance on flesh. Men shouted in triumph, screamed in agony, or cursed as they died. The sounds and smells of battle rose around me.

On our left flank, Jack and his horsemen were embroiled in their own battle with the men of von Felsingen and Harzmann. The Almains were giving back against Jack's furious assault, as he was keen to avenge Werner's sneering remarks about his peasant birth. I realised that there lay my chance to turn the conflict our way.

"Albrecht, I'm taking my reserve to weigh in with Jack. Together we can drive Werner from the field."

He drew his sword. "I'll try my luck on our right, but we will have to skirt the marshy ground, so will take a little longer."

My own company gathered about me, and we rode like demons to join Jack. Marco and Huw were on either side of me. We picked our way through the edge of the trees and reformed on the other side, thus outflanking Jack's small battle. With flailing sword and

Hawkwood's Sword

mace we crashed into the side of von Felsingen's Almains. They crumpled like reeds, and despite angry shouts from Werner they broke away and began to ride from the field. I was confronted by the raging figure of Werner von Felsingen, bloodied sword in hand, a battered shield on his left arm.

"So, John Hawkwood!" he gasped. "This is the end of this battle. Fear not; we shall meet again. You have killed my dear friend Conrad, and that I shall never forgive! The day is yours, as far as I care now." He turned and rode after his fleeing men.

As for us, we swept on, killing as we went, and crashed into the flank of Landau's main battle. Albrecht's men were coming in from the right, and we were rewarded by the sight of a sizeable contingent of the Count's Hungarians and the remaining Cuman horse archers leaving the field. More and more of the Count's men flung down their arms and sued for mercy. I met Albrecht in the midst of the carnage. His face was grim, but I saw that much of his old fire had returned. Mayhap the effects of his bad night visions were wearing off in the light of our victory.

"Another bloody day, but another victory for the White Company, my friend," he said, stripping off his gauntlet and holding out his hand to me. I took his hand in mine, and so that solemn handshake signalled the end of the battle for us both.

One other matter remained. As we stood by on our horses, an Almain squire from Landau's guard approached us under a flag of truce. He was accompanied by another, bearing a standard. Speaking German, he addressed himself to Albrecht in this wise:

"My beloved master, the illustrious Count Conrad von Landau, has fallen upon this field of battle. Therefore the victory is yours. We seek permission to bear him and other noble dead from the field, for decent burial at another place. If you would claim his standard as a trophy of war, it is yours." As he said this, tears streamed down the battle-weary soldier's face.

"What is your name?" said Albrecht, leaning down and placing a hand on the man's shoulder.

"I am Lutz von Landau, the Count's son," he said proudly.

Frank Payton

"Very well then, Lutz," said Albrecht. "Take the standard with you, to wrap about your father's body when you bury him. He was a brave and noble opponent. No one shall say that we of the White Company are aught but chivalrous to the dead. God save you, and farewell."

As the late Count's son and his comrade trudged back to the place where lay their dead leader, Albrecht looked across at me. "A bold and noble youth," he said. "We shall have to beware of him in the future."

We both turned our horses away from the field to ride up to the heights again. As we left, the larks were singing their joyful song of Spring.

Chapter 13
Canturino

In later years, the action at which we defeated and killed Conrad von Landau would become known as the Battle at the Bridge of Canturino, but in truth I saw no bridge over that stream which proved such an obstacle to our enemy on that day. With the collapse of his military forces, Bernabo Visconti's campaign against Montferrato ceased, and for a spell the good Marquis could rely on a period of peace.

The final departure of Werner von Felsingen from the White Company was something I welcomed. Albrecht however, I knew, still felt deeply bereft of his former principal marshal. He promoted von Auerbach to the position, but was never really at ease with him—mainly, I think, because Hannes was older than himself.

In the battle the Company lost about two hundred men killed, in addition to those whom von Felsingen had lured away to the side of the Visconti, who were almost all Almains. We were left then with some three and a half thousand men of all sorts, both as to nation and place on the field of battle. Added to these were the crossbowmen of Genoa.

In the aftermath of the battle the men roamed the field, gathering whatever of value they could find, and burying our dead where they had fallen. Von Landau's men had ridden away and left their own dead. It would be for the country people to bury them, and if they reaped any reward in the way of money or goods, then I

Hawkwood's Sword

wished them luck of it. For Albrecht and myself, the problem was to secure employment for the Company once we had recovered and regrouped.

"Was Conrad Harzmann's body found?" Albrecht asked me, as we ate our evening meal in my quarters on the evening after the battle.

"No. I asked Jack and the others to make a thorough search, but no sign of him was found," I said. "It may be that Werner knew where he fell, and had the body taken away when they fled the field."

"I wonder if we shall see Werner ever again," said Albrecht, seeming to me to regret his going.

"Would you wish to?" I asked, somewhat taken aback. "I'd only welcome him at the point of my sword. Great God in Heaven, Albrecht, he was a caitiff and a traitor, who would have happily handed us over to Bernabo Visconti in exchange for gold. No, we are well rid of him, and that pale, sly fox who was ever at his side whispering God knows what evil in his ear."

" I suppose you to be right, Jack," Albrecht said morosely. "But I have a feeling that we have not seen the last of him. Remember, there are other companies of my fellow countrymen here in Italy, who would perhaps welcome Werner and his followers."

"They might, but they'd be fools if they did," I said. "Have some more wine and forget Werner von Felsingen. We have weightier matters to think about. Do not forget, either, that I am sworn to return to Savignone and take the Lady Proserpina to wife."

Albrecht stroked his neatly bearded chin, an old habit with him when considering what he should say on any serious subject. He looked across the table at me, a small smile on his lips.

"So, you are still resolved on this alliance, this adventure of the heart?" he said at last. "And after the ceremonies, the banquets, and the whole business of the nuptials, what then? Will your Lady follow you into the field, and ride at your side as did the Amazons of ancient legend?"

Frank Payton

"Now you are foolish, Albrecht," I said. "I will have none of it. Proserpina is a highly spirited young lady, but she will not join me on campaign. My wife-to-be has property of her own, and will take up residence there, where she will be mistress in her own house. That will be a resort of peace for me, when not on campaign. In time, I hope, there will be sons and daughters to come after us. You know well that I have a daughter, Antiocha, who still lives in England, although her mother is dead of the plague. A bastard child she may be, but she remains my daughter—and someday I shall see her again in England, or perhaps I shall bring her here to Italy. No more of this nonsense, I pray, or I shall grow angry."

He shrugged his shoulders, sighed as if giving me best on the subject, and poured wine for both of us. He raised his cup.

"Very well, Jack. I drink to your Lady and to yourself. May your marriage be long, happy and fruitful. *Zum Wohl!*" He tossed down the wine in one mouthful, and rose to his feet. "I shall see you in the morning, when we must begin the return to Romagnano."

"I thank you for your good wishes, old friend, for myself and my Lady." I swallowed the contents of my own cup, and thus we parted that night, I think in no small degree of cool unfriendliness, but I cared not.

*****

We returned to our principal camp at Romagnano, riding through the gates on a fine Spring day, to the welcoming shouts of the reserves who had been left as a garrison. Riders had been sent on ahead of us, and there was already a festive air amongst the men. Extra wine and food rations had been made available, and Albrecht and I had agreed to hold a grand banquet in the open during the evening.

Before any such festivities, however, every man was required to appear before his company's constable and show himself as

Hawkwood's Sword

having in his possession a full complement of weapons and armour associated with his rank and place on the field of battle. Each man also had to satisfy the Horsemaster or his deputies of his horse's wellbeing and equipment.

As for myself, I retired to my pavilion in the company of Jack Onsloe, John Brise, and some others of my staff, including Marco and Huw. Seating myself at the head of the table, I gratefully accepted the cup of wine which Huw placed in front of me. He was swiftly followed by the cook's lads, who in addition to wine brought nuts, fruit and sweetmeats to the table. Before long, a merry mood spread through the assembly.

"What next, Sir John?" came a voice from further down the table. "Whither away for more booty and riches?" sang out another.

"Have you never enough of fighting and loot?" I laughed. "I'll wager some city or noble will be looking for our services ere long. For the present, take your ease; the call will come soon enough. We ought now to empty our cups to the memory of the brave lads who fell in the last battle against von Landau, and will ne'er see England again."

A quiet then fell over us, and we all stood and drank the cups dry in memory of our companions lost in battle. As we sat down again a voice asked, "Has any man here seen Dickon Rhymer, or John Reeve, or Ned Shaw?"

There was silence, then: "Dickon went down to one of von Felsingen's company," said Jack Onsloe. He was a good man, one of my best."

Will Preston spoke up. "I saw Jacky Reeve shot through by those little devils on black horses, God damn their eyes!"

Giles added that he had lost Ned Shaw to a lance-thrust from an Almain knight who had ridden with von Landau. There were others who spoke up, but not all the deaths were witnessed.

"Huw!" I called to the boy, "Bring more wine for all. Now then, my friends, I have some happier news for you. As some few of you already know, I am shortly to marry a young Genoese

328

noblewoman. She is known to those who were in Genoa with me earlier this year. If they wish, they may be amongst my guests at the wedding."

There was roar of approval at this proclamation, followed by the laughter and ribald jesting common between menfolk on such occasions.

It was John Brise who stood up, with a brimming cup of wine grasped in his enormous right hand, and ordered the whole company to stand, which they did. "We, your comrades in arms, wish you and your Lady all good fortune, Sir John, in your marriage. May you be blessed with many sons and few daughters."

Having delivered himself of the longest speech I had ever heard him make, John sat down heavily, and buried his face in yet another cup of wine. The rest emptied their cups in the toast to marriage, and resorted to more laughter and jests.

"I thank you all, for myself and my Lady Proserpina," I said, which few words I thought were quite enough.

*****

As the wine and the sweetmeats disappeared from the table, the talk of lost comrades and the prospects of future employment ebbed away, and with it my companions. At last I sat alone save for Marco, with Huw hovering in the background. I waved him over to the table.

"Sit down, boy," I said. "Have some wine, and some of whatever else is left. You have both carried yourselves well today."

"Thank you, Sir John," he said, "but I will just take a cup of wine and a little to eat, and go to my sleeping place." With that he left me alone with Marco.

"Shall we have more trouble from Milan, do you think, Sir John?" he asked.

Hawkwood's Sword

"I doubt it. We have broken Bernabo's army, which has also lost its leader. He will have to find a new general, gather men, and equip them, before he can take the field again."

"So, what shall we do now?" he persisted.

"What is in your mind, Marco?" I asked in return. "Would you leave my service?"

He looked startled, shocked almost. "No! Never, Sir John. I swore allegiance to you for life. I would not go back on my oath. But there is something else I wish to ask of you." He hesitated.

"I can guess your desire," I said with a smile. "And yes, you may go to visit Genevra da Lucca, wherever she is. In addition I will give you an escort, unless you wish to go secretly."

Marco sat as if struck dumb. A wide grin spread over his face. "Thank you, Sir John. You make me very happy. Thank you also for the offer of an escort, but perhaps to travel alone would be best for me. Your men would be too obvious in Milan. Besides, I can keep my eyes open for anything of note much better if I am alone."

"Very well, Sir Spy," I laughed. "Go when and as you will, only tell me when you go, and return in six days' time."

"I shall leave in the morning, after a good night's sleep for myself and the old nag I shall request from Tom Steyne." He finished his wine and got up to go. "It would perhaps be better if I saw him now."

"Do not forget the banquet," I said. "I shall need you by me then."

He laughed. "I would not desert you at such a time, Sir John. You will need Huw as well. I shall tell him."

"Away with you, then," I said. "Go and see Tom about the horse. I need to rest now before this evening."

*****

There is little need to tell much of the remainder of the day, or of the banquet in the evening. Whilst there was the will, and the light lasted, the men held running races for purses of gold or silver, or richly fashioned cups of the same metals. Archers and crossbowmen shot with and against each other, for distance and marksmanship. There were wrestling matches, mock fights with wooden staves for weapons, and so on, until all were sated by the effort and excitement. Many a wager was won and lost. Money changed hands like water running from one vessel into another.

The dusk saw in the evening meal, with tables stretching away at some length from the one where Albrecht and I sat in some state surrounded by all our marshals, constables of companies and lieutenants. We had all dressed in our most sumptuous clothes and made a glittering show, but I had feelings of regret that my Lady Proserpina was not present to grace our company as Queen of Honour at our high table.

Seemingly mountainous quantities of food were distributed along the tables. Huge portions of roast mutton and beef, roast fowl of every description, stews, pies, puddings, sweetmeats, fruit, nuts, and gallons of good red wine.

Amongst those at the tables were crowds of women, brought in by more daring, or possibly romantically inclined, souls who craved female company and dalliance. Some were harlots from the nearby town, intent on filling their purses with hard-won gold or silver from the woman-hungry men of the Company. Others were the camp-followers of any marching army, who were tolerated for whatever skills they had in the way of being helps for our healers, washerwomen, cooks and suchlike.

In addition, several singers and musicians appeared from the night into the glow of torches and wax candles. Their loud singing, piping and twanging filled the air, and at times almost silenced the hubbub of voices from the tables.

The feasting and merriment continued into the night, until most men and their female companions either fell asleep over the tables or crept away to engage in the intimate pleasures of the night.

Hawkwood's Sword

Finally I gave it my best and, wishing the few companions who were left at the top table good night, with faltering feet and spinning senses made my way to my own quarters, falling asleep at last to dream of Proserpina.

*****

True to his word, Marco returned to Romagnano on the sixth day, slipping almost unnoticed past the guards—although, by then, most would have recognised his shadowy comings and goings and his changes of appearance. To any curt challenge he always gave the same short reply, "Marco", and rode straightway towards my pavilion.

That night, he ducked through the door flaps in the late moonlit evening.

I was sitting with John Brise, Jack Onsloe, and Giles Ashurst, talking of tactics and battles long past. I looked up at his entrance.

"Welcome back, boy. Is all well at Milan?"

"Very well indeed, Sir John, and I have much to tell you." He paused and looked around with an anxious air. "Is there aught to eat and drink? I am sore famished."

We laughed at this—except Jack, who merely took another gulp of wine and got up to go. As he went, he slapped Marco on the shoulder and muttered, "Good lad," and disappeared into the fading light.

"Take Jack's place here," I told him, and called for Huw to have some food and drink brought in.

Between mouthfuls Marco gave us an account of his journey to and from Milan, and of his warm welcome in the da Lucca household. As he ate he rambled on in such a fashion, and at such great length, but saying little of any consequence at all, that John and Giles grew tired and decided they had better things to do.

Frank Payton

When they had left the pavilion, I said, "Now, Marco, what do you have to tell me of real interest? I guess you have held back information for my ears alone. Am I right?"

He grinned, and took another gulp of wine. "You are right, Sir John. I do have important news for you. The Florentines are preparing for war against Pisa."

I sat bolt upright at this intelligence. Here was an opportunity perhaps for further profitable employment. "What is their reason?" I asked.

"It is an old quarrel," he said. "Florence's trade has to be conducted across Pisan territory, to and from the port of Livorno. Not unnaturally, the Pisans exact tolls on the passage of goods. That is the bone of contention. Fighting will begin again between them this summer."

So, I thought, *Which city will come to us first for aid, Pisa or Florence?*

"Who has told you this?"

"Paolo da Lucca. He had the news from his agent in Florence. We had long talks about affairs of this nature. He appears to hold me in some high regard."

"And Genevra? How does she hold you?" I asked with a smile.

"We are in love with each other," said the boy in all seriousness. "She is ever accompanied by her old nurse, somewhat like Taddea and the Lady Proserpina. We were not often left alone together, but once when we were, we declared our love."

"You think then that da Lucca would accept you as a son?" I asked.

"I am sure of it; he gives every indication." He took another sip of wine.

"Very well then, I shall see what I can do to help you in this matter. Such an alliance would be good for you, and also valuable for me," I said, to his evident joy.

"Let us return to this coming war between Florence and Pisa," I continued. "Have there been any hostilities yet?"

"Nothing beyond sporadic bickering and scuffling on a small scale, between those guarding merchants' goods in passage and Pisan officials."

"I think we will keep the news of these matters to ourselves for the present," I said, "And see what happens. It may come to nothing; in any case, we cannot move until approached by one side or another."

The alternative, I told myself, would be to secretly approach both sides to see which one would offer the most for our services. I thought the matter warranted further consideration.

"In the meantime you and I have other matters to discuss, touching upon the Lady Proserpina."

"Of course, your marriage to her. When will it be?" Marco asked, eyes shining.

I told him then that, the day after he had left for Milan, I had sent Matt Sayers with a small detachment to Savignone to give the news of our success at Canturino, and to deliver letters to Proserpina and Ludovico.

"Matt should be back any day now. I have requested that Niccolo come with him, for I wish you and he to return to Savignone with my gifts to Proserpina and others. You will also be able to say when I shall travel there myself, and who will accompany me. Stay there until I arrive. Ludovico will need to know all this."

"You will need to allow at least two weeks for the Count to arrange everything for the wedding day, Sir John," said Marco, "For all his household must be provided with new clothes. That is the custom amongst the great families."

"Very well, two weeks," I said, grudgingly, "but no more. Much as I am eager to marry Proserpina, I must look to the affairs of the Company, like it or not. This pother between Florence and Pisa must be turned to our advantage in some way. But all that can wait until the morn. Now, get to your bed, my lad. I see your eyes closing, even as I speak to you."

Frank Payton

He rose from his seat to obey, then turned, saying, "Thank you, Sir John, for the hope you have given me."

When I looked up again, he was gone.

I sat on alone to finish off the contents of the wine-jug, and to crack and eat the few nuts remaining from the evening meal. Should I tell Albrecht of Marco's news? I wondered. Strange thoughts had recently arisen in my mind concerning my old comrade. He had of late begun to place barriers between us. I will not say that he had not done his duty by the Company, but however much he tried to conceal it, his old fire and the friendliness between us was absent.

Was he jealous of my ambition to return to England rich and as some great lord, or was it due to my intention to marry Proserpina, I asked myself. I knew he had never married, and had no children, not even any born out of wedlock. As he had once said, he had been wedded to the sword for too long to change. All members of his family were dead, and whatever lands and riches they had once enjoyed were gone. Like many of his men, he was no more than a landless swordsman, owing fealty to none.

I reached out once more for the jug, but on lifting it realised it was empty. I decided it was time for sleep.

*****

In the afternoon of the following bright Spring day, Niccolo stood before me as I sat in the sun in front of the entrance to my pavilion. He swept off his black velvet cap with its jewelled clasp, and bowed low. I marvelled that on each occasion when I saw him, he appeared to have shed more of his boyish ways and to have grown older. He was clad that day in sober dark red and black velvet, with high leather riding boots. A plain sword hung at his left hip, a slim-bladed dagger at his right. Behind him towered the tall figure of Matt Sayers.

Hawkwood's Sword

"I bring greetings from the good Count Ludovico da Savignone," he began very formally. "Also from his sister the Lady Proserpina. I have letters for you, Signore Giovanni." So saying, he stepped forward and placed the parchment rolls in my had. I passed them to Marco for safe keeping.

"You are very welcome, Messer Della Sera. Will you take some refreshment after your journey?" I said gravely, and indicated a table just inside the doorway, which had been laden with food and drink against their arrival.

"That is most kind. Some refreshment would be very welcome, would it not, Matteo?" He looked back at Matt, then lost his reserve and laughed merrily. Matt had earlier caught my eye, and slowly closed and opened one eye to me with a grin as if to say, "See here our young ambassador."

"It would that, Master Niccolo," Matt replied.

Formality disappeared as the new arrivals helped themselves from the table. We all laughed and applauded Niccolo for the way in which he had carried out his duties. I was glad to see that the boy in him had not vanished altogether.

"Well, Niccolo," I said, when hunger and thirst seemed to have been at least partly satisfied in all present, "Tell me, how is my Lady Proserpina's health, and that of her brother?"

"They are both in very good health, Signore. The Count is busy with his estate affairs, and also attends the Doge's court regularly. I am sure that his wound is completely healed."

"And my Lady?" I asked.

"She is returned to her usual mischievous, happy self again, and blooms as a Spring flower. She rides about the countryside, with an escort of course, just as she used to do."

"I am relieved to hear it, Niccolo," I told him, and I was. A great weight had been lifted from my mind at his news. I knew I could look forward to the joy of seeing my beloved again.

*****

FRANK PAYTON

I recall that time at Savignone as if it were only days ago. Spring that year was near perfect: blue skies, small white and cream-coloured clouds, bright green fields and the darker green of the trees. The estate gardens were alive with flowers, and the small birds went about their business of mating, loudly proclaiming their joy in Life.

Three weeks had passed since Marco and Niccolo had left Romagnano, and I had later joined them at Savignone—the day previous to that upon which the wedding ceremonies were to take place. As I expected, Ludovico had wanted the marriage held at the Palazzo Lucanti in Genoa, but—typically—Proserpina had won her own way, and insisted upon staying in the country. She told me later, "The Palazzo is so dark and gloomy, and closed in by the other large buildings. I wanted bright skies and sunlight for our wedding day."

The party which had travelled with me included John Brise, Andrew Belmonte, Giles Ashurst and Huw. Jack Onsloe had refused to come with me, saying that it would evoke too many bad memories for him. However, he sent what proved to be a princely gift to Proserpina on the occasion: a small ivory chest, brimful of the most beautiful and delicate precious gem-encrusted jewellery I had ever seen. Proserpina was moved to tears, as I had told her previously of how Jack had lost his own family, wife, children and all. "To send me this," she said, "After his own loss.... And I always looked upon him as such a grim, unsmiling and frightening man."

Marco was already at the di Lucanti estate with Niccolo. Later, Ludovico privately acknowledged to me their great help and assistance with the preparations. I also brought with me an escort of ten men-at-arms and five archers, including Alain Malwe.

My own gifts to Proserpina had delighted and enchanted her. Marco had told me that diamonds were especially prized as wedding gifts; I had therefore sought out the finest I could, sending to Florence and Genoa for those who traded in such gems to visit me with their wares.

Hawkwood's Sword

Also present at the formal ceremony were various members of the di Lucanti family, the old uncles Domenico and Matteo, Ludovico's brothers Paolo and Muzio and their wives, accompanied by a drove of young male and female cousins whose names I cannot now remember.

To my surprise, Proserpina had insisted upon Rafaello and Lorenzo Scacci attend, saying to me later that, as they had helped to rescue her from the clutches of Orlando, they deserved some reward. "Then perhaps, dear Gianni, our families will again be friends and allies, as they once were in our grandsires' day."

Finally, to bestow upon us the blessing of God and Holy Church, there was Father Pietro, brought in by a special request from Ludovico to his bishop, and by virtue of the part he had played in Proserpina's rescue. We clasped hands in a glad greeting to each other, little knowing that the wedding would also be the occasion of our last meeting.

*****

The evening meal on the night we arrived was a quiet affair. Proserpina and her girl cousins did not appear, nor did her two aunts. Thus we were left to ourselves, and enjoyed a merry carouse with a good dinner—and, for some, an excess of wine. As on a previous occasion, the ancient uncles left the table early and retired for the night to their books and to sleep. As for myself, I tried to keep a sober head, but retired late, leaving a still merry company at the table.

On the morrow there were many late risers, myself amongst them, and so we broke our fast in ones and twos, some early, some late, according to how the wine of the previous evening had taken us. By midday though, we men were all arrayed in our finest attire, and in deference to the occasion went unarmed save for solitary daggers, without which I think most of us would have felt almost completely naked. With an eye to safety, however, I had arranged

FRANK PAYTON

that the men who had accompanied me would form a discreet guard around the estate house and gardens.

Towards noon we all converged on the Great Hall, which had overnight been transformed, decked out with heraldic flags, banners and pennants, together with flowers and flowering plants from the gardens. Tables were bright with white napery, cups and plate of gleaming silver gilt, and more decorations of flowers and fruits, cunningly arranged. Large silver gilt flagons of wine were arranged on side tables. There would clearly be no shortage of wine to wash down the rich repast which awaited us.

One end of the hall had been left clear, and there stood Father Pietro, clad for once not in his dull brown habit with the belt of rope and with coarse sandals upon his feet, but garbed in rich vestments of gold, green and white. I went forward and stood before him. Behind me stood John, sweating and uncomfortable in his unaccustomed finery, and Andrew—much younger, and well used to fashionable attire. Giles completed my trio of supporters, handsomely dressed in red and white.

Proserpina approached from my right, followed by a group of young female cousins and friends, all most sumptuously attired in a rainbow of colours. She wore a dress of simple white, but adorned with a myriad of precious crystal gems. Her honey-dark hair was braided and coiled into a heaped confection into which had been worked more precious gems and pearls. She came and stood beside me, and I took her hand. Behind her stood Ludovico.

According to custom, I turned and faced her and asked: "Proserpina, do you consent to be my wife? Declare it now before this concourse of witnesses."

She answered boldly, as I knew she would: "Yes, I do so consent to be your wife, and will remain faithful unto death."

We both then faced Father Pietro, who, after a short prayer for our future happiness and well being, bestowed upon our union the blessing of God and Holy Church.

Hawkwood's Sword

The thing was done: we were man and wife, Proserpina and I, and I then led her and the whole company to the tables for the wedding banquet.

What shall I say of that afternoon and evening? Course after course of rich food followed one upon each other, accompanied by a veritable river of wine. Between courses, musicians played and minstrels sang for our entertainment. There were tumblers and jesters, acrobats and performing animals. As hour followed hour, the whole blended into a tapestry of pleasure which no artist-weaver could capture.

At long last Proserpina was able to retire to her chamber—our chamber to be—accompanied by a bevy of her young maiden friends and cousins. When these latter returned to the hall, I made my excuses, wished those about me good night, and went to my own quarters. There I stripped off my wedding finery, and donned a long robe of rich red and white brocade which Huw had laid out for me. I went over to the window and overlooked the garden. It was the same moonlit scene which I had looked upon on my first visit to Savignone, the previous year. A full moon bathed the garden with its brightness and turned everything—house, statues, plants and all—to silver. The black sky was cloudless.

Thoughts of Orlando Scacci came unsought into my mind, and I shivered despite the thick brocade about my nakedness, to think of how I had so nearly lost my love.

Turning away from the window, I went to the door. I opened it and walked out into the passage, and made my way to the bridal chamber. I entered and, closing the door, placed my back against it and slid the bolt into its place.

Proserpina was standing by the window, as I had done, gazing into the garden. She was bathed in moonlight, and as she turned towards me she allowed her silken robe to slide back from her shoulders, revealing her naked beauty. Between her perfect breasts nestled a single pear-shaped diamond on its golden chain. She came open-armed towards me. I enfolded her in my own embrace, and felt her warm softness against my body.

Frank Payton

"My silver goddess," I whispered, before kissing her. "I love thee so much."

"And I love thee, my brave Gianni," was her tremulous reply.

I lifted her then and carried her to the bed.

Later, much later, after a tempestuous lovemaking, we slept, still entwined in the lovers' embrace.

FINIS

ABOUT THE AUTHOR

Frank Payton was born in Nottinghamshire and educated at Queen Elizabeth's Grammar School, Mansfield, Nottinghamshire. After leaving school he entered the Army on a Short Service regular engagement with the Intelligence Corps; he served in Germany and Cyprus.

On leaving the Army he joined the British Coal Corporation, in the Finance Department, moving eventually into the field of Industrial Relations, which would now be termed Human Resources, eventually achieving senior management status.

He took early retirement from British Coal, and opened what eventually became a very successful book-selling business in Mansfield, dealing with antiquarian and newly published books. He retired to Lincolnshire in 2001, where he began to write.

His abiding interest and passion over many years has been history, and over the years has covered a diversity of periods and countries. He became in turn the founding Secretary of the Nottinghamshire Family History Society, and later the Society's President.

The Assassin's Wife

By
Moonyeen Blakey

Fireship Press
www.FireshipPress.com
Sales@fireshippress.com
ISBN-13: 978-1-61179-218-8 (paperback)
Found in all leading Booksellers and on line eBook distributers

Second Sight is Dangerous

Nan's visions of two noble boys imprisoned in a tower frighten her village priest. The penalty for witchcraft is death.

Despite his warnings, Nan's determination to the save these boys launches her on a nightmare journey. As fifteenth-century England teeters on the edge of civil war, her talent as a Seer draws powerful, ambitious people around her.

Not all of them are honourable.

Twists of fate bring her to a ghost-ridden house in Silver Street where she is entrusted with a secret which could destroy a dynasty.

Pursued by the unscrupulous Bishop Stillington, she finds refuge with a gypsy wisewoman until a chance encounter takes her to Middleham Castle. Here she embarks on a passionate affair with Miles Forrest, the Duke of Gloucester's trusted henchman. But is her lover all he seems?

"…a vivid and visceral journey into the darkest hearts of men during the Wars of the Roses… An incredible, unforgettable story, surely made for the screen. Moonyeen Blakey is a major new talent to watch."
— Sally Spedding
Winner of the Cornerstones "Wow Factor" Writing Competition

*If you enjoyed this book
you'll love David Glenn's
other de Subermore mystery novels*

The Queen's Sword

> "*The de Subermore Mystery Series is a must for any devotee of the Elizabethan Era.*"
>
> **December 1599.** A grimy, plague-ridden London is beginning its painful emergence into a great city; but there is treachery afoot as yet another plot is developing to assassinate Queen Elizabeth I.
>
> Young, impetuous Michael de Subermore, is summoned to Whitehall palace, ordered to infiltrate the suspected conspirators, and uncover their plans. Amid plots, counter-plots, bouts of amnesia, duels, and back-alley murders, Michael survives by using his sword to defend the Queen, his honour, and the life of the woman he loves.
>
> Historical people and events are beautifully interwoven into a hard-to-put-down, fast-paced, gripping story.

www.FireshipPress.com

All Fireship Press and Cortero Publishing books are available directly through www.FireshipPress.com, amazon.com and via leading bookstores from coast-to-coast

**For the Finest in
Nautical and Historical
Fiction and Nonfiction**

WWW.FireshipPress.com

Interesting • Informative • Authoritative

All Fireship Press books are now available
directly through www.FireshipPress.com, amazon.com
and via leading bookstores and wholesalers from coast-to-coast